T0268515

ACT LI
A LADY,
THINK LIKE
A LORD

ACT LIKE
A LADY,
THINK LIKE
A LORD

CELESTE
CONNALLY

MINOTAUR BOOKS
NEW YORK

This is a work of fiction. All of the characters, organizations, and events portrayed in this novel either are products of the author's imagination or are used fictitiously.

Published in the United States by Minotaur Books, an imprint of St. Martin's Publishing Group

ACT LIKE A LADY, THINK LIKE A LORD. Copyright © 2023 by Stephanie C. Perkins. All rights reserved. Printed in the United States of America. For information, address St. Martin's Publishing Group, 120 Broadway, New York, NY 10271.

www.minotaurbooks.com

Design by Meryl Sussman Levavi

Map art © Catriona Phillips

The Library of Congress has cataloged the hardcover edition as follows:

Names: Connally, Celeste, author.
Title: Act like a lady, think like a lord / Celeste Connally.
Description: First edition. | New York : Minotaur Books, 2023. | Series:
    Lady Petra inquires
Identifiers: LCCN 2023028081 | ISBN 9781250867551 (hardcover) |
    ISBN 9781250867568 (ebook)
Subjects: LCGFT: Detective and mystery fiction. | Novels.
Classification: LCC PS3616.E7469 A65 2023 | DDC 813/.6—dc23/eng/20230626
LC record available at https://lccn.loc.gov/2023028081

ISBN 978-1-250-86757-5 (trade paperback)

Our books may be purchased in bulk for promotional, educational, or business use. Please contact your local bookseller or the Macmillan Corporate and Premium Sales Department at 1-800-221-7945, extension 5442, or by email at MacmillanSpecial Markets@macmillan.com.

First Minotaur Books Trade Paperback Edition: 2024

10 9 8 7 6 5 4 3 2 1

For my friends who have been there for me
since we were kids

ONE

Monday, 17 April 1815
Buckfields, seat of the fifth Earl of Holbrook
Newmarket, Suffolk

"MAY I REMIND YOU, MY LADY, THAT DAUGHTERS OF EARLS ARE not normally dressed by their lady's maids amongst the saddles and bridles of a harness room."

Lady Petra Forsyth, seated on a large wooden trunk painted with the Earl of Holbrook's coat of arms, held out her booted foot and wiggled it for Annie to grasp. "Yes, but at least this time I did not walk through muck in the stable yard first."

Annie took the heel of the knee-length boot with both hands, pulling with an indulgent roll of her eyes. "A small consolation, my lady. You do smell mightily of horses."

"This is to be expected after one has been on a horse all day, is it not?" Petra replied while holding out her other boot, the pair of which once belonged to her older brother, Alexander. As had the buckskin breeches still hugging her legs, the black frock coat with gold buttons she had shrugged out of moments earlier, and the frilled white shirt and cravat, both now loosened at the neck.

"And I would still be on my horse if it were not for my uncle," she added. "To believe he arrived four hours earlier than scheduled! Disagreeable man." Then, as Annie pulled her second boot, Petra's eyes widened. "But, oh, my poor papa! His injured ankle continues to pain him, and now he will have Uncle Tobias strutting about to add to his vexation."

"This is why we must hurry and get you into your riding habit, my lady," Annie said, panting slightly as Petra's leg was finally freed. "For both his lordship and Lord Allington will be awaiting you."

Indeed, upon the next trunk was a lady's riding ensemble. The soft blue of the long skirt and matching fitted jacket were embellished with embroidery in a deep cobalt, all of which would set Petra's eyes, coloring, and figure to their best advantage. The garments were also constricting and impractical, which was why Petra preferred to ride in her brother's old togs. When safely on her father's lands, of course.

"At least my *parfum de cheval* will serve to distract my uncle from noticing my riding habit will not have the smallest amount of dirt on it," Petra said, frowning over at the costume.

"I should hope it is pristine, my lady." Annie's reply was quick, and affronted.

Petra dipped her chin, lips pursed, but her tone was kind. "Dearest Annie, I know you take my meaning. You always ensure I am most beautifully turned out, but in this case it is less desirable that I should appear so clean."

A mollified Annie helped Petra stand and step out of her breeches. Petra's cravat was then pulled away, and over her head came the white shirt in a rush. Reddish-blond curls, having escaped her plait during her brisk ride, flew forward, sticking to her cheeks. Petra pushed them away irritably.

"Damn and blast! Why did my uncle have to arrive early?"

"My lady, your language does deteriorate with each visit home to Buckfields," Annie said, though this time her reproach was tinged with amusement as she helped Petra slip on a chemise. Then she held out the riding stays.

Though quite an adult at four and twenty, Petra allowed herself the childish act of pulling a face at the garment. Despite its lovely primrose-pink sateen and a higher cut at the hips, allowing for more comfort while riding sidesaddle, the boning still made her chemise bunch uncomfortably, leaving red marks on her skin.

"If only stays, and all like it, would deteriorate at the same rate as my language, we women would rejoice."

Yet Petra slid her arms through, then allowed Annie to lace it tight. A high-collared shirt of cambric was added, then a petticoat, before Petra was finally donning the riding skirt and jacket, both constructed from a merino wool that was suitable for the still-cool spring weather. As with all her daytime dresses, discreet pockets were sewn into the skirt rather than relying on those separate pockets attached to strings and tied about her waist under her dress. Though her modiste continued to be remonstrative of these requests, Lady Petra would not be swayed. Pockets were simply a necessity.

"The post boy arrived nearly the same time as Lord Allington," Annie was saying as she worked the laces of Petra's half boots, each with blue tassels at the ankles. "You received three more invitations." She lifted clear hazel eyes briefly to Petra's, adding, "I brought them directly to your bedchamber."

"Away from the prying eyes of my uncle, and his like-minded valet," Petra said approvingly. "Well done. And were there no letters?"

Annie shook her head. "Were you expecting one from Lady Caroline?"

"No, not at all. Lady Caroline was only due back in London today from seeing her Captain Smythe off at Portsmouth. And as much as my dearest friend excels at accumulating new gossip and passing it on to me, I must allow her a modicum of time to apply it to paper."

Petra picked up her hat, which was small with a flat top and short brim, and matched her riding habit perfectly, down to a cobalt tassel at the crown's center. "I may guess that one of the invitations is from Lady Milford for a picnic at Strand Hill. When we had tea after Easter, she was a bit poorly, suffering with her nerves again, and said she wished to invite me for a meal out in the spring air when she felt better. As the days have been so grand and much warmer lately, with the daffodils coming up all over, I cannot help but think her spirits may be lifting."

"A picnic does sound lovely, but I'm afraid an invitation from Lady Milford has not yet arrived," replied Annie as she selected a boar-bristle hairbrush and began to gently work out a tangle in one of Petra's curls. "Of the three, one is from Lady Watson, and another is from Lady Wyncroft."

Petra, who had been frowning thoughtfully at hearing her friend Gwen had not yet written to set a day for her picnic, now lifted her eyes heavenward at hearing Lady Wyncroft's name. "It is likely another of my cousin Lynley's tedious teas. However, Lady Watson's is no doubt for her annual masque, which will make up for having to be in the company of Lady Wyncroft on some other date. And what of the third?"

"It bears the Duchess of Hillmorton's seal," replied Annie. "And I would wager it to be to her spring ball."

"How lovely," Petra said. "It was kind of Her Grace to send another invitation to me here at Buckfields after the first was sent to Forsyth House. And if I recall from Lady Caroline's last letter, the ball is to take place this week—on Thursday, I believe. Caroline said she would gladly accompany me if I arrive in London in time, for her Captain Smythe will be at sea for some months and she will be free to be my companion."

"Have you decided whether or not we will be returning to town for the remaining season?" asked Annie as she smoothed Petra's plait.

"Not yet, I fear," Petra replied. "Just this morning, the earl's ankle was pronounced properly mended, but his physician recommended Papa wait another fortnight before riding out with the string. I confess I have been rather enjoying riding in his stead and taking notes on how his horses go each morning. Continuing for another two weeks would be a great pleasure—and you know I do enjoy being in the countryside." Giving the tassel on her hat a flip, she added, "Of course, London is always a delight to me as well. I understand the British Museum will be displaying Titian's *Diana and Actaeon*, in fact, which I would quite like to see again."

"And you do enjoy a good ball, my lady," Annie said, working Petra's plait into an appropriately ladylike coiffure.

Petra, who had pulled off one riding glove, clapped her bare hand to her still-gloved other. "Oh, I do. I have not danced once since just after the New Year, before Papa became injured. I should love to dance again." She paused, glancing over her shoulder at Annie. "And I think you would enjoy seeing a certain footman in the halls of Forsyth House once more. Maybe have another early morning dance in the library, when no one else is about?"

"You mean to tease me, my lady, but I will not have it," Annie replied crisply, but her cheeks had a pretty flush to them. "Now sit still, if you please. The earl wishes you to help him entertain your uncle, and we are already late."

Dutifully, Petra sat still as Annie inserted the first hairpins, but held her tongue only briefly.

"Since I am dreading spending time with my uncle and have had no gossip from London for almost a month, you must tell me what you have learned as of late. Oh, come now, do not be silent in an attempt to persuade me I am mistaken. I saw you reading a letter with great interest yesterday. And I think I have done rather well to wait a full day before asking you what news."

"My lady, sometimes you are quiet as a cat and I could not say how you manage it."

Petra heard the familiar sound of Annie's good humor. She only had to display a bit of patience now. Annie would first need to act as if revealing such information was beneath the code of a proper lady's maid. It was the done thing. Yet anyone who claimed they did not need to unburden themselves to at least one other person could not be considered wholly in their right mind, in Petra's opinion. And Annie was as steady as any person Petra had ever known.

"The letter was from Maggie, Lady Sloan's lady's maid, if you must know," Annie said finally, as if she would face the pillory otherwise. Yet her tongue was duly loosened, and she began to chatter away as she continued pinning Petra's hair.

"It seems Lady Sloan hired away her sister Lady Elizabeth's underbutler," Annie began. "Lady Elizabeth then responded by offering two of Lady Sloan's housemaids better wages—and only days before Lady Sloan was due to host the entire sixteen-member party that is her husband's family."

"Those two are *shocking*," Petra said, making Annie giggle.

"Maggie also wrote that Lady Sloan hired a new gardener for their estate in Oxfordshire," Annie continued. "He is said to be quite handsome and previously improved the gardens of Sir Hugh and the late Lady Thacker. Did you know her ladyship had passed? Maggie wrote that it was said to be some sort of a miasma, possibly from traveling in late February."

"No, I had not heard this sad news," Petra said. "But I was little acquainted with Lady Thacker, though I always felt her to be a kind, gentle sort. Sir Hugh I know a bit more as he is often at the Rowley Mile races—though he rarely gambles more than a shilling on any horse. I shall remember to send him a letter of condolence on the earl's and my behalf." Removing her second glove, she said, "Have you any other news, then? Maybe some of a happier variety?"

Annie eagerly complied, recounting Maggie's story of her mistress, Lady Sloan, being gifted a new spaniel puppy who had wreaked havoc on her mistress's rugs, counterpanes, and any piece of wood the little dog could discover.

"Oh, Lady Sloan was at her wit's end! But having instantly adored the puppy, could not give it up. Then her ladyship was told of a young gentleman's daughter from Yorkshire—a Miss Reed, as I recall—who has such a way with dogs, and who was currently ensconced at her family's London home. The puppy was sent to Miss Reed, and her ladyship and Maggie both look forward to its return. Is that not diverting, my lady? A young woman who trains dogs?"

"I think it is wonderful," Petra said, handing her riding hat to Annie to pin into place.

Annie paused, not yet placing the hat on Petra's head. "Maggie wrote that it was Mr. Shawcross who recommended Miss Reed to Lady Sloan, as he has sent a puppy intended for the Duchess of Hillmorton for training."

"*Duncan?*" Petra said, rather too quickly. She ignored the vexing little frisson that came with hearing his name again. "Has he returned to England?"

"Last week, my lady, as I understand it," answered Annie. "In time to celebrate the wedding of his brother the marquess. Though Maggie claims she heard Mr. Shawcross say he has returned for good. That the work he has done on the Continent over the last three years in securing and improving the Duke of Hillmorton's lands is now complete, and local men have been hired to protect His Grace's interests. I expect Mr. Shawcross shall be at Her Grace's ball, too, considering he is her grandson and she dotes upon him."

"Hmph," Petra replied. "And *I* expect he should count himself lucky that he has Her Grace's favor, considering he has not had mine for some time."

There was a silence of two heartbeats while Annie slowly began pinning the hat into place. Her voice was filled with hesitation when she spoke.

"My lady," she began. "I have been at your side since you were a girl of fourteen and I barely seventeen. I know you to be compassionate and forgiving, even when someone close to you has behaved unkindly . . ."

Petra arched one eyebrow, yet mild was her reply. "Though your words are appreciated, Annie, it is not like you to express unnecessary praise—especially when I am not always deserving of it. If you have something you wish to say, I would prefer that you do as normal and simply speak your mind. I daresay I find it much less disconcerting."

"Indeed I will then," Annie said, her confidence returning. "It is true you and Mr. Shawcross had a terrible row the day he left for the Continent, but so much time has passed since then. Three years, in fact. What are a few harsh words surely neither of you meant compared to the extraordinary friendship the two of you have enjoyed since almost your earliest days?"

Mulishly, Petra wished to refute these claims of a long-lasting affinity, and knew she could not. Especially now that she was here, at Buckfields. For throughout the earl's ten thousand acres, with its eighteen buildings that included expansive, Palladian-inspired stables, private gallops, and the twenty-eight-room house that had been the seat of the Earl of Holbrook since 1633, there was not one square foot where Petra and Duncan had not played together and tormented each other in equal measure. Since she was four and he a year older, to be precise, making Annie's words maddeningly true.

The only daughter of Thaddeus Forsyth, the fifth Earl of Holbrook, and Lady Maria, née Allington, Petra was born ten years after her brother Alexander, long after the earl and his countess had given up hope of another child, and was thus treated from her inception as the happiest of surprises. Yet before Petra could even begin to toddle about on pudgy legs, she was left motherless, Lady Maria having contracted consumption not long after Petra's birth.

By contrast, Duncan was not to know his true surname until the age of five, when Robert Shawcross, sixth Marquess of Langford and heir of the Duke of Hillmorton, once more rode into the tiny Perthshire hamlet of Struan in the Scottish Highlands. A restless soul who traveled often, Langford had come back to Struan after nearly six years with two thoughts on his mind: to find the ideal parcel of land on which to build himself a house, and to once more tup the pretty lass with auburn hair he'd enjoyed on his last visit.

Instead, Langford would find the lass now wedded to a burly, fair-haired Highlander who cared not for the English. Especially not for a marquess who whose thick dark hair and eyes a distinctive shade of green were repeated with uncanny perfection in the first child his wife had borne five years previous.

In one of Langford's few moments of selflessness, he offered to take Duncan to London, promising to raise him as a Shawcross alongside James, his younger son by his marchioness. Duncan's mother, with child again for the third time and wishing for a better life for her eldest, had tearfully encouraged her son to claim his birthright and become a gentleman.

The Marchioness of Langford, however, was said to have flown into a tear-filled rage. She refused to allow her James to be passed over for the marquessate by her husband's Scottish by-blow, and told Langford that Duncan should never return to Langford House so long as the boy lived, or risk her wrath. Because Lady Langford was not known to make idle threats, Duncan was quickly shunted off to Hillmorton House.

To the surprise of every servant employed by Their Graces, the duke and duchess quickly took to their young grandson. Nevertheless, Her Grace felt it best to send the charming but unmannered Duncan out of London to begin his education. As Her Grace had recently assisted the widower Earl of Holbrook in acquiring a new nursemaid for his young daughter, she looked no further than Newmarket and Buckfields. She felt Duncan would do best in the fresh air, and Lady Petra—one of Her Grace's many goddaughters—would thrive with the company of another child of about her own age.

Whether or not the duchess had anticipated how quickly Petra and Duncan would go from warily eyeing each other to escaping the nursery in an attempt to discover if a secret glade existed in the earl's forest, Petra had never asked. An excellent tutor was brought on for Duncan and gradually he learned to suppress his Scottish burr in favor of the round tones of an educated Englishman. And along with Petra, who soon had the first of several governesses, he would also learn his letters, as well as read, write, and speak French, German, Greek, and Latin.

These accomplishments, however, did little more than allow the two children to taunt each other in multiple languages, much to the chagrin of their perpetually exhausted nursemaid.

Further worrying Nanny, as they called her, their brickbats almost always ended in one challenging the other to a race on their respective ponies. Duncan and his chestnut pony called Pirate would attempt to best Petra and Rhubarb, her brave little bay with a white blaze down his face, as they galloped across the fields for the line of pear trees at the edge of the earl's forest. Victory spoils were varied and usually inventive, occasionally resulting in further challenges that had poor Nanny clutching at her heart. But most often, the loser was required to engage in a spot of petty theft. Specifically, of the confectionary drops made in the earl's kitchens, Petra's choice always being chocolate, while Duncan unfailingly preferred lemon.

To Petra, those were halcyon days, but soon Duncan was sent away to Eton while she continued her education at Buckfields through a series of governesses. Each was more dour than the one before, and none approved of the earl allowing his daughter to spend as much time as she liked riding horses.

Only when Annie was taken on as Petra's lady's maid and showed herself willing to bring her darning out to the stables to keep an eye on her young mistress—more than once poking a stable lad with her needle when he forgot his manners in Lady Petra's presence—did Petra feel as if she had found something of an ally. With Annie to talk to, her days were a little less tiresome while waiting for Duncan to return and assume his role of sparring partner.

Time and time again, Duncan traveled to Buckfields in between terms at Oxford, where he was proving himself to be a Shawcross worthy of the name and illustrious lineage. Though it was here, Petra knew, that Duncan had never felt any pretense were required of him. Even now, she could recall the visit where Duncan learned his father died, the marquess having succumbed to malaria during his travels to South America. In the company of the earl and Petra, Duncan freely mourned his father's passing, but the loss of the marquessate to his younger brother, James, not at all.

While the relationship between Duncan and James remained tenuous—largely by the design of the dowager marchioness— Petra and Duncan's once-forced companionship had evolved into a unique but close bond. So much so that, just after Petra's twentieth birthday, Duncan made introductions between Petra and Emerson, Viscount Ingersoll, who was Duncan's most trusted friend from Oxford. The introduction swiftly became a love match, and soon Petra was to become the luckiest viscountess in all of Britain, in her opinion—and even more so due to the generosity of her late mama.

For Maria, Lady Holbrook, had left her daughter a gift the likes of which few women would ever know: an inheritance. Not a dowry to be settled onto Petra at the time of marriage, but monies that would belong to her no matter her circumstances. The earl had even duly promised his countess that any man who wished to marry their daughter would be required to sign away his rights to Petra's inheritance or receive her hand not at all. And he would stay true to his word, along with offering a generous dowry in the marriage contract between Lady Petra and the handsome, blue-eyed, broad-grinned Lord Ingersoll.

No one, however, could have foreseen that neither provision would be needed. For the viscount's life was lost to a tragic fall down a set of town house stairs mere weeks before the nuptials.

There were only three people who would know that at the moment Emerson died from a broken neck, Petra had been upstairs, asleep, covered only by a linen sheet, not yet cognizant that the warmth of her beloved's arms was no longer enveloping her. One was Annie, who had continued to be the most loyal of lady's maids. Another was Lady Caroline, the most steadfast of confidantes. The third was Duncan, who had been a true friend to both betrotheds, lending his London town house as a place of privacy for the young couple. That night, Duncan came running as soon as he was summoned by Petra, whisking her to the safety of Forsyth House at the south end of Berkeley Square before she could be seen. His quick and admirable actions freed Petra to do nothing but feel her grief and be pitied by the ton for her great loss, without a whisper of scandal or ruination floating about her.

Though Duncan, too, would soon be gone from Petra's life, leaving for the Continent and his new role as the duke's agent only a day after Emerson's funeral.

Petra, still pale and drawn with mourning, had accompanied Duncan on a ride at Buckfields when he delivered the news. Even now, she could still feel how her brow had furrowed with disbelief. How could Duncan leave her when she most needed his friendship? His rakish sense of humor to make her laugh? As she hotly questioned his decision, Duncan responded by questioning her right to do so, his Scottish vowels reappearing like they always did when he was under strain. Tempers that had been taut on both sides in recent days then became rapidly untethered, their voices rising with each moment.

Their horses unnerved by the shouting, the two friends had circled each other on their prancing steeds, like opposing warriors moments before battle. Verbal spears made of the harshest words were thrown, faults of the other hurled back and forth, the row like no other they had ever had, each feeling they were being used most grievously.

In the end, Petra, her blue eyes blazing, would demand that Duncan be gone from Buckfields by the time she returned from her ride.

"If you wish it, my lady," Duncan had said with the utmost formality. He was galloping from Petra's sight in moments, and was gone from Buckfields within the hour. Petra was left feeling angry, terribly bruised on the inside, and truly unmoored for the first time in her life.

Before losing so much so quickly, Petra had never thought overly much on her inheritance, having never felt she would require it with such an amiable future husband as Emerson. The altering of her views on the matter did not come as a result of her mourning period, however. Rather, because of her contemplations that began a year later, when she finally felt ready to reenter society. At almost the same time her naturally buoyant disposition began to overtake the darker days, a notion had begun to slowly take seed. So slowly, in fact, that when it finally became a fully fledged thought, the guilt that would naturally accompany it was tempered with a curiosity to know if it would have merit.

That was, Petra began to wonder if having lost her chance of being advantageously married, if she might have—in a way—been given an opportunity. One that would allow her to view her inheritance through new eyes. Specifically, as it pertained to what was afforded to her as a woman; to what it could afford her life going forward.

Over the next year and some months, Petra contented herself with enjoying society, never eschewing dancing or the introduction to a gentleman, while her mind quietly considered other matters. Namely, what women were allowed and not allowed to do—both legally and according to the standards of feminine etiquette established by society. And with each topic on which she ruminated, Petra made certain she thought on both sides equally—often debating them with Caroline, who was always willing to take the opposing side for the sake of argument.

The earl, whose only thoughts on eligible matches centered on which of his thoroughbred stallions and mares would best produce a winning foal, never insisted Petra entertain suitors if she did not care to. And as eligible gentlemen came her way—two of whom proposed marriage, leading Petra to swiftly but kindly refuse—she was left in no doubt of one thing. That the freedom to remain her own woman—to hold her own reins instead of having them legally in the grip of a husband—had become of the utmost importance to her. And thanks to her mother's gift, it was a freedom she did not have to relinquish.

But it was not until June of 1814 when, surprising even herself, Petra finally announced her decision to society. It was at the Countess of Ardley's ball, a mere quarter of an hour after Petra had turned down her second proposal—this one from Lady Ardley's sweet if rather totty-headed son, a viscount whom everyone called Tibby. When Lady Ardley, not yet knowing Tibby had proposed, insinuated she knew Petra's surname would soon become Wyncroft, what Petra had been feeling manifested into words that somehow managed to sound both respectful and laced with a strength of conviction.

"Lady Ardley, as much as I respect your distinguished family and surname, I can truthfully say I have never found another man I love as much as my late Lord Ingersoll. And, as I am possessed of my own fortune courtesy of my late mama's will, I intend upon my own eventual death to be referred to as the late Lady Petra Forsyth, and by no other name."

And then like flames hitting kindling, her news spread throughout *le beau monde*.

"My lady? Did you hear me? I rather wonder if your head hasn't been in the clouds these past moments. Or were you simply conducting a quiet diatribe against Mr. Shawcross?"

Petra gave her head a tiny shake as Annie's voice broke through her memories, then heaved a sigh with deliberate theatrics.

"You must know I have never been able to call Duncan a sly boots or any other name that he deserves due to your sisterly tendresse for him. Even when he did not reply to my heartfelt apology letter, you would not join me in calling him a heartless cur."

Annie knew of the letter Petra had written some weeks after her row with Duncan. Petra had even posted it in the way they had since childhood, as a locked letter, which used a thin strip cut from the writing paper itself that was then twisted and passed twice through a small hole made into the folded letter. Petra had confirmation that Duncan had received her letter, but no locked-letter reply ever arrived with Petra's name scrawled in Duncan's untidy hand.

"It is only because I felt you never truly wished to call Mr. Shawcross a heartless cur despite it all, my lady," Annie said.

Petra looked over her shoulder at Annie, eyes narrowed. "*Hmph.* But to think you are just now disclosing your knowledge of his whereabouts. Maybe you are as sly as he."

"I knew at some point you would wish to hear the contents of my letter, my lady," Annie said. "For you are not quite as light on your feet as all that, and you do so enjoy convincing me to divulge gossip."

"Oh, Annie, you are wicked!"

As she knew they would, Annie's cheeks rounded with a barely suppressed grin at Petra's unconvincing exhortation.

Outside the harness room, clattering hooves reminded them of the time, and of Uncle Tobias waiting in the earl's study, likely tapping his long fingers in impatience.

"My lady, I do not think I should be seen carrying your brother's breeches, boots, and shirt inside," Annie said. "What if Lord Allington's valet sees and reports back to his lordship?"

"Mm, yes," Petra mused, then dipped her head to look down at the trunk on which she sat. Rising, she then reached up into her now smartly coiffed hair and pulled out a hairpin, eliciting a sigh from Annie's lips.

"My lady, must you have selected that one?"

"I shall endeavor to remove one less instrumental next time," Petra said, as she felt a curl sag. Turning, her tongue between her teeth, she bent, inserted the hairpin in the iron lock, and gently worked it. The padlock obligingly opened to reveal the trunk was half filled with extra stirrups, bits, and various bridle parts. "In here should do nicely."

Annie hurriedly folded and stored away all the unladylike riding clothes. Then Lady Petra faced front once more, smiling while Annie reinserted the hairpin and she put on a fresh pair of leather gloves in the same York tan as her first.

TWO

A QUARTER OF AN HOUR LATER, PETRA WAS STANDING WITH her back to the wall just outside her father's library, her riding gloves now clenched in one hand.

Her decision to take the shortest route to her father's side had led her to the little-used south entrance of his study. This rendered Petra unannounced by Cudmore, the butler, and her approach unheard by the two men sitting in leather chairs that faced the north wall, its bookshelves offering literary works and stud books, and its fireplace offering warmth. Petra had stopped at the threshold to remove her gloves, but had quickly swung around to her present position when she registered the topic of conversation. Uncle Tobias was giving Papa another treatise on the unladylike state of the fifth Earl of Holbrook's only daughter.

"You must see that Petra is thoroughly headstrong, Holbrook," Uncle Tobias said, the cutting edge to his voice almost as familiar to her as the subject matter. "I witnessed her riding astride with impunity as I arrived, wearing breeches like a man. Breeches, I give you!"

Drat, Petra thought, *he* had *seen me*.

She looked down at her blue riding skirt and tasseled boots. Insisting to Annie that she look authentic, she had walked into the nearest horse box and performed two twirls, sending straw dust upon her boots and several inches of her skirt while the gray thoroughbred blinked bemusedly at her with limpid brown eyes. Annie had watched her, too, sighing and saying something about Lady Petra never doing anything by halves. All this effort had been for naught.

"Come now, Tobias, it is not as bad as all that," said her father's voice. It was calm, but with a tightness Petra rarely heard. She imagined his cheerful blue eyes looking weary. His graying eyebrows knitting. Possibly a slump in his broad shoulders. "My Petra only does so when here, on my lands, and amongst—"

Her uncle raised his voice a notch and carried on, a creak of leather making Petra guess he had leaned forward for emphasis. She could see his face in her mind, too. High forehead emphasized by a receding hairline. Pale blue eyes set deep in a thin face. A slash of a mouth. He looked nothing like the portraits of her late mother, and Petra could almost see his upper lip curl as he spoke.

"And I daresay it is still difficult for me to believe, but Lady Petra has declared herself to the Countess of Ardley—which is to say all of London—as never wishing to marry. By God, Holbrook, Petra has become a spinster *by choice*. Recently she was even depicted as all but a crone in the latest broadsheets! My dear late sister would never have allowed such behavior from her daughter. She would have been mortified, and I should declare you a fool if you do not count yourself concerned."

Petra raised her eyes heavenward, then lowered them to stare out the window, over the green expanse of lawn to a large paddock. Uncle Tobias's speech on her independent ways was a tiresome rendition. One that had been honed over the years with each extended visit from Allington House, his residence in London, to Newmarket and Buckfields, where he made himself equally at home.

In truth, for the past three years, she'd enjoyed something of a respite while her uncle was with His Majesty's army in the wars against Napoleon, and Petra had hoped his time in the service of England would have given his viewpoints a measure of clarity. Yet since his return—the wars not yet won, but Uncle Tobias having sold out of his commission with the rank of second lieutenant—the only change seemed to be that he'd added the rather horrible word "spinster" to his diatribes. And with no small amount of relish.

Petra pressed her lips together to keep her sigh from escaping and giving her position away. She once more cursed Uncle Tobias for arriving early. She and Papa should not have had to hear her uncle's drivel until this afternoon, after they had enjoyed some cakes and tea.

No, cakes and tea laced with brandy. She and Papa always required brandy when Uncle Tobias came to visit. And by thunder, her uncle was still working his jaw, wasn't he?

"I do not know how you withstand such an obstinate daughter, Holbrook," he was saying. "If she had been mine, I would have used that horse whip over your mantel until she gave up such foolish notions."

"Yes, but she is not your daughter, Toby." Though the earl's voice remained unheated, he used Uncle Tobias's nickname only when his agreeable nature was running its last furlong. As was typical, however, Petra's uncle ignored the subtle warning.

"If you recall," Uncle Tobias returned, "as my sister, Maria, lay dying and Petra was crawling at the nursemaid's feet, dearest Maria asked me to help you look after your daughter. She knew you would allow Petra too much leeway."

As if to emphasize this, Uncle Tobias added in another of his irritating habits by thrusting the end of his walking stick onto the floor, causing a cracking noise that served to signal he was heading into full cry.

"If the French conflicts had not taken me away, Holbrook, your daughter would be like her brother. Advantageously married and helping to continue the Forsyth and Allington lines."

"And this coming from the last Allington, and a bachelor at that," said her papa dryly, causing Petra to cover her mouth and nose lest her other unfeminine trait of snorting while laughing alerted them to her presence.

"Ahh," replied Uncle Tobias, relating such smugness in that one sound that Petra felt he had been waiting for just such a barb to be thrown. "But I am not to be a bachelor for much longer, Holbrook," he said. "For Miss Alice Brown, whom I first met a year ago whilst on leave and staying with acquaintances in Kent, has agreed to become my wife. We shall be married in one month's time."

"Indeed?" replied her father, sounding as thoroughly surprised as Petra felt. "Well, congratulations to you, Allington. I wish you both very happy."

"Thank you, Holbrook," replied Uncle Tobias. "It shall be a quiet wedding in Chartham, near Canterbury, for that is Miss Alice Brown's wish. But it is also her wish—and mine—to start a family right away. Thus, *I* am fulfilling my duty and my role as an Allington. But what of Lady Petra?"

"What of her?" replied her father. "She is a Forsyth, and proudly so." To this, Petra nodded her head with vigor, but could not fault her father when he added, "Though she takes pride in being an Allington as well, I am sure."

"As she should, on both counts," Uncle Tobias said. "And had I been here, I could have helped her to further understand her place regarding both lines. But as I was away and unable to guide her . . . well, sir, let me be so bold as to put it in the equine terms you understand."

The earl began to bluster a reproach, but was once again cut off. Petra was clenching both hands now, her nails digging into her palms as she struggled to hold her position and her tongue. Uncle Tobias rapped his cane on the floor twice more. His words held perverse pleasure.

"Holbrook," he began, "for all your accomplishments in raising and training the best racehorses in England, if not all of Great Britain, you are singularly lacking in the same excellent instincts and firm hand when it comes to your own offspring. And now, while you have an heir worthy of the Forsyth name in Alexander—who's sired a grand colt himself to inherit the earldom, plus two more—he has taken residence in the north and is no longer the prize stallion for you to parade through society."

This time, the earl was quick in his reply. "I say, that is most unfair, Toby. And you know I do not give a fig about London, the ton, and everyone in it." Yet it was without the earlier threatening undertone. Uncle Tobias must have heard this as well, because now there was a barely suppressed note of victory in his voice.

"Now, regarding Lady Petra—a thoroughly pretty filly indeed. We all had the highest hopes for her, did we not? Especially when she became engaged to the late Lord Ingersoll three years ago." There was a soft rap of his cane on the floor. "They were indeed a match, both in bloodlines and in matters of the heart, and I know she suffered in his untimely loss." Another rap sounded, once more brisk. "But she has now mourned and recovered, only to what end? While I admit Petra has not yet lost her sprightly carriage or shown signs of unsightly swayback, I must say with the utmost sadness that she has turned into a thoroughly willful mare to whom no man cares to hitch his cart."

This pronouncement was met with silence. Petra realized she was breathing heavily, but it did not block her hearing. She'd heard no response from her father. The man who had taught her everything. Who had shown his pride in her through shining eyes and quiet nods of his head even when he never said the words. And with the faint sound of another door opening and a soft clearing of the throat, Petra relinquished her hopes of that pride being spoken aloud and silencing the odious man who was unfortunately her kin.

"Pardon me, my lord." Cudmore, an excellent butler, always appeared when the earl needed him most. "You asked me to remind you that the farrier is due at the stables at half past two. It is a quarter past now."

"Of course. I shall be along directly." Petra again heard the tightness in her father's voice, plus the multiple creaks of leather as he rose from his chair. There was a pause, then he said, "Yes, well. Care to join me, Toby?"

His words held a politeness even a child would recognize as forced, but Uncle Tobias's responding voice seemed unaffected.

"No, no, Holbrook," her uncle replied, all easiness. "You go on.

I'll just stay here and await the arrival of my niece. She may entertain me while you tend to your horses." There was a pause, then he added, "Actually, there is a gentleman I'd like Petra to meet, and I wish to have a few words with her about him. In fact, I hope you do not mind, but I have invited him here to Buckfields. He is due to arrive on Monday."

"Someone who would be willing to, as you say, hitch his cart to my headstrong daughter, I take it?" replied the earl, a note of anger finally pulsing through his voice.

Petra was momentarily gratified to hear it, though she could no longer be sure if it was due to her uncle's comments about her person and her choices or Uncle Tobias asking a guest to Buckfields without securing the earl's permission first.

Her uncle was emitting a soft chuckling sound. "Something like that, yes. He is a very interesting man, and I have no doubt Petra will make an impression on him."

The earl gave no discernible reply. Outside the library, however, Petra lifted her chin, and whispered under her breath.

"We shall see about that."

She pushed off the wall, her jaw set. She would be damned if she would accept the attentions of any man who associated with her uncle.

Yet just before her gaze shifted away from the paddock in the distance, a figure within it moved slowly into her line of vision. It was a small bay pony, lazily cropping the green grass.

It was Rhubarb, her very first pony. The one who had taught her everything a human could not. Who had taken her galloping over fields, leaping over hedges and fallen logs, never failing her.

By the earl's design, Rhubarb could always be seen from Lady Petra's bedroom and sitting room, as well as from the view outside of the earl's study. Petra loved being able to visit her pony and bring him apples to enjoy, happy that he remained in abundant health and fine spirits despite his nearly thirty years.

Petra watched Rhubarb now, suddenly seeing him in a different light. She already knew that his head was flecked liberally with gray. That the rest of his mahogany-bay coat, once so shiny, seemed to have dulled into an ashy brown with age. But as he walked another few steps, his former sprightly carriage forever lost to the stiffness of age, Petra noticed something new.

Her pony had gone swaybacked.

This put too fine a point on things. Petra turned, hitched up her skirts, and tiptoed silently away until she knew her boot heels would not be heard on the marble floor. Then, reaching the staircase that would take her to her suite of rooms, she hurried up the steps and to her bedchamber, making a beeline to the fireplace mantel.

Hastily grabbing the invitations she'd received, Petra riffled through them. With a cry of delight, she extracted one that was most beautifully engraved. And accompanying it was a folded piece of stationery with a well-known coat of arms and the salutation *My dearest goddaughter*.

Lady Petra Forsyth was but one of eight ladies of her age who could claim to be Her Grace's goddaughter, yet she still enjoyed being addressed as such by the formidable and canny duchess—even when Petra guessed the note would be requesting a favor, and she was not proven incorrect. Petra rarely minded these errands, however. Some of them had even been rather exciting. But today the request was simple, yet most welcome, and a smile spread across her face.

If an invitation to the Duchess of Hillmorton's ball in three days' time would not give Petra good reason to leave Buckfields for London, escaping her uncle and the possibility of having to entertain the unknown gentleman he had invited to save her from a life of spinsterhood, a personal request from the duchess would.

It seemed Her Grace had become rather enamored of the fine linen handkerchiefs woven south of Newmarket, a set of which

Lady Petra had gifted Her Grace on her last visit to Hillmorton House. Her Grace would like more of them, and had already written to Otley's Fine Linens to place the order for several sets, including some for her dear Shawcross, who had delighted her in returning from Spain in time for the ball. Would Lady Petra be so kind as to collect the handkerchiefs on her journey back to London?

It would mean traveling an extra fifteen miles, adding upward of another three hours on to an already full day's journey. Lady Petra would be *delighted*.

"And as for Duncan Shawcross," she whispered to herself with defiantly narrowed eyes, "I shall not let his presence at the ball irk me for even a moment." She then called out for Annie.

"My lady?" Annie rushed out of Petra's dressing room, the pair of shoes she'd been polishing still in her hands. "What is the matter?"

Petra whirled around, holding the two pages aloft as if they were a winning cup at Ascot. "Annie, you must pack my things with haste. It is time to return to London."

THREE

FLICKERING CANDLELIGHT THREW SHADOWS ON THE DUCHESS of Hillmorton's face as she frowned at Petra, who was rising from her curtsy, a slim papier-mâché box held in both hands.

"My girl, you have been out in the sun again. Riding your papa's horses every day, I'd wager. It has brought out your freckles. You look as if you have the pox."

The duchess was one for strident tones, and they carried her voice over the jaunty Irish air the orchestra was playing as her guests continued to arrive.

Petra ignored the titters from the Greely-Wilke sisters, who were several steps behind her, waiting to greet the duchess. And from the corner of her eye, the slightest telltale movement from Lady Caroline indicated her dearest friend was restraining a grin.

"Will such an affliction prevent you from accepting a kiss from your goddaughter, Your Grace?" Petra asked with studied seriousness.

The duchess's lips pursed and her eyes narrowed. "Do you see, Shawcross? Lady Petra is not even moved that I find her complexion wanting. I believe she may even like her freckles."

Lady Petra turned to finally acknowledge the gentleman in a dark coat over a silver-blue waistcoat standing at the duchess's side, hands clasped behind his back. "Yes, I should like to hear Mr. Shawcross's opinion, too, Your Grace." She let her lips curve into a smile that matched her honeyed tones. "If he would be so kind as to reply."

Duncan regarded her steadily, his eyes a mélange of greens beneath black brows as he held out one hand to stop a footman in golden livery carrying a platter of fat purple grapes. He addressed the duchess as he expertly pinched off a small bunch.

"I daresay, Grandmama, the freckles over Lady Petra's nose do resemble Cassiopeia in the nighttime sky. Was the mythological queen not known for being rather vain in regard to her beauty as well?"

One of the Greely-Wilke sisters gasped. Likely Miss Miranda. Duncan briefly held a grape between strong teeth before it disappeared between his lips. There came a longing sigh. Miss Millicent, no doubt. Petra could almost feel the mirth emanating from Caroline, who did so love a spot of drama.

Instead, Lady Petra gave her attention to the duchess. "Your Grace, I have been away from London for three months, returning with freckles. Your grandson has been away for as many years, returning with, it seems, a penchant for speaking ill of the stars and Greek goddesses, as well as his childhood friend. Which one of us do you suppose is most changed for the worse?"

There was a profound quiet from the sisters. Shocked whispers could be heard from farther back as the greeting line continued to grow. Even Caroline did not move.

"You both are steadfast in your horrid behavior," snapped Her Grace, her nostrils flaring. Then the edges of her mouth drew back, creating a series of ripples on her powdered cheeks as she broke into a cackling laugh. "And I am glad of it, my dear. It reminds one that not all of society is full of dullards."

Her Grace looked pointedly over Petra's shoulder at the Greely-Wilke sisters, who were tittering once more. They were instantly silenced.

The duchess then offered Lady Petra her hand, but Petra still held the papier-mâché box, painted in rich detail and depicting an

English setter and her puppies frolicking in the lush spring grass. The footman having hurried away, she held it out to Duncan to hold for Her Grace.

"If you will, please, Mr. Shawcross."

His gaze raked over the box's glossy exterior, then Petra, as if both were filled with equal impertinence. There was a heartbeat when Petra thought he wouldn't take it, but his grandmother gave his arm a light rap with her silk fan. Scowling, he reached for the box, needing only one gloved hand where Petra had needed two.

"They are your handkerchiefs, Your Grace," she explained. "I chose this box because the setters reminded me of your Willow and her pups from my childhood." She sent a quick, pointed look toward Duncan. He matched her expression in contrary fashion, then held out the box for his grandmother's inspection.

"Oh, they do indeed. How utterly delightful," Her Grace said, clearly pleased. Petra clasped the duchess's proffered hand, and leaned in to kiss her cheek.

"I added an extra set for your youngest granddaughter's sixth birthday," she said. "They're embroidered with the loveliest pink rosebuds."

"She will adore them, my dear, thank you," said Her Grace, then gave Petra a nod of dismissal. Keeping her eyes firmly on the duchess, Petra curtsied again and turned with a swish of her cerulean-blue gown to take Caroline's arm.

"Dearest, Mr. Shawcross will not like that you made him your personal footman," Caroline said in an undertone as they walked nearer to the growing crowd of guests. She glanced over her shoulder. "Yes, if looks were arrows, you'd have one stuck dead center in your back. At least, if he could shoot as well as I, you would." A thrum came into her voice. "Though I profess it makes his eyes greener when he glowers in such a way."

"I care not one small turnip what Duncan Shawcross likes or dislikes anymore," Petra said with a lift of her chin. "As we have ceased to be friends, he may lump it if he is displeased with me."

"And *I* am displeased that you and Shawcross will not simply talk to one another again," Caroline said, pulling Petra around the elaborate chalk design in symbols of spring that marked the dance floor. "And further because you insisted I be ready early so that you could deliver *a box of handkerchiefs*. Dearest, have you no respect for my reputation as one of the finest-dressed ladies in London?"

But Petra would not be deterred.

"And did you hear how he made sure to use a constellation named after a Greek goddess in his description of my freckles?" They'd reached the table laden with dance cards and each slid a golden cord onto her wrist. "He knows of my penchant for the mythological world and that now I shall have to use a looking glass to know for sure. And, by thunder, that will only make him sure of his claim and then he will smirk like he always does when he is right."

Hearing Caroline's suppressed giggle, Petra just stopped herself from giving a defiant toss of her head, knowing it would be unladylike—and that there would be eyes on her after her interaction with Her Grace, even if they weren't Duncan's.

"And as for his eyes," Petra continued, her lips barely moving as Lady Easterly and her ever-present quizzing glass came into view. "I have always told him they are the color of a common garden toad no matter what his expression." Noting Caroline looking back a second time, with a certain amount of appreciation despite having just heard his eye color likened to unattractive amphibians, Petra sighed and increased her pace, pulling her friend with her.

"What?" Caroline asked, the picture of innocence. Then, mistaking Petra's exasperated expression, her laugh escaped. It was a throaty sound that made the heads of several handsome gentlemen turn, then allow their gazes to linger on Caroline's long neck, mahogany hair piled high, and lively brown eyes. "You need not worry, dearest. Shawcross and I, we would never suit." She leaned to whisper in Petra's ear, "Though I do believe Her Grace might be contemplating whether you and he might."

Petra emitted a groan. "Please do not say such things." Still, she could not claim Caroline was mistaken. For only moments earlier, as Petra and Caroline had approached Her Grace, Petra could have sworn she had seen the duchess give a speculative glance toward her unmarried grandson, then at Petra herself.

Could Her Grace secretly be feeling the same way as Uncle Tobias—horrified that Petra had announced her intention never to marry? Was it possible Her Grace now intended to exercise her considerable powers of persuasion upon Petra to alter this decision, and then orchestrate a match between Petra and Duncan?

No, Petra thought, and quickly banished these thoughts as she recalled Lady Ardley's ball. When the news of Petra's announcement that she would remain unmarried was causing whispers so loud that Lady Easterly had checked the windows with her quizzing glass for signs of an impending windstorm, Petra had looked across the room and met the duchess's eyes. Godmother or not, Her Grace had never bestowed her good favor on anyone she felt unworthy. Then, with nearly the entire beau monde watching and with Petra's knees shaking beneath her gown of marmalade silk, Her Grace had inclined her head.

Caroline had been at her side then, too, and had even clutched Petra's hand and whispered from behind her glass of wine, "Darling Petra, that was as good as the Queen's approval. Well done, you. And for heaven's sake, do remember to breathe before you faint dead away."

Inwardly chastising herself at the absurdity of her own thoughts, Petra returned to herself as she and Caroline stopped to speak with one of Caroline's aunts. After brief pleasantries where Petra was greeted with unencumbered delight, she wandered away to get a better look at the ballroom's floral centerpiece.

At least, that is what she told Caroline. In truth, Petra needed a moment to collect herself, to calm her emotions at seeing Duncan again.

Since returning to London, she'd been so busy paying calls and helping Mrs. Ruddle, the capable housekeeper of Forsyth House, with devising menus and making other household decisions that she'd had little time to think on what it would be like.

Was it her, or had the angles of Duncan's face become more pronounced? Was he a bit broader in the chest as well? Or was it that he was trimmer in the waist from all his travels?

Petra hated that she longed to go to him, to have him give her that big smile that he could never hold back when he was truly delighted. They should already be at the lemonade table, jesting with one another and making plans to meet for a ride in the Green Park tomorrow. If all were well, afterward, he would return with her to Forsyth House for one of Mrs. Bing's huge breakfasts or risk breaking the heart of Petra's cook. Later, they would take a walk in the gardens with Annie so she could fuss over Duncan's leaner appearance and demand all the news of his travels. Instead, Petra felt as though she and Duncan were truly as strangers to each other.

Damn and blast! she thought heatedly as she pretended to gaze at the huge flower arrangement. *If that stubborn man will not forgive me after all these years, especially when he said equally hurtful things? Then by the bollocks of Pegasus, he may take his smug self back to the Continent without my friendship!*

With these defiant thoughts, Petra willed herself to focus on the beautiful arrangement dominating a round table in the middle of the duchess's grand saloon, which was serving as the ballroom for the evening. Spanning the width of two men, the flower-filled centerpiece was nearly as tall as one, and held all the colors of spring. There were heavy pink peonies, dainty yellow buttercups, stalks of arching bluebells, and so many more—flowers that bloomed naturally in the vernal season as well as those grown specially in the duchess's hothouses. Petra let her eyes feast on the textures and colors as snatches of gossip came to her from milling guests.

". . . and did you ever think Her Grace would invite Mrs. Richfield again?"

"My dear, you will never guess what Miss Sayers said to me just yesterday . . ."

"I could not believe it when I heard. Lady Milford? But with her nerves, well . . ."

Petra frowned at this news, delivered by the Marchioness of Rockingham with a level of ghoulish sympathy. She'd seen Gwen only last month, so whatever could be the matter? Petra turned her head to strain her ears toward the marchioness, but other voices shifted her attention.

". . . and I told Lady Caroline, 'I saw that yellow damask first.' And do you know what was her reply? She said that while yellow favors her, I would look like someone had doused me in sick. The impudence! Oh, sometimes I think that if she were not the daughter of the Duke of Carlingford and the wife of the handsome Captain Smythe . . ."

At this, Petra's furrowed brow eased and she had to work to keep a smile at bay. Caroline's exquisite gown was indeed made of a lovely yellow silk damask. The color made her friend's brown eyes appear almost amber and enhanced the warm tones in her skin. Yellow suited her, it was true. And her status as one of the most highborn ladies of Petra's age—which included marriage to a celebrated captain in His Majesty's Royal Navy who would eventually also ascend to the rank of earl—did indeed give Caroline much leeway.

Petra turned, only to find the two ladies hurrying away. A moment later and the yellow-damask thief herself was back at Petra's side, the note of triumph in Caroline's face telling Petra she had heard the whole exchange and did not feel the need to deny a word of it. She once more linked her arm with Petra's.

"Were we insolent little chits like that?"

"Undoubtedly," Petra replied. "You recall our coming-out ball."

"Ah well," Caroline trilled with a lighthearted shrug. They both then directed their gaze to the orchestra, where a violin player wearing all black had risen from his chair.

"My lords, ladies, and gentlemen," he announced, "we begin the night with the minuet."

Petra, noticing more than one gentleman casting their eyes her friend's way when the music started, asked, "Have you grown bored of . . . who has it been since I went off to Suffolk? Lord Whitfield, as I recall?"

"Bored? Heavens, no," Caroline replied, then began leading Petra through a doorway not far from the orchestra. "Let us go into the portrait gallery and have a proper palaver," she said. "There I can better explain the many inventive reasons why I keep Whitfield around. Now, whatever is that look for, dearest Petra? My Captain Smythe does not mind my taking a lover, as you are aware, and the marble statues will not blush. Most of the gods and goddesses they depict did far more licentious things than I." Caroline's dark head tilted to one side and she leaned in to whisper, "My captain and his acting lieutenant undoubtedly have when they secrete themselves away in that cottage in Surrey, though possibly not by much."

"*Caroline*," Petra chided through her laugh. "You know I adore your captain."

"Oh, you cannot be missish with me, Lady Petra, even if you have declared yourself a perpetual miss," Caroline rejoined as they crossed the wide passageway that was thankfully free of guests. "For I know better, even if your own debauching was tragically cut short . . ."

She trailed off. Caroline's words of teasing were accompanied by one of her rare gentle smiles. She squeezed Petra's hand in the true sympathy of a devoted friend.

Once, any reference to Emerson and the night he fell to his death had felt to Petra like a thousand sharp knives taking their turn to slice at her heart. Now the feeling was more like a concentrated, quick pain, such as the kind that came from the sudden prick of a finger.

And while Petra felt she would forever know that ache, on one level or another, time had taught her another lesson. She had learned that the little, almost secretive smile that came to her lips at the still-intoxicating memories of her four months in Emerson's arms was much more diverting than damp eyes and a running nose.

Caroline's eyes sparkled at the sight. "Missish be damned. Does this mean you will consider taking another lover in the future?"

The music was lessening, as was the babble of talking people. "Hmm, I cannot say," Petra said, enjoying being coy for once. "Yet if I do, it shall be on my own terms—and the man I choose will know it and accept it before I go to his bed."

"Or maybe you should just take him to yours," Caroline said. "I, for one, have never seen my Lord Whitfield's bed, and let me tell you just how lovely it is that he is the one required to go home the next morning. Or, indeed, in the middle of the night . . ."

They were now quite alone except for the footman standing guard directly inside the entrance to the portrait gallery. Petra chose a small candelabra from the selection on a long table and lit the candles as Caroline waxed lyrical about Whitfield's considerable talents while in her bed. Seeing the footman gaping, Petra shooed her friend past paintings hung on walls covered in red silk damask toward the far end of the gallery. They didn't stop until they reached the portrait of Farnley, the champion racehorse Petra's father had trained for the duke, which was hung in a pride of place.

"Now, as we have not exchanged letters for one whole month, tell me of your recent weeks in Newmarket," Caroline said as she eyed the painting of the gray stallion. "And whether or not old Farnley here had the bad luck of being painted with grotesquely overlarge withers as Her Grace continues to claim."

Petra laughed, admitting Farnley's withers were overlarge, but only a bit. Then she told Caroline how she had ridden out to the gallops in her father's stead, and how much she had loved being back home at Buckfields with her father and the freedom to ride as much as she wanted.

"But then Uncle Tobias arrived for one of his visits . . ."

"Ah, Allington," Caroline said, taking the candelabra from Petra and placing it on a nearby plinth holding a bust of Cicero. "Is he in danger of being as much of a prig as ever?"

"Oh, he is not in danger of it," Petra said. "I believe he's been crowned the king of prigs. Only now His Priggishness is to be *married*."

"Lawks, are you in earnest?" Caroline said, wrinkling her nose at the thought.

"I am, though in his letters he has never written a word about the poor woman, whom he met some months earlier whilst on leave, as I understand it."

"And I am in no doubt that it took him that long to convince her to look twice at him," said Caroline. "She must have few prospects indeed to accept him. However did you manage to steal away from Buckfields, then? I would have expected Allington to imprison you there for another fortnight at least, simply to force you to hear him gloat over finally finding a wife."

Petra gestured toward the ballroom. "I have Her Grace to thank for this timely invitation. Though you should have seen my father when I told him at dinner that night I would be leaving the next morning. I fear not even the saddest spaniel could have had more affecting eyes."

Caroline grinned. "And your uncle? How did he react?"

"Oh, Uncle Tobias's eyes looked as if they would pop from their sockets," Petra said. Then she deepened her voice and recounted her uncle's next words.

"'Holbrook, I demand you forbid my niece from leaving!'" she spluttered, just as Uncle Tobias had as he gestured toward Petra at the dinner table. "'Why, I have only just arrived, and she did not even greet me after my travels. And now she means to leave not even a day later? I will not be disrespected in this manner!'" Returning to her own voice, Petra added, "He followed this with a banging of his fist on the table, rattling the china. It was quite rude, I must say."

"Capital rudeness," Caroline agreed.

Petra lifted her chin. "If I were to give myself an accolade, it would be that I made a rather convincing show of contrition toward my uncle." She widened her eyes, batting her lashes innocently at Caroline, just as she had at her father's dinner table, holding one palm flat over her heart. "'Dearest uncle,' I said, 'you are quite correct. I am wholly at fault. Please do forgive me for not joining you earlier. The Duchess of Hillmorton had sent a request of me along with her invitation and it was of the utmost importance that I reply immediately.'"

Caroline gestured to a nearby small still life in a gilded frame. "Do tell me Allington went as purple as these plums."

Petra nodded with delight. "He refused to eat his soup, he was so vexed. And it was delicious, too. I feel he rather missed out." Then she gave an exasperated sigh. "Though in his petulance, he attempted to convince Papa that I should not be allowed to run Forsyth House as if I am the countess instead of merely the daughter."

"And how did the earl respond?" Caroline asked with a roll of her eyes.

"Only with the truth," Petra replied. "That I have been making decisions for Forsyth House since I was sixteen years of age, and I run its entirety on a small but loyal complement of servants who keep the house in excellent condition. He even added that it was I who hired Mrs. Bing—who is the best cook in London, in his opinion—and Charles, who, though a footman now, will make an excellent replacement for Cudmore one day. Just as Allen, the new underfootman I took on, will one day replace Charles. I hired Rupert as well, who is a most excellent groom and coachman. And not only are they still with us, but Papa wishes he could convince them to work at Buckfields." Petra grinned. "But not Mrs. Ruddle, as the earl likes his housekeeper to have a sense of humor, and our Mrs. R is rather dour. Or Smithers, because Cudmore does not approve of the way Smithers decants the earl's wine and Papa would never wish to anger Cudmore."

"Dearest, that is most diverting," Caroline said, amusement

threading her voice, "but I meant how did the earl respond to your bit of theatrics?" She then reached out to straighten the still-life painting. This gave Petra just enough time to set the smile on her face so that she did not show the worry she felt that Uncle Tobias may be, at that very moment, continuing to lead her father's mind toward further repellent thoughts.

"I think it is possible I detected a note of appreciation in Papa's eyes for my tactics, for he capitulated and asked me what time I should like the carriage ready," Petra replied, hoping she was indeed speaking the truth. She could not really say for sure, as her father had quickly turned his attention to his soup, which had been a cold green pea and tasted like spring.

Talk of the carriage then reminded her of what she'd heard in the ballroom, about Gwen. Her friend had always been prone to nerves, melancholia, and various other small ailments—one of which was the feeling of sickness on long carriage rides.

"Caroline," Petra began as she retrieved the brightly burning candelabra. "In the saloon, I heard the Marchioness of Rockingham imparting some news about Lady Milford. Do you know the nature of this account?"

Caroline seemed surprised. "Heavens, did no one tell you when you paid calls upon your return to London?"

"I only had time to pay three calls, and with only a quarter of an hour to be had, talk of the ball took up most of the conversation." Petra laid her hand on her friend's arm. "Caroline, do tell me the news."

"Well, I'm afraid it's rather sad," Caroline said. "When Captain Smythe and I were in Portsmouth, the very day before he shipped out, we took a stroll down the high street. There we encountered Lord Milford, who was there for some, as he put it, 'soothing sea air and healing respite.' Naturally, we inquired as to why he wished for time by the sea, and though he had looked quite cheerful when we first laid eyes on him, Milford seemed positively shattered as he imparted the news. My captain said he never cared for Milford—and you know Gwen and I rarely enjoyed a moment in each other's company—but we both agreed it was dreadful."

Petra gave her an exasperated look. "Caroline, do go on. What did Lord Milford say?"

"Dearest," she said, "We were given rather scant details, but I'm afraid Gwen had some sort of fit and died."

FOUR

PETRA GAPED, THE CANDELABRA WOBBLING IN HER HAND, making the flames dance dangerously. "Gwen—she has died? When?"

Caroline took the candelabra and steered Petra toward a nearby bench. "Sit," she commanded, and sat down as well, glancing toward the footman at the far end of the gallery. "Shall I have some lemonade fetched for you? Some wine? You know I do not carry a vinaigrette on me, so you must do with a libation of some sort. I myself would recommend the wine."

Petra waved this suggestion away. "When did Gwen have this fit? I had tea with her only last month, only a day or two after Easter, at Strand Hill. She seemed quite well, I assure you."

Only this was not true, she reflected. She had even said as much to Annie. Gwen's nervous disposition had seemed to affect her more than usual that day. Her friend's gray eyes had darted repeatedly to the door of her drawing room, and she'd started each time footsteps could be heard in the hall. Gwen had eventually settled once Petra had persuaded her to eat a slice of seed cake and then walk with her in the back gardens. Petra had put her friend's excessive nerves down to a lack of proper eating and fresh air, nothing else.

"Milford said his wife passed just over a fortnight ago. On the fifth of this month, I believe," Caroline said. "He said they had a small funeral, which had been Gwen's wish."

Petra nodded sadly. This would have been fitting for Gwen, who'd always been uncomfortable having the eyes of society on her. Even in death, Gwen would have wanted her privacy.

Petra closed her eyes for a long moment, her heart heavy. She would cry later, she decided, when she could be alone to think of her sensitive, gentle-hearted friend. Gwen, with her hair the reddish-brown color of teasel, her lovely gray eyes that showed as much happiness as they did worry and pain, and her sincere compassion for others. But Petra could admit to herself that Gwen had never been of a strong constitution. As much as Petra truly wished to be surprised Gwen had died, she could not be.

"Dearest, are you well?" Caroline asked. Petra nodded.

"Thank you, I am. I shall simply miss Gwen's friendship greatly." She said this on a sigh as she gazed down the north end of the gallery. "But I cannot claim to be wholly shocked, I must admit."

"My captain and I said much the same," Caroline said.

When Petra stood, she linked arms with Caroline once more. "I shall write to Lord Milford tomorrow to convey my sympathies," she said as the two began walking slowly back up the gallery. "Though I feel I must rebuke him for not sending news of her death to Buckfields. Why, it is but eight miles from there to Strand Hill. I could have ridden to the funeral with nothing but the company of one of the stable lads, if needed. And been back again in the same day."

"True. Yet all of society knew Gwen and her husband did not have the happiest of unions, even if they seemed to have been happier as of late. Perhaps Milford was simply content to give her the quiet send-off she requested and get on with living."

Petra pursed her lips. "What a rather callous thing to say, Caroline."

"You think it so? Even though you have long disapproved of Milford as a mate for your friend?" Caroline tilted her head and gazed thoughtfully at the ceiling, painted with the scenes of the Greek god Helios refusing to look at his former lover, Clytie, who is turning into a heliotrope, forevermore following the path of the sun as it arcs across the sky. "I seem to recall you declaring Milford would never be good enough for Gwen even if he had inherited a dukedom instead of a barony, had fifteen thousand a year, and was twice as handsome as he already is."

"That is only because it was true," replied Petra with a touch of mulishness. Then she stopped, turning to face Caroline. "You said their marriage had been a happy one as of late. What did you mean by that?"

"Well, of course there had been rumors of discord between the two for some time, but that you already know," Caroline said, her eyes going a golden amber, as they always did when she was recounting gossip. "In fact, Lady Katherine told me she and her lady's maid witnessed Gwen's husband leaving Milford House early one morning just before Christmas, valise in hand, and in a towering temper. But then, not a few days later, all seemed to be well between husband and wife. My captain even said Milford had been smiling on the regular at White's."

"And smiling at one's club is something strange, is it?" Petra asked as they began to walk once more.

"I think it rather is with Milford," Caroline countered. "Since he came from humble beginnings, he is always trying to be seen as the epitome of an aloof nobleman, would you not agree?"

"Yes, that is true," Petra conceded. Before inheriting the barony when he was one and twenty, Milford, along with his late mother, had run a small inn near Plymouth until the eighth Baron Milford died without heirs and passed the title to his distant cousin. With Strand Hill so close to Buckfields, Petra had been witness to Milford's efforts to shed his former self, which had included taking elocution lessons, finding an excellent tailor, buying one of the earl's best riding stallions, and marrying Lady Gwen, the only child of the late Lord Selby.

Caroline had already continued. "Lady Katherine then said that she had seen Gwen actually outside, strolling along Mayfair with her lady's maid. In *January*, looking quite calm and serene. You were in Suffolk at the time, if I recall."

Petra did not find this so odd, and said as much. Caroline merely tutted.

"Maybe Gwen was willing to accompany you on a walk, dearest, but you must know she is rarely seen in public otherwise. And

I don't recall ever seeing her out of doors during the bitter cold months. You may have seen her at her best, but to the rest of us, she always appeared to rather be like a rabbit who knows she's in the sights of a pack of hungry foxes." To emphasize this, Caroline widened her eyes in fear and darted them around the room as if looking for an exit.

Petra sighed. Caroline's imitation of Gwen was painfully accurate. "And you take this to mean that their marriage had improved?"

"I think everyone took it as such," Caroline said, making a small motion in the general direction of the ballroom, and thus society.

Petra thought on how to reply, finally saying, "As much as Gwen was a dear friend to me, and I to her, she spoke little of the troubles in her marriage. We saw each other with much less frequency than you and I, and I only knew that which she wished to tell me. Which is likely true of most in marriages."

Caroline, who was half a head taller than Petra, leaned sideways, lowering her voice to a whisper. "At least tell me this, for I know you are able. At Lady Oakley's musicale—the one in 1813, not the one last September, which I do contend was like listening to braying donkeys for half the night—is it true Gwen and Milford had a nasty quarrel on the balcony, and Gwen went to claw at his face like an angry cat?"

"Oh? Was that the tale you heard?" Petra said, her face as blank as the bust of the goddess Ceres they'd just passed. For the answer was yes, but as Gwen had lost her head at her husband's cruel lack of sympathy that her courses had come when she had believed herself to be with child, Petra had always felt that discussing it would be beneath her.

"Oh yes. The rumors of this still persist—on occasion when Gwen was mentioned in society, which was not often as of late. Yet you were the only witness—that much you yourself have confirmed—and you have never spoken a word, which is just like you. You are a rather horrid friend when it comes to gossip, dearest."

Petra replied with a beatific smile, but Caroline remained undaunted.

"Oh, I do wish I had attended that musicale, but, if you recall, my captain and I were in Dorset for the month—" Her next words dissolved on her lips as two men came striding into the gallery.

"I tell you, contact Drysdale," drawled the taller one, who had a strong jaw, a lean build, and the relaxed, swaggering gait of an established, confident rake.

"Are his rates reasonable?" said the other, who was rather broader of build, with black hair, blue eyes, and a trim beard that did not disguise an attractively full mouth.

"I think so, considering," said the first. "Though I decided it was not my wish to use him, I know several who have." The two men came to an abrupt halt upon seeing Petra and Caroline, and exchanged a brief glance between them before the taller said, "Excuse me, ladies. We did not know we would be interrupting your enjoyment of the gallery. Lady Caroline, Lady Petra, good evening."

"Lord Langford," Caroline responded with an elegant curtsy. "And Lord Whitfield, good evening."

Duncan's half brother, James Shawcross, the seventh Marquess of Langford, responded with a bow, as did the gentleman who was Caroline's delectable Lord Whitfield. He gave Caroline a wolfish smile, but not before glancing quickly at Langford, as if wondering how much the two ladies had heard, and finding Langford unruffled.

"My lords," Petra said, applying a smile to her lips and curtsying as well, thinking as she always did how much Langford resembled Duncan, and their father, the late marquess, in handsome countenance, though not whatsoever in color. Instead of dark hair with a bit of curl, Langford's was a straight, fine golden brown. His eyes, too, were a light brown instead of the distinctive Shawcross green. He was also lankier than his brother, though about the same height. "How lovely to see you both," Petra added. "Yes, Lady Caroline and I enjoyed some time in the gallery, but were about to return to the ball. Please, do not let us keep you." And to Langford, she added, "And may I congratulate you again on your impending nuptials, my lord. Lady Horatia is a lovely girl and will make an excellent marchioness."

Langford inclined his head with a satisfied smile. "Your good wishes are most appreciated, and I am indeed a fortunate man. Though it has been too long since we have seen you in London, Lady Petra. I do hope you will dance with me this evening and tell me of the latest from Suffolk."

"I should be happy to, my lord," Petra replied, her smile as polite as his. She knew as well as Langford that they would never dance together, that these pleasantries were merely out of the politeness ingrained in both of them.

In truth, she and Lord Langford had always been easy enough in each other's presence, but Petra had never encouraged a truly friendly connection. Not after so many years of witnessing his sour countenance when he was in any proximity to Duncan, no doubt encouraged by his waspish mama. To Petra, Langford's disinterest in her was welcome, for she knew too much of his proud ways and dissolute exploits to wish for anything else.

In these traits, Langford resembled the previous marquess more than Duncan—though Petra reminded herself that Duncan could never be accused of abandoning his own rakish ways. Still, she could not deny Duncan had matured into a gentleman of standing, though with a continued indifference toward society.

That was not to say Duncan did not play his roles well when required. In situations such as tonight's ball, he would dance, though he cared little for it. He would flatter the ladies and laugh at the stories the older men would tell. And he would converse pleasantly with his brother if and when required. Not for Langford's sake—and especially not to make the dowager marchioness happy—but out of respect and affection toward his grandparents, and his two paternal aunts, Lady Endcliffe and Lady Catesby.

Now if only he would apologize to me out of respect, Petra thought irritably.

"And you, Lady Caroline? Would you do me the honor of saving a dance for me, or three? Perhaps the supper dance as the third?" This came from Whitfield, his blue eyes, so stark against his black hair and beard, seeing only Caroline, which included an appreciative glance at her décolletage.

"I should be delighted," Caroline purred. She took Petra's arm again, with a glance over her shoulder at Whitfield, and they began walking back to the saloon and the ball, which was now swollen to the corners with guests. A new dance was about to begin and a handsome young gentleman with a gingery mustache was there in a trice.

"It is only 'The Bourbon Hornpipe,' Lady Caroline," he said, "but I do recall you saying you enjoyed it."

"Go on, then," Petra said to Caroline. "I am in need of refreshment, and I wish to say hello to more of our friends."

As Caroline allowed herself to be led away, Petra's mind went back to the discomfiting news of Gwen, feeling as if a shawl of guilt were wrapping itself about her shoulders. She had known Gwen was unwell, hadn't she? *Yes*, she told herself. *I should have gone to Strand Hill to see my friend no matter if Gwen and Milford did not care for uninvited guests.*

Her heart was heavy once more. She must never let such a thing happen again with any other friend. With thoughts of writing Lord Milford tomorrow to express her sympathies—and, she admitted, with hopes he might write back with some news that would help assuage her guilt—Petra finally made to move toward the lemonade table. Her throat was feeling dry and constricted as she thought of Gwen, saying a silent prayer that her friend had not suffered.

Only steps later, however, she was compelled to stop again and greet a lady and gentleman of her acquaintance. Then she clasped hands with two more ladies, and then greeted another gentleman.

Her dance card began to fill. More friends soon called her name, and by the time Petra could once more set herself back on course for a cooling drink, her heart felt somewhat lightened again as "The Bourbon Hornpipe" was replaced by "The Knight of the Lakes."

FIVE

THERE WERE CERTAIN ADVANTAGES TO HAVING DECLARED SHE would never marry, Petra found herself thinking as she finally reached the lemonade table. She could now arrive to a private ball without a true chaperone and she could speak to whomever she pleased without the risk of ruin to her reputation.

It might just be worth being called a spinster for this joyous level of freedom. Not that she would admit as much to Uncle Tobias.

Walking around three potted lemon trees, she found a footman carefully filling glasses with lemonade. Petra chose one and drank eagerly, all the while admiring the riot of color that was the ladies' dresses, grateful that it was finally spring and Annie could pack away the darker shades and heavier fabrics once more. Even though it would be another two months before it was truly warm enough outside to forgo a wrap.

She put down her empty glass, which was whisked to a silver tray by the footman; he bowed respectfully when she glanced his way. In his livery and powdered wig, he was unremarkable, until he straightened, revealing a tall man with a long, thin nose.

This particular feature would have meant little to Petra, but for the day nearly one month earlier at Strand Hill. When Petra, concerned for Gwen after seeing how nervous her friend seemed, had called for some cake and asked for assistance in walking Gwen out to the small garden at the side of the house. Gwen's footman, Martin, had assisted with both requests.

As such, Petra had seen much of Martin's profile and noted his calm manner. Thus, she spoke before she could remind herself that, to most of those in attendance at the ball, it would be insupportable to be seen conversing with a footman.

"Why, it is Martin, is it not?" Petra said. "I am surprised to see you here. Has the duchess borrowed footmen from as far as Suffolk for this evening's entertainment?"

"It is a pleasure to see you again, my lady," Martin said in greeting, giving her another bow. "I am in Her Grace's employ now. I 'ave been for nearly a fortnight."

Petra nodded with sympathy. "Yes, yes, of course. I expect you left after the death of Lady Milford. I have only just heard, and I am so terribly saddened."

Martin's eyes, which were a pleasant brown and had been gazing into the middle distance as befitted a good footman, snapped momentarily to Lady Petra's. They registered confusion.

"No, my lady," he said. "I were dismissed only a few days after you visited Lady Milford. But—"

"Dismissed?" Petra repeated. Then she caught herself, revised her tone to be noncommittal. "Well, I am sure her ladyship had her reasons for letting you go, Martin."

Martin was just as quick to reply, his voice taking on a measure of indignation. "No, my lady. That is not true."

"I beg your pardon?" Petra asked, regarding him coolly now.

"I mean, I don't believe it were her ladyship who let me go, my lady. She were very happy with my work, she was." He gestured toward Petra with her empty glass, his words coming faster now. "You heard her when you last came to tea, my lady. She told you right in front of me that I were her best footman. She trusted me, and I earned that trust."

Petra looked at the outstretched glass, then back at Martin without a word. The footman, recognizing his gaffe, flushed beet red. He put the glass down and stood at attention, lowering his voice once more to a respectful level. "I am terribly sorry, my lady. Please forgive my impertinence."

Petra was silent, looking to see if anyone had noticed the footman's outburst. Between the music and guests greeting one another—not to mention that the potted lemon trees had provided a bit of screening—it appeared as if she and Martin had both remained overlooked. For the time being, at least.

Petra knew others would insist she shouldn't be listening to Martin's grievances. Yet something about the footman's reaction piqued her curiosity. For, at the very least, what Martin had declared was the truth. Gwen had told Petra in front of Martin that he was an excellent footman. Privately, Gwen had added with a troubled expression that she wished all men of her acquaintance were as trustworthy as he.

Finally, she inclined her head. "Pray tell, Martin. Why were you dismissed?"

Spine straight, and with eyes cast just over her head, the only sign of Martin's feelings now was the tightness in his voice.

"I couldn't tell you, my lady, because I weren't told myself. It were his lordship who gave me my notice. Me an' about eight others. All of us were all loyal to her ladyship, we were. It were right after that physician came to visit, leaving her ladyship in distress and taking to her bed. Lord Milford only said it were her ladyship who decided she had no more need of us, that she would be hiring new servants. He said she didn't need to explain her reasons, but we were to leave the next morning."

"Without any explanation?" Petra asked, frowning.

Martin shook his head. "I wondered what that physician could have said to her to make her wish to dismiss those servants which she liked as opposed to the ones she didn't, but I couldn't see no reason for it. He'd never visited before, and knew nothing of us. It were all very strange, my lady."

Petra could only agree. This was most definitely not like Gwen. Petra had known her friend to be as loyal to her servants as they to her. That Gwen would dismiss that many at once, and without good reason, sounded like madness.

Then she remembered what Caroline had told her—that Gwen had died after some sort of fit. And Gwen had been acting strange when she, Petra, had visited as well.

Lady Petra's stomach felt suddenly hollow with an unwanted thought. Could her friend have been displaying signs worse than simple nerves and melancholia? Was it possible these afflictions were coupled with the onset of something rendering her touched in the head?

She was brought back by Martin's voice, in which thrummed anger and confusion. "We all agreed—there weren't nothing to say her ladyship was ever unhappy with us, my lady."

"And what of her new lady's maid?" Petra asked, recalling that Dorie, Gwen's former lady's maid, had retired only a few weeks before Easter. "Was she dismissed as well?"

"She were, my lady, a few days before the rest of us." Martin said. "Fiona was her name, and she never liked being in service. His lordship said Lady Milford would rather find a more experienced lady's maid, like Dorie had been."

Petra nodded distractedly. Martin looked like he was holding his tongue for his own good now, yet his eyes flicked to Petra's once more. They were pained, and his voice came out as a hoarse whisper.

"My lady, you said Lady Milford died. When did this happen? Even though she dismissed me without a word, she were still kind enough to send us all off with good references. For that, and for the good years in her employ, I'd like to pay my respects."

Petra felt a rush of sympathy for the footman. "That is very kind of you, Martin. However, I'm afraid it has been two weeks at least since Lady Milford's passing. And it will not do to keep the truth from you—it seems Lady Milford's death was caused by a fit of some sort. There was only a small service in her honor afterward. I did not even attend."

Martin frowned. "That cannot be true, my lady."

"I assure you, Martin, it is the truth," Petra said, but kindly. "A small funeral would have been to her preference."

"No, my lady," he said, shaking his head. "I mean she could not have died when you said. I saw Lady Milford but two days ago. Standing not far from Milford House."

"Here in London?" Petra said with no little incredulity.

Martin nodded. "Early in the morning, it was, while I were exercising His Grace's gray mare. Her ladyship were looking up at the house as if she barely knew it and had no lady's maid at her side." The footman frowned as he thought back. "She weren't dressed like her usual self, neither. I called out to her when I saw she looked to be in a state of distress, movin' her hands like she does when she's havin' one of her bad days."

Petra watched as Martin pulled his hands together and to his chest, curling and uncurling his fingers in a rapid pace while rolling his shoulders back, almost as if he were trying to rid himself of his own skin.

A sense of unease was rippling through Petra. She had seen Gwen make those very hand movements that day during tea at Strand Hill. And often enough before that.

"I called out to her ladyship," Martin continued, two lines of concern forming between his eyes, "but she just turned and walked away in haste, as if she were frightened. I went to call after her again and—" He stopped, eyes going rigidly to front.

Petra was at first inclined to demand he explain himself and his absurd notion of seeing Gwen alive, until an understanding of the footman's response made her glance with practiced dispassion over her shoulder.

Trenworth, the duchess's butler, was swiftly approaching, his dark eyes boring into the poor footman with fiery disapproval. Without a word, Trenworth gave an almost imperceptible motion toward the tray of half-drunk glasses of lemonade, then jerked his own powdered head in the direction of the servants' stairs. When she turned back, Martin was already hurrying away, the bright tinkling sounds of glass hitting glass mingling with the strains of the violins.

Trenworth bowed at the neck. "Lady Petra, I am terribly sorry for Martin's intrusion on your moment of respite. He is new, and tends to forget his place at times. I shall be sure to reprimand him thoroughly."

"No, no, Trenworth," Petra replied as she selected another glass of lemonade. "Martin did nothing wrong in this instance. It was I who engaged him in conversation. I recognized him as being formerly in Lady Milford's employ, you see."

Trenworth's expression remained politely unconvinced of Martin's innocence, but he tipped his head in acquiescence, murmuring, "Of course, my lady." One more slight motion with his hand and a new footman was manning the lemonade table. The opening notes of a quadrille had begun as well.

It was one of Lady Petra's favorites. She would love to dance. It was what she should do, and she had seen a couple of gentlemen of her acquaintance who were usually kind enough to offer to partner her when the dance was not already taken on her card.

Petra told herself to go find Caroline. To forget what Martin had said and ignore the unsettlingly strange comment about him seeing Gwen two days earlier—made further troubling by the idea that Martin had wanted to say more to give credence to his claim.

No, she decided. Martin had probably concocted a story about Gwen to suit some unknown purpose of his own after being dismissed for reasons he felt were unwarranted.

Yes, that is likely the case, Petra thought firmly. Gwen was dead, and Petra would do well to forget her concerns that something was not ringing true. After all, an unmarried earl's daughter who had recently declared herself as never wishing to marry should not court additional talk by asking questions about anyone's death, much less that of a friend who might have been experiencing some level of madness.

The music swelled. On the far end of the saloon, the duchess continued to greet her guests, the handsomely craggy face of His Grace now at her side, while on the dance floor, couples came together and moved apart in time. Duncan was amongst them, partnering Miss Arabella Littlewood, the beautiful young ward of Lord and Lady Potsford.

Petra watched the dancers, somewhat expecting to meet with

Duncan's imperious gaze as she did, for she'd felt the oddest sensation of having eyes steadily on her. But he showed not the slightest sign of knowing her whereabouts. Instead, he was smiling—*actually smiling, the lout*—as he made conversation with Miss Littlewood, who blushed prettily as she responded.

Glancing around, Petra could not see anyone paying attention to her at all. Not even Trenworth, who was instructing the new footman to line up glasses of lemonade in perfect rows.

Her eyes slid toward the servants' doorway through which Martin had disappeared. She did not believe he had truly seen Gwen alive, but something was compelling her to be certain. If nothing else, Petra wished to forbid the footman from spreading false gossip that might add to the distress of Gwen's husband and remaining family members, few and distant as she knew they were. And if he indeed could produce more pertinent information regarding Gwen, then Petra decided she must find some way to discuss the matter with him privately in a way that would not cause either of them to be looked upon as doing something untoward.

Yes, that would do. Now, all she had to do was to find Martin once more.

She felt it likely that Martin would be delivering the glasses to the servery room, where another servant would then take them downstairs. Petra would need a reason to follow the footman from the ballroom, one that would allow her the freedom to walk through Hillmorton House without Trenworth or anyone else thinking her motives suspicious.

Inspiration soon came, much as it had a couple of days earlier in the harness room at Buckfields. Discreetly, she reached up and pulled out two of the hairpins from her chignon, then loosened one more. Annie would again not be pleased with her.

"Oh, dear," she said, with just enough anguish to sound correct. "I am afraid my hairpins have become loose."

At this pronouncement, the dutiful Trenworth immediately faced her. "My lady?"

Petra held up the pins. "Her Grace has set up the lavender drawing room for ladies to retire to when needed, yes? Splendid. No, no, I remember the way. I'm certain one of the maids there can assist me very well."

SIX

KNOWING MARTIN WOULD LIKELY BE IN THE SERVERY WAS ONE thing. Knowing where the blasted servery was located was another thing entirely. Though liveried footmen and other servants were at nearly every corner, asking them for directions would cause gossip, so she simply kept walking as if she did not require their assistance.

After two wrong turns—one where she stopped briefly to inspect her freckles in a large mirror before scowling at what she saw and moving onward, and the second where she came upon a dead end—Petra ended up, coincidentally, where she had first claimed to be headed: the lavender drawing room.

Named for the hue of its striped wallpaper, the drawing room was the duchess's least favorite—owing to a draft that always chilled Her Grace's ankles and, somehow, the tops of her ears. But tonight it had been turned into a warm and cozy place with several sofas, chairs, and chaises longues for Her Grace's female guests to sit, rest their feet, gossip, and have their hair touched up or their cosmetics reapplied. At such an early hour of the ball, the room was largely empty save for two ladies and several maids. The maids stood along the back wall in their starched black dresses, white aprons and caps, and plain faces, waiting to be called forth by a woman of noble birth wearing bright spring colors and jewels that sparkled in the candlelight.

And one of these ladies, her ginger hair curled into tight ringlets, was the last person Petra wished to see.

Slowly, she turned around, but it was no use. There were some predators in the wild who had the ability to sense their quarry long before their desired meal knows better, and Lynley, Lady Wyncroft, had long been one of them.

"Could it be my dear cousin?" Lynley exclaimed in apparent delight, turning in her seat, away from the mirror that had served her keen eyes all too well.

Petra offered a smile, then suppressed a sigh when Lynley held out a hand, knowing Petra must cross the room to take it or risk slighting her. Wending her way around two bergère chairs and a chaise, she clasped hands with the only child of sixth baronet Sir Oswald Allington, her mother's sole male cousin. The former Miss Allington was now a viscountess, having married Viscount Wyncroft the previous July, less than a month after Lady Ardley's ball.

Petra's relationship with Lynley had not always been strained. As young children, they had played together well in the nursery when Sir Oswald, a widower himself, had brought Lynley for stays with a cousin of her own age. That was, until Lynley's desire to rarely venture out of doors beyond the occasional turn in the garden clashed with Petra's appetite for riding horses, reading under the dappled shade of the oak trees, catching ladybirds in the garden, and playing on the lawn at having the powers of a god or goddess from mythology—almost all accomplished alongside Duncan and the earl's various dogs.

Over time, Lynley's pretty violet-hued eyes increasingly assessed Petra in narrow fashion. The ability to converse with one another on even the smallest of matters was fractured. And after she had ascended to a rank above Petra with her marriage, her cousin's tongue, sharp from even her earliest days, had been honed to have the bite of an asp.

When Petra had declared herself as never wishing to marry, Lynley had been one of the first to declare to any lady of distinction—and talkative servants as well—that she always thought Petra strange. Overly willful. And, as of the last time Caroline had deigned to attend one of Lynley's teas and then wrote Petra to recount the news, likely entertaining sapphic tendencies.

Initially, several women of the ton had taken heed of Lynley's words. For a brief time thereafter, Petra's invitations had reduced in number, especially by the patronesses at Almack's. Yet as those same patronesses continued to notice Her Grace extending her good favor to Petra, it soon became clear that Lynley's opinions were falling on ears that were, if not deaf, at least willing to listen with some level of dubiety.

"I'm absolutely delighted to see you, cousin," Lynley said, not sounding delighted at all.

"As am I. You look lovely tonight, Lynley." Her cousin's gown was indeed beautiful. The pale pink silk was embroidered with white leaves about the bodice, forming into vines that trailed down the length of her skirt.

"Lady Wyncroft, if you please, Petra," her cousin returned crisply, and loud enough for the maids to hear. She turned back to the mirror and used one finger to push a stray strand of dark red hair. "I have not given you permission to use my Christian name now that I am married . . ." She swiveled her eyes to Petra in the glass, the unspoken words being, *And you are not.*

Petra met Lynley's eyes steadily, holding her gaze just enough to see a bit of pink on her cousin's cheeks, then said, "If you wish it, Lady Wyncroft. And how is dear Tibby? I saw him earlier, but have not yet been able to greet him."

"Breckville," Lynley corrected coldly. "I shall not have anyone calling my husband by that horrid nickname."

"Why? When it is the name the viscount himself prefers . . ." Petra lifted one eyebrow just enough, though her voice remained sweet. "When he gives his friends permission to use it."

Lynley huffed, then her pinched little mouth widened. "Why were you skulking outside the door just now? You do know the wall a spinster sits along whilst everyone else dances is not here, but in the ballroom, yes?"

This produced a gasp from some of the maids, no doubt as Lynley had wished it from the satisfied look in her eyes.

"Mm," replied Petra, resisting the urge to display her dance card. "I think I shall have enough dances tonight to suit my tastes, but I thank you for your concern."

Lynley grasped Petra's hand, cocking her head to one side in a display of gentle sympathy. "And I am glad of it, dear cousin," she cooed. "For a dance or two will do you some good."

"Pardon me, my lady."

Petra looked over to see one of the maids bobbing a curtsy.

"Tansy, my lady. I was your lady's maid the fortnight you spent at Hillmorton Castle in Warwickshire last summer, when your own lady's maid was taken ill."

Petra's lips curved into a smile. "Indeed, and I recall you doing an excellent job, Tansy."

"Thank you ever so much, my lady," Tansy said, flushing with pleasure. She looked like a little chickadee, with bright dark eyes, black dress, and golden hair visible beneath a white cap. "I noticed you were carrying your hairpins. If you would come with me, I should be happy to return them to where they belong."

"You have read my mind, Tansy." She turned to Lynley, who had not quite hidden the shock at knowing Petra had spent two weeks at the duke and duchess's estate in Warwickshire, and gave her a smile. "Seeing you always does me a good turn, Lady Wyncroft. Thank you. I shall see you and Tibby in the ballroom. Though if I am dancing too much to speak with you again, I look forward to your tea the first week of May."

"Oh, my lady," whispered Tansy a few moments later from their place at a mirror in the corner, out of earshot of the other maids, as they watched Lynley rise and sail from the drawing room with her nose all but aimed at the ceiling. "If you will permit me to say so, that was well done."

Petra allowed herself a brief grin as she held up the hairpins for Tansy to reinsert. Then she had an idea.

"Tansy, are you acquainted with the new footman, Martin?"

The maid's cheeks reddened prettily. "I am, my lady. He is

very kind, quite handsome, and most intelligent. I enjoy talking with him very much, when there is time. Do you know him as well?"

"Only a little," Petra said. "He was the trusted footman for my late friend, Lady Milford."

Tansy's face went somber yet confused. "Late, you say, my lady? I'm afraid I did not know her ladyship had died. Martin had said he'd seen her but two days ago. He did say she looked unlike herself, but she hurried away when he attempted to speak to her. He was most disconcerted, but then she had dismissed him so cruelly . . ." She trailed off, her cheeks ablaze.

"It is all right, Tansy," Petra said, meeting the girl's worried eyes via the mirror. "You did not put a foot out of step. Martin explained to me he was dismissed for reasons he does not understand. While I have no information to give him on that score, I was hoping to speak with him again regarding his seeing Lady Milford in London. Do you know where I may find him?"

"I'm afraid he could be anywhere at present, my lady. I know Mr. Trenworth had him in the ballroom, at the lemonade table, but I passed by him a few minutes ago and he said he'd been sent away."

"Yes," Petra mused. "I am afraid I must shoulder the blame there."

Then, via the mirror, she saw someone rushing into the drawing room. It was Lady Potsford, clearly upset and flustered. While this was not an entirely new way of encountering her ladyship, Petra wondered if she had come across Lynley in the halls, for the older woman was another of Lynley's favorites on whom to test her verbal barbs. Especially as Lady Potsford had managed to wear a color that was unsuited to her, again, with her hair, as per usual, styled in unbecoming fashion.

Inwardly suppressing a sigh, Petra felt compelled to go to Lady Potsford's side, for her ladyship had always been kind to her, and had been a good friend of her own late mama. Though that did not mean she enjoyed too much time in Lady Potsford's company. For when one did, one was subjected to a near-constant discourse regarding young ladies and how their propriety was constantly in danger of being compromised.

This rhetoric had increased greatly when, some six years earlier, Lady Potsford, childless herself, had taken in as her ward Miss Arabella Littlewood, the daughter of her late cousin.

In doing so, the maternal instinct to protect a young female had risen up out of Lady Potsford with the strength of a lioness—if a lioness were prone to fits of near swooning if her cub so much as coughed once, complained of a headache, pricked her finger while completing a needlepoint, or, heaven forbid, ventured outside when it looked like rain.

Sadly, Petra felt, this tendency to worry about Arabella had only grown worse as the girl, who had grown tall and willowy with laughing blue eyes and soft brown hair, was now of marrying age.

I expect Duncan might have noticed this fact as well, she thought while Tansy carefully smoothed and pinned a final curl. Using the mirror, Petra met the housemaid's eyes and spoke softly.

"Tansy, I must go and speak with Lady Potsford. Might I ask you to pass along a message to Martin for me? One that must be kept in the strictest of confidences, you understand. Only to be revealed to Martin and no one else."

"Of course, my lady," she said with a brightened face. "I would be happy to. And I will be the soul of discretion. I want to be a proper lady's maid, I do, and for that to happen, I must be able to be trusted. You can count on me, my lady."

SEVEN

PETRA DID NOT WASTE TIME. "PLEASE TELL MARTIN I SHOULD like to speak with him regarding Lady Milford, and what or who he feels he saw, and I should like this conversation to happen as soon as possible. For it concerns me that I am hearing Lady Milford is alive, when everything points to the fact that she sadly passed away."

Tansy nodded, looking suitably serious, and Petra continued.

"Tell Martin I will hear him out and take what he says into consideration. However, until I speak with him, I would ask that he not continue going about saying that he has seen Lady Milford, for doing so might cause unneeded talk and Lord Milford undue pain."

"Of course, my lady," said Tansy. "I believe Martin has only told me about seeing Lady Milford. Would you like him to come to Forsyth House to speak with you?"

Petra thought on this, finally shaking her head.

"Ask Martin to simply deliver a note to me at Forsyth House. In this note, he should tell me what day and time he can meet me at the stand of trees near where the Temple of Concord stood last year in the Green Park." When Tansy blinked as if in confusion, Petra explained. "That is where I exercise my horse when I am in town and wish not to endure the chaos of Rotten Row. It is generally quiet after one o'clock in the afternoon, when most people are having a meal at midday. Tell Martin that it would be an ideal time. And as His Grace's footman, no one will stop him from entering its grounds, especially if he claims His Grace has suggested exercising the gray mare at the more quiet parkland."

"But why should he not come to speak to you at Forsyth House, my lady?" Tansy asked, then promptly looked chagrined. "I'm ever so sorry, my lady. It was out of turn for me to ask."

Petra rose from her seat at seeing Lady Potsford across the room, looking pale as she she all but slumped in a klismos chair upholstered in lavender velvet.

"It is simple," Petra said, not unkindly. "I do not wish for further gossip to spread, even if unintentionally, by my own loyal servants, or Her Grace's, by bringing a footman to my drawing room—though it would not be suspicious for a footman from Hillmorton House to deliver a note to me. And should Martin simply write his account down and have it delivered to me, I may have additional questions, and I'm afraid I cannot be seen in a constant exchange of letters with a footman, either."

"No, my lady," Tansy said, wide-eyed with earnestness. "It wouldn't do."

"Quite. However, at the Green Park, Martin and I can meet as if by accident. I can pretend my horse has a stone in its foot, and ask him for assistance, that sort of thing. It is rather for the best this way. Now, do you understand all I have asked you to say to him?"

Tansy nodded. "Yes, my lady. I shall do so immediately."

Petra pulled a coin from her reticule and pressed it into Tansy's hand. The girl tried to say it was not needed, but Petra insisted. "You've done well, and you shall make a fine lady's maid one day."

She watched as the maid bobbed a curtsy and hurried from the drawing room, and then she made her way to Lady Potsford, and just in time. Her ladyship had risen from her chair, seemed to make an effort to gather herself, and begun to walk unsteadily to the door.

"Please, Lady Potsford, take my arm," Petra said, then added in an undertone, "I do hope my cousin, Lady Wyncroft, is not to blame for your current distress."

Lady Potsford's eyes, which were grayish in color, large, and quite pretty, widened in brief surprise at this, but she shook her head as she took Petra's arm and they left the drawing room.

"Thank you, my dear. No, Lady Wyncroft passed me without a word, and for that, I was thankful. I simply do not . . ." Petra watched her swallow and try again. "I simply cannot . . . I confess I am in a state of constant worry."

Petra stopped and turned to face Lady Potsford. "You have always been kind to me, and I should like to help you, if I can." Upon recognizing where they stood, Petra said, "Do look, we are near His Grace's small library. It is a delightfully calming place. Why do we not go in there, and you can tell me what it is that is putting you into such a state."

Lady Potsford's eyes filled with tears, but she composed herself and shook her head.

"I thank you, Lady Petra, but no, there is nothing you can do." Then she clenched her fists and exhorted, "They have seen to it! *He* has seen to it!" Her hands went to her mouth. "Oh, my poor Arabella! What am I to do?"

Petra pressed her lips together. It would seem Lady Potsford was merely becoming overwrought again about her ward. And with all the handsome young gentlemen here tonight at the ball, Arabella's dance card would be full quickly. She recalled the way Arabella had been watching Duncan as they danced, with her eyes verging on besotted.

"I am sure that Mr. Shawcross has honorable intentions regarding Arabella, Lady Potsford," Petra said hastily. "I should not worry."

Without warning, Lady Potsford reached for Petra's hand, taking it in both of hers.

"You are as brave as your mama always thought you would be." Her grip tightened. "I, too, once had an opportunity never to marry. I could have lived in a pretty little cottage on my aunt's estate in Wiltshire. I had two thousand a year to my name, and I could have lived my life tending to some of the most magnificent rose gardens you have ever seen. But I decided to marry instead. In hopes of so many things, I admit, including children of my own. But I wish I had been as brave as you, Lady Petra. If I had, I might have saved others as well. Both then, and now."

"Do not say such things, Lady Potsford," Petra insisted, squeezing her ladyship's hand. "Why do we not have tea in the coming days and speak further? Would you come to Forsyth House on Saturday, perhaps?"

Lady Potsford looked close to tears. "I would be delighted—"

They both stilled when voices could be heard from His Grace's library as the door was opened.

"No, no, Bellingham," one said in plummy tones, making him easily recognizable as Lord Potsford. "As I've said before, just meet with the man. Tell him your concerns. He'll explain your options, and do the rest."

Another voice replied, "I think I shall, my lord." Petra nearly made a face at the unctuous voice of Josiah, Lord Bellingham, causing her not to notice that Lady Potsford had shifted to stand behind her.

"What, ho? Is that Lady Petra?"

One would never know to look at Lord Potsford now that he had once been handsome. For Petra had known him since her childhood, when his lordship had kept a string of racehorses for her papa to train. Of Potsford's once-thick head of brown hair, nothing but a ring of gray-brown that started above his ears and ran round the back of his head remained. His fine nose and smooth cheeks now held so many fine red veins that he looked perpetually flushed with anger. And even his eyes, once a warm hazel, now looked small and dull, instead of full of good humor.

Now, while the width of him from the front remained slim, when seen from the side, his middle bulged almost as if he were in the last stages of being with child. His tailor had done the best he could, though, and Lord Potsford cut a fine picture as he strode forward with the slow swagger of a man who'd once been handsome and powerful, and still believed himself to be both, even if he only somewhat remained the latter.

"You are correct, my lord," Petra said with a curtsy. Reluctantly, she then looked to the other man with a nod. "Good evening, Lord Bellingham."

Josiah Bellingham's brown eyes locked onto Petra's form with a particular greediness of a former suitor who, though now married, had yet to stop acting as if Petra might accept his suit. But Lord Potsford had noticed his wife, and his own eyes narrowed in a heartbeat.

"How long have the two of you been standing here?" he snapped. "What did you hear?"

Behind her Lady Potsford emitted the softest of whimpers as Petra replied, "I do not know what you could mean, my lord. Her ladyship and I have just come from the lavender drawing room. It was naught but a coincidence that we encountered you here."

"Then what were you speaking of just now? I demand to know!"

Lady Potsford was shaking at Petra's side and looked like she was going to cry.

"Cakes," said Petra hastily.

"Cakes?" barked Lord Potsford.

"Yes, my lord," Petra confirmed. "I was recalling the delicious cakes Lady Potsford served at her dinner party last season, and I wished to ask for the recipe for my Mrs. Bing."

Lord Potsford looked Petra up and down, then did the same to Lady Potsford with a sneer.

"The only thing my wife *can* do well is eat cakes. Come, Mary. Back to the ball with you so you can further watch Arabella's every move."

Before Petra could do anything, he'd taken Lady Potsford's elbow and shunted his wife away, leaving a leering Josiah Bellingham at her side.

Petra did rather detest the idea of being near Josiah while devoid of a companion, for each of the last three times it had happened, he had attempted to pull her into a secluded corner. She had been able to evade him the first two. And the third?

Discreetly running her gloved thumbs across the tips of her fingers, Petra pressed to feel her fingernails. They were not quite so long this time, but she would still readily embed them in Josiah's flesh again if the situation required it.

"Were you really in the lavender drawing room with Potsford's wife, Lady Petra?" Josiah asked with a smirk that made his snub nose twitch. A bit like a pig's, she always thought. Yet most ladies of the ton found Josiah, with his slim build, broad shoulders, clear brown eyes, and thick hair the color of honey, to be quite handsome. His wife, Fanny, certainly did, and rarely left his side at balls, possessive of her husband and visibly despising the unwritten rule that married men were not to dance with their wives.

"Of course," Petra said. "My hairpins had come loose, and I had to ask one of the maids to help me."

"Hmm," Josiah said, an irritating tinge of doubt in his voice. "True, Trenworth said as much, yet I noticed you talking to that footman he sent running. One I believe used to work for Lord Milford. You were rather animated in whatever you were discussing, my lady, and then followed after him with more haste than I would have expected."

So I was not wrong, thought Petra. *There* had *been eyes on me— and they were from this swaggering cur.*

But Josiah's eyes had moved to a place over Petra's head, warming with a sight. "I say, hello there."

Petra turned to see Tansy. The maid bobbed a curtsy to Petra, then one to Josiah, a flush on her cheeks. "Pardon me, my lady. I just wished to say that I did as you asked."

"Thank you, Tansy," Petra said, wishing the girl had not stopped at all. "You may go now."

She curtsied again. "I do hope you will enjoy the ball, my lady. You as well, my lord."

"Oh, I plan to," Josiah said. "Though there will be few there as pretty as you."

Tansy blushed, but could not contain a smile as she hurried away.

Josiah then offered Petra his arm, but she had already pretended to be more concerned with patting her hair to notice anything else, and began walking. A long stride meant Josiah was immediately at her side, but she ignored him. His conduct, however, could not be so easily overlooked.

"You should not do that, you know," she said.

Josiah looked unabashed. "Do what, exactly?"

"Flirt with a housemaid," Petra said. "Why do some men always feel as if pulling the attention of a female onto them makes them more of a man? In my opinion, it only lessens you, and makes fine and innocent young women fall prey to potential ruin."

Josiah let out a bark of a laugh. "And you think that maid is innocent? With the way she smiled at me? Highly doubtful, my lady."

They had reached the main corridor, stepping onto a pristine carpet of reds, golds, and creams—the colors of the duchy of Hillmorton. Petra came to a halt, turning to face Josiah.

"First, lower your voice, sir," she snapped. "And second, how would you come to know whether a housemaid you have only seen once was virtuous or not? Or do you just enjoy making assumptions about a woman, and then feel that, by voicing them, you can make others believe badly of her as well?"

Josiah watched her with amusement, then leaned down so his lips were only inches from her ear. "You seem to be overly concerned about the reputation of a housemaid, Lady Petra." He backed off just enough to ensure that his eyes met hers. "Or is it possible that your concern is for someone else's reputation, hmm? Possibly one who rushes after a handsome footman?"

Petra's right hand was clenching into a fist, but her inclination to bring it swinging upward was stopped short by the sound of someone clearing their throat. Josiah returned to his full height and slowly turned sideways to reveal the form of Duncan Shawcross some five steps away, arms crossed and leaning against a carved Roman pillar said to have been from Caesar's own palace.

"I see you laid eyes on our Lady Petra," Duncan said. Glancing at Petra's right hand, he added, "Though if I hadn't interrupted just now, you might only have one eye that's still capable of seeing her."

Josiah snorted. "You jest, Shawcross. She would not dare."

"Scoff if you like, Bellingham," Duncan said. He wryly brushed the side of his thumb over his left eye. "It was many years ago now, yes, but believe me, I speak from experience. And I believe you bear the scars on your wrist from what you felt Lady Petra would not dare to do, so I wouldn't be so sure."

Petra watched as Josiah's cheeks turned splotchy with a building anger as he turned to face her directly. "Such an unattractive trait to have in a woman," he said in tones barely above a whisper. "It no longer amazes me that you are a spinster, for no man wants a woman who acts with so little femininity. Or maybe it is not a man's touch that you crave." He lowered his voice further. "Or maybe you are simply mad, too."

"I say, Bellingham, I would appreciate it if you spoke up," came Duncan's voice, all lazy ease, before Petra's shock could abate enough for her to form a response.

Josiah stared down at her, his eyes bright with malice. "I merely told Lady Petra that I am glad to see her looking so well, and I will allow you, Shawcross, to escort her back to the ball."

With a bow that was more condescending than polite, Josiah stalked off. Petra realized she was shaking with suppressed anger, and ordered herself to stop. When her body did not comply, she channeled it into a fierce glare directed at Duncan.

"I do not require you to come to my aid, Mr. Shawcross."

"You did not require it tonight, no," he returned, looking steadily at her.

"Don't you be a boor as well," she snapped, rolling her eyes and crossing her arms over her chest.

"Now, lass, you canna call me a *hoore*," Duncan admonished in a low voice, though from his lips was heard a brogue so thick Petra's mind was transported. To the day when Duncan first arrived at Buckfields, all tousled hair, wary green eyes, and the barely intelligible speech of a wild Scottish boy with no proper schooling.

Just as Petra's eyes flew wide, Duncan reverted to his normal voice, saying with feigned contrition, "Do forgive me, my lady, you said 'boor.' Well, yes, that I can be from time to time."

"Quite so," she replied through gritted teeth. "With respects to your boorishness, I demand that you stop repeating that tired story of the day when we were children and I gave you a blackened eye. You make me out to be a woman with no intelligent qualities who uses her fists and her claws instead of her words and her brain. I do not care for it, mostly because it is far from the truth."

"Fair enough. All the same, I enjoy putting Bellingham in his place as much as you, so I did it for my own amusement."

Of course you thought of only yourself, Petra thought hotly.

"Was Bellingham correct?" Duncan asked as he extracted a lemon drop from his pocket and popped it into his mouth. "Were you following the new footman? For while I do not believe that you did so out of some amorous intent—I have seen for myself the way you look at a man who has your heart—I have also seen the way you look when you wish to discover the root of some matter." He raised an eyebrow in request of a response.

Petra was feeling her ire rise, but kept her voice sweet. "And do tell. When tonight did I look this way?"

Duncan flashed the briefest of smiles. "You must recall that I know every secret passageway and shortcut in this house. The dance had just ended, and I sought a moment to myself before Lady Potsford admonished me for choosing too energetic a reel for Miss Littlewood's 'delicate temperament.'" He rubbed the back of his neck in a brief show of exhaustion. "Sometimes I miss the days of being reminded that I am a bastard, when the young misses were shunted to the other side of the room at the very sight of me, despite my grandparents' favor."

"Oh, but I am happy to remind you that you are a—"

"As I was saying," Duncan continued. "I was about to go into His Grace's library, then had to retreat to evade Lord Potsford and Bellingham. I saw you looking about, determining your next direction—but not before you checked your reflection in a mirror." Casually, he tapped the bridge of his nose, right where her freckles were smattered, and Petra scowled. "Nevertheless, not wishing to alert Potsford or Bellingham to either you or me, I did not call out." He paused. "You are well aware of the way to the lavender drawing room, Petra. Whom or what did you wish to find instead?"

She wanted to tell him about her concerns that Martin was speaking of seeing Gwen alive. That she was looking for Martin only for that purpose, and to ask for Duncan's help. The words were forming on her lips as easily as they would have three years earlier, but she bit them back.

"Whom or what I wish to find is no longer your concern," she said. "You made it quite obvious that you wished it that way when you chose never to reply to me." Then she turned on her heel and followed Josiah's path back to the ball, ignoring the pang of misery that was attempting to nudge aside her vexation.

EIGHT

PETRA CONTINUED TO FEEL NETTLED AS SHE RETURNED TO THE music-filled saloon, but at least Josiah Bellingham had thankfully vanished into the throng of guests. Duncan, too, had not come near her again after entering the ballroom a respectful full step behind her. For her part, Petra had immediately found Caroline and attempted to relate Martin's strange tale to her friend.

However, she soon discovered she and Caroline would not have two moments put together to speak privately. Sometimes it was due to friends wanting to talk and gossip. Other times, both ladies had offers to dance. In the end, Petra only had time to tell Caroline that she had much to impart to her, and then finally gave herself over to enjoying the simple pleasure of being back in London and indulging in the feast of music and friendship.

Though the crowd of nearly four hundred had thinned by half or more as the clock edged closer to striking a new day, Petra danced and talked until it was finally time to indulge in the sumptuous banquet from Her Grace's kitchens.

The supper began at one o'clock in the morning, and Petra followed the crowd into the dining room, thoroughly famished and happily exhausted from dancing, which had the added benefit of helping to abate her worries.

Here was one time that being without a partner made no difference, for the rules were relaxed, other than the notion that those gentlemen and ladies who had danced the final dance before supper—the supper dance, as it were—would continue to accompany one another into the dining room and sit together. As Petra had been earlier waylaid by His Grace, who was determined to hear every second of how his two young thoroughbred colts were coming along, the supper dance had been enjoyed without her.

Looking for a seat so she could rest her throbbing feet, Petra cared little for whom she sat next to, be they friend or relative stranger. Wishing only to sit far from Josiah Bellingham, Petra waited until she saw him choose a seat, then went in the opposite direction, taking possession of the first chair she saw empty that was out of Josiah's line of sight. An aged vicar, one Petra recognized as being kin to Her Grace, was already occupying the chair to her left. He smiled kindly, giving a quick nod of his head, and then began to wolf down a bowl of white soup.

Unoffended, especially as it meant not hearing a sermon of sorts on, well, anything, Petra turned to find a young man of no more than eighteen standing at the chair on her right, looking somewhat uncertain.

"Hello," she said with a smile, picking up her wineglass.

"Good evening—though I suppose one should say good morning, Lady Petra," he said, giving her a bow. His voice was as timid as his stance, and sounded as if he were still becoming used to its lower registers. "I am Judson Bellingham, my lady. May I sit?"

"Bellingham?" Petra repeated, eyes instantly narrowed.

"Indeed, Lady Petra. Josiah is my older brother. I, ah, understand you are acquainted."

"It is rather all one could say," Petra replied. "However, it is true your brother was briefly one of my suitors during my debutante year."

Judson looked like he wanted to tug at his collar. "I'm afraid I was not witness to it, Lady Petra, as I am more than nine years his junior, and was rarely around Josiah as a child. That was as much my desire as his, I must confess." With this statement, a small spark of defiance could be seen in Judson's eyes.

At first glance, Petra had seen a thin young man with hair the color of straw, a pale, oval face, and brown eyes. But she could see the distinct resemblance now that marked him as a Bellingham.

Judson had grown an inch or two taller and had hair a shade lighter than Josiah, but he had the same well-formed features and snub nose. Though in Judson's face, Petra could not see an ounce of guile. Not yet, at least.

"Then I must confess that I consider you most intelligent in that sense, and I am glad to make your acquaintance," Petra said, inclining her head. "Yes, please sit, Mr. Bellingham."

He did, saying, "I thank you, Lady Petra, and I would be honored if you would call me Juddy. It is what all my friends call me, and I should hope to count you as one of them." With this, he smiled, making him look nothing at all like his older brother, but instead like a kind young man.

"Then I shall be honored to count myself amongst them, Juddy," she replied, then looked smartly left at hearing an odd sound.

It was snoring. The vicar on her other side had promptly fallen asleep after eating his white soup. His last spoonful was teetering on the edge of his bowl, ready to splash onto the napkin the vicar had tucked into his collar. Gently, Petra removed the spoon from his hand and pushed the bowl away, lest the vicar slump down onto the table itself.

"Can't say I blame the old chap," said Juddy. "I've had a rather lovely time tonight, but I've had little shut-eye this week with sitting for exams. I'm a first-year at Cambridge, you know. Anyway, I feel as if I could touch my chin to my chest and start snoring at any moment, too." When the vicar gave a particularly loud snore, making Petra giggle, Juddy said, "In fact, I might just take a quick kip after supper like him. Then I shall be fresh once more for all the dancing that is to come. Josiah and Fanny have said we will stay all the way through breakfast. This will be my first ball where I've stayed to the bitter end, and I am rather looking forward to it. Will you be staying as well?"

"I should think so," Petra replied. "Her Grace's ball has long been my favorite, for it ushers in spring, so I wish to stay as long as my poor feet will allow."

"Yes, I do believe I may need to soak my trotters tomorrow, too," Juddy said, "but it shall be worth it."

Petra began to fill her plate as she looked around the room. Dozens of tables were placed one next to the other and formed a rectangle, giving her a grand view of Her Grace's guests. They had danced all night in their finery, becoming livelier as the wine flowed, and were now still moving about, taking chairs, and exclaiming about how hungry they were.

At the far end of the room, Lady Caroline looked right pleased to be sitting next to Lord Whitfield, whose mouth had remained within an inch or two of Caroline's ear for some time now. Nearby, the Marquess of Langford was paying little notice to his lovely fiancée, Lady Horatia. Instead, Langford chatted merrily with the beautiful and recently widowed Lady Norbury on his opposite side. Farther down was seated Miss Arabella Littlewood, next to Duncan. Arabella was looking as if she'd had more wine than she should have, but drank the glass of barley water Duncan poured for her without incident.

And not too far away was Lady Potsford, keeping a worried-looking eye on Arabella, who had stumbled when walking into the room, only to be rescued by Duncan. He'd managed to grab her before she fell, set her upright in one swift move, and offer her his arm. This was lauded by everyone near them, and the whispers about Duncan and Arabella had begun immediately, prompting Lady Potsford to cast a look—a hopeful one, Petra felt—in the direction of her husband, who steadfastly ignored his wife.

Turning toward Juddy Bellingham, Petra was eager to set her mind upon subjects more pleasing.

"Are there any balls or parties you are anticipating in the coming weeks?" Petra asked, taking a bite of a jelly that was quite good.

"*Rather*," Juddy said with enthusiasm, naming Lady Watson's masque, the Marchioness of Endcliffe's ball, and two others. "And then there is Lord Milford's deer-stalking party in eight days' time. He told me about it when I saw him on Rotten Row yesterday morning. Oh, do you know the baron, Lady Petra?"

"Why, yes," Petra replied. She'd brought her fork, on which was speared a roasted potato, to a sudden stop on its way to her mouth. "His late wife was a dear friend of mine."

Juddy nodded. "Yes, very sad, that. Although I must admit I did not know Lady Milford. But why do you look so disapproving? After all, it is just a stalking party, with the requisite feast."

"I suppose I find it odd that he should hold one barely weeks after her untimely death," Petra said tightly. "And out of season at that."

"I cannot disagree on your first point," said Juddy judiciously. "Though I suspect you would be less angry with Milford if you knew it is because the prince himself requested the stalking party."

"The Prince of Wales? No, I was not aware." Some of her irritation faded, for it was not as if Lord Milford would have been able to refuse a request of Prinny himself.

"Indeed. Josiah said that Milford is feeling rather smug, for he has been hoping to come under the notice of His Royal Highness for some years now without his level of favor budging even by a notch. It turns out all Lord Milford really needed was a stellar red-deer herd on his Suffolk lands. I myself was simply delighted to be invited. For you see, Lady Petra, stalking is one of the few things I do better than my brother."

Because Juddy was looking at her as if worried he had offended her, Petra gave him a smile, and began asking him questions to ease his discomfort.

What was his favorite subject at Cambridge? Philosophy, much to the dislike of his late papa. Did he enjoy the theater? Yes, rather too much, he was afraid. What about the races? Again, rather too much, he must admit.

Juddy drained his second glass of wine, saying morosely, "It is why I have had to live with Josiah and Fanny when I am in London, instead of getting lodgings of my own at present." He turned eyes that were becoming glassy to Petra, and let out a dry laugh. "I have learned my lesson, at least with the horses, for I cannot live without the theatre. Haven't placed a bet on a race in a month now. Living under their roof has been the torture I needed to confess my sin of gambling and learn to be happy with the other vices I seem to have been born with."

Once more, he filled his wineglass, then topped off hers and briefly raised his in a wordless toast. Petra took a small sip, thinking Juddy looked a bit miserable, and it was likely for more reasons than being forced to live with Josiah and Fanny.

Only minutes earlier, Petra had asked Juddy to pass her a slice of chocolate torte and was forced to ask twice. He'd had to tear his gaze away from Duncan, who'd briefly stood and flung his arms out wide before bowing with great ceremony to his young cousin, Lady Claire. It was an act that unintentionally emphasized the breadth of Duncan's shoulders and the rather more muscular arms and thighs than Petra knew he'd sported even three years ago.

Yes, she'd seen the longing in Juddy's eyes, and noted that he had looked with a similar expression toward another young man closer to his own age—and had then looked down shyly when the young man had returned his gaze. Juddy had then gulped the rest of his glass of wine and poured himself another, his pale cheeks flushed.

"What is life like with Josiah and Fanny?" she asked over the faint sounds from the saloon of the orchestra tuning their instruments once more.

As she thought he might, Juddy began to release the frustrations that had been within him. He spoke of things Josiah had told him he should do that were manly, which seemed to include driving a four-in-hand, making sure the housemaids were the prettiest in London, getting accepted into White's, and not allowing a woman to take over a house or the expenses. At this he snorted.

"Our dear Fanny would have much to say about that. Rules with an iron fist, she does—though I admit she has always been kind to me."

Surprised, mainly because her knowledge of Fanny Bellingham was based mostly on seeing her disapproving face at balls like this, Petra fought to find a reply to give, but soon found Juddy was not expecting one.

"To my dear brother, however, Fanny is rarely kind. I have heard Josiah call her temperamental and frigid on the regular. And though I get on with her, I do see why." He cast a gimlet eye Petra's way. "In public, Fanny guards their union like a jealous cat protecting her handsome tom, but when at home, Josiah is lucky to get a second glance from her."

"Indeed?" murmured Petra, thinking she rather did not blame Fanny Bellingham.

"Oh yes," Juddy said. His words were beginning to slur now, but it did not stop his tongue from wagging. "In fact, on my eighteenth birthday, all but a fortnight ago, Josiah took me to his club as a treat."

"Many happy returns to you," Petra said, raising her glass to him. "And how did you find . . . White's, was it?"

"Yes, White's. *Most* enjoyable, Lady Petra," Juddy enthused. "I shall be joining soon, I hope, though Fanny does not wish it. She does not like it when Josiah visits, but it is the one thing he says he will never acquiesce to any woman. They quarreled when he took me on my birthday, you know. He was rather cross about it, complaining to anyone who would listen, including Lord Potsford. In fact, his lordship said he might be able to assist Josiah in the matter."

"Oh?" Petra said as she looked over at Caroline, noting her friend was still enjoying the attentions of Lord Whitfield.

"Well, I was not supposed to listen, you understand, but I did, rather." Juddy put his fingers to his lips just as a giggle escaped. "Josiah and his lordship were in an alcove, taking snuff. His lordship said he understood unstable women—yes, that is the term he used, Lady Petra, though it raised my brows in quite the same fashion as yours, I will not lie. And then he suggested that maybe

Fanny could use some time in the country. For her health, one understands."

"Certainly," Petra said when he glanced her way, clearly expecting a response.

"Potsford then told my brother that he knew of a man he could recommend," Juddy continued. "A physician of some sort. Said that the man could come speak with Fanny, and attempt to discover the reasons for her ill temper. And if the man felt it necessary, he could take Fanny for a stay in the country. Has a place called Tradewinds or Westwinds, I believe." He snapped his fingers. "No, it is Fairwinds. I recall because, dash it all, it did sound rather like a peaceful place. Nearly asked if I could go there myself."

Petra recalled earlier in the evening when Langford used much the same words, saying he had "a man he could recommend" to Whitfield. From somewhere in the back of her mind, Petra then recalled hearing a rumor several months earlier. It involved Lord Whitfield and an opera singer who was with child. Petra looked once more to see Caroline tipping her head back and laughing. Heavens, Whitfield looked like he wanted to devour her right there.

And then she remembered the words of Martin the footman. That Gwen had been visited by a physician who had left her in some distress. Suddenly, Petra was more curious about this man known to Lord Potsford.

"Yes, it's lovely, I am sure," she repeated. She did not know exactly what to ask, so she chose the first thing that came to mind. "Did he say where this Fairwinds could be found?"

Juddy had frowned. He was becoming loose-limbed from drink and tiredness, and he yawned widely.

"Not that I recall. Though north of London, I expect, for I believe he said something about it being a quiet place. Yes, I recall him saying it is a two and one half hour drive with fresh horses, and near the River Roding. Though that may mean it is in *Essex*." He gave a little shudder at the thought.

"Mm," Petra said. "Is this doctor someone known to society?" Juddy's eyes had begun to close, a soppy smile on his face.

"Hmm, Lady Petra?" he said thickly.

"Will you tell me his name?" she asked. "For, ah, I may know of someone who may wish to use him as well."

Juddy murmured something she felt was "Rather doubtful, my dear," but she could not be sure.

With a suppressed scowl, Petra made sure she was not being observed, then used her thumb and middle finger to flick Juddy's left thumb as hard as she could. Sure enough, the action caused Juddy's eyes to fly open. "Ow," he mumbled.

"The physician's name, Juddy?" Petra said, smiling at him as his eyes began to lower once more.

"Right. My apologies. Ragsdale, I think it was."

Petra, not recognizing the name, shrugged inwardly but gave him a smile nonetheless as she began to rise from her seat. "Thank you, dear Juddy. Now, get that kip in."

But Juddy was sluggishly holding up one hand, one brown eye opening briefly once more. "No, no, I have it wrong," he said on a yawn. "It wasn't Ragsdale. I'm afraid I was rather thinking of a very handsome . . . well, never mind. The name, I believe, was Drysdale." He smiled again, and, not a moment later, had slumped in his chair, chin to chest, fast asleep, never seeing Petra's lips part at hearing that name twice in one evening.

NINE

"A Mr. Drysdale? Why, I have never heard the name," Caroline said as she and Petra took a turn about Her Grace's rose gardens. "Or of any physician who helps women recover their health in the country, though I do believe some exist."

The clocks had struck four o'clock in the morning when Petra was finally able to have a few minutes alone to speak with Caroline. Both ladies having enjoyed the rather scandalous notion of four more dances each, they had decided a walk in the gardens would be a welcome respite. The grass was soft on their aching feet, the cold air was refreshingly crisp, and the darkest hours of the night were lit by not only the nearly full moon, but also enough lanterns and torches so as to make it almost as easy to walk in the gardens as it would be in the light of day.

"Hmm, that is what some of the other ladies I have asked said, though none knew of any specific names," Petra said, then added, "As I did not wish for Josiah Bellingham or Lord Potsford to know it was Juddy who spoke of their private conversation, I felt the need for discretion and only introduced the subject to those few ladies I felt might be the most knowledgeable, including Her Grace."

"I should think that if Her Grace was not aware, most women would not be."

"I agree, and that is what made it rather strange." Petra then tilted her head from side to side. "However, it is possible she did not hear most of what I said, for we were too near the dancers, and one of them nearly toppled Miss Littlewood, who was passing by and accidentally crossed into the young man's path."

Petra did not add that she had felt as if Arabella had startled upon hearing the name "Drysdale," but she could not be sure. What was for certain was that Duncan once again had come swiftly to the pretty young miss's aid and had asked Arabella for the next dance. This had earned him an approving nod from his grandmama, who had then turned back to Petra and said in a rather booming voice, "Never heard of the man, my dear. Ah, here comes His Grace, for it is time for us to thank our guests and retire. We are no longer the young pups who merrily dance until the sun arises once more! Now, come, give your godmother a kiss and we shall see each other in the days to come."

Petra now let her fingers pass over the blooms of two cream-colored roses that had just opened, catching just a whiff of their perfume released by her touch as Caroline spoke.

"However, I will tell you one thing I *have* heard, and that is very little of the truth. I'd wager what that footman said was all but a bag of moonshine. How could Lady Milford still be alive?"

"But why would you not believe Martin?" Petra asked, if only to be contrary. "Because he is nothing but a footman with no education to speak of and little to recommend himself?"

"Certainly not," Caroline replied. "I am merely saying that this Martin must have been mistaken, just like you said. He must have seen someone else, and mistook that woman for Lady Milford."

Plucking a leaf from a rosebush about to flower, Caroline seemed to think for a moment, then turned quickly to Petra. "A woman confidence-trickster, for instance. Maybe someone who knew Lord Milford had lost his wife, and intended to pretend to haunt him in order to demand money." Caroline blinked earnestly. "It has happened, you know."

Petra bit her lip in an effort not to laugh, but then sobered herself.

"No, you are correct, Caro," she said. "I agree that some woman could very well be trying to trick Lord Milford. Not that I would feel inclined to stop her if this were the case," she added dryly. "But how would such a woman exist who looks that much like Gwen for a loyal footman to believe it?"

"We do not know," Caroline countered. "Gwen could have had

a long-lost sister. Even the nicest of noblemen have been known to stray from their marriage bed." She lowered her voice, nodding up ahead toward the darkened outlines of a gentleman and lady who could be seen emerging from one of Her Grace's secret gardens, the gentleman raising the woman's hand to his lips. The two did not see Petra and Caroline, but rushed off, hand in hand, in the opposite direction. "And we both know the idea of the pure and virtuous lady is as much a myth as it is the truth. It could have been Gwen's own mama who had an indiscretion many years ago that resulted in a bastard look-alike. One who, upon hearing of her highborn sister's demise, decided she was entitled to some of what her sister enjoyed in life."

"Your mind is rather more devious than I have ever supposed, Caro," Petra said.

Caroline grinned, unperturbed that her idea was being dismissed. "I still think you should be wary of Martin's story. But let us see the opposite side, merely for the sake of it. What if Lady Milford is indeed still alive? What does that mean?"

"I agree," Petra said. "It is what has been on my mind, crowding in upon the delightful time I have been having at the ball. I cannot help but think, could Gwen have run away from her husband? And where is Gwen now, if she is indeed alive? Is she safe? Has she found shelter? Or is she hurt, hungry, in pain—" Petra stopped, her voice quite choked now and unable to continue on those lines. She turned to face Caroline instead. "If I knew, I would do anything I could to help her."

"I know you would, dearest," Caroline said, patting her hand. "And I would assist in whatever way I could."

Petra brightened somewhat, an idea having formed. "If I found Gwen—if she is alive and wishes not to return to her husband—I could send her to live with my aunt Ophelia for a time. As I did two summers ago with Georgina, that servant girl with child by . . . well, by that peer I found out was threatening to have the poor girl and her unborn babe drowned."

"*Horrid* man," Caroline said. "I am glad Georgina and her child are now living happily as the wife and son of a Dales farmer on your aunt's estate. You did indeed save a life—two, in fact—that day."

"*We* saved two lives," Petra corrected. "I could not have done it all without you distracting his lordship by flirting with him and pretending to be untrained with a bow and arrow when you could have outshot him from fifty paces farther away."

"And do not forget to give yourself credit. Your secret skill at picking locks came in handy as well, if I recall."

Petra laughed. "How else was I to ensure Georgina saw the safe return of the letters he wrote that proved he knew he was the father of her child? She ended up not needing them, but it was a distinct possibility."

"Yes it was. I must agree, then. We did truly do something special that day," Caroline said, "using abilities we must largely hide from men in order to keep our ladylike reputations, I might add. I quite enjoyed myself."

"I did as well," admitted Petra, though her attention had been caught by a brief glimpse of candlelight from the entrance to another secret garden some ways away. Moments ago, she'd seen the silhouette of a gentleman enter. Now another gentleman was walking with furtive excitement in the same direction. He passed by a torch, briefly illuminating his light hair, thin frame, and snub nose. Juddy Bellingham, she would wager, revived after his earlier nap in the dining room.

A separate part of her mind smiled for the lad, and hoped he would be careful not to get caught. For though Petra now knew many men who were like Juddy, society chose to ignore that fact. If caught, Juddy would be arrested, with a multitude of punishments possible. If not arrested, but still seen, he would be considered by many as immoral, a wastrel, and even touched in the head. Some would call him lunatic . . . a madman . . .

Madness.

"Caroline," she said. "What if it is true?"

"What if what is true?" her friend replied, looking perplexed.

"Martin . . . he said Gwen looked like she was in such distress when he claimed to see her. And this fit she had—if she *is* alive, it all has begun to make me feel as if she has gone mad. But, oh, dear Caro, what if she has? Gwen had always had bouts of nerves and other ailments—but has she progressed into bouts of hysteria, or even lunacy as well? For that is almost what it sounds like. What shall I do for her then if she is alive and I find her? How am I to be around her?"

Caroline turned as well, taking one of Petra's hands in each of hers. "Dearest Petra, do you recall what you asked me that day, after I told you I had finally come to understand the truth of my husband? Of the workings of his heart? And then, once I did, I asked similar things as you? Do you remember what you said?"

Petra nodded, but it was Caroline who said the words.

"You asked me if my captain ceased to be a person worthy of my friendship, my trust, my respect, and my love—even if it be platonic—simply because I now understood how he differed from what I was taught to believe a man was."

"I remember," Petra said, looking down at their clasped hands. "You barely thought on it for two seconds put together before answering that of course your captain was still worthy." She let out a light laugh. "In fact, I believe you shouted the words."

"I learned much from your wisdom then," Caroline said, "and now I think it is time for you to ask yourself much the same question. Though I realize it differs in some ways—especially if Gwen's mind has indeed deteriorated to a point where nothing can be done—at its core, it is the same."

"It is, I agree. And if Gwen should be alive, but no longer herself, I can still treat her as my cherished friend, be kind to her, respect her, and attempt to understand her in whatever way she is now," Petra said, giving Caroline's hands a squeeze before letting them go. She looked up into her friend's face. "And I will endeavor to do so. Thank you, dear Caro. It is good to be reminded of such things."

"How do you plan to proceed in discovering whether Gwen has passed or if she is alive? And if she is, what of her whereabouts?" Caroline asked as the two turned to make their way back through the rose garden.

"That is another question I have been asking myself," Petra replied. "I have requested a meeting with Martin, and that is a good first step. Maybe he can tell me some other information I have been lacking."

"And if not?" Caroline asked as, up ahead, Josiah Bellingham came storming out of Hillmorton House, looking all around him.

Petra was feeling reckless all of a sudden. "Well, then, maybe I shall do all manner of unladylike things—do the things a man might do—and see what I can discover for myself."

Caroline's throaty laugh was all but lost as Josiah bellowed out, "*Judson!*"

"I believe I saw him go in the direction of the orangery, Lord Bellingham," Petra called out, pointing in quite the opposite direction of the secret garden where Juddy was currently ensconced. Josiah gave Petra a sneering look, and then strode off through the rose gardens toward the orangery. Petra turned to Caroline.

"There is another friend I must help at the moment," she said. "I shall see you inside directly." Without waiting for a reply, she lifted her skirts, turned, and rushed in the direction of the secret garden.

Upon reaching the wrought-iron gate that was shut yet had no lock to secure it, she was out of breath, but her gasps for air were little compared to the gasps of pleasure from within. But there was no time to let them come to a crescendo.

After politely clearing her throat, she called out just loudly enough for the occupants within to hear. "Juddy? It is Lady Petra. Your brother is about. I have sent him toward the orangery, but I suspect you should come back to the house with me. Ah . . . promptly."

There were several quiet swears, the sound of clothes rustling, and a few moments later, Juddy came stumbling out, fastening the final button on the flap of his trousers, his pale cheeks flushed even in the low light. He opened his mouth to speak, but she shook her head.

"You have neither shocked nor upset me, but we must go now. Give me your arm, do." Turning in the direction of the house, she called back over her shoulder. "Sir, you should give us an ample head start, please. And do be careful in returning yourself. Do not let Lord Bellingham see you."

"Of course," said a voice that sounded weak with relief.

She and Juddy hurried back through the gardens, then she pulled him into a more stately stroll just as Josiah came crashing back through a wisteria bower about to bloom.

"Oh, there you are, my lord," Petra said. "No sooner had you rushed off than I encountered your brother about to walk through the rose garden, and I joined him whilst waiting for your return. My apologies, sir, it must have been another young gentleman I saw earlier."

Josiah looked suspiciously at his brother, then at Petra, but any conversation was thwarted when four thoroughly soused gentlemen came out of the door, roaring with laughter.

Blast it, thought Petra. All four were Josiah's comrades and she tended to avoid them when possible, having never had an enjoyable conversation with any. One pulled off from the rest, holding up a bottle of amber liquid and calling out, "Bellingham, there you are! Come! Come with us. Randolph here has some damn fine snuff and I've got the last bottle of that excellent whisky. No need to stay out here with a spinster and your whiny pup of a brother. Let Lady Petra take him back inside and put him under Fanny's wing again."

Josiah grunted, hands on hips and still eyeing Juddy and Petra. "Hmm, yes, excellent suggestion, Kirkby," he drawled, lazily straightening his cuffs as he took the steps up to stand alongside the other four men. "In fact," he said, leering Petra's way, "maybe that's where the lady would rather be, too, hmm? Fancy having the arms of *Lady* Bellingham about you, Lady Petra?"

The other men guffawed, including the one named Kirkby, who

swiveled unsteadily, thrusting the bottle of whisky into Josiah's hands. "For she certainly doesn't wish to be in your arms, Bellingham. Much less have you between her legs."

To this, Josiah gave a bark of laughter, but his upper lip curled as he took the bottle. "And I would rather give consequence to the beautiful and willing little housemaid Lady Petra was speaking with earlier than the spinster herself, so you should not count me unhappy that the lady does not wish to feel my considerable pleasure."

"I say!" said Juddy hotly. But the other men were laughing so hard, Juddy's voice was all but drowned.

Petra stayed outwardly calm, though her heart was pounding in her ears. These sorts of comments about who she wished to love had begun almost immediately after Lady Ardley's ball. She had been somewhat ready for these barbs, understanding as she did that a different path taken from what was generally accepted was always the subject of speculation and gossip—and that those who feared just such a different path often used cruel words to mask their unease.

Petra had decided from the first not to give too much thought to those who attempted to degrade her, for she had known her own heart since she was a small girl, and nothing had changed. Yet she had felt that by staunchly defending that she was a woman who wanted the love of a man, she was diminishing the hearts and feelings of friends like Juddy, Captain Smythe, and even a dear female cousin on her Forsyth side who had lived in Dorset with her companion, Dorothy, for the last twenty years. Therefore, Petra continued to go on allowing people to think exactly as they wished.

Curiously, she had found other women tended to question Petra's motives as much as men. It was the men, however—and especially those in their cups—who tended to be the most outwardly cruel and vocal.

Keeping her head high and her arm securely in Juddy's, Petra began ascending the steps without comment. It was at the top that

she stumbled. Pitching sideways, she fell right into Josiah Bellingham as he was laughing and attempting to pull the cork from the
whisky bottle.

There was a crash of glass and two low *glug-glug* sounds, and
then the peaty smell of whisky was perfuming the air. All six men,
Juddy included, went silent with shock as they stared at the broken
bottle releasing its amber goodness onto the marble steps of Hillmorton House. Petra, having deliberately landed with her hands
securely on Josiah's arm, had already pushed off him, righting herself easily—even before Juddy, who had belatedly lunged to assist
her, could do more than take her elbow.

"Dear me," Petra tutted, shaking out her dress, "I'm afraid I made
you drop your whisky. And it being the last bottle, too. Rather a
shame. But you still have your fine snuff, my lord—and each other.
And that is a good thing, for I know not one lady here tonight who
would wish any of you to be between their legs."

Without another word, she took Juddy's arm again and they
walked toward the set of doors that had been opened by a footman.

As they stepped inside, Juddy stopped. He turned to Petra and
gave her a bow, his eyes shining with the respect she hadn't seen
from his brother. "I am ever so glad I met you tonight, Lady Petra.
You are everything I have ever expected you to be, and more."

Petra smiled. The thorn that was threatening to dig deeply into
her skin in the form of the ugly words and taunts from Josiah Bellingham and his cronies felt merely like a scratch with the young
man's words.

"Then let us go back and enjoy the rest of the ball, shall we?"

Juddy offered his arm once more, but Petra stopped when the
footman spoke.

"My lady?"

She turned, at once recognizing Martin's long nose and kind
eyes beneath his wig. She smiled. "Yes, Martin?" When she saw him
glance at Juddy, she said, "You may speak in front of Mr. Bellingham, Martin."

Yet the small foyer they were in had three hallways leading off it, and down the one that led straight back a young man hovered in the shadows, glancing worriedly their way. "Ah, why don't I wait for you just down the hall, Lady Petra?" said Juddy.

She nodded her thanks and turned back to Martin.

"I hope you will not think me improper, my lady, but Tansy passed on your request to speak with me. I'd planned to send a note as to a time to meet, as your ladyship requested, but as you are here . . ."

"Yes, quite. Can you tell me a day and time?" Petra said, glancing around to make sure they were not overheard.

"Indeed I can, my lady," he said. "I am allowed to exercise His Grace's mare, and do so on Friday afternoons, which is my half day." He stood even more proudly. "His Grace knew of my way with horses and trusts me with the gray, he does."

"That is a great honor, for I know His Grace only allows the best riders to work his horses," Petra replied.

Martin smiled. "And though there will be little time for your ladyship to recover from the events of the ball, if you can help Lady Milford, then I believe time may be of the essence."

Petra bit back a sigh, still not knowing who to believe. "Yes, of course" was all she could say.

"Excellent, my lady. Would two o'clock this afternoon at the Green Park then be acceptable? Near where the Temple of Concord stood, as you suggested?"

At the very moment Martin spoke the words, Josiah Bellingham and the other four gentlemen barged through the doors.

"Two o'clock, this very afternoon, at the Green Park, eh, Lady Petra?" jeered Josiah. "You are planning an assignation with a *footman*? Is he the man who shall finally make it between those thighs of yours?"

Petra saw the flash of anger in Martin's eyes, but he went ramrod straight once more at the sight of someone coming from the hall behind her.

As if divined into being within the candlelit foyer, one man with a trim lady half his height and some twenty years older stepped around Petra. Duncan, a muscle pulsing in his jaw, was escorting his aunt, the Marchioness of Endcliffe. Her ladyship wore a gown of pale, shimmery green that emphasized the Shawcross eyes she had inherited, and the sapphire necklace about her neck sent sparks dancing on the walls as she passed a candelabra. No more than a heartbeat later, Lord Whitfield and Caroline also came into view, from the opposite hallway.

Silence reigned in the suddenly crowded foyer, and then the marchioness spoke.

"If you must know, Lord Bellingham, Lady Petra is considering purchasing one of my father's horses, and His Grace asked Martin here to put the horse through its paces for her. As Martin's half day is this afternoon, it was the most sensible suggestion." She clasped her hands in front of her and took another step closer. "As such, do you feel as if your vulgar and most ungentlemanly question is still warranted, now that you are aware of the circumstances? And let me be clear—what I am asking is whether your vulgar and ungentlemanly question was warranted in any way, shape, or manner—to any woman, no matter her marital status or station—ever." Without so much as a breath, she snapped, "Well, Lord Bellingham? What is your answer?"

Josiah had sobered almost instantly, and began to stutter, going redder in the face by the moment as all eyes stayed upon him. "No, Lady Endcliffe. I do heartily apologize. It was indeed a rude and ungentlemanly thing to say." He turned to Petra, giving her a stiff bow. "I am indeed sorry, Lady Petra."

"Yet I do not think you are, Lord Bellingham," Petra replied coldly, turning her head away. She knew the proper thing to do was to accept his apology, but she could not. And while she was not certain of it, she thought she saw a brief nod of agreement from Duncan.

"I agree with Lady Petra," Lady Endcliffe said as Josiah's mouth gaped like a red-faced trout forcibly hooked and pulled from the water. "I wish you to leave Hillmorton House, Lord Bellingham. You have benefited enough from Their Graces' hospitality for one night, and it is time you went to your carriage and returned home. Lady Bellingham and your brother may stay if they wish." She raised her voice and her chin further, sounding altogether like her venerable mother, the duchess. "And do not turn up at my own ball in a month's time without both your wife and the Dowager Lady Bellingham at your side to keep you in check." Still staring unflinchingly at Josiah, she addressed Duncan. "Shawcross, please see that Lord Bellingham takes the most efficient route to the courtyard and his carriage."

"I know a shortcut," Duncan said, as he stepped to Petra's side and then gestured with his arm toward the hallway where Caroline and Whitfield waited, both standing with respectfully muted expressions.

Josiah looked around the foyer, his angry eyes saying what the rest of him did not dare. He then gave a curt bow to Lady Endcliffe, turned on his heel, and stalked off, Duncan at his heels.

"You may leave, gentlemen," the marchioness said, her eyes boring into the other four men. "Please open the door, Martin." With four identical bows, they hastily exited in the direction of the gardens. Whitfield and Caroline left as well, but with smiles and much less haste.

As the marchioness watched them go, Petra gave Martin a quick, grateful nod, receiving an almost imperceptible one in return. Then she turned to the marchioness. "I'm very grateful to you, Lady Endcliffe. Thank you."

"Bah! That Lord Bellingham is nothing more than an overgrown child, is he not?" Lady Endcliffe replied, whipping open her silk fan to wave it gently in front of her. "But I feel as if you would have had everything in hand without my arrival, Lady Petra. Nevertheless, it is a good thing my nephew heard your conversation with Martin here and knew what it was about." The marchioness's green eyes danced with humor. "For it did sound like a rather tawdry assignation was being planned, my dear. I'm afraid I had no idea His Grace was looking to sell that mare." Then she gave one elegant little shrug. "But I do not have the fascination with horses that you do. However, if you should like the gray, then I hope His Grace gives you a fair price."

Petra could only manage a weak smile, but Lady Endcliffe did not seem to notice. "Come, Lady Petra. Let us return for the last of the dancing and merriment until the breakfast, shall we?" And Petra allowed herself to be led away, back to the ball.

TEN

ANNIE WAS TUTTING AS SHE FINISHED SECURING THE BUTTONS of Petra's riding habit, one in a claret hue that managed to be becoming despite bringing out the ginger tones in Petra's hair.

"You have not had enough sleep, my lady," she said. "You arrived home at half after seven this morning, and now it is barely half past noon. Why should you not wait to go out riding until this afternoon?"

"I promise I will rest later, before going to tea at Lady Caroline's," Petra replied. "You must remember, I have been rising much earlier for the past three months to ride out with the earl's string and take notes on the gallops. I am used to it, and one late night has not changed my habits."

"So you say, my lady," Annie replied. She tilted her eyes up to Petra's. "I expect Lady Caroline will not wake for several more hours."

"Lady Caroline rarely wakes before noon no matter what the day or the circumstances, so that argument will not work on me," Petra countered. "Besides, Arcturus needs to be hacked and he does not care for the rain." Angling her head toward her window, she glanced out at the sky again. It was blue, but the clouds were already forming. "I expect I will be home again by no later than a quarter to three. I may even be able to nap for a bit before teatime. Will that make you less disapproving?"

Annie used a brush to remove some lint from Petra's coat and said, "Only if you promise to come home without even one splatter of mud for me to clean, my lady."

"Then I expect you shall remain disapproving," Petra said, flashing her lady's maid a smile before making her way out toward the door to the mews, but not before stopping first by her drawing room and extracting something from a small locked drawer. Mere minutes later she was breathing crisp spring air as Arcturus, a chestnut gelding with a diamond-shaped star between his eyes, was led to her by Rupert, her head groom and coachman. He nodded with his usual unflappable calm when Petra explained that she intended to meet one of Her Grace's footmen in the Green Park for a short conversation.

"Shall we go there now and wait for the footman, my lady? Or ride somewhere else first?" Rupert assisted Petra with a leg up into her sidesaddle, tightening the chestnut's girth by one more hole and then easily vaulting from a mounting block onto a second gelding, this one a bay with not a speck of white on him. The bay stood a lot more patiently on the cobblestones than Arcturus, who was already moving in quick sidesteps in anticipation of stretching his legs.

"Oh, the Row first, I think," Petra said breezily, hoping he would not suggest differently. Rupert was not overly fond of the tree-lined horse path in Hyde Park that was Rotten Row, preferring to exercise the horses in areas that were less frequented by riders whose main thoughts were to be seen riding, rather than riding well.

While Petra was generally of the same mind, she had awoken this morning with an instant knot of worry formed over the fate of Gwen. Could her friend still be alive? Or had Martin simply seen, as Caroline suggested, a woman who resembled Gwen in some way?

While hearing Martin's information later in the day was of the utmost importance, she realized the first thing she needed to do was to speak with Gwen's husband, the ninth Baron Milford. And, thus, she had devised a plan.

Rupert had no objections to Rotten Row, it seemed, and they began riding in the direction of Hyde Park. Petra complimented Rupert on how well her horses were looking, which Rupert accepted with his usual good grace and a pleased gleam in his button-brown eyes.

He had a calm way with horses that Petra had rarely seen the likes of, and she liked Rupert all the better for the fact that he was as quiet on their rides as he was in the stables and with Clancy, his own apprentice groom. When riding out with Rupert accompanying her, Petra felt safe in his presence, knowing his eyes were in constant motion and looking out for any issue—whether it would be one that would upset Lady Petra, or one that would upset her horses.

Thus, she could usually simply enjoy losing herself in the rhythmic sound of horse hooves, creaking saddle leather, and the occasional softly puttering sneeze or bridle-jingling neck shake from one of their mounts. It allowed her to think of little but how her heart was freer, her soul calmer every time she was on her horse.

Today, however, Petra's mind was elsewhere, on all that had happened at Her Grace's ball. She thought on many things, her mind listing them off, one after the other.

First in her contemplations was the news of Gwen's death. Then on hearing Martin's tale that countered the sad news. Lady Potsford's great distress was replayed in her mind, as was how Lords Langford, Whitfield, and Potsford had seemingly referenced a mysterious man named Drysdale. She mulled with a frown over her encounters with Josiah Bellingham and his four soused friends, her frown then easing a bit with thoughts of young, sweet Juddy Bellingham and all that he had revealed under the influence of so much wine and melancholy. She felt there was a common thread somewhere in these thoughts, but didn't know quite what it could be just yet. Petra was still musing on this when Rupert spoke.

"We are nearing the Row, my lady."

Petra was glad Arcturus had behaved himself so far. She surely would have been tipped unceremoniously to the ground otherwise, her mind had been so far away from the present.

"If I may, my lady," Rupert said. "I suggest you start him at a trot and keep him there for a while. He needs to be reminded that he won't always be allowed to go haring off at a gallop the minute he sets a hoof on the path."

Petra arched an eyebrow with good humor. "What you are not saying, Rupert, is that I am the rider who allows him to gallop the moment we reach the path, when galloping is frowned upon here. But, yes, I quite agree with your suggestion."

Despite his earlier good behavior, Arcturus was nevertheless jumping out off his skin, and clearly expected to be given his head upon reaching the wide horse path. Yet after a few minutes of Petra expertly keeping him in check at a slower pace, he settled into the smooth trot that had led her to buy him in the first place. A half-length behind, Rupert followed on his bay.

There were few riders out on the path this morning after Her Grace's ball, but Petra's eyes roamed over each one of them. She saw a few acquaintances, nodding politely at some, and gracing a couple others with a smile. Yet none had been the rider she was seeking.

"Lady Petra! Hallo!" came a booming voice.

A two-wheeled cart pulled by a shiny, high-stepping trotter came from the opposite direction and slowed to a halt. Petra pulled Arcturus into a walk and stopped so she could better meet the cheerful eyes of the Dowager Countess Grimley, who preferred to be called Lady Vera owing to, as she often laughingly put it, "the rather grim nature of my husband's unfortunate surname." Beside her sat a thin, long-faced lady's maid who looked as if she would rather be anywhere else than crammed onto the cart's rather small seat next to the ample-hipped dowager countess.

"Good morning, Lady Vera," Petra said. "My, your trotter is looking quite fine. I have never seen horses shinier than yours. How are you this lovely morning?"

"Oh, but you do flatter me so," the dowager said, laughing with her usual gusto so that her bosom moved up and down in time with her shoulders. "And I am well, my dear. Very well. And so is Mozart here. Aren't you, boy?" She wiggled one of the pony's long reins and he turned his head inquisitively toward his mistress. "We decided to take a turn on Rotten Row this morning because we knew we'd all but have the place to ourselves until everyone recovered from Her Grace's ball. And I was correct, wasn't I, Horton?"

The lady's maid nodded her head, but said nothing.

"I admit, I felt the same," Petra said, "even though I attended the ball. But I am used to waking up early to ride, so it was no hardship."

"Of course, of course," Lady Vera said. "I never go to balls any longer, though. No sense in getting dressed up just to mill about in a crowded room, smelling the *odeur* of so many others, especially after they have been flinging themselves about to music all night long." She shook her head, the frills edging her bonnet wiggling as she did so. "No, I am most happy in my little dowager's house, near my son and daughter-in-law, with my dogs and my Mozart here."

"And I am glad to see you continue to be most happy, Lady Vera," Petra said. "A life with dogs and horses is indeed a blissful one."

"I hear that is what you have decided on in your life as well, my dear," Lady Vera said, tipping her chin down and looking up at Petra with shrewd eyes.

"It is true," Petra said, though she did not quite know that she would wish to liken her life to that of the dowager's just yet. "I have decided to remain unmarried."

"You have decided to become a spinster." Lady Vera's voice was not harsh, but it was still strange hearing it put so straightforwardly from one of the kindest ladies of her acquaintance.

"I suppose I have," Petra said, though it was with effort that she kept her voice light.

Lady Vera regarded Petra for a moment, then said, "Well, Lady Petra, if you are going to be a spinster, do not be embarrassed by it."

Petra was momentarily startled, but then smiled. "That is excellent advice, Lady Vera, and I shall take it. Thank you."

Lady Vera waggled one thick, beringed finger her way. "Ah, but I have one more piece of advice. Do not close your heart off, Lady Petra. I, too, lost my first love as a young woman. But then I found the earl—and I did not want to take a chance, but I did. The earl could drive me into fits of insanity, but he also made my life a wonderful adventure. I do not regret it, my girl." She inclined her head. "But then again, I chose wisely, and I agree that makes all the difference."

"Indeed it does, Lady Vera," Petra said, thinking of how Lady Potsford's experience had been quite the opposite. "And thus far, the choices I have had would not have been wise ones, of that I am certain."

Lady Vera gathered up her pony's reins again. "Well, you have always had a good head on your shoulders, Lady Petra. Must have gotten it from your mother, as I say every time I come across Holbrook at the racecourse." She winked at Petra. "If you have said no to a suitor, I expect you had good reason to do so."

"Could I convince you to apply those words to a letter and then misdirect your post so that it reaches Allington House?" Petra asked, feigning seriousness.

Lady Vera chuckled so hard her whole cart bounced gently up and down on its springs. "Allington giving you trouble again, is he?"

"I'm afraid my Uncle Tobias is rather displeased with my decisions, Lady Vera," Petra replied. "Before I left for London, he had even invited a man to Buckfields without Papa's permission. I felt rather lucky to have received Her Grace's invitation so I could slip away to London."

Lady Vera's eyes narrowed in distaste. "Did he now? The shamelessness of that man. He was never kind and trustworthy like your mother, you know. Even as a child. Used to ask for one of my cook's marzipan confections when your grandmama came to visit me in Warwickshire, bringing Allington and your mother with her. I'd tell Allington he could go to the kitchen and ask for *one*, and then my cook would later say I'd told him he could have three. That was the type of child he was, and I expect he has not changed much."

Petra was about to concur when Lady Vera then pushed out her lips almost as if she wished to kiss the air.

"Hmm, in fact, I saw that same smirk on his face recently."

Arcturus was beginning to fidget again, and sidestepped away from Lady Vera's cart. Petra guided him back into place, but he was tossing his head like he did when he was about to misbehave, so her reply was perfunctory.

"Oh? Did you see my uncle here in London?"

"I did indeed," said Lady Vera. She tilted her head toward her lady's maid. "Horton and I were at the milliner's on Oxford Street, and I had only just left when what did we do but turn left instead of right. Walked a good half a block before we realized we had gone in the wrong direction!" Lady Vera was chuckling again. Horton merely blinked as Lady Vera went on.

"But just as we were turning back, I saw Allington alighting from a doorway, smiling rather suspiciously. He was coming out of a solicitor's office, so one could only assume he had arranged for some legal way to deprive someone of something," Lady Vera said with a wry smile. "Yes, Allington looked far too pleased with himself not to have been winding the law about his finger to better suit his purposes."

"I think it may be possible my uncle was handling some legal matters pertaining to his upcoming nuptials. Yes, indeed, for we were as surprised as you to hear the news ourselves. My uncle is to be married in the upcoming weeks to a Miss . . . well, I cannot recall her surname, but I think it is Green, or Brown, or White. I recall it being a color. Anyhow, she is from somewhere near Canterbury."

"So someone with a name as common as rain in England, eh?" said Lady Vera. Then she frowned thoughtfully. "But I thought Allington's solicitor was Mr. Murray on Bilton Street, is it not? Allington and I have used the same solicitor for years now. Your papa does as well."

"You are correct, now that I think of it," Petra said as Arcturus tried to sidestep away again. "Maybe my uncle was visiting the London solicitor of his bride-to-be?"

"Every family I know from Kent uses Mr. Townover, off Drury

Lane, and this solicitor's name on Oxford Street started with an *F*. Ferrars, maybe? Forster?"

"Fawcett, my lady," said Horton.

"Indeed, Horton? Look at me, Lady Petra, being just as unable to remember names as you," chortled Lady Vera, then gave a merry shrug. "But, alas, I do not know every Kentish family who does business in London, so your aunt-to-be's family may very well be using this solicitor." She gave a sideways glance at her lady's maid. "When was this that we saw Allington, Horton? Tuesday?"

"Wednesday, my lady," said Horton.

"Wednesday?" Petra repeated. "You do mean from a week earlier, yes? For my uncle had just come to Suffolk to stay at Buckfields when I left for London. And he always stays at least a month. Surely you do not mean the Wednesday of two days ago."

Horton nodded her head, as did Lady Vera. "He must have returned early, my dear," she said. "Yes, for if Horton is confident it was Wednesday, but two days ago, then it is so."

Petra was curious. Could Uncle Tobias have returned to London in order to speak with a solicitor about something other than his impending marriage? For what purpose, if so?

Both Lady Vera and Horton were watching Petra with interest until Arcturus caused a diversion. Irritable now, the chestnut tried to bite the rump of Lady Vera's trotter, who, even with his blinders on, sensed the act and jerked sideways, jostling Lady Vera and her maid in her cart. Yet as a true horsewoman herself, Lady Vera remained unruffled when Petra offered her apologies.

"No need, my dear, no need. Mozart can handle himself, can't you, Mozart?"

And as if to prove his mistress correct, the little trotter flattened his ears at Arcturus and let out a squeal of rage.

"I think that is our cue," Lady Vera said gaily. "It was wonderful to see you again, my dear. Please give my best to your dear papa— and Allington, too, if you should wish. But I will not fault you if you do not!" She clucked to Mozart and the horse went easily into its high-stepping trot, leaving Petra biting her lip to keep from laughing.

"Would you like to continue your ride, my lady?" Rupert asked. He had been steadfastly observing the heavens as Lady Vera had eviscerated Uncle Tobias, but it seemed it was not all out of an effort not to laugh. "I expect it shall rain before too long. But we still have time to get old Arcie a good canter in, if your ladyship is of the mind to."

Petra gave her horse a couple of pats on the neck. "Yes, I think he's shown he needs some more exercise, and the path is not at all crowded. Let us take the last stretch at a forward trot, then turn and canter halfway back."

"Excellent thinking, my lady," said Rupert, and they set off, easily covering the last part of the nearly mile-long path. It was when Petra took Arcturus into a turn to head back, urging the chestnut into a controlled canter, that she saw him.

ELEVEN

IT TOOK HER NO TIME AT ALL TO CATCH UP TO THE HANDSOME and distinctive horse that had just been slowed to a walk. He was a tall, lean thoroughbred stallion, his color a solid dark gray, with a mane of jet black. Petra's eyes didn't stay long on the beautiful animal, however, instead going to its rider.

Tall and lean himself, Russell Milford, the ninth baron, had removed his top hat to wipe a white handkerchief over his perspiring forehead, further pushing back the already retreating line of fair hair.

He had a most handsome face despite it, Petra could readily admit. Angular in nature, with full lips, eyes of the darkest blue, and cheekbones that made admiring matrons whisper to one another and wonder as to the last time he had eaten a good meal. There was also his mustache, which was neatly trimmed to a shape that flattered his face. And though Petra did not think it an attractive addition, she was in the minority in regard to views on facial hair on men. Caroline would all but fall into a swoon.

Still, here he was. She now had a perfect, and socially acceptable, reason to speak with Milford. Almost exactly as she had planned it this morning—though the planning took place only after Annie brought her morning tray and inadvertently imparted information Petra realized she had never gleaned at the ball. Specifically, whether Lord Milford was still taking the sea air in Portsmouth, or if he had chosen to continue his mourning period either at his house here in London or in Suffolk at Strand Hill.

"Charles was dispatched to Bardwell's Apothecary to fetch some ingredients for Mrs. Ruddle's cabinets this morning," Annie had said as she placed the breakfast tray holding a rack of toast and a pot of jam across Petra's lap. "While at the apothecary, Charles encountered Mrs. Macwherter, the housekeeper at Milford House, who was waiting for a special remedy to be drawn up for his lordship. After hearing from your ladyship the sad news of Lady Milford, Charles felt free to express the condolences of the servants at Forsyth House. Mrs. Macwherter agreed that it was a terrible thing before going on to say she always felt you were the most steadfast of friends to her ladyship, and was grateful for the sympathies of this house."

"That was kind of her, and of Charles," Petra had replied. "And I am glad to know Lord Milford is back in London, for now I know where best to send my letter of condolence."

Then, while Petra sipped her tea, wishing that she could speak to Milford in person, feeling irritated that it was considered unacceptable for a woman to call upon a man, even to express condolences, Annie had thrown open the curtains. And as the lovely morning was revealed, Petra remembered that Milford enjoyed a daily ride when in London, and almost always did so on Rotten Row, where both his skills as a rider and his handsome thoroughbred could be seen at their best advantage.

Thus, she now angled Arcturus at a trot toward the gray, determined to take her chances where she could find them.

"Good morning, Lord Milford," Lady Petra said. She didn't fully slow her horse to a walk until Arcturus was head and shoulders in front of the gray, whose sides were expanding and contracting heavily from having finished an all-out gallop. Milford, she recalled, had never cared that the practice was forbidden. "I was rather hoping I would see you here."

Lord Milford stopped wiping his forehead, surprise registering in his flushed face before bowing at the neck and replacing his top hat. He gave her a smile that was inexorably polite.

"Why, Lady Petra. How lovely it is to see you. Is your father well? His ankle mended, one hopes?" He said this while pushing the square of white linen back into his coat pocket, adjusting the cuffs of his coat sleeves, repositioning his cravat, and keeping his gray stallion in check. No doubt in hopes of completing the portrait he had cultivated over the last six years, since he had been plucked from near poverty to inherit the title of his distant relative.

"The earl is indeed well, thank you, with an ankle that has been pronounced shipshape," Petra replied. "And he is much happier for it. But I wish to speak with you about—"

Milford brought his horse to a halt, and thus, so did Petra. Milford's shoulders heaved a weary sigh. "About my wife, I know. And I have much to say."

"Do you indeed?" she asked. "I should like to hear it."

"And so you shall," he returned, but rather quietly. "Lady Petra. Please let me apologize for not informing you of my wife's death. You, who have always been so kind to her—well, I should have written to you. I should have asked you to attend the funeral." Lord Milford then gazed over her shoulder, blinking as if in a trance. "But I could not, I'm afraid. Gwen would have wanted a private funeral, and I found the lack of people who would offer me their pity when I only wished my wife back to be a comfort."

"Lord Milford—how did she die?"

The question surprised Petra, even as it crossed her lips. She had been ready to coldly dress him down before going smartly into another scolding for the way he handled the sacking of his servants. And only then would she bring up the still absurd-sounding story that Martin had told her. Once that was done, she would question his declaration of wishing to have his wife alive once more. Yet the soft anguish in his voice had stopped her, changed her course.

Milford's voice was strained. "It was a fit—though of what kind, I could not tell you as I was unfortunately not there. In truth, Lady Petra, I have shared the exact details with only a few, but as my wife's dear friend, I believe you have earned the right to hear them. You see, it happened when she was visiting Chipping Ongar."

"Chipping Ongar?" Petra repeated blankly.

Milford supplied the answer easily enough. "She had gone to pay a visit to Dorie, her old lady's maid. Dorie had gone to live in the village with her sister, who had also retired from service."

"I see," murmured Petra.

"Yes, it was quite unexpected, both the desire for my wife to visit Dorie and her falling ill later. But then, she had been mourning the loss of her maid, so I could not feel as if it were wholly strange. Yet almost as soon as she arrived, Dorie wrote to say Lady Milford had taken to her bed with one of her black moods." Milford's blue eyes cut to Petra's for a moment. "As you know, she would have days at a time like that on occasion—and her melancholia had, at times, seemed worse in recent years—but Dorie wrote that this bout seemed different somehow. However, then my wife seemed to improve." Milford paused, his voice going husky. "On the day she . . . left us, she wished to have some fresh air and walk on her own a bit, by the river." He gave Petra a sad smile. "Dorie explained that her ladyship felt hovered over for so many days that a bit of time to herself was in order. A footman was sent to stay near her—"

"Oh, was it Martin?" Petra blinked as if innocently unaware that Martin and others had been cruelly dismissed.

"No, no," Milford said, a crease coming between his eyes. "It was a footman from the house where Dorie's sister had once worked, borrowed for the day. My wife had me dismiss Martin and a handful of other servants not long before her tragedy. It was odd, because she seemed so close to them, but she refused to give me a reason."

"How odd indeed," Petra said, and this time her confusion was real. She had been sure he would deny dismissing them, or would have blamed the servants themselves somehow. "My apologies for interrupting you. Please go on."

Lord Milford was staring into the middle distance as he obliged.

"The footman was sent, but he was ordered to stay some distance away. To give my wife some privacy, you understand. It was he who was witness to her last moments. I'm told Lady Milford began shaking all over as if in a fit, then she was swooning, and . . ." With one hand, Milford made a pantomime of a person falling in slow motion, as if gently slipping into the water, and his voice had a faraway, dreamlike quality. "She simply fell in."

Petra's fingers went to her lips.

"The footman ran to pull her out, of course, but she had gone under," Milford said in a strained voice. "She was wearing a simple dress, and he found part of it a short distance away, ripped and—if you'll pardon me, Lady Petra—a bit bloody. It is believed my wife, already unconscious from her faint, may have hit her head going in the water, and the current took her away too quickly." Milford hung his head, adding quietly, "One of the other reasons we had a quiet funeral is because there was no body. But I have been to the site, seen the strength of the water. There is no possibility my wife survived."

"How terrible," Petra said, her throat tight, as Lord Milford's eyes squeezed shut. Then he seemed to compose himself, speaking as he stared down the horse path, where more riders were beginning to make an appearance.

"You must forgive me, Lady Petra. Over the last fortnight, I have somehow been able to remain calm whilst relaying the facts to others. It was as if I were outside myself at times. As in many marriages, my wife and I had differences, yet the strength of my affection for my wife was one I did not truly understand until she was gone. I do not know if that sounds sensible, but it is how I feel."

"Yes, of course," Petra said, pulling her handkerchief from her pocket to dab at her eyes.

"Despite my anguish," Lord Milford continued, "I have agreed to plan a deer-stalking party in a week's time, as the Prince of Wales has expressed a desire for one on my lands. I admit that the planning has helped me retain my calm." He gathered his reins again, looking suddenly overcome. "Forgive me," he repeated, "it is not your fault, but I cannot talk of my wife any longer, and I must return to the house as I am traveling back to Suffolk today."

"Of course. I quite understand," Petra said. "I shall miss Gwen very much, and I thank you for your willingness to speak to me." But she did not know if Lord Milford even fully heard her. After the briefest of nods, he and his gray stallion trotted away.

"My lady? Is there anything I may do for you?"

It was Rupert, riding up to where she and Arcturus still stood in the middle of the horse path.

Petra watched the rapidly receding back of Lord Milford. Her heart felt heavy, yet a sense of unease she could not yet name swirled within her gut at the same time. Lord Milford had been so convincing, but Martin had seemed so sure of himself as well.

Who was telling the truth? Milford, with whom Gwen had a marriage that was never happy? Or Martin, whom Gwen supposedly trusted but had dismissed only days before her death? Petra felt at once tired, out of her depth, and not sure which way to turn next. And still, curiosity continued to make her want to push on. The only thing she could do now was meet Martin and hear his side of the story.

"I am well, thank you, Rupert," Petra said with a weary sigh and checked the watch pinned to her riding coat. "I think I have had enough of the Row for today. And it is a good thing, for we are almost late to meet Martin in the Green Park."

"Very good, my lady," Rupert said. "We shall make our way there now."

Owing to Petra going over the conversation with Lord Milford in her mind—occasionally interrupted by the nagging thought that Uncle Tobias had returned early to London and, by Lady Vera's assessment, was up to no good—the half mile or so they covered down Piccadilly to the entrance to the Green Park was all but a blur.

"I suggest we move to walk nearer the trees for some shade, my lady," Rupert said as they passed through the gates.

"I agree," Petra said, touching her handkerchief to her brow and upper lip, the sun having emerged gloriously from the clouds as they rode. As she had hoped, the park appeared sparsely populated, on account that it was almost exclusively the dominion of the upper classes, and the bulk of them were only just now beginning to stir in their beds after Her Grace's ball.

Tucking her handkerchief in her pocket, they rode onward past a row of plane trees in the direction of the spot where the enormous folly known as the Temple of Concord had briefly been erected for the three-day Grand Jubilee in August of the previous year. Petra recalled its theatric revolving temple that was a backdrop for glorious fireworks, only for the temple to be dismantled and sold off in parts a couple of months later.

While the grass and surrounding foliage had not been much damaged by the fireworks, the space was still somewhat forlorn-looking at present and largely avoided by those wishing to stroll the park. Therefore, it made for a more private area where Petra could conceivably have a conversation with a footman and have the news not reach the scandal sheets within the hour.

Goodness, it has become warm. Reaching for her handkerchief once more, Petra's fingers came up empty.

"Rupert, do you see my handkerchief?" she asked, looking around as best she could. Rupert did as well, saying, "I see it, my lady. Just a bit back; I'll fetch it now."

If Petra hadn't been pulling Arcturus into a stop, what happened next might have led to a disaster. But when the rock came flying through the air, it didn't strike her horse's flank, potentially causing Arcturus to bolt; it was Petra's right shoulder blade that took the full hit instead. She uttered an exclamation of pain, then immediately wheeled Arcturus around to see from where the rock had come.

TWELVE

RUPERT WAS ALREADY CHARGING TOWARD THE TREES ON HIS bay, pulling up short at a rather magnificent black poplar. In a flash, he'd swung down to the ground and was yanking what looked to be a dirty set of flailing arms and legs from the tree's lower branches. The young boy of not more than ten years of age—for Petra felt sure that's who her rock thrower was—was then hauled by the scruff of his grimy shirt to the edge of the path, where Petra and Arcturus waited.

"How dare you attempt to hurt Lady Petra," Rupert growled, giving the boy a shake, further tousling a mop of dark blond curls. "You'll apologize, you will, you little scoundrel, and then I'll see you to the Bow Street station for assault upon a fine lady!"

"L-Lady Petra?" said a worried voice. "It were Lady Petra? I wouldn't hurt her, guv'ner! I swear it!"

As dirty hands brushed at the hair flopping into his face, Petra recognized him.

"Teddy?" she exclaimed, leaning as much as she dared from her saddle to get a better look at the boy. "Whatever are you doing here?"

"You know this—this boy, this street urchin, my lady?" Rupert asked before the boy could answer, his eyes dark with suspicion as he looked from Teddy to Lady Petra and back.

"I do—and I thank you, Rupert, for so quickly coming to my aid and catching the person who threw a rock at me. However, I believe you may let Teddy go. He will stay and answer our questions and not run away as a coward would. Am I correct in saying so, Teddy?" She dipped her chin while raising her eyebrows, encouraging a positive response.

As expected, Teddy's little chin thrust out, and his eyes, which were blue as a clear sky, were further brightened with indignation.

"I ain't no coward. Of course I'll tell the truth, my lady," Teddy huffed. He turned his head to glare at Rupert. "And I'd never hurt Lady Petra, so let me go!"

"Teddy," Lady Petra said, calling upon her patience. "Please apologize to Rupert. He is my head groom, exceedingly trustworthy, the finest horseman I've known, excepting my dear papa, of course, and would be an excellent friend to you—but only if you are respectful to him." She looked to her groom. "Rupert, this is Teddy. I met him last year when he rather helped me out of a pickle. He earned my trust, and has continued to do so by running the occasional errand for me. He is very intelligent for a boy his age, and loves horses, so I would not take his actions of a few moments ago as indicative of his general nature."

Teddy's chin was set, but it quivered once at hearing Petra's description of him. And then once more when he looked up into Petra's face and saw kindness and patience there, along with a strong will that said she would not give in to his bad behavior, even with the kind things she had said about him. The fight went out of his face and his voice.

"I'm sorry, guv," he said finally. "I promise I would have never hurt Lady Petra. Never, I tell you. Lady Petra's the kindest person I know."

"That she is," Rupert said, his voice only slightly less of a growl as he released the boy. Teddy looked up at him, and Rupert held the boy's gaze with assessing eyes before giving him a brief nod.

Now Petra got the full beam of Teddy's blue eyes, which turned worried in the next second as he addressed her, speaking at a rapid pace.

"Please forgive me, my lady. I swear I didn't know who I were aimin' at when I were throwin' that rock. I was just given a thruppence to throw it at the chestnut ridden by the lady with the silly red hat." He looked momentarily stunned at his own words.

"Begging your pardon, my lady. It's a fine hat—it's just that's what he called it."

Petra kept her countenance unconcerned, but she was instantly on her guard. "And, pray tell, who is this 'he,' Teddy?"

Teddy shrugged, but she could see the worry in his face. "Barely saw but a bit of him, my lady. He came up to me just on Piccadilly, when me back was turned, see, and grabbed my collar, like this one here—" He thumbed in the direction of Rupert, who, Lady Petra noted, found it amusing, especially when Teddy added, "Mr. Rupert, that is. He—the man—held the coin in front of my face and told me to run to the Green Park. That a lady would be comin' by on a chestnut wearing a—"

"A silly hat. Yes, Teddy, I know. It is quite all right. I think my hat silly, too," Petra said with a wan smile.

Teddy swallowed, but forged on. "He said that he and the lady play jokes on each other from time to time, and she would not mind. He said your chestnut wasn't likely to spook too badly. He said you would laugh, my lady."

"Hmm. Rather the opposite, I'm afraid." When she saw Teddy continuing to look distressed, she added, "But I am not hurt in any way, I assure you. Tell me, was this man's voice recognizable in some way?"

Teddy's face screwed up. "How d'you mean, my lady? He sounded a dasher, but otherwise just like any other man who were grown." Now his lips pursed as if in disapproval. "Though I think he were changin' his voice somehow. You know, deliberately talkin' differently to disguise himself." He deepened his voice, adding, "Lower-like, if you take my meaning."

"Of course." Thinking darkly of Lord Milford, she asked, "Was he on a horse? A dark gray stallion, perhaps?"

Rupert cut his eyes toward Petra, but she kept hers on Teddy.

"No, my lady, he were on foot," Teddy said confidently. "There were horses about, but where I was, I would've heard if he'd ridden up on one. Seen it, too."

"Of course," Petra said, knowing Teddy must be right, for she had just remembered that Milford would not have known of her plans to go to the Green Park. "Did you see any part of him, then?"

"No, my lady," Teddy replied again. Then cocked his head to the side. "Well, the bit I did see was his hand, when the thruppence appeared. It were his left, being as he had me by the collar with his right, see? He had his gloves on, but I could see part of his wrist. Had scars on the inside of his wrist, he did."

Petra felt herself take a quick, shallow breath. Scars on the wrist? *Josiah Bellingham.*

Damn and blast. Josiah had known exactly where she would be today. The exact time, in fact. Had he truly paid Teddy to spook her horse? In, what? Hopes that she would fall and hurt herself in revenge for making him look like a fool the night before at Her Grace's ball? Anger began to well up inside of her, so quickly that she almost didn't hear Rupert speak.

"What type of scars, lad?" he said. "As in those from a knife, perhaps?"

"Or those from fingernails?" Petra asked darkly. She ignored another brief look of surprise from Rupert and focused on Teddy.

"Nay," Teddy said, shaking his head. "Like from someone's teeth, they were."

Petra was momentarily stunned by the very thought before saying, "Teeth, did you say? Surely you mean a dog's bite, or some such." She could easily imagine Josiah evoking the anger of any dog enough that it bit him.

Teddy grinned and lifted his knee pointing to a space just above his left ankle, several inches below where his well-worn, too-short trousers stopped. "No, my lady. Like when Gully Gulverton bit me when I fought him. I were six and he were eight, or so he claims. I ain't never seen nobody that big who were eight years old, not in London, at least. But it don't matter—I won."

"Quite," Petra replied, equal parts horrified and pitying, but with a touch of amusement at how proud Teddy was to show off his scar. Even from her perch atop a horse, she could see the two curved scar marks on his leg that still bore the look of human teeth indentations. "Well done, then."

"I can take care of meself, I can," Teddy replied, puffing out his chest.

Rupert's dark eyes were gleaming now. Petra could tell he liked the lad's hubris. Good. She had been planning on attempting to introduce Rupert to Teddy in hopes of securing Teddy a better life as a stable lad—if he wanted it, of course. Teddy had thus far refused her offers to help him by sending him to the country to live at Buckfields. She suspected that he had a parent or a sibling somewhere to whom he wished to stay close, but he had never yet opened up about his circumstances. Still, at present, her questions about the man who commissioned Teddy to do her harm were overriding her pleasure in Rupert and Teddy forming a bond.

"I have seen that for myself, Teddy," Petra replied, knowing instantly it was the correct thing for her to say. "Was the man's scar much like yours?"

Teddy shook his head. "No, my lady. It were naught but a few teeth marks—some from the upper teeth, some from the lower—from what I could see. Maybe more. Didn't even look that bad, neither, 'cept for one, that looked a mite worse, like his cuff were causing it distress." Teddy examined his own wrist, then shot the cuff back into place smartly, as if his yellowed, bedraggled shirt was as pristine and white as any nobleman's. "All 'n' all, looked like he got his arm away before the bloke he were fightin' got his teeth in but good. Bet no one will even notice them marks in a few months' time. Won't likely leave a real scar like mine."

"How do you mean, a real scar?" Petra asked, even as a memory from the ball came back to her. Of Josiah walking up the steps to stand in drunken solidarity with friends while straightening his cuffs.

"Well, my lady, they were fresh, weren't they?" Teddy replied, as if it should have been obvious. "Probably no more than a week old,

I'd say. I could smell he'd put some of that special salve Bardwell's does up, too. You know, the one that smells a bit like lemon drops."

"I'm afraid I don't know it, Teddy," she replied, wondering with an unpleasant feeling in her stomach if the distinctive smell did indeed come from the salve or from someone who happened to be extremely partial to lemon drops. Someone with green eyes and a history of playing pranks on her as a child. She only felt a bit better at the thought that Josiah could still be the culprit, if the old scars on his wrist from Petra were now joined by a fresh set of bite marks no more than a week old. "How do you know it's Bardwell's Apothecary that makes the salve?"

"Because Miss Frances made some for me one time when she saw I'd cut my foot." Teddy held up his bare right foot and pointed to the top, near the arch.

"And who is Miss Frances?"

"She'd be the daughter of Sir Bartie, the herbalist. Miss Frances runs his apothecary on Jermyn Street. Makes up all the salves and what not."

The sound of horse hooves made Petra, Teddy, and Rupert all look down the path. No more than twenty paces away, a beautiful dapple-gray mare was trotting across their line of vision. The gray was riderless, with her reins flapping on her neck and the stirrups of her saddle bouncing against her sides, but Petra recognized her all the same.

"Why, that's His Grace's mare. The one Martin was to be riding. Oh, Rupert, we must catch her before she comes to harm!"

Rupert, though, was already in action. "I'll fetch 'er, my lady, don't worry! Teddy, stay with her ladyship." He'd swung back up on his bay and was galloping off after the mare.

"Right, guv'ner!" Teddy called out. He had already begun looking through the trees as if on the lookout for brigands, and then his neck craned as he caught sight of something. "My lady, I think I see someone on the other side of these trees, and a bit farther on. On the ground, like."

"Oh, it may be Martin," said Petra worriedly, as she tried to peer through the tangle of branches and flowering spring leaves and found her view all but blocked. "Teddy, please go and see if he's hurt."

Teddy nodded and dashed away, only to return a moment later, his elfin face pale under the dirt streaks. He pointed emphatically back through the trees. "My lady, there's a man there. He's dead, he is. With a knife in 'is chest!"

THIRTEEN

PETRA MOVED SWIFTLY, PULLING HER RIGHT LEG UP OVER THE fixed head of her sidesaddle, and half slid, half leapt off Arcturus's back.

"This way, my lady," Teddy said, pointing to a space between two trees big enough for her horse to fit through, and she and Arcturus followed Teddy at a quick pace.

"Oh!" The exclamation was out of Petra's mouth before she could stop it.

It was indeed Martin, dead, just as Teddy had claimed. The footman lay twisted to one side, as if he'd fallen forward, then managed to turn partially sideways at his last breaths. His eyes were open and staring, one arm flung out to the side while the other curled over to rest protectively on his torso. A long finger still touched the hilt of a knife protruding from his blood-soaked chest.

Teddy was at her side. "What should we do, my lady?"

With trembling fingers, Petra pulled a coin from her pocket, plus one of her calling cards.

"Teddy, you must run for help. You must find a Bow Street Runner and bring him to us." She handed him the shilling, and her card. "They'll require the payment, and here is my card. Tell the Runner to come straightaway."

"But I cannot leave you, my lady," Teddy said, his blue eyes wide. "I promised Mr. Rupert."

"Who will be here any moment," Petra said in a firm voice, turning him around to point him toward Piccadilly. "Now, *go.*"

With one last look of worry, Teddy did as he was told, his quick footsteps fading into the trees in moments.

Feeling a bit light-headed, Petra tied Arcturus to a nearby tree limb as thunder rumbled in the distance, clouds once more covering the sun. Then she heard the sound from behind her. Footsteps—the long, sure stride of a man wearing boots, not the sound of two horses, which would indicate the arrival of Rupert.

She froze, the fingers of her right hand going beneath the left sleeve of her riding jacket. And when she felt the man's presence two paces behind her, she whirled, pulling forth a small dagger as she did.

She was right. It was a man, and his hands went slowly up, top hat in one of them—though fear was not upon the face that looked as if it had been chiseled into place.

"You mean to defend yourself with that wee dagger, my lady?" The Scottish burr was back, taunting her.

"*Duncan*," she exhorted, her breaths now coming heavily. She looked from Martin's body, up into Duncan's too-calm expression, and fear suddenly overtook her. She lunged forward, making a thrusting gesture with the knife. "Move away from me. I shall not let you take my life as well!"

He'd leaned away from the dagger thrust, smiling at her flimsy attempt to frighten him. Then his eyes narrowed to look straight at her, becoming glittering green orbs behind a feathering of dark lashes.

"Petra, you are in earnest?" A huff of disbelief escaped his lips. "No, you cannot be."

She'd moved away from him, still pointing the little dagger in just the way Duncan himself had taught her. Palm side up, thumb on the hilt edge, and aiming directly where it would do the most damage: at his groin.

"Oh, I am very much in earnest," she said. "How is it that you come across me here if you did not know the place where Martin was felled?" She glanced at the body of the footman, pity for him overwhelming her. "The poor footman was stabbed. Only a handful of people knew he was to be here, waiting for me, and you were one of them." Her voice grew stronger, louder in hopes that Rupert was near and would hear her. "Of all of the men present last night, Martin would have trusted you the most. Would have let you get close enough to do that to him. But, why? What reason would you have to kill him at all, much less in such a horrific manner?"

Duncan had suddenly become blurry to her eyes. By thunder, she had teared up. "Was it because of what he knew of Gwen?" She stretched out her arm, the little dagger trembling in her hand. "Answer me, Duncan Shawcross. What could Lady Milford have done to warrant you killing her loyal and kind former footman?"

Frustrated, she went to wipe her eyes with the back of her other hand, and that's when it happened.

Duncan grabbed her right wrist, making her cry out in pain. Her grip on the dagger lessened. The next moment, she was being swung around. Then he was at her back, the full length of him pressed up against hers, his right arm about her waist. His left hand was splayed over the front of her rib cage, her little dagger held fast beneath his open hand, the sharp tip between her breasts, facing upward to her face.

His voice was in her ear and she heard him emit a sigh. "This is truly a tragedy, Petra, I agree with you wholeheartedly. But look at him." Then he said it with more command. "Petra, *look at him.*"

Petra struggled, thinking she might try to bite him, but her mouth couldn't reach. In response, he held her even closer. He'd thoroughly hobbled her in a matter of heartbeats.

"Petra," Duncan growled. "*Look at him.* He has cuts in other places than just where the knife went in. He fought back, and fought back with all his strength."

"Good!" Petra returned, attempting to squirm away, and failing. "I am glad he tried to hurt you."

"And yet I do not have one speck of blood on my person," Duncan snapped. "Nor is any of my clothing torn, ripped, or damaged. Look at his outstretched hand, Petra." She was jerking her head back against his chest. He merely laid his jaw against the top of her head to still it. "Look," he said again, only in a softer tone.

She did, and saw it, stilling as she did. "It is . . . is it the flap of a coat pocket?"

"I believe so," Duncan said. "And as you saw, my pocket flaps remain firmly in place—or maybe you did not have enough time to notice my well-maintained attire, with wanting to plunge your dagger into an area I would most like to remain undamaged."

Petra struggled once more against him. "This is not a time to be jesting. Martin has been killed, and most terribly. Let me go, you brute."

"Do you believe me?" he asked, only loosening his steellike grip on her person a small amount.

"By the bollocks of Pegasus," she huffed, wanting to stamp on his foot. It was a desire she just barely resisted. "You do vex me, Duncan Shawcross."

"Lord, I have not heard you say either one of those statements in far too long," he said. She felt against the whole of her back his stomach muscles pulse with two short, dry laughs. "But that does not answer my question."

When she only replied with a *humph*, he sighed. "All right, you are intelligent to desire more information. Then may I present you with it?" Without waiting for a response, he began speaking.

"After the events of early this morning, I knew that Bellingham was most unhappy with you. I decided it would then be best to come to your meeting spot with Martin. No, do not make that disapproving noise, Petra. I did not intend to listen in, only to keep a lookout for Bellingham. Anyway, I arrived at the stroke of two, only to see my grandfather's gray mare without her rider. I started after her, but saw Rupert doing a much better job, as he was on a horse and I was not. He pointed me in your direction, calling out something about a street urchin named Teddy. When I saw the boy crashing through the trees, looking like the devil himself was after him, I did the same, but toward you instead, assuming the boy had hurt you and run off."

"Teddy would never hurt me," Petra said. "I sent him for a Bow

Street Runner." Then her brow furrowed. "But why did you not call out to me?"

"I did, Petra," Duncan said patiently. "Though I only did once before you turned with this dagger in your hand." She felt him lightly tap the dagger still held to her rib cage with his thumb. "And it was at the moment the thunder came, which may have been a factor in your not hearing it. Now do you believe me?"

Desperate now to be out of his embrace, she said the words through clenched teeth.

"Yes. I believe you. Now release me this moment—and give me back my dagger."

His arms went wide, and she spun around to find he'd stepped back with her dagger laying on his palm, as if he were presenting her with the little weapon—for it did indeed look tiny in his hand, with its blade, though sharp, barely hanging off the side of his palm. No wonder he had laughed at her.

Plucking it from his palm and finding it still warm from his hand, Petra stored the dagger back in her sleeve. She then turned away to walk to Martin's body, though she did not object when Duncan moved to her side. He didn't speak as she bowed her head, granting her the silence. Petra hoped Martin's soul was still nearby, lingering for a few moments more, and could see, feel, or sense the anguish in her heart, and know her intense sorrow. Then she could hold in the words no longer.

"Oh, poor Martin! This is my fault, Duncan, for it was I who brought him here. I do not think I shall ever forgive myself."

"It was not you who killed him, Petra," Duncan replied. Petra looked up, surprised at the anger in his voice. He met her eyes briefly before looking away. "But the feeling of guilt that cannot be driven away is one I understand, so I cannot fault you for it."

Petra wanted to ask him what he meant, but when she looked back at Martin, she knew this was not the right moment. Then her hands flew to her face.

"Oh! But Her Grace! What will she think? She will be so disappointed in me for leading her footman here, and putting him in danger." She turned horrified eyes to Duncan. "What if Her Grace is in danger?"

"On the latter account, you need not worry."

"But how do you know?"

"It is my job to know, for I am entrusted with her security," Duncan said as his eyes roamed every inch of Martin's form and the area around where he lay. "On the former charges you have set against yourself, you need not worry on those, either. At least, not at present. My grandparents can no longer bear the sounds, the smells, and the destruction of Hillmorton House that happens at a ball that lasts twelve hours and welcomes roughly four hundred guests." His eyes cut to Petra's and she saw amusement in their depths. "Grandfather escapes to his club. And Grandmama to a more reasonably sized town house nearby, on Mount Street."

"I did not know Their Graces owned property on Mount Street."

"*His* Grace does not. *Her* Grace does. She keeps it very quiet, though occasionally she holds salons there for women she trusts."

"Then how do you know of it when other women do not?" Petra asked, curiosity taking her mind away for a moment.

One of Duncan's dark eyebrows lifted. "I am entrusted with her security," he repeated.

There was something in the way he said those words, as if the trust given to him was something he felt to his core, meaning more to him than whatever riches he would be entitled to as the duchess's grandson. Something in Petra made her feel as if he were speaking to the trust Petra once had given to him as well, and it produced a tiny bubble of something like longing in her chest. Yet it burst when her eyes fell to the ground and the tragic loss of life evident upon it.

"Be that as it may, Her Grace is still in town and will soon hear of poor Martin's demise. She may wish for me never to darken the doorstep of Hillmorton House again."

"Actually, she will not hear—at least, not for a few days. The house on Mount Street is having new windows installed this week.

Thus, she decided a short trip to the seaside was in order. I came here after seeing her carriage off to Brighton—and as I shall be the one informing her of this tragedy, I will also be making sure that the news does not reach her with great haste."

Petra looked up at him, wanting to ask, *Why are you doing this for me?* Instead, she dropped her gaze back to the ground and said, "I am grateful, truly," before adding, "also for not treating me as some weak female who will swoon at the sight of blood."

This produced the ghost of a smile. "I recall when you were ten and I eleven and we came across your father's gamekeeper after he had been gored by a stag," he said, squatting down and gently pulling the short length of material from Martin's hand. "If seeing a man's intestines flowing out from his body did not send you into a dead faint as it nearly did me that day, well . . ."

Petra felt the smallest amount better with his words. She watched him curiously, saw his eyes roving over every inch of Martin's form. "What are you seeing?" When he glanced up, she said, "Please tell me. I should like to know before the Runner gets here. For you must know he will not allow me to stay."

Duncan rose to his feet, studied her for a moment, then gave a brisk nod. "All right. First, I will tell you that Martin has not been dead long."

Petra checked her watch fob. "I would have expected as much, as I was to meet him at two o'clock, and is not yet a quarter past."

"Yes, but he could have been out riding for an hour already," Duncan countered.

"That is true, of course," Petra said.

"Did you take notice at how easily I was able to take the pocket flap from his fingers? And do you see how his face is just now beginning to pale? That tells me he has been dead less than a half hour."

Petra looked up at Duncan, then back at Martin's body. "Please, do go on," she said.

"Look at the knife hilt," Duncan then said, pointing. "Notice that it is simple and the handle wood. Though I cannot see the entirety of the blade, to be sure, I would expect the knife is from a kitchen. This means it can be found almost anywhere, and even a woman could easily obtain it."

"A woman?" Petra said, startled. "Do you think it could have been a woman who did this?"

Duncan shrugged. "If a woman were angry enough, it is possible. But plunging a knife into a man's body is a lot harder than one believes. A woman would have to be in the throes of some sort of hysteria or mania to have the level of strength needed for this act."

Petra's brows came together, her mind on Gwen. Did she indeed drown while experiencing a fit, as Lord Milford asserted? Or was she alive, as Martin had claimed? And if she were, was Gwen off her head to the point that she could have deliberately hurt her own former footman?

"Yet I do not think it was a woman," Duncan continued. "Footmen are generally tall and strong, as they do so much carrying. Martin was a bit taller than most, and very strong, judging by the day I saw him lifting a cask of ale for the ball with ease. While it is not impossible, I think it unlikely that even a woman experiencing madness would get so many knife wounds into his person without him being able to also fend her off and keep her from administering the fatal wound."

"So you believe the perpetrator to be a man?"

"I do, and I will show you why," Duncan said. Then he gently grasped Petra's shoulders and turned her to face him. "Now, lift your arm, if you would. As high as you can. You are about the average height for a woman, yes? An inch or so over five feet, I would wager?" When she nodded, he gave her a wan smile. "Right. Make a fist and pretend to stab me, knowing you would have to aim somewhat downward to do so with the most effect."

Petra gave him a curious look but did as she was asked, though feeling very silly while doing so.

"What do you notice?" he asked.

"That at my height, and aiming the knife properly, it would be difficult for me to pierce you above your clavicle," she said. She looked back at Martin's form, guessing what Duncan would ask her next and answering in advance. "You are tall, but Martin had likely another inch on you. Besides the obvious stab wound, he has others in his upper arms, neck, and cheeks. And even one horrible gash on his forehead. But what is it that makes you believe he did not sustain these injuries whilst on the ground?"

"Take a look around him, at the ground and the grass."

Petra did, taking in for the first time the height of the grass, which was at about four inches or so, with smatterings of small, white daisies.

"There is little disturbance of the grass overall. Yet I can see some boot impressions about, and the grass is all but trampled here." She pointed to the space not far from Martin's feet, clearly churned to the point of showing dirt and crumpled daisies. "That is where Martin must have stood and fought for his life. But I do not see areas around the body where the grass is greatly agitated, as I expect it would be from someone on the ground, shifting from side to side to avoid blows." She looked back at Duncan for confirmation of this.

"Excellent," he said with a brief nod. "Go on."

"All right," Petra said. "Then, after taking these facts into account, I think one can safely assume the blaggard who did this to poor Martin was much taller than I am." She bit her lip thoughtfully, then said, "Likely a man of average height or more, but possibly not as tall as you."

"Well done," Duncan said. And though he did not smile, there was appreciation brightening his green eyes.

No, they were not toad-like in color at all.

She blinked. "But how was it that you learned to look at . . . situations such as these? And how did you learn to think in such ways as you have encouraged me to do?"

"It has been three years since we have been in each other's company," Duncan said lightly, but his eyes had gone flat.

Then Arcturus, still tied to the tree, lifted his head, ears pricked toward the way Duncan had come.

She and Duncan both heard it as well—hoofbeats. Coming at a brisk trot. They had little time now to speak privately.

"What of the pocket flap?" Petra asked. She plucked the scrap from his left hand, noting with a crashing sense of relief as she did that she could see his wrist beyond his gloves and there were no scars, scratches, teeth marks, or wounds of any kind. No salve smelling of lemon drops, either. Duncan had not been the man to pay Teddy to spook Arcturus.

"You did so well just now, why don't you tell me?" Duncan said. The one dark eyebrow that raised further issued the challenge, even as another, louder rumble of thunder sounded from the heavens.

Petra felt the fabric, turning it over with her fingers. "It is wool. The color looked to be black, but I can now see it is the darkest of aubergine."

"Will that make it easier to find the wearer?" Duncan asked, sounding curious rather than like one who knows the answer and is simply testing another.

"Possibly," Petra said. "I suspect this color will not be in every tailor's shop. Must we give it to the Runner when he arrives?"

"I should think it best. However, give me that little dagger of yours again. Quickly."

She once more pulled it from her sleeve, and Duncan used it to begin cutting away a two-inch piece of the fabric.

"Wait—cut it so some of the stitching is showing," Petra urged, pointing to the loose threads where the flap had been torn from the rest of the coat. "I can tell my own needlework from that of others. I wonder if it is possible a tailor might be able to recognize who may have done the stitching."

"Good thinking," Duncan said. Petra held out her hand for the bit of fabric, stitching and all. But Duncan had turned to assess the nearness of Rupert and the horses, pocketing the scrap as he did so.

He was not going to let her question any tailors, as she had hoped. She glowered up at him, but he did not seem to notice as he met her eyes.

"Petra, Rupert is almost here. I must insist you explain about Lady Milford."

She did not want to answer, not yet. For he would likely tell her not to keep looking, not to keep asking questions, reminding her that she was but a woman, and what could a woman do? Give but some fine, intelligent answers, discover some clues, and then be told to leave?

Duncan's hands went to his hips. The growling voice was back. "Petra . . ."

It was Rupert and the arrival of Teddy with a Bow Street Runner in tow who first saved her, then the rain did much of the rest.

"Holy 'ell!" Rupert exclaimed at seeing the knife lodged in Martin's chest, completely forgetting himself for once. Even as Rupert stumbled backward, from the opposite direction came Teddy, crashing through the trees once more, followed by the Bow Street Runner, whose wool greatcoat flapped about his heels. Introduced as Townsend, he was a blustery fellow who, as Petra expected, objected to having a woman present as he looked over Martin's body, even if she was the earl's daughter and had once seen a man gored by a stag.

Petra called Teddy over and bent to whisper to him while Duncan and Townsend spoke, the Runner continually looking back at Petra as if he wished she would go away. Finally, he appealed to Duncan.

"It just wouldn't be right, Mr. Shawcross," said Townsend, as droplets of rain started falling. "Just wouldn't be right. An' it's rainin', sir. I'd like to get on with my duty, but havin' a lady present . . ."

Duncan scowled, but encouraged Rupert to help Petra back up onto her horse.

For his efforts, Teddy received two farthings and a penny from Lady Petra—which was the sum of what she had left in her pocket—and another two groats from Duncan, plus a small handful of lemon drops from his own coat pocket.

"This almost makes up for having been taken in by that blighter who paid me to spook your horse, my lady," Teddy said through a mouthful of lemon drop and with a charmingly crooked grin that showed an equally crooked canine tooth.

"What was that, Teddy?" Duncan asked sharply. Teddy's eyes went wide with apprehension.

"Never mind Mr. Shawcross, Teddy," Petra said. "Now, be on your way to somewhere safe while it rains. And I shall tell Mrs. Bing to expect you at Forsyth House at teatime."

Petra knew Mrs. Bing would get some hot broth in him and Smithers would not object to Teddy sitting by the fire in the servants' hall while he ate. Mrs. Ruddle would even see him off with some apples and a thick slice of Mrs. Bing's pork pie. It was all Teddy was willing to accept, and would likely be shared with other children who slept rough on the streets of London.

Thus, leaving the gray for Duncan, Petra rode toward home in the rain, Rupert riding protectively at her flank, her thoughts coming at the speed of the sudden downpour.

If there was one thing she felt sure of, deep in her bones, it was that Martin was killed—no, murdered—because of Gwen. But did that mean Gwen was still alive, and Martin knew where she had been, and where she might be now? Or was Martin murdered because Gwen had been killed, too, and he could have offered Petra the proof she needed to confirm it?

Somehow, she must discover the truth.

"My lady!"

They were barely outside the park's boundaries when Teddy came running up, though stopping well short of Arcturus, who loathed the rain and had his ears back against his head.

"Were you able to secure it?" Petra asked.

His curls now plastered to his head from the rain, Teddy pulled out a small piece of wool in the darkest of aubergine from inside his sleeve. "Couldn't 'ave been easier, my lady. Mr. Shawcross ain't the wiser."

Petra stowed the scrap in her own pocket, and thanked Teddy, who grinned and was off like a rabbit once more. Petra and Rupert, now fully drenched, picked up a trot for the final distance home, Petra's determination increasing the closer they came to Forsyth House.

Yes, somehow she must discover the truth—not only for Gwen's sake, but also for Martin's. And now she had a small scrap—with distinctive stitching, or so she hoped—on which to start her journey.

FOURTEEN

"My lady? It is half past four o'clock. Lady Caroline is waiting for you in your drawing room." There was the sound of curtains being flung open. "I would have much liked to allow you to sleep more, but she arrived in such a worried state for you." Petra's warm counterpane was pulled back. "If she were anyone else, I would have sent her away, telling her to come back when your ladyship sent word that she could, but—"

"Yes, yes," Petra mumbled. "I have instructed the house that Lady Caroline should always be allowed and welcomed."

"And so we did, my lady," Annie said. "I have asked Mrs. Bing to send up some tea things for her."

"Lovely," Petra mumbled, slipping back into sleep. "If you would only give me five more minutes of silence put together."

She was then jerked back awake by a forceful snapping noise that was Annie shaking out one of her dresses. Annie's cheerful voice did not help matters.

"And 'tis a good thing, too, that Lady Caroline was here, or I would have had to send away the other woman waiting on the doorstep. Do you recall me telling you of a Miss Reed, my lady?"

"*Muhunh.*"

"That is absolutely right, my lady," chirped Annie. "She *is* the young woman I told you about who works with dogs. Smithers asked her business, and she said she was sent here at the request of her benefactor. And, oh, my lady, at her feet were the two sweetest dogs, sitting quietly like little ladies. Only one might be a boy, for it is a darling little terrier she calls Fitzwilliam—or Fitz for short. I must say, he is the best behaved terrier I have ever seen in my life, my lady. She says she has bred him herself, crossing two types of terriers. Oh, I do love how his little ears fold over. And his coat looks like it would be wiry and rough, but instead it is very soft. But the other dog, my lady, is a beautiful little miss of a pointer. She's sleek and nearly all brown, with no spots on her at all except for a bit of white on her chest. Even Lady Caroline—"

"All right, all right!" Petra grumped loudly. "I shall get up if you would simply hold your tongue."

Annie's next words proved that she was unmoved, especially as Petra's eyes were still closed.

"If you had come home earlier, my lady—and not soaked through, with mud covering your boots, leaves in your hair, and quite the frightening tale to recount—you would have had two hours' rest instead of only one. So you have no one to blame but your ladyship."

Petra cracked one eye. "I tell everyone who will listen that you are a gem, but you are, in fact, a harpy."

Annie's hazel eyes danced with merriment. "I have chosen your pink calico dress with the yellow flowers, my lady." She took Petra's hand and pulled her into a sitting position, giggling when Petra let out a groan of dramatic proportions.

Petra stood, swaying sleepily, as Annie pulled the dress over her head, but was somewhat revived when she sipped on the small cup of hot, spiced chocolate that was put in her hands. "I felt you could use it, my lady," Annie said.

"Thank you, Annie," she said. "You are indeed a gem."

"Drink it, my lady, or I shall turn into a harpy again," Annie returned.

Petra sipped Mrs. Bing's frothy chocolate drink that was spiced with cinnamon and cloves and thickened with a bit of gingerbread, but still walked sleepily until she entered her drawing room to find a small circus in play, with both Caroline and another woman sitting—heavens, directly on the floor.

Lady Caroline was laughing as she held out one of Petra's riding crops, and a small brown terrier leapt over it. Each time he flew over the apex, he caught a small bit of chicken tossed by the woman looking just a bit younger than Petra and Caro. This must be Miss Reed.

With a striped yellow bonnet hanging at her back, Miss Reed had tight curls in such a pale blond that she almost looked to have a bit of cotton fluff at the top of her head. Even sitting, Petra could tell Miss Reed was short and a bit on the stocky side. She had full, merry cheeks, and, Petra could tell by listening to her explain to Caroline how she'd trained the terrier, a disarming mode of speech that sounded to be equal parts well-bred lady and Yorkshire country lass.

Miss Reed then spoke another few words in what sounded like Gaelic, and the terrier moved to sit at her side while a dog three times his size, yet still a fine-boned and small brown pointer, took to leaping over the riding crop. Her silky ears flew like wings as she bounded up and over like a jackrabbit, catching the bit of chicken easily. Both dogs were shiny, clean, and the very portrait of happy and well-mannered.

And it was the pointer who noticed Petra first. She trotted right up to Petra and sat with a wagging tail, waiting like a little lady for Petra to make the first move.

"What a beauty you are," Petra said, stroking the dog's soft head and ears. The pointer was indeed sleek, like those spotted pointers of German origin, with, as promised, only a bit of white on her chest. She leaned into Petra's touch, looking up with sweet brown eyes that looked already devoted.

"Took to you right away, she did, my lady," said Miss Reed, beaming as she rose quickly to her feet and gave a curtsy. "He seemed to think she would. Bet me a ha'penny that he'd be right, in fact. I took that bet, being as it Sable there tends to be a bit standoffish until she meets you proper-like, but now I do believe I am out two farthings!"

"And who might 'he' be, Miss Reed?" Petra asked. Smithers had given her Miss Reed's calling card, and thus she was certain the young woman's name was Miss Charlotte Reed. It was Caroline who answered, though.

"Why, Shawcross, dearest. He has been Miss Reed's benefactor for some months now, it seems."

Miss Reed's head bobbed up and down, though she looked with some uncertainty between Caroline and Petra, having heard the particularly amused tone in Caroline's voice and seen the flash of surprise, and then the wariness that Petra could not hide.

"I am delighted to finally meet you, Miss Reed," Petra said, offering her hand to the woman, then reaching to stroke the adorable terrier gathered in Caroline's arms, "for I have heard through other sources that you have quite the way with dogs. I was thinking of hiring you myself for one of my papa's newest spaniels, who seems to be determined to be quite naughty. But I cannot imagine what Mr. Shawcross has to do with you bringing this sweet pointer here today. Sable, did you say her name was?"

Miss Reed nodded as the pointer wagged her tail again and trotted a little circle around Petra to sit at heel at Petra's right leg.

"Sable it is, my lady. She's a part German bird dog—which is in itself descended from a Spanish pointer—which has large liver-colored spots and head, with brown and white speckles over its whole body, and part all silvery-gray bird dog first kept in the German court of Grand Duke Karl August of Weimar. I have been hearing the dogs called the Weimaraner. You mix the two and she came out with that lovely all-brown color and the sweetest nature. Mr. Shawcross said she's the color of a sable, which he saw in Russia. But I have yet to see one except dead and on the collar of a woman's coat, so I told him I would take his word on the matter."

Duncan had traveled to Russia? And had become the benefactor of a girl who works with dogs? Petra had not known any of this, and it made her feel untethered somehow. Her Grace had never even said as much—and the duchess, knowing things were not quite as they were between her grandson and Petra, but little more, had always made certain to slip in some news of Duncan's life. Petra wondered if even Her Grace had given up, just as Duncan had.

"How fascinating," she managed to say. "And what is Sable doing here?"

Miss Reed beamed. "She is yours, my lady. Mr. Shawcross originally bought her for himself as a hunting dog, along with her brother. But whilst her brother took to the birds right away, Sable here did not care for the sound of the guns. He then sent her to me to train as a companion dog instead. Was to be given to Her Grace as a present next week. But Mr. Shawcross turned up on my doorstep but an hour ago. Soaked through from the rain, he was. He told me he'd changed his mind, and Sable was to go to you, as you would be outside more, and give her the exercise she needs. For she requires quite a bit, my lady. These hunting dogs can run all day without tiring."

Miss Reed's voice had been confident and jaunty, but with the vehement shaking of Petra's head, she continued only with an uncertain gameness. "She gets on well with horses and knows her manners, as you can see. Plus, a handful of tricks. Would you . . . would you like to see all she knows, my lady?"

"I thank you, Miss Reed," Petra said, ignoring the look of dismay on Caroline's face as her friend cuddled the little terrier, "but I cannot accept this dog, as lovely as she is."

"But why, dearest?" Caroline asked, challenge in her tone. "No, let me guess. You are thinking that a gift from Mr. Shawcross would likely add further gossip to that which is already filtering through the ton."

Petra stared daggers into her friend's eyes, but all that came from her mouth was "How do you mean?"

Caroline gave her a look of only mild exasperation. "The news is already out about the fate of that poor footman. Lord Whitfield and I were outside the Green Park ourselves when three Bow Street Runners came, well, running. Whitfield stopped one, and we were told of the horrid news, that one Runner was already on the scene, and that you had been the one to find the footman, with Shawcross not far behind."

Petra sighed. She should have expected as much. And could not help feeling a sudden wave of suspicion that Lord Whitfield, who also knew the time and place she was to meet Martin, simply happened to choose that time to stroll with Caroline in the very area. "And was anyone else about?" she asked.

"Oh, a good dozen at least." Caro's brown eyes flashed. "Including Lord and Lady Wyncroft, so the news is sure to be the talk of the Row tonight."

Lynley and Tibby. Petra suppressed a groan at hearing mention of her cousin and her former suitor. The one thing the couple truly shared in common was an inability to hold their tongues when it came to gossip.

Miss Reed spoke up. "I have already heard the news as well, my lady. Not from Mr. Shawcross, but from my maid, who was at Bardwell's Apothecary when Lady Wyncroft's own maid arrived to select some cosmetics for her ladyship."

It seemed Lynley's servants could not keep quiet either, and the very thought caused Petra's already thin patience to dissolve completely.

"Bloody hell!" Petra exhorted. Her eyes went to Caroline. "Do you not see? Duncan—Mr. Shawcross—is gifting me a dog to show that I am incapable of taking care of myself. That I need a dog for protection as I am a weak woman who does not even know how to properly use a dagger to defend myself. No, do not ask. It is a mortifying tale and nothing more."

"If I may, my lady," Miss Reed began, after a pause where Caroline tutted and rolled her eyes. Miss Reed had not looked shocked at Petra's unladylike language; instead her light green eyes had gone bright with merriment. "I had the impression Mr. Shawcross thought you quite brave and capable and simply thought you might like a companion of the canine variety who would make you feel . . . further as if your endeavors could be carried out, whatever they may be, knowing that a loyal dog would wish to protect you, if the case ever arises."

Damn and blast, Petra thought weakly. Miss Reed had made her feel quite foolish indeed. Yet before she could think twice upon the compliments Duncan had paid her to Miss Reed, she changed the subject.

"Tell me, Miss Reed. How did you come to have Mr. Shawcross as your benefactor?"

Miss Reed's smile was rather infectious. "Oh! My father, Mr. Reed, is the fifth son of a viscount who had been very close indeed to His Grace many years ago. Our lands in Thirsk, near the Dales, were a gift from His Grace for my grandfather's service, in fact. They abut lands His Grace still owns, and though my papa remains quite penniless, he does manage to keep our family respectable through renting out the lands to others." She gave a shake of her head, her curls springing out in all directions.

"But that does not answer your question, my lady, and so I shall now. Last year about this time, Mr. Shawcross briefly came to stay in Thirsk before returning to the Continent. Business of some sort. Anyway, he came upon me as I was training my papa's newest Labrador to retrieve in the far fields, and was mightily impressed with my abilities. He then recommended me to two gentlemen in the area. Oh, they were skeptical at first, but I soon showed them when I returned their Labrador and spaniel, respectively, with excellent manners and rather champion at flushing and retrieving."

Her cheeks went pink, though Petra somehow felt it was pride in herself and not from holding romantic notions for Duncan.

"The two gentlemen attempted to abscond with their dogs and not pay me, however, but Mr. Shawcross would have none of it. I got paid my due, and he made sure my money became my own, and not my father's." Then she hurried to add, "Though my papa is a kind man, of course. But a coin in his possession disappears faster than a pint of bitter in the Drover's Arms. After that, Mr. Shawcross became my benefactor—though it is but in name only, you understand, my lady. To keep those who send their dogs to me, or who buy one I have bred, honest in their payments." She let out a short, satisfied laugh. "For offending the grandson of the Duke of Hillmorton would not be good for any man with an ounce of sense to his name!"

"Do you not agree, dearest?" Caroline asked, her tone and look suggesting that Petra had responded to Duncan's gift in a rather childish manner. Caroline was swaying gently side to side, holding the terrier called Fitz close, as he looked up at her with eyes both adoring and contentedly sleepy.

Petra met Caroline's gaze, hating that her friend was right, then looked down at Sable, still sitting at her side. The dog's eyebrows, if one could call them that, were going up and down as if concerned and attempting to ascertain Petra's mood. As if she already knew Petra and wanted the best for her. It was humbling—and, she must admit, adorable.

"Then I thank you, Miss Reed," she said, stroking Sable's head. "She is indeed the loveliest dog I have seen in some time, and I am already taken with her. You are extremely talented, it is clear, and I am honored you would bring her to me."

Miss Reed's face lit up, much like the sky had outside the windows of Petra's drawing room. "You are very welcome, my lady. And I would be most honored if you would call me Lottie. It is short for Charlotte, my given name, and I prefer it greatly to the formal 'Miss Reed.'"

Petra smiled. "I should like that very much, Lottie."

"Now, I must go, my lady," said Lottie. "I have a smart little French bulldog named Bruni I am training for a Miss Railey, and he is waiting in the dog cart outside. I have promised his mistress I would bring him to Wimpole Street this afternoon so she may walk him before going to promenade with her mama. But first I must make a stop at Bardwell's Apothecary for Frances—Miss Bardwell, that is—to draw me up a salve that will tend to a little cut Bruni received when playing a bit too hard with Fitz here." Pulling out a lead for Sable from her haversack, she added, "Nearly forgot, my lady. I am instructed to say one more thing from Mr. Shawcross, though I cannot think what it might mean."

Petra held her breath. It seemed Caroline did as well.

"He said to tell you that he would have given it to you, and he wished you would have asked."

Petra only just stopped herself from looking chagrined as she thanked Lottie politely for the message.

Arrangements were then made for Lottie to show Petra all of Sable's commands. The two women were to meet in Hyde Park the following day, after Petra completed some shopping on nearby Oxford Street. Then Lottie took her leave and Caroline and Petra sat down for tea, Sable going to sleep at Petra's feet as if she had done so already for years.

"Now," Caroline said, accepting a cup of steaming tea from Petra. "You must tell me everything I do not already know about the poor footman's death. Including the meaning behind that mysterious statement that, you must admit, sounded rather like an assignation had been planned between you and Shawcross. Does this mean you two are finally talking again? And whatever was the 'it' he would have given you if you'd only asked? Do tell me it would lead to another thorough debauching."

FIFTEEN

CAROLINE WAS ALTOGETHER DISAPPOINTED TO DISCOVER THE "it" Duncan would have given Petra if she had asked was a mere scrap of fabric.

"I rather think one or both of you should be reminded on the workings of immoral behavior," Caroline said dryly before encouraging Petra to begin her explanations of the afternoon.

Petra selected a shortbread biscuit and began her tale.

"Do you think it was Lord Milford who paid Teddy to throw that rock at your horse?" Caroline asked some minutes later.

"I could not say," Petra said, pinching the crumbs of a shortbread between her fingers.

"What about Bellingham or one of the others with him that night? I should think Bellingham at least devious enough to do so."

"Again, I do not know, Caro," Petra said, feeling a tad impatient. "I am more interested in who might have killed Martin than who played a silly prank on me."

"Oh, but darling, I only ask because I believe the two are much connected."

"As do I," Petra replied. "But I cannot think on who might have done both in such a short span of time. Meaning that they would have had time to kill Martin and then found time to locate a street urchin to play a malicious prank. Teddy was not particularly near the park when he was given his assignment."

Caroline nodded. "Yes, you make a good point. Street urchins are everywhere, until you have need of one. This man would have had to search to find Teddy."

"And Teddy only just had enough time to get up in that tree and wait for me to ride by," Petra said. "For once the prank Teddy had been assigned had been foiled and Rupert rode off to catch His Grace's gray mare, Teddy saw the body through the trees with fair enough speed. I believe if he'd been waiting long, he would have seen Martin on the ground before that."

"True, if not the fight and *la mort horrible* itself," Caroline said, narrowing her eyes and staring out the window to the gardens in thought.

"*Exactement*," Petra agreed with a heavy sigh.

"From what you said Duncan taught you, I think it likely the man who killed Martin might have had blood upon his person— and assuredly on his cuffs as well," Caroline mused.

"Which Teddy, too, would have noticed," Petra said. Then shivered a bit. "That means there might very well be two men out there who wish me harm."

At these words, Sable lifted her head, eyes alert toward the door of the drawing room. Yet it was only Charles, bringing in a letter on a silver salver. It seemed he had already met Sable in the hallways, and she walked up to him with delight, sat on her haunches, and lifted her front paws in the air.

"Already making friends, I see," Petra said as Charles spoke to Sable in soft tones and used one gloved finger to give her a scratch, before bowing and removing himself from the drawing room. Petra slid a finger underneath the wax seal and read the short note with a slight groan.

"Oh, bother. I had forgotten I had asked Lady Potsford to tea tomorrow." She explained to Caroline about having seen her ladyship in the drawing room of Hillmorton House. "Though I confess I also wished to ask Lady Potsford about this man, Mr. Drysdale, after hearing his name mentioned between his lordship and Josiah Bellingham." Petra glanced at the letter again. "Only she has asked that I go to Potsford House, and for a midday luncheon instead, which will make it more tedious as I will not be in my own home. I always find that her ladyship's sofas are too hard, her tea too weak, and her decor much too dark for my tastes. Hence why I had asked her here."

"Maybe Lady Potsford will be able to tell you where Fairwinds is located," Caroline said, dabbing at her mouth with a napkin. "For all Juddy Bellingham was able to tell you was that it is, what, two or more hours outside of London, and likely in Essex?"

"You are correct, of course. I will go to tea at Potsford House tomorrow with a more purposeful mind in hopes I may discover more information. Perhaps Miss Arabella Littlewood will join us for some more lighthearted conversation. Speaking of Miss Littlewood, she danced twice with Duncan at the ball, and I saw her on his arm twice more."

"Yes, I saw that as well," Caroline drawled. "And did this vex you, dearest?"

"No," Petra said with a fluttering of her eyelashes. "But I can give her instruction on how to best vex him, if she so desires."

"Liar," Caroline said lightly, then rose from the sofa. "Shall we go to Hyde Park together later, then? I suspect we shall see all of society out tonight, as most will use it as their first glimpse of the outdoors today after recovering from Her Grace's ball."

Petra, however, was feeling the effects of little sleep again combined with an excellent tea.

"No, I think I shall allow them to gossip without me tonight," she said with a yawn hidden behind her hand, then ran her other over Sable's soft head. "Plus, I shall like an evening to get to know my new companion and write some letters."

Sometime later, after Caroline had left, Petra was startled awake by a sound of some sort. She realized she had dozed off on her sofa, likely not long after she had begun to reply to the letters of her Aunt Ophelia and Sylvie, Alexander's wife. Sable had been asleep beside her. The dog's calm warmth and the peaceful quiet of the house had succeeded in permeating her busy brain, which was preoccupied with memories of Martin and no small amount of guilt over his death.

The room was all but dark. The servants would be having their evening meal. No doubt Annie had checked on her and left her sleeping, for a candle was burning nearby, the tea things had been cleared away, and a small dish of water for Sable had been left by the door to the garden.

The sound came again. It was a soft whine, and it was coming from Sable. The dog was sitting up and looking out the window with great interest, her ears perked up and the little noise coming from her throat. Having had animals her whole life, Petra knew it was not the sound of a dog who needed to be allowed outside to relieve herself. Nor that of a dog seeing a quarry—for the very purpose of a pointing dog was to silently indicate the sighting of quarry by their stance, not by whining or barking.

Petra ran a hand over Sable's back, turning around to look out into the darkened garden with her.

There was a flash of something, and then it was gone. A chill ran across Petra's arms. The something had been like the ghost of a woman in a pale dress.

Rising from the sofa, Petra took up the candle and opened the door to the gardens. Sable dashed out and toward the spot where Petra had seen the apparition before Petra could call her back. But there was no sound other than the slight rustle of the trees, the wind having calmed after the earlier storm.

"My lady? Is everything well?"

Petra whirled to see the tall, stalwart form of Charles, and for a brief moment and still thinking on ghosts, she was thankful he looked nothing like Martin, instead having dark brown hair and blue eyes. She asked him to go out into the gardens to see if someone was there, explaining that Sable had alerted her to a presence.

"I wonder if it was Mr. Teager," Charles said, referring to the somewhat reclusive gardener at Forsyth House. "He has been working later recently with the milder days, and may have come out to retrieve a tool he left out by accident."

This sounded sensible, but ten minutes later, Charles returned, Sable bounding back inside.

"It must have been a stray cat, my lady," Charles said as he closed and locked the door. "For I can say with confidence there was no one about in the gardens. Now, I shall get a fire going for you, and then I'll send Annie in with a fresh cup of tea."

For a few minutes after Charles had left her drawing room, however, Petra continued to rub her chilled arms and stare out the window. What she had seen had been too big to be a cat. Had there been someone out in the garden? Or had her mind been playing tricks on her?

"Or maybe you are simply mad, too." The comment made by Josiah Bellingham at the ball came back to her, unbidden and unwanted. And it changed the focus of her thoughts. Why would Josiah have even said such a thing? Was it in some reference to spinsters? Did he think she and all spinsters must be touched in the head to wish to remain unmarried?

Petra sank onto her sofa once more, reminding herself of many of the reasons why she had made her decision.

First and foremost was because women had almost no rights—and fewer once they married.

When Sable sat at her feet and blinked her sweet brown eyes as if to indicate she was interested in hearing these reasons, Petra smiled and spoke softly.

"Do not misunderstand me. I have a great affinity for men in general and I have never thought ill of the male sex simply because our laws favor them. It would be preposterous. And I also adore children, believe very much in love, that love matches do exist, and that happy marriages are always possible." Petra sighed. "Yet even in the case of such a happy match, by law, we women are the property of our fathers first, and then later, our husbands.

I think every woman who feels as I do has said this at some point, but we women are little more than possessions. Objects. Vessels in pretty dresses that are to be used to produce children, often simply in order to carry on a family name. And if we do bring children into the world? Well, they are the property of our husband the moment they are born. Though, if we do not bear children—or if we cannot—we are considered nothing but dried husks who become a financial burden on the men who are our supposed protectors."

Once more, she rose and began pacing her drawing room, her words coming quietly, but with vehemence.

"Then there is the subject of monies—for there are far too few women like me who have an inheritance to their name. And if a woman has a dowry, or even if she has somehow earned her money like my new friend Lottie has, that money goes into her husband's coffers once they become man and wife. Oh, there are supposed rules—a husband cannot deplete the principal and a wife is guaranteed pin money, or property, or a stipend for her widowhood, or whatever is agreed upon by the men who drew up the marriage contract. And for many, it remains true. But it is never guaranteed. For though the husband may claim he will not misappropriate the monies his wife brings to their marriage, excepting those instances with excellent legal binds, the law says those monies are his."

Sable had trotted at her side the entire time Petra had been pacing, and sat down smartly when Petra abruptly came to a halt.

"Why?" she whispered with heat. "The answer is but a ridiculous one. Because some man named Mr. Blackstone decided that, once married, a woman and a man are one, and thus, whatever belongs to the woman belongs to the man."

The angry noise she made had Sable leaning against her legs as if to offer comfort. Petra stroked the dog's silky brown ears as she frowned.

Yes, one false move on a woman's part—even sometimes after many years of relative happiness—and everything can be taken from her. A woman can be cast out, with nothing to her name.

Do I know of women who exercise significant control over their husbands? thought Petra. *Why, yes, I do. Fanny Bellingham is one, to hear Juddy tell it. And yet it is Josiah Bellingham, the husband, the master of the house, who has the final say in the end.*

Petra stared at her reflection in a nearby mirror, her cheeks flushed with anger. "And if it makes me a madwoman to wish to make decisions for myself, for my home, my body, and my money, then so be it. And Josiah and all like him may rot."

Yet one other question remained as Petra turned away, going back to her sofa and her unfinished letters.

What other woman had been deemed mad by Josiah, and likely other men? Or could it be there was more than one woman?

SIXTEEN

Arriving at Potsford House at number Thirty-seven St. James's Square the next day, Petra ascended the steps as Annie was driven off in the carriage, sent on errands for Petra's household, to return in one hour. As the carriage rolled away, Sable hung her head out the window, ears flapping in the brisk wind, watching Petra with a devoted look and making her smile. She had not yet written to Duncan to thank him for Sable, and she knew she needed to.

What was of more importance at present was finding the man who had killed Martin, and discovering the truth about Gwen. If Duncan could assist her in these, she would endeavor to work in a thank-you in person for Sable. Maybe over tea and biscuits. And maybe Duncan might finally return the favor with information of his own; namely, why he never wrote back to her in three long years.

Petra took hold of the door knocker in the shape of an acorn and gave it three brisk taps. An aged butler answered the door to Potsford House, bushy gray eyebrows raising in brief surprise at Petra's lack of a lady's maid and her carriage disappearing down the street, but he stepped back and admitted her into the house. At least she was wearing a bonnet. Petra rather disliked bonnets, but had worn one today as Lady Potsford felt all women should be diligent in wearing them when out of doors.

"This way, please, Lady Petra. His lordship has been awaiting your arrival."

"Lord Potsford?" said Petra, a smile playing at her lips as she made to unbutton her coat. "Is he joining her ladyship and me for luncheon?"

The butler, however, had already stridden several steps down a black-and-white marble hallway, and did not answer or offer to take her coat. Perplexed, Petra was forced to hurry after him, eventually turning into a library, where the butler said, "Lady Petra Forsyth, my lord." The door was quickly and quietly closed as soon as she stepped over the threshold.

Lord Potsford rose unhurriedly from a desk at the far end of the room.

"Good day, Lord Potsford," Petra said, giving him a curtsy, then clasping her hands in front of her.

His bow to her was perfunctory at best. "Thank you for coming, Lady Petra. I am afraid my wife is unwell and cannot receive you today. I only discovered you were to come a few minutes ago, or I would have sent word."

"I am very sorry to hear that, my lord," Petra said. "I had been looking forward to a lovely meal prepared by your cook and Lady Potsford's excellent company."

Petra's eyes went to a nearby chair, expecting to have it offered to her. Potsford saw this, and a thin smile played about his lips.

"Yes, well, it may be some time before you have the pleasure of sampling Mrs. Fell's cooking, Lady Petra. For I must tell you that my wife has been very ill and will be leaving within the next few days for a respite in the country."

Petra did not have to feign surprise, for she was very much aghast. "I am all astonishment, my lord. I saw her and spoke with her at Her Grace's ball and she seemed much the opposite. Did something occur in the recent hours to cause her to become so unwell as to require time in . . . my apologies, is it Durham where your land holdings are located?"

"You have an excellent memory, Lady Petra," Lord Potsford said.

"Indeed I do, my lord," Petra replied. "Please tell me, what is ailing her ladyship? I should like to help in any way I can."

Lord Potsford gave a huff of dry laughter. "I thank you, but I am afraid there is little you can do. For my wife . . . well, she has become less of herself in recent years. Once, Lady Potsford was the pillar of stability, and lately she has become erratic. Happy and serene one moment, and then she becomes a mountain of energy and nerves the next."

"I am afraid I have not seen evidence of this, my lord," said Petra, though she knew it was somewhat untrue. She'd seen some of it the night of the ball.

"And she cannot stop worrying over Arabella," Potsford said, his voice growing more fervent. "Did you not see how upset she became at the supper over nothing but a small stumble the girl took? Why, I thought my wife might fly through the air to reach Arabella's side. And when the girl pronounced herself well—assisted by Mr. Shawcross, who was most attentive—my wife would not calm with any speed. She had hysterics about it later in the carriage ride, in fact, and her lady's maid had to give her a dose of laudanum to induce her to sleep that night."

"I am sorry to hear Miss Littlewood's stumble affected Lady Potsford so," Petra said.

Though Petra did indeed recall Lady Potsford hurrying forward to assist Arabella, she did not recall seeing any sign that it was worse than her ladyship's general state of worry. And while this doting would be irritating for Petra herself to experience, she had grown up with nannies who did not rush to her side unless she was bleeding or crying uncontrollably. And she felt that Arabella understood her guardian's need to fuss, and accepted it with as much good grace as any young lady could.

Potsford laid one hand on the top of a wingback chair and shook his head. "My wife has formed an inordinate attachment to our ward, and cannot see Arabella for what she is—a woman of eighteen who will likely be married soon."

"Indeed? Is there happy news to report, my lord?" Petra asked.

Lord Potsford shook his head, but would not meet her eyes, blustering, "No, no, not as yet. But my wife, she cannot bear the thought no matter when it occurs. Why, she came barging into my library the day after the ball without my consent, whilst I was entertaining one of my men of business. She demanded to speak about Arabella, insisting she should not marry. I decided then that something had to be done."

"And so you are sending her away . . . ?" Petra said.

"I am indeed, Lady Petra," Potsford responded. "I do not wish to, but I believe it is—"

"For her own health?" Petra finished, one eyebrow raising.

Potsford looked at her, his eyes narrowing. "Yes, that is true."

"And you are sending her to the country." It was a statement, not a question.

"As I said," his lordship snapped.

"But yet you did not confirm she was going to Durham, my lord," Petra said sweetly. "For my memory also serves me well in recalling that you were forced to sell your property in Durham last year. Might it be that you are sending her to a place run by a man called Drysdale?"

Lord Potsford's eyes looked like those of a startled bullfrog in the way they suddenly bulged outward. And the redness on his face increased fivefold. The sight caused gooseflesh to pop up on her arms at Potsford's physical response to her question.

"How did you hear that name?" he barked.

Anticipating his shout, Petra did not shift where she stood, though it was difficult, especially when he advanced two steps in her direction. She lifted her chin, hoping it made her seem unwilling to be intimidated by him.

"I merely heard two peers discussing him, my lord, and your name was mentioned in conjunction," she lied.

She thanked the heavens she had not mentioned the name Fairwinds, too, for it might have given away her informant. And protecting Juddy Bellingham from being discovered as the source of her information was of the utmost importance.

Plus, she did not lie completely. Lord Langford and Lord Whitfield had been discussing the mysterious Mr. Drysdale. But for what purpose, she was not sure. Neither peer was yet married, so they had no wife to send to this man. Though Whitfield had been linked to that opera singer who had become with child. Could Whitfield have arranged for his former lover to be taken away? And to what end?

Potsford's jaw was clenched, and she saw his fingers curl into a fist.

Hastily backing up a step, she put her hand to her heart in the most feminine of shocked gestures, adding, "And as I have no knowledge of Mr. Drysdale beyond his name and the understanding that he is a physician and assists women in recovering their health in the country, I do not understand why you are looking so vexed, my lord." Almost belatedly, she widened her eyes for a most helpless look.

Luckily, it was directly into her eyes where Lord Potsford looked last.

He cleared his throat, relaxed his hand. "Yes, do forgive me, Lady Petra. I felt you might have been accusing me of something untoward."

"That was never my intention, my lord," she said, hoping that she looked suitably distressed. "But forgive me for asking, but what will happen to Miss Littlewood? For I know she loves Lady Potsford and depends on her guidance greatly, despite her ladyship's becoming, well . . . rather overprotective."

Potsford's flush deepened again, but this time it seemed to be of a different nature. "Arabella will be looked after by her lady's maid until my sister, who is currently visiting friends in Norfolk, meets us in Suffolk next week, after I attend a stalking party."

"Lord Milford's, do you mean?" When he looked a bit startled, she said, "I saw him on Rotten Row yesterday. He explained about His Royal Highness requesting the stalking party specially. My father will be in attendance, I expect."

"And will you accompany him?"

"I am not certain yet, my lord, but I believe I would feel strange being there without my dear friend Lady Milford to welcome me. I have only just learned of her passing, you understand."

Potsford seemed to calm a bit at this. Now he walked past her and opened his library door. "Yes, I understand most heartily. You shouldn't distress yourself by attending if that is the case. I'm sure Holbrook will understand. Now, I'm afraid I must bid you a good day now. I have much to do—yes, much to do before my wife leaves London."

"Of course, my lord," Petra said. "Will you be so kind as to tell Lady Potsford that I look forward to drinking tea with her upon her return?"

Potsford was looking distracted now. "Of course, of course. Though I cannot say when that will be. Now, if you will. Framstead! Yes, here he is. Framstead will see you out, Lady Petra."

She stepped back over the threshold and turned to give Lord Potsford a parting curtsy, only to find the heavy library door shut firmly in her face by his lordship himself.

Framstead, with much dispassion, asked Petra if she would like him to hail her a hackney. She thanked him, explaining that she would be going to Lady Caroline's house, which was but a short walk away. Though would Framstead be so kind as to let her carriage know where she had gone when it arrived to pick her up in three-quarters of an hour?

"Very good, my lady," he said, bowed, and shut yet another Potsford door on her. She resisted the urge to stick out her tongue at the door, knowing Framstead was likely watching her. Instead, she stood on the doorstep, taking her time adjusting the sleeves on her coat and retying the ribbon on her bonnet. Then, just to be contrary, she went down two steps and stopped once more, making a show of checking the contents of her reticule.

Sure enough, she just caught a slight twitch of a curtain from the front window. Smiling with satisfaction to herself that she had sufficiently vexed the butler, she descended the final steps and turned in the direction of Caroline's house. It was not as nearby as she had made Framstead believe, but she would rather find a hackney on her own than wait in Framstead's presence until one arrived.

She glanced up at Potsford House again, thinking of all she had learned, and feeling concern for the safety and health of Lady Potsford. Petra wondered if she might locate Juddy Bellingham and attempt to discover the exact location of this place called Fair-winds—if for no other reason than to be able to write to Lady Potsford while she remained there.

Then, over the sounds of the street and a carriage passing by, she heard an upstairs window being opened. Petra stopped just beyond the corner of Potsford House and looked up. Could it be Lady Potsford? Would Petra be able to tell if she was well or not?

Instead, it was Miss Arabella Littlewood who met her eyes. The young woman put a finger to her lips, then she awkwardly pitched something out the window. Petra watched helplessly as the small, round object that looked to be a shade of blue and had fluttering edges fell short of the street. Instead, it dropped unceremoniously down into the lower servants' area.

Petra looked up. Arabella's profile could be seen speaking to someone who had entered the room. Arabella was shaking her head emphatically, as if she were terrified. Petra moved swiftly away, onto the steps of the next house at number thirty-five and behind one of its large Palladian columns when she realized the someone who was putting Arabella into such a state.

Lord Potsford.

Petra was at a loss as to what to do as she hid behind the column, her mind in a swirl. What if Potsford planned to assault his ward? Petra waited for as long as she dared, listening hard for screams from the inside of the house.

Minutes passed, and she heard nothing. Glancing up, she saw Arabella standing at the window again. She was crying, but quite alone. Then the girl slowly moved away, a handkerchief to her nose.

Petra knew she must move or risk being discovered by the butler of number thirty-five, who might well alert Framstead next door if he felt Petra were a Cyprian looking to bring shame upon the well-bred inhabitants of St. James's.

Slowly, Petra went back down the stairs, creeping as close as she dared to Potsford House again to try and see if she could locate what Arabella had thrown. Just as she moved to take the stairs down to the servants' entrance, she stopped in her tracks when a carriage came from the nearby side street at a fast rate. She heard a man's voice shout, "Stop here, man! I said number thirty-seven, you imbecile!"

As the carriage came to a halt, Petra ducked her head—grateful now to have worn a bonnet that shielded much of her face—and dashed back up the stairs of number thirty-five. From behind the safety of the wide column, she watched a man alight from the carriage.

He had the arrogant posture and the fine clothing of a gentleman, but there was something different about him as well. As she watched the man look up at Potsford House, he briefly removed his hat, giving Petra an excellent view of his face.

The man dressed like an aristocrat, but he had a weathered face and shifty, shrewd eyes. His hair was well cut, a darker brown on top but generously threaded with gray, increasing to the point that the sides and back were nearly white. Despite this, Petra would put his age at no more than thirty-five.

His eyes roamed to the window that had, minutes before, framed Miss Arabella Littlewood, and Petra saw how he stared at the window for two long moments as his mouth slowly quirked up.

He was satisfied with himself, and the whole of him sent a chill through her person.

A moment later and he was walking up the stairs with a studied air of confidence, knocking on the door with the elegant silver handle of a gleaming oak walking stick. The door opened, and she heard Framstead's voice.

"Good afternoon, Mr. Drysdale."

SEVENTEEN

PETRA FOUND HERSELF WALKING, WITHOUT A COMPANION AND without a true sense of her direction. Irritation that she had not been able to retrieve whatever Arabella had thrown out the window made her walk quickly, in a way that would not be considered ladylike if anyone were watching. How would she go about finding the object without being seen, or questioned?

Her mind was filled with so many questions, she hardly knew what to do but to simply keep moving. When she finally looked around to get her bearings, she found she had not walked in the direction of Caroline's house but instead turned onto Jermyn Street. Carriages abounded, and people were on the pavement, going in and out of shops, yet the number was few in comparison to places like Oxford Street.

A few steps away, Petra caught the words on the window of one shop. Bardwell's Apothecary. Two women were exiting, chattering away to each other as they stopped in front of the latest broadsheet affixed to the window and adjusted their bonnets and gloves.

"I must say," said one as Petra came upon them and looked into the window, "that Miss Bardwell does have a way with herbs and plants. This cream is but a miracle at easing the pains in my joints. I don't know what she puts into it—marshmallow, for one, I think— but it is rather worth the eight pence."

"Mmm," said the other with a sour expression. "I do agree, but it is a shame."

"What is a shame, Ermintrude?"

"Well, you saw her, did you not?"

"Miss Bardwell, you mean? But of course I did, Ermintrude. She assists me each time I am in the apothecary. A fine girl. Bit shy and reticent unless talking about her tinctures and whatnot, but very intelligent and pretty. A credit to Sir Bartie, I am certain."

The second woman, Ermintrude, sniffed. "But Violet, you must have noticed."

The first woman, Violet, made an exasperated noise. "Noticed what, Ermintrude? I cannot read your mind, so you must speak plainly."

"Well, her mama is from Spain," said Ermintrude.

The first woman seemed unconcerned. "Yes, I noticed her darker complexion and dark eyes. What of it? My Mr. Dimsdale is much the same, and I know his parentage from four generations back. He's as English as you and I. Plus, the Spaniards are a lovely lot. Even King Henry the Eighth took one as his bride. His first bride, at least."

"Queen Catherine was not a Moor, though, Violet," Ermintrude said darkly. "But a good Christian Spaniard."

Violet tutted. "And why would you think Miss Bardwell's mama was a Moor? Preposterous."

"Did you not see how the girl wrote down notes to herself? In those funny squiggles?" Ermintrude insisted.

"Indeed. Looked like stenography to me. My brother uses it to catalog his notes on the birds he watches. Says it's faster than writing the whole word."

"It is not stenography, though. Lady Bardwell writes that way as well, even though she speaks Spanish to her daughter. It is the way those who practice Islam as their religion write. Those like the Moors."

Violet was silent for a moment, then Petra could hear her words as the two turned and walked in the opposite direction.

"That's as may be, but I do not find it very vexing. Did you know they spread much learning about the world? Mathematics, and libraries, too. Very intelligent. And I read the Moors are who brought apricots to Europe. You love apricots and will eat them all day long, Ermintrude. So I wouldn't be too quick to think Miss Bardwell being a Moor a bad thing, lest you wish to give up your daily serving of apricot jam . . ."

Petra entered the apothecary, finding herself all alone with heady scents of herbs and hanging bunches of dried flowers. The counter ran across the back, and the wall to her right was lined with shelves and bins, most containing more dried flowers or herbs to be scooped into paper cones before being weighed at the counter. Others contained herbal lozenges, twisted up into papers. Then there were bottles of rosewater and rose oil to be had, as well as a small section of fresh flowers, likely from the hothouses of Sir Bartie himself. Amongst them were delphiniums and peonies, both having yet to bloom in Petra's own gardens, looking lush and fragrant.

"Which was it this time, my lady?" came a voice from behind her, her tone light and wry, her pronunciation very proper and English. "Am I part Moor, part Romani, or simply a bit exotic and strange, and therefore most fortuitous to have my father's good name and the Queen's patronage of our shop to keep me from being an outcast to polite society?"

"You heard, then—Miss Bardwell, I presume?" Petra asked, turning to find a lovely young woman with hair of the darkest black pulled back into a simple chignon, fringe going across her forehead. She had tawny skin and dark eyes that stared directly into Petra's. Her angular chin was set with slight defiance, but Petra did not feel as if Miss Bardwell was wishing to be insolent. No, this woman had self-possession despite what others thought of her, and Petra liked her immediately. "It was talk of possible Moor from your mama's side. Though the woman called Violet was not vexed by it and seemed to be disappointed by her friend's prejudices. Can you really write as the Arabs do?"

Miss Bardwell smiled at the interest in Petra's voice. "I can, my lady, though it may be somewhat imprecise, I readily admit. My mother taught me. Her family traces back to the Moors who lived in Granada, Spain, but converted to Christianity and remained there after the final expulsions in the early seventeenth century. They kept their customs alive in secret, mostly the writing and some recipes. I confess I only speak a bit of Arabic, though I can, indeed, write it." She gave a light laugh. "It seems Mrs. Tomkins—the one called Ermintrude—is one of the few correct about my parentage. She reads much, but learns little, I am afraid to say. Most people are like Mrs. Dimsdale—that would be Violet—and think my note-taking a form of stenography, and my looks from Romani blood, or simply those of a Spaniard." She paused, then asked, "Would you like me to write your name in Arabic?"

Petra nodded and was about to introduce herself, but Miss Bardwell had quickly used quill and ink to make a series of softly curving marks and dots on a small piece of paper. She turned it around, sliding the paper across the counter.

"With my compliments, Lady Petra Forsyth."

Running her finger along the foreign marks, Petra said, "How is it that you know me, Miss Bardwell, when I have never been in your apothecary?"

"Oh, it is not so mysterious. And I would be honored if you would call me Frances. Your lady's maid does, as does your aunt Ophelia on the occasions when she is in town, and thus I shall like it very much if you do as well."

"I should be happy to, Frances," Petra said, though she raised her eyebrows in request of more information. Frances replied, looking a bit shy now.

"I know everyone in London society, my lady, whether or not they come into my father's shop. Mostly because their servants do, to stock their cabinets with herbal remedies. They speak openly with other servants, greeting each other and asking after families. One begins to place them after a time. And then I place the names with faces from the broadsheets, of course. It is the simplest way. And I have found it behooves me, as the woman behind the counter, as much as it does my father's business."

From somewhere beneath the counter, Frances pulled a sheaf of broadsheets, some but black and white, some colored by hand. Her eyes shifted up only briefly to Petra.

"The new artist seems to like you, my lady. I can tell he is new because his portraits are more lifelike than those of the previous artist, who rarely depicted you, drawing you as an aged spinster when he did."

"Mm, yes, he did indeed," she said dryly, thinking of Uncle Tobias referencing it that afternoon at Buckfields. "But this is the first I am seeing of the new artist's work."

At the top was a print that was so bright in color as to have been very recent. This was further indicated by its depiction of Her Grace's ball from two nights earlier.

The unknown artist had depicted one of the dances, at the part when the women came together while the men stood at the edges. Petra saw with some surprise that, while other women were depicted in the scene—including Lady Horatia, Miss Arabella Littlewood, and even Fanny Bellingham—she, herself, seemed to be at the center, a bit brighter than the rest. Her head was held high, a smile upon her face, and she was looking every bit as youthful as Miss Littlewood, who was six years Petra's junior. The men's faces were all in shadow, unrecognizable, though their builds gave them something of an identity. All but one had the same expression. They looked haughty—no, almost angry and predatory—as they watched the women enjoying themselves. Only one had a smile upon his face as he watched Petra dance. Beneath the print was the title in bold block letters: *Breath of Fresh Spring Air*.

"I am glad to know I was not depicted as a crone again, as I am now six months older than I was at the last unflattering rendering," Petra said.

The bell over the door to the apothecary tinkled and in hurried a lady's maid.

"Yes, Lilly?" said Frances smoothly. "What does Lady Covington require today?"

"Some of your ginger syrup, if you please, Miss Frances," came the reply.

Petra moved away to select a small bottle of rosewater to

purchase, but could smell the ginger as the thin syrup was poured into a brown glass bottle from a large jug with a spigot, and the maid produced the two farthings required. Then Petra was once more alone with this very interesting woman, whom she had decided was about Lottie's age. One and twenty, or two and twenty at most.

"Now, what is it I can do for you, my lady?" asked Frances. "Besides the rosewater, of course."

"I understand you have a lovely salve that smells of lemon drops," she began. "Or so says my young friend named Teddy."

Frances was too quick by half. "The street urchin with the eyes the color of cornflowers? Yes, he's come back for it twice more for some of his fellow rough-sleepers. Gave me all his money to buy it both times. I refused his money, of course, but he spent the rest of the day both times sweeping out our back storeroom to compensate me."

Petra smiled. "Thank you for helping him. I am monstrously fond of Teddy, but he will only accept so much."

"More should be like him, my lady. Now, about that salve. Do you wish me to make you some?"

"Actually, no," Petra replied. Frances had shown herself to be a straightforward person, so Petra felt she could be the same. "I am wondering if you might recall making some for a gentleman as of late. One who might have had teeth marks on his left wrist."

Frances's demeanor changed with such abrupt fashion, it was as if a wall had come down in front of her. "I believe I could not recall, my lady."

"Could not, Frances?" Petra said. "Or will not?"

Now a flash of anger passed over Frances's face. Yet it seemed to be accompanied by something else. By fear.

"Why do you wish to know, my lady?" she asked, glancing toward the window outside. Petra had not wished to explain her reasons to this woman, but she spoke them anyway.

"Because a man paid Teddy a threepence to throw a rock at a horse and spook it, likely to cause the rider to fall and hurt herself.

Though the plan was thwarted, I am that rider, though Teddy was unaware of this until later. He did not see much of the man, except for a wound on the man's wrist. One that was receiving treatment from the salve Teddy recognized as coming from this apothecary."

Frances was silent, and then the door opened, ushering in two women with a footman at their heels. The three went immediately to the bins of dried flowers.

"I'm afraid I cannot help you, Lady Petra," she said in a quiet voice. Taking the broadsheets from the counter, she straightened them into a pile and turned away to put them in a cabinet fitted with a lock. She pulled at the door, whispering an epithet when it did not open.

Quickly, as the two ladies were not watching, Petra moved around the counter, pulling out one of her hairpins. "Let me," she said, and made quick work of the lock.

"Thank you, my lady." Frances looked impressed, and chagrined, but did not meet Petra's eyes again.

"I am happy to have met you, Frances," Petra said truthfully. "If your recollections become clearer, I would be grateful if you would let me know."

The two ladies were at the counter, asking in loud voices for their regular orders.

"Of course, Mrs. Taylor and Miss Taylor," Frances said. "Straight-away."

She was gone into the back of the store before Petra could say another word.

Frustrated, Petra swept out of the apothecary and down Jermyn Street, looking for a hackney.

"Need a hack, my lady?" asked a small, toothless, and shabbily dressed man leaning up against a lamppost. He pointed with two dirty fingers down the next street. "There be a couple waiting down that there street."

"Thank you," Petra said. She hurried in the direction the man indicated when something brushed against her leg and dashed away, barking. *Sable.* Turning the corner, Petra found herself not on a commercial street, with hackneys waiting, but facing a darkened alleyway.

"Sable!" Petra called out. The dog had raced down the alley, making haste after a man running at top speed. Petra saw a glint of something falling to the ground, then a door slamming shut, as he dashed into a doorway. Sable reached the door a moment too late, but stood there, growling at it even as Petra rushed after her. Petra tried the door, but it was now securely locked. Sable was sniffing at the thing he'd dropped.

It was a knife, one with a simple wooden handle. Just like the one that had ended Martin's life.

"My lady!" Annie was rushing down the alley in a rustle of skirts. "Sable saw you and jumped out of the carriage! She was gone before—oh!"

Annie's hands went to her face in shock at seeing Petra picking up the knife. It was not as long as the one she'd seen protruding from Martin's chest, Petra realized, but narrower. Like the one she'd seen Mrs. Bing once use for boning a fish. And it had recently been sharpened.

"I am well," she confirmed to Annie, one hand holding the knife, the other stroking Sable's head in gratitude. "But I think I can now confirm that someone truly wishes me harm."

EIGHTEEN

WHILE PETRA AND ANNIE SAT IN HER CARRIAGE, PRAISING Sable, Rupert made inquiries up and down Jermyn Street to see if anyone had seen the man with the knife. No one had, and the little toothless man was now unsurprisingly gone.

"Likely paid to say what he did to you and then leave, my lady," Rupert said. On this, Petra had to agree as she helped Annie wrap the knife in a handkerchief and stow it safely out of sight. She had considered asking Rupert to go back into Bardwell's Apothecary to ask Miss Frances Bardwell if she might have seen anything unusual. But upon recalling the fear in the young woman's eyes as she had looked over Petra's shoulder and out onto the street, Petra felt as if Frances had been compelled to remain silent.

"We shall go on to Oxford Street, then," Petra said, glaring out of the carriage window in irritation. "I will not be frightened by whoever is attempting to intimidate me. No, Annie, I appreciate that you wish to keep me safe, but I must continue now."

Annie looked mulish, but went silent as Rupert turned the carriage north.

When finally navigating the bustle of Oxford Street, it was while passing a food stall that Petra called out, "Rupert, please stop!" She handed Sable's lead to Annie and alighted from her carriage, nodding when Rupert said he would have to move up a bit and wait for her. He had seen what she had, and was not worried.

Teddy was disappearing down a side alley with two other young children, both biting hungrily into apples. Petra called out his name, and Teddy turned around, pulling the two younger children, a boy and a girl, behind him.

"Teddy, it is I, Lady Petra," she said, and saw his wary stance relax. He said something to the other two children and handed the boy another two apples. They trotted off, looking back every few steps in curiosity.

"Are you feeding yourself as well as the other children, I hope?" she asked him, giving him a once-over as he hurried up to her.

"Aw, now, my lady, you ask me that every time, and my answer ain't changed," Teddy said, a hint of a flush marking his cheeks.

"Then I shall understand it that you are not as often as I would like you to, and then remind you that Mrs. Bing will always give you what she is able, if you come to the house and ask politely."

Teddy looked down at his feet, which were bare as it had been a warm day, and nodded. Petra then spoke briskly, so as to not embarrass him further.

"I am very happy to have come across you today, Teddy, for I am in much need of your assistance."

Teddy's head whipped up and his blue eyes were fierce. "Did someone try to hurt you again, my lady? Just tell me where to find them, and—"

Petra held up a hand. "I thank you for the gallant offer, but no," she said. It was a lie, she knew, but she needed Teddy's agile mind to concentrate itself elsewhere. "However, I am hoping you can locate something for me, and it is most important that you be discreet and not caught."

"Haven't been caught yet, my lady," Teddy said, puffing out his thin chest.

Petra explained about the small blue object that Miss Littlewood had thrown out her window, reminding Teddy that he should not be seen, even if he must wait until nightfall to retrieve it.

"I'll find it and bring it to you at Forsyth House. On my honor, my lady."

"Excellent. Thank you, Teddy," she said. She held out a halfpenny—her usual payment to him—but had to say, "Take it, or I shall consider it an insult," when he hesitated, mumbling that she and Mr. Shawcross had already given him more money at the Green Park than he'd ever had in his life.

But no sooner had he accepted the coin than Petra pulled him out of sight behind a stack of empty crates that hugged the alleyway.

Teddy attempted to look around her. "What is it, my lady? A constable? A Runner?"

"No," Petra hissed. "The man who drew up in the carriage at Potsford House. He is here."

Before she could stop him, Teddy had slipped around to her other side and was looking through the slats of an empty crate near Petra's knees.

"Tare an' hounds, my lady. That'd be Mr. Drysdale."

Petra was aghast. "You know this man, Teddy?"

Almost as if he had heard his name, Drysdale began scanning the street as he closed the door of the hired carriage. When he turned toward the alley where Petra and Teddy stood hidden, she got her first look at his eye color. They were blue as Teddy's—or hers, for that matter—but, oh, how they looked as cold as a frozen lake. She held her breath as his eyes passed over the alley.

"He often buys from the food stall, my lady," Teddy whispered. "I'll see if he's gone."

Petra reached out to grab his collar and stop him, but Teddy was too fast. He'd moved out of the alley and onto the street, slipping through well-dressed ladies and dapper gentlemen like an eel. Moments later, he was back.

"He's scampered, my lady. Bought an apple and then walked off, toward his place of business."

"Goodness, he has an office on Oxford Street?" Petra asked.

"He does, my lady," Teddy answered. He pointed off to his right. "Down there. There's three men who have their businesses in the same space. Mr. Drysdale has the whole first floor. A tailor, Mr. Cuthbert, and a solicitor, Mr. Fawcett, are on the ground floor."

Petra couldn't believe her ears. Fawcett—the very solicitor

Lady Vera claimed Uncle Tobias had consulted? And he held office lodgings directly beneath Mr. Drysdale? And what's more, a tailor operated out of that building, too?

"Do you know anything else of this Mr. Drysdale, Teddy?" Petra asked, almost breathless with excitement.

"All I knows is that he's as likely to give someone like me a swipe with that cane of his as he is to say good mornin'," Teddy said darkly. "Though it'd be almost funny, wouldn't it? As respectable as he looks, and tries to act, I don't think 'e's respectable at all."

"How do you mean?" Petra asked.

But Teddy only shrugged. "I hears things, you know? About people in society. Nobody pays any mind to a street urchin, see?"

"Sadly, I do," Petra said.

But Teddy was looking to explain, not to receive pity, and went on almost as if Petra hadn't replied at all.

"For instance, I heard that Mr. Shawcross was born . . . well, if you'll excuse me, my lady . . . on the wrong side of the blanket. And he herded sheep with his granddad until he were five and the old marquess came to—well, I won't say what I heard the men say—but the marquess came back to the village and realized Mr. Shawcross were his own son."

He looked up at Petra and she gave a brief nod of her head. "It is not wholly common knowledge, so I shouldn't go about repeating it, but you have the gist of it."

Teddy, however, didn't look happy to know of Duncan's past. Instead, his elfin face was serious.

"Well, Mr. Shawcross weren't born much better than me, the way I see it. But he's a true gentleman, ain't he? But Mr. Drysdale? He'd be another matter, my lady. I don't know nothin' about his past, but I'd wager he weren't much better than me when he were younger. He grew up to look like a gentleman somehow, too. But while he looks the part, he and Mr. Shawcross ain't nothin' alike."

"From the little I have seen of Mr. Drysdale, Teddy, I would have to agree with you. Do you know anything of how he made his fortune?"

Teddy shook his head as he looked toward Mr. Drysdale's place of business. "Couldn't tell you, my lady. But I can say that I've seen several gentlemen you would know coming out of his office with him. Looked mighty pleased with themselves, they did."

"How do you mean, gentlemen I would know?" Petra asked him, her eyebrows coming together in confusion.

"Well, they're part of your lot, my lady. Lords and such. All of 'em."

"All of them?" Petra asked. "Is there anyone you could name?"

Teddy seemed to think on this, and Petra stepped over to the food stand, purchased another apple, and handed it to him, for the boy looked in need of sustenance. He thanked her and he took a bite, speaking through a mouthful of apple.

"Well," he said, and then so many names of distinction rolled off the boy's tongue that Petra was made weary by them, though she could not admit surprise at hearing Lord Whitfield, Lord Potsford, and Lord Bellingham amongst them. Mercifully, the Marquess of Langford was absent, as was Duncan's name. Then she held up her hand to stop him.

"Teddy. Did I hear you say Sir Hugh Thacker? The husband of Lady Thacker?"

Teddy nodded emphatically as he chewed another bite of apple, but over his crunching noises, all Petra could hear was Annie's voice, recounting gossip from a letter.

"Did you know her ladyship had passed? Maggie wrote that it was said to be some sort of a miasma, possibly from traveling in late February."

Teddy nodded, then cocked his head to one side. "I like Lady Thacker, I do. She's like you, my lady, when she's in town. Always kind and willing to help us out with a bit of bread and cheese, or a coin allowin' us to buy our own."

Petra gave him a sad smile. "I am honored you think so, Teddy. I am terribly sorry to have to impart such news, but Lady Thacker sadly passed away. It seems she fell ill whilst traveling with Sir Hugh in late February of this year."

Teddy stopped chewing, and his little brows pulled together. "I am very sad to hear it, my lady." Then blue eyes were blinking up at her. "Late February, you say? That must have been just after the day I saw her comin' out of her house on Wimpole Street, escorted into a carriage by Mr. Drysdale."

"Are you certain?" Petra asked, a chill tapping its way down her spine.

Teddy nodded. "I were on Wimpole Street that mornin', my lady. Early-like. For occasionally, after Lady Hewitt has a midnight supper, her cook'll leave some scraps out for my lot. Doesn't happen often, but we get word of it when it does. Anyhow, I were hidin' in the one spot where I can see everything I need to, but no one can see me, if you know what I mean."

"I do indeed, Teddy," Petra said.

"All the carriages from the supper had left, except one, which were in front of the house two down from Lady Hewitt—Sir Hugh's house. I saw the door open, and a man comin' outside, leading Lady Thacker." Teddy paused and took another bite of his apple. "Course, I thought it were Sir Hugh, but when they were about to get into the carriage, she stumbled, knocking into the man. His hat fell to the ground, and I saw it were Mr. Drysdale. All that white hair on bottom and darker on top, see?" He looked up at Petra expectantly. "Why would she be goin' somewhere with Mr. Drysdale at such a time?"

Petra did not quite know herself, but she was beginning to believe it was for very bad reasons indeed. However, she did not wish to tell Teddy her fears just yet, for she was not sure what they were herself. Though as the concern for Lady Thacker was evident on his face, she felt she owed him something. "I do not know for certain, Teddy, but it is possible Lady Thacker was taken away because she was already having issues with her health."

The boy nodded, the hand holding the apple moving away from

his mouth and down to his side. "I don't think Sir Hugh minded one jot that Lady Thacker died."

"Why would you think that about Sir Hugh?"

"Because one of the places we sleep at night is near a brothel, my lady. Not too close, mind. But close enough that I sees who comes and goes, you know?"

Petra did not wish to know, but she gamely said, "And Sir Hugh is one of them."

Teddy nodded. "Almost every night, my lady. And when I saw him on the streets, he looked happy, as if a burden had been pulled from his shoulders."

A knot had formed in Petra's stomach. "Yes," she said, thinking, *That is what many women are to men. Simply a burden upon their shoulders.*

Teddy had dipped his head, and his voice was small when he spoke.

"If it were me, my lady, I don't think I would be happy at all to have someone I loved taken away, even if it were for their health." There was a pause, and his voice was but a whisper, giving Petra the impression he was picturing someone he'd never spoken of to her in his mind. "No, I don't think I would be happy at all."

NINETEEN

PETRA WONDERED IF TEDDY HAD SOMEONE HE LOVED WHO might be taken away from him "for their health" as she watched him disappear down Oxford Street.

At the same time, his words from moments earlier repeated in her ears.

"They're part of your lot. Lords and such."

Petra was beginning to suspect Drysdale was earning his living from helping men of the ton send their wives away to Fairwinds. Yet were the fates of Gwen and Lady Thacker due to causes brought on by their respective poor healths? Or was something wholly more sinister happening?

With Drysdale's place of business down the street, Petra hoped it would be possible to discover some answers to her questions. Though she decided she would not attempt to speak with the so-called physician. Not yet, at least.

But Mr. Fawcett, the solicitor, and this Mr. Cuthbert, who was a tailor, would likely have some information. In situations such as these, the other proprietors would know much of their fellow businessmen. Maybe they knew where this place called Fairwinds was located. And the true purpose of it.

She stopped at her carriage to tell Annie and Rupert of her direction.

"My lady," Annie said, holding on to Sable's collar. "I must tell you I do not care for it that you are being so single-minded. I feel as if you may be doing something foolhardy."

Petra bristled, but bit back a snappish reply. "I shall return hopefully within a quarter of an hour," she said, then turned and walked with intention toward the two-story gray building.

As she neared, she saw the plaques announcing the businessmen working inside. H. CUTHBERT, TAILOR, and G. FAWCETT, ESQUIRE. She felt it strange there was no plaque announcing Mr. Drysdale.

Reflexively, she clutched her reticule, in which still resided the scrap of pocket fabric torn from the jacket of the man who had killed Martin. The scrap Teddy had stolen from Duncan's own pocket. She could ask this tailor if he recognized the stitching. But her eyes were trained on the name of the solicitor. She hoped that, with Mr. Fawcett, she could kill the proverbial two birds with one stone. If all went well, Mr. Fawcett would tell her the nature of Uncle Tobias's business with him as well as the location of Fairwinds.

She was hurrying up the steps when, through the semisheer curtains of the uppermost floor, she saw the shadow of a man passing by. Guessing that shadow was Mr. Drysdale, she knew she must complete her business here quickly before he came downstairs and took notice of her.

The door for the tailor was to her left, the solicitor's to her right. Briefly, she went to the tailor's door first, but could hear two men speaking inside. Instead—and keeping an ear out for Drysdale coming out of his upstairs office—Petra knocked at the door marked with G. FAWCETT, ESQUIRE.

No answer. She put her ear to the door and heard only silence.

Without thinking, her hands went to pull out one of her hairpins—and then she stopped and bit her lip. Was Annie right? Was she becoming foolhardy in her actions?

Breaking into the office of a solicitor would qualify, yes, she thought.

In truth, she knew a solicitor would be unlikely to divulge her uncle's secrets. So might searching his office when Mr. Fawcett was not in residence actually be the better way of obtaining the answers she needed? She might even find the address to Fairwinds amongst his papers, especially if he assisted Mr. Drysdale in legal matters— which Petra felt might be highly likely.

Several other reasons for and against such action raced through her mind, including that Fawcett might return at any time, but still her fingers itched to pick the lock. It would be so easy.

Pushing her better judgment aside, Petra inserted her hairpin in the lock. Then she snatched it out again, whirling around at the sound of a drawling voice from the direction of the tailor's door.

"You'll have my coat ready for me by Wednesday, Cuthbert?"

It was Lord Bellingham. He was concentrating on adjusting his cuffs even as the small, wiry man behind him ran a brush over the shoulders of Josiah's dark blue coat.

"Of course, my lord. Wednesday, by no later than ten o'clock."

"Excellent. For I will be leaving for Suffolk by noon. I will send my man to come fetch it."

Petra spoke coolly. "Lord Milford's stalking party, I expect?"

Bellingham looked up, his right fingers still pulling the cuff straight over his left wrist.

"Why, Lady Petra," he said with a smirk. Mr. Cuthbert, the tailor, hovered behind him, showing wispy white hair and a thin face above his own impeccably tailored suit. "Did you come looking for me? Or are you here to have yourself a pair of trousers made? A waistcoat, perhaps?"

"No indeed, Lord Bellingham," she said, moving toward him, the little scrap of pocket fabric between her gloved fingers. "My brother's old buckskin breeches suit me just fine when I choose to wear them. And I would not ever come looking for you, to be sure. I would rather look for a tarantula, in fact. But since you are here, I thought I would check and see if you had lost something from your coat?"

Bellingham's countenance was at first confusion, then irritation. "What the devil do you mean, Lady Petra?" This swearing caused an intake of breath from Mr. Cuthbert, but Petra ignored it. She had seen a flash of something like concern in Bellingham's eyes.

"And yet you are here to have your coat mended, yes?" Petra's eyes shifted to Mr. Cuthbert, who was blinking rapidly, but nodded when she lifted an eyebrow.

"A wool coat, perhaps?" Petra asked the tailor.

Again, he nodded, saying in a rather squeaky voice, "Indeed, my lady. And in one of my finest wools, too."

"You will be quiet, Cuthbert," snapped Lord Bellingham. "And hand me my hat."

Petra felt a smirk coming to her lips. "Possibly a lovely one in the darkest of aubergines?" she asked, holding up the fabric scrap. "Such as this?"

There was a pause as both men's eyes went to the scrap, and Bellingham's expression went from controlled to triumphant. He let out a chuckle, snatching his top hat from Cuthbert's hand.

"No, that is not mine, Lady Petra." He stepped aside so Petra could see past him to the tailor's neat workshop, where a coat hung on a wooden valet stand. "My coat—which you can see with your very eyes—is a very fine wool, but merely black."

Petra felt a bit deflated, and Bellingham noticed. He came toward her in two lazy steps. Behind him, Mr. Cuthbert looked in need of some smelling salts.

"I had the pleasure of seeing Lord Allington yesterday," Bellingham said, "and he, too, spoke of your odd behavior as of late. I saw a bit of it at Her Grace's ball, but now I believe I can tell him that I fully agree with his assessment." He glanced up the nearby stairs. "And with Allington's ideas on how best to deal with this . . . development." He gave the most condescending of bows. "Good day, Lady Petra."

Petra did not move, or speak. But when he reached for the foyer door, she said, "Oh, Lord Bellingham? I can see you have a bandage about your left wrist." She merely turned her head, looking him up and down disdainfully, her eyes landing briefly on his outstretched left arm. "I understand bite marks—especially those sustained within the week—will heal best with a salve. Let us hope that it will not cost you more than a mere thruppence to purchase one."

His lips parted, and then he snapped his teeth shut, yanked

open the door, and stalked out. Petra walked into the tailor shop without a backward glance, closing the door behind her.

"My lady," Mr. Cuthbert said, his voice quavering a bit. "I'm afraid this is a shop for men. I do not make trousers for . . . well, for ladies."

"And I do not wish to have any made, Mr. Cuthbert," Petra replied. She held out the scrap of pocket fabric. When he took it, she then held out a coin. "I simply wish to know if this is your work, or that of another tailor."

The tailor hesitated, but as the coin was an entire shilling, his resistance was short-lived, his pride as a tailor taking over.

"This is not my work, my lady, I am glad to say." Some of the squeak was gone from his voice, telling Petra he was likely being honest. He took up Bellingham's coat and lifted the pocket flap, enough that the manner of stitching could be ascertained. "I always use a pick stitch for lapels and pocket flaps, and I am known for my evenly spaced stitches. I can tell even from the little piece you brought that the stitches are imprecise and poorly done." Now his manner was almost as derisive as Bellingham's. "The fabric may indeed be lovely, but the workmanship is not."

"Do you know who would have such workmanship?" she asked. And when he hesitated, she said, "I gave you a shilling, Mr. Cuthbert. I think it buys me more than just the knowledge that your skills at pick-stitching are excellent, does it not?"

Cuthbert looked nervous, but his voice rang true, even if disgruntled. "There's a tailor on Chancery Lane, near Fleet Street, by the name of Plympton, who does work like that. Plympton's work looks well enough, but is half the price and half the quality. I can't be sure, for this is but a scrap, and there are many tailors who don't put their whole effort into their work, but I'd bet this shilling that it might be his."

"Does the gentleman who has his place of business upstairs use Mr. Plympton?" Petra asked, glancing up toward the ceiling so there was no doubt to whom she was referring.

But Cuthbert walked smartly to his door and opened it once more.

"I could not tell you whom the gentleman used before me, my lady," he said tightly. "But I would doubt he used Plympton, knowing the gentleman's penchant for excellent tailoring. And I know for certain he does not have a coat of this color, nor have any of his coats been damaged lately. Now, if you will. Good day, my lady."

From somewhere upstairs, she heard a door open and close and the sound of a lock turning. Mr. Drysdale was leaving his office. She had no more time to press the question.

Quickly, Petra went out the front door, down the steps, and into the throngs of people on Oxford Street before she turned around to observe a carriage arriving. Moments later, Drysdale was in the carriage and it pulled away smartly, thankfully keeping him from seeing when Petra nearly jumped out of her skin at hearing a voice ringing out with delight.

TWENTY

"LADY PETRA! THERE YOU ARE!"

She turned to find Lottie, beaming at her. On one lead was Fitz, the little terrier. On the other was Sable. Lottie explained before Petra could even ask.

"I saw your carriage, and Annie told me you were nearby. There is a new tea shop just down the street, and I'm famished. Let us go and have tea and then we can go through Grosvenor Gate at Hyde Park, where I will show you all Sable can do. Annie is just a few shops down, choosing some new ribbons for your hair. She has sent your carriage to wait by the tea shop."

With that, Petra allowed herself to be led into a bright and cheery tearoom. In a corner table, over cups of soothing China tea and slices of fruitcake, Petra found herself unable to keep quiet about all she had learned. Possibly because Annie was unhappy with her and Petra wished for someone sympathetic to tell her she was doing the right thing, yes, but she could not cease talking once she had started.

Plus, maybe it was the knowledge that Duncan had trusted Lottie enough to become her benefactor, but Petra instinctively trusted her, too.

She told Lottie of visiting Bardwell's Apothecary, of Frances's unwillingness to confess which man had purchased her salve. Then she went on to tell her of seeing Teddy, of her uncle's suspicious conversation with the solicitor, Mr. Fawcett, and of seeing Lord Bellingham having his coat mended by a tailor. And with grateful rubbing of Sable's ears, she spoke of how the little pointer likely saved her life in the alley off Jermyn Street.

"I am appalled to hear this happened to you, Lady Petra," Lottie said darkly, before her face lightened and she offered Sable a bit of fruitcake. "But I am most happy to know you were unharmed and that Sable here is already so attached to you that she would wish to protect you. Oh, whoever that odious man was, I'd love to set Fitz onto him! And onto Lord Bellingham, too. He has always been rather rude to me."

"I cannot claim astonishment at this," Petra said.

"Indeed. He insulted my figure and said that the only dogs that sniff around me were those of the true canine variety."

"Oh!" Petra exhorted, furious on Lottie's behalf. "If I didn't already wish to strike him, I would now. How did you respond?"

Lottie's cheeks turned the color of prawns. "I replied that, actually, I preferred gentlemen to rakes, and that at least females, both human and canine, still liked me, whereas only the bitches of the human variety were willing to give him a second look." Lottie bit her lower lip, and her eyes the color of spring leaves brightened with mischief. "Then I said that I rather liked my plump parts, and that the man I eventually marry will be quite pleased with them as well—and I was ever so happy that he, Bellingham, would never see just how lovely they are."

"Lottie, you are a wonder!" Petra exclaimed, grasping Lottie's hand across the table.

"I would still love to set Fitz upon him," Lottie said. "Did you know I've taught Fitz to literally spring into the air and bite someone's bottom?"

Petra nearly choked on her tea, and had to laugh with her napkin over her mouth. "You must be joking."

"I am not," Lottie said with a grin. "I taught him the trick when I was in Yorkshire these past weeks, after my brother's twin sons kept using a slingshot to pelt small rocks at me own bum. Fitz took to my commands in one day and those buggerlugs haven't shot rocks at me since." Lottie looked around to make sure they were not being overheard and asked, "Does this mean that, ah, his lordship was also responsible for the other incident? With the footman?"

Petra shook her head. "I do not think he is, though I would have been happy for it to be the case, for the man does indeed deserve Fitz to bite him on the bum. I know where to ask next, however." She then told Lottie about Mr. Plympton on Chancery Lane.

"Why, I must be in that area on Monday," Lottie said. "Why do I not make the inquiries, my lady?"

After assurances from a beaming Lottie that she would be exceedingly careful, and be accompanied by her father and thus have more protection than Fitz, Petra passed the scrap of fabric to Lottie, saying, "I will accept your help if you do me the honor of calling me Petra."

Lottie and Petra spent the next half hour in Hyde Park, Lottie putting Sable through her paces and teaching Petra all the commands to use, most of which were in Gaelic—for no other reason, explained Lottie, than because she liked it after hearing Duncan speak to her other canine charges that way. Petra found herself smiling at the thought despite herself.

Later, as Petra and Annie traveled back to Forsyth House in Petra's carriage, uncomfortable silence reigned between the two. But Annie, never one to hold a grudge and incapable of remaining quiet when she could learn exciting news, could contain herself for only so long.

"You must tell me, my lady. For I am positively weak with curiosity. Yes, I know, at first I was unhappy with you for putting yourself in potentially dangerous situations, but then I reminded myself that Lady Petra Forsyth never does anything by halves. That you are doing this to help others."

"Oh, Annie," Petra said with no little emotion, but Annie would not be contained by sentimentality.

"What happened after I left you at Lady Potsford's? And I am especially curious to know what role Lord Whitfield played in your scheme."

"Lord Whitfield? Was he on Oxford Street today?" Petra asked, surprised, as Sable laid her head in Petra's lap with a contented sigh. "I do not believe I saw him."

Annie nodded. "He had been standing outside Mr. Drysdale's place of business, looking up at it. He was frowning with a bit of a concerned look. I confess I had wondered if you sent him to speak to Mr. Fawcett, or asked him to be a lookout in some way, being as he is Lady Caroline's . . ."

"He is her lover, yes," Petra said, too distracted to be scandalized, or allow Annie to be so. "But no, Lord Whitfield was not part of my scheme," Petra said. "Though I am wondering if he has schemes of his own. Annie, I must think on what to do, and how to handle this new issue regarding Lady Caroline. I worry that he may have ties with Drysdale, and may entangle Lady Caroline in some way."

But as they drew up to Forsyth House, her thoughts of Lord Whitfield were dashed aside, for another unforeseen problem had presented itself.

"My lady," breathed Annie as Rupert expertly drove the carriage into the small courtyard. "Did you know?"

"That the earl was due to arrive today?" Petra said as their carriage came abreast of the rather larger one pulled by four sleek black Friesians imported by the earl from the Netherlands. "No, it is all a surprise to me—but what a delightful one at that! I shall be most happy to see him."

TWENTY-ONE

THE EARL OF HOLBROOK WAS ALREADY ENSCONCED IN HIS library when Petra walked in.

"Dearest Papa!" Petra exclaimed, rushing to his side. "It is wonderful to see you. Why did you not tell me you were coming today?"

The earl, upon seeing his daughter, smiled and held out his hands to her. She kissed his cheeks, and his blue eyes looked bright and cheerful. And he chuckled as he caught her looking around with some apprehension.

"Do not alarm yourself, my girl. Your uncle is not skulking about this time." He gave her cheek a gentle pat. "You look well, my dear. I am most happy to see your face, as always."

Petra pulled a nearby chair closer and sat, laughter in her voice as she chided him.

"Should you be expecting me not to look well, Papa? And how is your ankle? You are not walking on it too much, are you?"

The earl lifted up his left boot and wiggled it a bit. "No, no, my dear. Not at all. I have been most solicitous in caring for my ankle, for I wish to be out with my horses—and I know you do not wish to take care of me for any longer."

Seeing that tea had already been laid on the low table along with two cups and saucers, both bearing a design of a green diamond pattern against a dark blue background after the earl's racing colors, Petra rose again to pour them both a cup and kissed the top of his head as she went past.

"Oh, now, Papa, you know that is not true. You were a very good patient, and you let me ride out with the string every day for three whole months! Excepting the fact that I knew you to be in some pain from your fall, it was a true joy to be at Buckfields with you."

The earl's eyes twinkled. "Is that what I must do to have my daughter visit me for more than a short fortnight? Well, then, it is nice to know that I may break any other bones I see fit and know that you will come running in order to be able to ride—and astride—as often as you like."

Petra fixed his tea with milk and one sugar and handed it to him, feigning a serious look. "Thank you, Papa. I am most obliged that you would schedule another bone break or two in the future, just to please me." Going back to pour herself a cup, she said, "Now, to what do I owe this unexpected delight in having you arrive unannounced? I did not encounter Cudmore at the front door. Did he and the full complement of servants not arrive with you?"

"No, no, my girl," the earl said, waving this off with the hand that held the saucer while his other hand brought the teacup to his lips. "I am only here for one night." After taking a slurping sip, he added, "Wasn't planning on being here at all until May, when I usually make the first of my twice-yearly appearances in town."

"Yes, and it is surprising you come twice, given how much you dislike being in town, Papa," she teased, and readied herself for one of his diatribes on the ills of London, which she always found diverting, even though the earl had no intention of them being so.

But when her father merely took in more tea, Petra was a bit surprised, but undaunted. "Well? Will you not tell me of your reasons for arriving then, if not to remind yourself of all the reasons you dislike coming to the fair city once known as Londinium?"

The earl gave a snort at hearing this, but put his teacup down with an "Ahh, a good cup of tea always does a man good."

"Papa," said Petra with a laugh. "You are teasing me."

The earl's blue eyes met her own, and she felt as if she were looking into a mirror at that point.

Petra would agree with those who claimed she took after her mother, for the portrait of her mother at twenty and the portrait of herself at the same age were almost identical. Blond curls that gleamed a honey color in all but the brightest of lights. A smallish nose and pointed, stubborn chin. And eyes set a touch wider than most, with light brown eyebrows that arched into a subtle point.

But it was the eye color where Petra differed from her mother. In the two portraits painted of Lady Holbrook as an adult, plus one from her childhood, Maria's had been the color that comes from glimpses of the sky through rainclouds. The earl's, though, were as blue as the stalks of *salvia azurea* Annie would bring Petra to brighten her favorite rooms in the late summer, and speckled with darker blue like that of a robin's egg. Petra's contained fewer speckles, but otherwise, she had her father's eyes. And at present, she could see his were full of some undisclosed hesitancy. Then he seemed to wave it away.

"Oh, but I am not meaning to, my girl. I have arrived because I was contacted by a man who's very interested in buying some of my racehorses and having me continue to train them."

Petra stared at him, for he did not look at her when saying this. "But I have never seen you come to London to meet with anyone about purchasing one of your horses, excepting the Queen herself. Even the Prince Regent was required to come to Buckfields—and he did, without so much as one word of complaint. That we were to hear with our own ears, at least."

The earl shifted in his chair. "Yes, you are indeed correct. Normally, I'd insist on the man coming to me, but he convinced me a trip to London would be worth my while. Said he'd introduce me to a couple of other chaps who have the money and the desire to own their own horses, too."

Petra sat down again and laid her hand over her father's. "Papa, why do I feel that you are not telling me all your reasons for giving into this man and coming here to London?" She hesitated, then spoke gently. "I handled your accounting as well as your stud books for weeks, Papa. I saw how the numbers did not appear as favorable as one would like in places, especially after we lost those two stallions last year to colic and two others have not been good breeders thus far . . ."

The earl fiddled with his teacup and was about to speak when

Smithers knocked twice at the door, opening it, and a well-dressed man entered, walking at an unhurried pace, his hand atop the silver handle of a highly polished walking stick. The earl rose quickly, causing Petra's hand to be thrown aside in his haste.

"Ah, yes, here he is," the earl said. "Petra, my dear, this is the man I was just mentioning. May I introduce you to Mr. . . ." He turned to the man. "Blast it all, I cannot seem to recall your Christian name. It is a rather unusual name. Italian-sounding, one would say. Is it Italian?"

"It is Luca," the man said, his voice soft, his delivery as smooth as silk. "I was told it means 'the bringer of light.' But if there is a drop of Italian blood in me, my lord, I am unaware of it."

"Quite so. Quite so," the earl said with a hearty chuckle before facing his daughter again. "My dear Petra, this is Mr. Luca Drysdale."

The smug smile and cold blue eyes she had seen looking up at the window of Miss Arabella Littlewood were now focused on her, vanishing only for a moment as he gave a correct bow.

"Lady Petra," he said, his head coming back up to once again emphasize the gray on the sides of his head as opposed to the dark hair on top. He was not as tall as she had thought when she first saw him. She had thought him closer to Duncan's height, but in truth, he was a couple inches shorter, closer in height to the earl, who was looking amiable and pleased.

"Capital!" the earl exclaimed, as Petra, after a moment's hesitation, gave the requisite curtsy. "Yes, very good," her father continued. "Drysdale here was just off using the—well, you know, my dear—as one does, and, as Smithers alerted me to your carriage nearing, I said I would wait here for you to arrive before I went upstairs for a fresh shirt. Travel does have a way of making one want to bathe, but there is no time. A fresh shirt will suffice." Before Petra could even attempt to protest, her father was striding toward the door. "Petra, offer Drysdale some tea, will you? My daughter will take care of you, Drysdale, until I return. And then we shall be off to my club for a drink and a look at my stud books."

TWENTY-TWO

PETRA'S EYES REMAINED ON THE LIBRARY DOOR, UNEASE MAK-
ing her feel as if something were flipping over in her belly. Under normal circumstances, Annie would be sent in to ensure Petra
was not left alone with an unmarried man. And if not Annie, then
Charles or Smithers would stand inside the door.

But not this time, and she could not feel surprised on the whole.
Annie was belowstairs with Sable. And it had been clear upon
Petra's arrival that the house had been in a bit of chaos owing to
the earl arriving without so much as a footman sent ahead to alert
the servants.

She put a hand to her stomach to settle it as, from the corner of
her eyes, she saw Drysdale take two strides closer.

"I have been looking forward to meeting you for quite some
time, Lady Petra," he said.

"Have you indeed?" Petra replied, letting her hand drop to her
side. She turned to face him. "Am I to imagine why, or will you
tell me?"

Drysdale dipped his chin, his eyes managing to look up at her,
his forehead wrinkling in concern. His voice held a touch of injury.
"Why, we have only just met, Lady Petra. Have I done something
to make you reply to me in such a harsh manner?"

"What?" Petra said, giving him an incredulous look. "I most
certainly did not speak in such a way."

Drysdale blinked at her as if confused. "Lady Petra," he said,
then paused. "Do—do you not recall what you just said to me?"

"I beg your pardon?" Petra said, her brows knitting. Had she
said something other than the words she knew for sure had come
out of her mouth?

A strange feeling was suddenly twisting in her belly and she felt quite unable to move and free herself from it. What was he playing at? She glanced back at the door, hoping for Smithers to come rushing in, realizing he had left Lady Petra alone with a strange man. Or maybe Charles or Annie would come instead.

Somebody, please come.

"Are you expecting someone else, Lady Petra? Or is it your habit to stare at the door when your father leaves?" Drysdale moved closer to her, but as if he were approaching a skittish filly, his smile both gentle and concerned as his gaze flitted to her midsection.

Damn, her hand had gone to her belly again without her even realizing it. Her vision was curiously becoming narrow, her breath unable to settle into calm. What was happening to her?

"Are you unwell, my lady? I had heard you were a woman of great strengths, but you appear quite fragile at the moment." And when she looked at him with a mixture of irritation and alarm— *Do I indeed look fragile?*—he took a slight step back, his expression one of anxious watchfulness. "Should I fetch you some water, my lady?" he asked, in a tone that suggested she might fly about like a frightened bird if he spoke louder.

Petra turned away from him, feeling too warm for comfort. She fanned at her face with her hand, needing the air. Her eyes went to a portrait on the earl's wall, but she was not truly seeing it. Her heart was pounding too quickly in her chest.

Drysdale edged closer, his blue eyes wide in worry. "I must confess I am rather concerned with how quickly your moods are going from one extreme to the other," he said gently. He gestured toward the chair she had vacated but minutes earlier. "Lady Petra, why do you not sit down?"

Two things brought her back to herself. The first was when she twisted away from Drysdale, causing her to stub her toe. She gasped and blinked rapidly, which brought the portrait into focus. It was a copy of the portrait of her mother at twenty that hung in

Buckfields. And in her mother's serene face that looked so much like her own, Petra saw herself as she knew in her heart she was: strong, no matter what her faults.

"Lady Petra, I feel as if I should fetch someone," Drysdale said, though as she turned toward him once more, she saw he stood with one hand leaning casually on his walking stick, in no rush to fetch anyone at all.

Petra wondered if it had been the same with Gwen. And Lady Thacker. And all the other women she did not know but who had dealt with this man, potentially been taken away by him. Had Drysdale made them question every thought, every gesture, every word that came out of their mouths within mere minutes, if not seconds, of being in his presence? It was as if he were a spiritualist—no, a mesmerist, convincing her with his words of things that were not true.

If only to give herself some time to think, she reclaimed the chair she had sat in earlier. She desperately wanted to pour herself some tea but was afraid that if her hands shook—for she could not be certain they would not—then Drysdale would use it to prey upon her fears again.

Drysdale lowered himself into the chair that sat across the low table from Petra. Casually, he took the teacup and saucer Petra had been wishing were in her hands and poured a cup, then added three sugars. He did not offer it to Petra, but took a spoon engraved with the Forsyth crest of a demi-griffin and lazily stirred as he spoke.

"I'd like you to know, my lady, that I am aware you were in Bardwell's Apothecary today, as well as on Oxford Street." The silver spoon went around in the teacup another circle, dinging against the porcelain like a clock striking the hour. "I know you have been attempting to discover my business." Another swirl of the tea by the spoon, another *ding*. "And that you have been asking about Lady Milford." One more stir of the spoon and he tapped it on the edge of the cup, just enough to make it sound as if it would chip the porcelain, and then slid it with infinite quietness onto his saucer. "Lady Milford is unfortunately dead, and I am giving you a warning that you should stop questioning this."

Petra bristled. Yet as an earl's daughter, she was brought up not to let her emotions show. To be commanding with those beneath her station. It was not something at which she had ever truly excelled, but she could do so when it was required.

She inclined her head toward Drysdale to let him know she had heard his threat. Then she laid her hands in her lap, and willed her voice to be as calm as his.

"Tell me about Fairwinds, Mr. Drysdale. If it is something I should not question, or fear, tell me why. I feel it is the least you can do after attempting to make me believe I had been acting erratically just now." She looked at him, her countenance composed. "For I know I was not."

One side of Drysdale's mouth lifted. "Yes, you were merely having what someone who studies the human mind and both its strengths and failures calls an episode of hysteria. Quite normal to happen on occasion, especially in women, whose tendency toward hysteria is always right under the surface, and all too easily brought about."

"Is that so?" she murmured.

"It is, Lady Petra," Drysdale replied. "But I shall answer your question, for I have nothing to fear by doing so. At Fairwinds, we study episodes such as these. Women of almost all ages are sent to me by their husbands, fathers"—he gave an elegant shrug—"and even brothers and uncles, when they can no longer control their episodes. When a woman is brought to Fairwinds, she is brought to a safe place, Lady Petra. One where she is given the best of care, the most modern of treatments, and is awarded with a healthful and peaceful life."

"I see," Petra said. Her body, having cooled down, was now feeling shivery from his words, but she willed herself still. "And are these women ever cured?"

Drysdale sipped his tea. "Occasionally, yes. Why, I was able to reunite one young woman with her family less than two months ago. She is now to be married and, by all accounts, already anticipating being with child. It merely took her a while to regain her calm, remember that she is a female, and accept the gentleman's hand."

"Pray, tell me, Mr. Drysdale, what do you mean by saying this woman needed to remember that she is a female?"

She watched as he pulled a silk handkerchief and dabbed at his mouth. "Well, Lady Petra, she was much like you."

"Indeed?" said Petra, her brows lifting just enough to show disdain for the statement. "How so? No, let me hazard a guess. She had decided to remain unmarried?"

"You should call it what it is, my lady. Or are you afraid of the proper term for a lady such as yourself?"

Petra knew better than to play as if she did not take his meaning. "I only dislike the word 'spinster' for the vitriol with which most people tend to utter the word. They do not speak the same way when they say 'bachelor,' do they?"

Drysdale's mouth now tipped down. "I suppose not."

"There. For until the word 'spinster' can be used without people saying it in derogatory fashion, or with the wrinkling of one's nose, or, worse, with *pity*, then I shall continue to dislike using the word and will use a synonym or a like phrase instead."

At this, Drysdale let out a laugh, but it was mirthless. "I expect two hundred years from now or more, the word 'spinster' will still call to mind a woman to be pitied."

"And I hope that will not be true," said Petra.

"One can always hope for the future, my lady," Drysdale said as if unperturbed. "But in the time we are living in, I doubt your wish will be granted. However, in regard to the lady who is to be soon married, she wished to walk around in trousers, like you. To ride astride, like you. To smoke cigars, to drink in pubs, and to make love to other women." He raised his eyebrows. The *Like you?* an unspoken question that he clearly felt was a foregone conclusion.

He had meant to shock her, and he had succeeded, but only for the smallest of moments.

"Is that indeed what you would like to do, my lady?" Drysdale asked, almost gently, as if coaxing a small child out of its hiding place.

"And what if I did?" Petra said. Everything within her was telling her she should not have said this, but she had the bit between her teeth now. She was unwilling to back down.

Drysdale merely smiled, changing his tactics once more. "Oh, you are enjoying your attempt to be bold, but I actually know you do not prefer other women—in the romantic sense, at least. I know of your love for Lord Ingersoll, God rest his soul. And I also know how you showed him your love prior to his death. I hear you were so very eager, and vocal in your enthusiasm, Lady Petra . . ."

Suddenly, her head was spinning again, like a top carelessly put to swirling around and around by a mischievous child. How could he have known?

Drysdale's soft voice was in her ears, as if he were leaning over her instead of sitting across the low table.

"Did you like the things he did to you, Lady Petra? Did you like the feel of his body covering yours? Turning you over and mounting you like the horses at your father's stables? I have heard you've watched horses enjoying their carnal lusts since you were a small child. No doubt it has influenced your ideas on love. You were impure in your mind for many years before you rode astride on Lord Ingersoll for the first time, weren't you, Lady Petra?"

His words left her feeling as if she could no longer breathe, even as a familiar face had become almost a shimmering mirage in front of her eyes.

Duncan. He was the only man who knew of her time with Emerson. Yes, Duncan often found her irresponsible, impetuous, and immature. He had all but called her a silly woman for bringing her little dagger to the Green Park. But would he have been traitorous enough to tell a man like Luca Drysdale of her wanton behavior with the man she had dearly loved? The man who was to be her husband until his untimely death?

Emerson had claimed Duncan would never give them away. But there was no one else who knew outside of Caroline and Annie. And while both knew of her delight in her time with Emerson, she had not confessed even to Caroline all the things she and Emerson had done in private. Of how she could not keep her hands from him the moment they were alone. Of how the rapture she felt became more and more vocalized with each subsequent night, when her experiences increased, and she became braver because of Emerson's care and tenderness.

Petra rose so fast from her chair that it nearly fell over backward. Inside, she was shaking with anger, but when she spoke, she was calm and commanding.

"I would like you to leave, sir."

Drysdale merely tutted, steepling his fingers together. "Oh no, I don't think so. I think I shall be staying—in one way or another."

The next moment, the library door had opened and the earl was striding in.

"Ahh, I feel much better now, and ready for some whisky and one of White's excellent meals. I do confess I am starving."

The earl stopped at seeing Petra standing. "Why, my girl, you look a bit flushed. Is something the matter?"

Drysdale had risen to his feet as well. "Oh, I think Lady Petra simply needs a rest, your lordship," he said silkily. "She had just been telling me of all the things she has discovered today."

"Discovered?" said the earl with a chortle. "It sounds as if you have been out on some sort of heraldic quest, my dear."

"I think she feels as if she was, in a way," Drysdale said, bringing up his walking stick and using it to make a slow slash through the air as if it were a knight's sword.

Petra gave the man a moment's hard stare. "And maybe I was."

Drysdale's lips curved into a smile. Petra's did not. The earl looked from one to the other, clearly disconcerted. Then he clapped his hands together once, saying with an attempt at brightness, "Yes, well, all ladies need their rest, even ones as full of health and joie de vivre as my Petra."

A knock on the door revealed Smithers, with news that the carriage was ready. Turning to Petra, he asked, "May I have some tea and cake brought to you, my lady?"

"Yes, thank you, Smithers," she said.

The earl was already walking away with Drysdale at his side. "Splendid! Get some rest, my girl, after taking some tea," he called back. "Eat some cake, too, for I know how much you enjoy it. I shall see you for breakfast in the morning!"

Neither her father nor Drysdale looked back as they left.

TWENTY-THREE

PETRA PACED HER DRAWING ROOM, THINKING ON ALL THAT had just happened. How easily Drysdale had made her feel as if she could not trust her own mind, her own thoughts. The bile increased with every recounting of his ugly words, and the realization of the likelihood that Duncan had been the one to give her away as no longer being virtuous. It hurt her like she had been unexpectedly kicked in the chest by a horse. Powerful, swift, and sending her sprawling to lie shattered upon the ground.

Annie knocked and entered, bringing a tray with tea things and cakes, plus a calling card Petra recognized from paces away as Duncan's.

"Mr. Shawcross wished to have an audience with you, my lady. I told him you were indisposed, having felt that you might have had enough of men speaking to you for one day."

Petra could not help but present a grim smile at this.

"You were quite right, Annie. I do not wish to have any man, especially one who has proven himself to be a false friend, speak to me for the rest of the day."

"Of course, my lady," said Annie, though sounding a bit confused. "Would you care to reply to Mr. Shawcross by letter? I saw him when he was speaking to Smithers and, in truth, he looked quite concerned."

"No, thank you," Petra replied crisply.

"Very well," Annie said. "But one thing you must do is eat some food." She picked up a plate and put two small sandwiches and one fairy cake on it, then handed it to Petra. "Take this upstairs with you, my lady. I will bring a fresh pot of tea to your dressing room and you will eat a bit and change into a fresh dress for Hyde Park. You will feel much better after eating something."

"I do not feel like eating," Petra said, sinking into a chair. "Or changing my dress." She held the plate out to Annie, who gently pushed it back toward her and then put her hands to her hips.

"You will eat something, my lady, or I shall leave you for a position with Lady Lynley, for you know she continues to try and hire me away."

"Blast that petty, thieving cousin of mine!" Petra exhorted. She pounded one fist on the edge of her chair. "Oh, this day simply will not give over to me!"

"I expect not, my lady," Annie said, her lips twitching as she held out a sandwich. Annie's threat, though an empty one, had worked. Petra took the sandwich, albeit with a grumpy huff, and bit into it.

Once she'd finished eating, and drank half a cup of tea, Annie spoke again. "My lady, I must tell you something."

Looking up wearily, Petra said, "Go on, then. It will not be the first harsh thing I have heard today."

Annie pursed her lips. "Now, I will not have you acting the martyr, my lady. I do not know exactly what happened when you spoke with Mr. Drysdale, but you are too strong to let him take up residence in your head."

Petra's lip trembled just a bit at this. "Do you really think so? Because I do not feel very strong at the moment."

"I know so, my lady," Annie said with a fierce expression, and held out another sandwich. Petra took it with a watery smile and ate.

"That is better," Annie said. "Now, what I have to say pertains to that odious man."

"To the devil with Drysdale," Petra growled, making go-away motions with her hand. "For he is as evil as the devil, and may they make each other miserable. I do not wish to hear any more of him."

"I should think you would wish to hear this, my lady," Annie said.

Petra looked at her with a baleful expression. Then sighed. "Fine. Go on, then."

"I went to the kitchens to get your tea things, and to check on Sable. But as I did not wish to continue getting in the way of Charles, Allen the new underfootman, and the other two footmen from Buckfields as they rushed to unload and bring the hampers downstairs, I came up the hidden staircase at the back of the house."

"All right. And?"

"And, again, as you know, the staircase comes out just down the hall from your bedchamber. As I came out into the hall from the stairs, I saw the door to your bedchamber was open and I thought I heard something in your dressing room. As everyone was either downstairs or in the earl's wing, including the two housemaids, I crept forward and peeked through the door. That man, Mr. Drysdale, was coming out of your dressing room, my lady."

Petra reached up and grasped Annie's hand. "Oh, Annie, tell me he did not see you." And she was relieved when Annie shook her head. Then her heart clutched again when Annie gave a mischievous shrug.

"Well, he did not at first, my lady, but I made sure he did a few moments later. I was able to make it to the main staircase and go down a few steps. Then I turned back and came up the stairs again, making as much noise as I could. As I expected, Mr. Drysdale came out of your rooms in a trice." She lifted her chin. "I stopped, acted surprised, and asked him what he was doing in my lady's bedchamber."

Petra gripped Annie's hand tighter. "What did he say to you?"

"He claimed the earl had sent him up to use the chamber pot in your wing, my lady, but he got lost. He was very convincing, I must say, but I could tell something was not right."

Petra had sagged with relief that Annie was not harmed. "What do you think he wanted in my bedchamber?"

"Had I not seen him come from your dressing room, my lady, I might not have found it. You might not have, either." From her pocket, she produced a slim blue glass bottle with a cork stopper. The paper label made it so no one had to guess its contents.

"Kendal Black Drop," breathed Petra.

Annie nodded, then held it up to the window, her mouth set in a grim line. "And made to look half-gone, too, my lady. I found it in the very back of the drawer in your dressing table."

Petra stood up, setting her plate of food aside as she did so. "I have never seen Black Drop, but I have heard it is akin to taking four times the amount of laudanum at once. Mr. Coleridge, the poet, is said to use it and to have written 'Kubla Khan' whilst in its horrible throes." Petra felt a shiver go through her. "Oh, Annie, Mr. Drysdale is hoping to make me look as if I use strong doses of opium regularly and cannot do without it—and that I keep it secret even from my lady's maid!"

She stopped, her eyes beseeching Annie's. But Annie only shook her head.

"Do not concern yourself, my lady. If you took a small dose of laudanum occasionally to help you sleep, I might be none the wiser. But someone who takes it regularly cannot be mistaken. And one who takes this Black Drop with regularity?" She tilted the blue bottle from side to side. "They can barely get themselves out of bed from day to day, and cannot hold a conversation with even themselves without sounding as if they are ranting." Annie's eyes then brightened with amusement. "You, my lady, rise much too early on a daily basis to have the opium habit—and if there be anyone in all of England who can claim you cannot hold a proper conversation with them, I should like them to prove it. Yes, for I am with you the bulk of every day, and I have too much respect for myself to be a lady's maid to anyone who whiles their life away on opium."

Petra, took Annie's free hand again in both of hers. "Thank you," she whispered, and then smiled. Yes, something had gone right today, finally. "You are indeed the rarest of gems, Annie."

This had the enchanting effect of making Annie blush. Slipping the bottle back into her pocket, she said, "I will dispose of this horrid concoction without anyone seeing, my lady. Everyone belowstairs will be having their tea and will never notice."

There was a knock upon the door, and Charles appeared, with Sable at his heels. "Lady Caroline is here, my lady."

Caroline glided in, with Sable trotting alongside her. "I came by to see if you would accompany me to promenade this evening, dearest. For the ton was positively buzzing yesterday with questions about the poor footman's murder, as distasteful as their interest may be."

"Yes, truly distasteful," Petra said shortly, her temper flaring once more despite herself. "For Martin was a kind man who died doing nothing more than a favor I had asked of him. Nothing more than imparting information that would help me understand what happened to Gwen. We should all feel respect for such a person, not gawk at the circumstances of their death."

Caroline raised her eyebrows at Petra's heated reply. "I certainly agree it is an ugly flaw of human nature. Though would I be correct in assuming that something else is adding to your vexation, dearest? Is it Shawcross again? You two must let go of your pride and speak to one another, you know."

Petra's anger gave way to a lump in her throat at the mention of Duncan. Knowing that he betrayed her was still too painful by half. She did not even dare to look at Annie, who would no doubt concur with Caroline, if asked.

"Did anyone question my motives for meeting a footman?" Petra asked instead, concentrating on giving Sable's ears a rub. "Or make any connection to Gwen?"

"Not the connection to Gwen, no. I think few, if anyone, on Rotten Row yesterday knew Martin had been Gwen's footman, except for Mr. Shawcross, of course."

"Duncan was promenading? That is unlike him," Petra said.

"Well, he was walking with Lady Horatia, his brother's betrothed. The Marquess of Langford, however, was nowhere to be seen." Caroline sighed. "Horatia is a lovely, sweet girl, and I am afraid Langford will not be good to her."

"And did anyone make any commentary about me meeting a

footman?" Petra asked, and to change the subject as well, for she found that, despite his betrayal, she did not care for the idea of Lady Horatia promenading with Duncan—and found it most frustrating that she should feel this way.

"I heard every rumor, including something akin to the truth—that Martin wished to impart some news to you. Only everyone I heard got it wrong. They all said he wished to grouse about working under Trenworth, who is known for his inflexibility, and that Martin was planning to apply to you for a position here at Forsyth House. Then others wondered if you had fallen in love with the footman, who was noted by the Greely-Wilke sisters as being *très beau*." Caroline's lips tilted upward. "Some wondered if you had even declared yourself a spinster so that you might take him as your lover."

Petra decided she was too tired to do more than roll her eyes. Instead, she asked, "However did you respond, Caro?"

"I did not have to," Caroline said, a bit of devilishness about her expression. "For Mr. Shawcross spoke up, saying that Lady Petra would choose as her heart dictates, and at present, it seems she has chosen no one but herself." Caroline grinned, letting her reticule swing back and forth on her wrist. "And he found that an *admirable trait*." She then stopped, stared out the windows. "Heavens—Petra, did you see that? There looked to be a woman in your garden!"

Petra swiveled around, saw the flash of a figure in a pale dress, and this time she knew she had not seen a ghost. Without even thinking of pulling the bell for a footman, she rushed outside, Sable at her side, Annie and Caroline at her heels.

TWENTY-FOUR

"WHERE DO YOU BELIEVE SHE WENT?" ANNIE WHISPERED.

"I cannot be sure," Petra replied. "I will go toward the wisteria tunnel. Annie, please look in the rose garden, and take Sable with you. Caroline, I think you should stay nearest the house in case of trouble."

"As my dress is new and very lovely, if I may say so, I agree it is best I stay here," Caroline said. "Though this is when I wish I carried my bow and arrows with me everywhere."

Petra wished the same as she made her way to the back of the garden, where there was a tunnel created out of a series of six arbors, all covered in wisteria. While not quite yet in bloom, the flowers were showing signs of being ready to burst forth in heavenly scented purple clusters. Some of the vines were already reaching over the shoulders of a white marble statue of the goddess Nike. Farther down were other statues of Apollo, Diana, and Eros.

Petra made her way into the tunnel. She didn't see anyone at first, but didn't stop until she was in the middle, next to the carved granite bench positioned near the life-sized Greek goddess of victory.

"My lady?" called out Annie in a low voice from the nearby rose garden. "Is all well?"

Petra drew in a breath to reply, and then heard a rustle behind her before a hand clapped over her mouth.

"Lady Petra, it is I," hissed a voice. Petra, half in shock, half in recognition, tried to turn, and the hand released her mouth and did not impede her.

What she saw made her let out an "Oh!" that was so loud and anguished she heard Annie cry out and come running in her direction.

Petra could not believe her eyes. Before her stood a thin,

bedraggled woman with lank hair the color of teasel hanging down to her waist. She wore an ill-fitting gown in a pale yellow that was wrinkled and covered in streaks of dirt. Her eyes, once such a pretty gray, now looked almost too big for her face, which was sunken at the cheeks. Dried, cracked lips, a fresh abrasion on one cheek, and dirt on the other completed the picture. Yet Petra reached for her and pulled her into an embrace.

"Gwen!" she said. "Oh, Gwen. You are alive. Is it truly you? However did you get here? However did you survive going into the river?"

It was like her arms encircled a skeleton, and one who had little strength to return the embrace. Petra gently sat Gwen down on the bench just as Sable and Annie dashed into the wisteria tunnel. Gwen's eyes immediately looked terrified.

"I cannot be seen," Gwen croaked, trying to rise and run, the urge to flee giving her strength that Petra did not know someone in such a state could possess.

"It is all right," Petra said. "It is only my lady's maid, Annie. Stay here. I will bring you some food and water, and we will decide what to do."

Gwen startled again at the sound of feet rushing their way, shrinking back against the curve of the wisteria tunnel. But before Petra could shield her, Caroline had arrived, and stood in shock at the sight of Gwen, whispering, "Heavens!"

For her part, Annie had rushed forward, immediately taking stock of Gwen's injuries.

"She needs food and water. Immediately. And something to clean her scrapes." Annie put the back of her hand to Gwen's forehead. "She is terribly feverish. There is no time to wait."

"I cannot be seen," Gwen said, even the effort of becoming agitated seeming to drain her. "If anyone sees me . . . if my husband . . . or Drysdale . . . if either find out I am alive . . ."

Caroline, Annie, and Petra all exchanged looks. Gwen's face now had a sheen of perspiration. She found Petra's hand and grasped it.

"Mrs. Nance . . . housekeeper at Fairwinds . . . she helped me escape. I went to Dorie . . . we faked my death . . . Dorie is being watched . . . I managed to make my way here. Been in hiding . . . Petra, I cannot be seen!"

"It is all right, dearest," Petra said soothingly. "We are going to get you to safety."

Gwen seemed not to hear. She now fairly clutched Petra's hand. "You must know. My husband . . . he sent me to a Mr. Drysdale. To an asylum for the insane."

"Fairwinds," Petra said. "It is an asylum? Not a place of recovery for one's health?"

Gwen made a derisive sound that led to a short spate of coughing that seemed to wrack her thin frame. She struggled to speak.

"The women . . . at the asylum . . . Fairwinds. He performs experiments . . . horrible things to them . . . to me. Mrs. Nance . . . she attempts to help us, but can do little. Some . . . their minds are sadly gone. Most . . . are not . . . mad. Just have difficulties . . . like me." Gwen's eyes looked fierce and hot. Her voice broke. "He is . . . hurting them . . . He enjoys it . . ."

"Shh, dearest Gwen," Petra said, feeling sickened by what she'd heard. She reached out and stroked Gwen's hair from her forehead. Her friend was positively burning. And at the same time, Petra felt a wave of hot shame rise up within her. Oh, she had been so bloody stupid to believe Lord Milford's anguish that day on Rotten Row! He had seemed most convincing, but it had all been false. Instead, what she had witnessed was a cruel performance masking the relief of a husband who, after sending his wife to an insane asylum, now was happy to believe she was well and truly dead. And that the blame for Gwen's death could be placed on her own frail mind and body, not his heartless actions.

Then Petra corrected her thoughts. In a way, Milford's arrogant willingness to believe Gwen's frailties was brilliant, for it enabled Gwen to find her way to London. *To find her way to me for help. And it is what I shall do no matter what.*

Petra blinked away tears as she attempted to soothe her friend. "It is all right. You can tell us everything once you have rested, and we will create a plan."

"No!" Gwen shouted, though it came out more of a hoarse croak. She kept shaking her head, and her words came out faster, even if weakly. "Petra, they must be saved. Men of the ton . . . they are making contracts with him. With Drysdale. There are more lives . . . at stake. Yours, Petra. And more."

"Mine?" Petra was aghast, and looked to a worried Annie and Caroline, then back at Gwen.

Her friend had exhausted herself, and her words slowed as her skin went clammy. "The duchess must know. The proof . . . it is in a ledger . . . and in . . ." Her eyes fluttered as she whispered, "Locked desk." And then she fainted, falling forward onto Petra, just as another form arrived at the entrance to the wisteria tunnel. The outline of a tall, very powerful-looking man.

Instinctively, Annie and Caroline stood closer together in an attempt to hide Gwen. Petra held Gwen closer. If it were Lord Milford, she would not allow him to take her friend.

"Do not come any closer, sir!" Petra said, then muttered, "*Ionnsaigh!*" to Sable, who instantly began growling. The Gaelic word, Lottie had said, meant an order to challenge a foe, and the pointer was more than willing.

"Lady Petra? What is the meaning of this?" Then the man lowered himself down on one knee and said something in Gaelic that had Sable dashing to him, wagging her tail, the growl replaced by a happy bark.

Petra recognized the voice, and the man. It was Duncan, and in that instant, she forgot his betrayal. Everything that had passed between the two of them was set aside. This moment was about saving Gwen.

"Duncan! Please help us!"

Duncan, however, was not alone. Steps behind him was a woman, whose dark eyes widened when she saw the scene in the wisteria tunnel. In a rustle of skirts, Frances Bardwell was at Petra's side, checking Gwen's pulse.

"Lady Milford is very weak, but she is still with us. We must get her inside. Mr. Shawcross, can you lift her?"

Annie spoke up. "I will go arrange a room, and make certain only Mrs. Ruddle knows for the time being."

"You are acquainted with Lady Milford?" Petra asked Frances, who was feeling Gwen's pulse even as Duncan lifted Gwen's limp form easily into his arms. Following close behind as he strode toward the house, Petra added, "And Mr. Shawcross, too?"

A ghost of a smile came over Frances's face. "Mr. Shawcross I have only just met when we arrived on your doorstep at the same moment, my lady." Two spots of color came into her cheeks. "I came to rectify my error in not telling you what I knew of the man who required my salve."

"It is all right, Frances," Petra said. "I was able to answer my own question soon enough, and I expect you had good reasons for keeping the information to yourself. But what of Lady Milford? Do tell me how you know her so well."

"She would often come into the apothecary herself," Frances explained, "looking for remedies to treat what she called her 'black days.' I would wager from your look you are not unaware of her troubles? I was most distressed to hear of her passing, and not a little skeptical of the news as well. Not least because I happen to know Lady Milford here had been terrified of her husband as of late—but also because I heard of her supposed drowning, yet I know her ladyship happens to be an excellent swimmer."

Petra felt a little stunned. In all her years of friendship with Gwen, she had not known this about her friend. Had she known it, she might have had stronger suspicions about Gwen's death in the first place. *Maybe I might have trusted Martin from the beginning*, she thought with a sinking heart, *and I could have saved him from being so horribly murdered*. Yet Petra did not have time to learn anything else from Frances. Gwen was placed in a bedchamber in

Petra's wing. Frances asked to stay with Annie to help Gwen. "I have much experience with the sick, Lady Petra, and Lady Milford is my friend. Please."

"I would be grateful, Frances," Petra replied. Caroline offered to stay as well, but as she had an appointment to promenade with Lord Whitfield, Petra assured Caroline it was right she leave.

"We must appear as normal as possible, Caro. I shall do my best to go to the Row and meet you," she added, trying not to pace about her drawing room as she did so. So many questions were crowding her mind—and with Duncan nearby and watching her intently, every nerve in her felt heightened. He took a step toward her almost as soon as Caroline departed.

"Petra," he said. "We must speak. Yes, now. There is little to go on in Martin's death. And I suspect the Bow Street man, Townsend, is not inclined to look into it further. It is imperative you explain further about Lady Milford. For it is clear now there is a connection."

There was a knock on the drawing room door, and Annie entered.

"My lady, Miss Bardwell is asking for you. I'm afraid Lady Milford worsens by the moment."

Petra looked at Duncan, her voice clipped and polite. "Thank you for what you did, bringing Gwen inside," she said. "But I am needed upstairs." She paused in following Annie out, and turned back. Duncan's countenance showed confusion, anger, and frustration. Everything she was feeling as well. Therefore, she said, "We shall talk soon, I promise."

The earl did not return to Forsyth House until well after midnight. And with Annie having enlisted the help of only Mrs. Ruddle, Charles, and one loyal housemaid, neither the earl, his valet, nor the two Buckfields footman were the wiser of the two women hidden in a bedchamber down the hall from Petra's own. No one knew of the young female apothecarist who, though the daughter of a knight who had the patronage of Queen Charlotte, was little more than a woman of trade in the eyes of society. Nor did they know of the unconscious and supposedly drowned Lady Milford.

Throughout the night and into early Sunday, however, Gwen worsened, thrashing around in the bed as Frances, Annie, and Petra all stayed by her side, pressing a damp cloth to her forehead and others upon her body to lessen her temperature. Well before the earl returned from his club, Charles slipped out with Frances to Bardwell's Apothecary, returning with a host of tinctures, herbs, teas, and other herbal remedies. Frances did what she could, and Petra was grateful, but her worries for Gwen continued to grow.

After much discussion, Petra and Frances made the decision not to call a physician.

"He would likely advocate bloodletting, and I feel it is a rather useless endeavor in fevers," Frances told her.

Petra felt Frances's abilities were as good as any physician's, and thus Gwen had as much of a chance as she did with a male physician who had fewer or no other remedies at his disposal than Frances.

By morning, Gwen was little better, with her fever lessening slightly, but not broken. Yet she finally fell into a restless sleep as the sun came up.

Annie, having had the forethought to put Gwen in a room that had a particularly large dressing room attached and featured a comfortable chaise longue, showed an exhausted Frances to it, as she insisted on being close to Gwen.

Once freshened and changed into a clean dress, Petra ordered Annie to rest.

"I shall have breakfast with Papa, attend St. George's Day services if he wishes, and then return home to sleep. We must continue to act as normal, until we know which move to make next."

Then, with Sable trotting at her side, Petra made her way through Forsyth House and into the cozy room her father called the little eating parlor. There, however, she did not find the earl. Only a letter from him waited for her atop her place at the table.

TWENTY-FIVE

IT ONLY TOOK READING A FEW LINES OF HER FATHER'S LETTER for Petra's hands to start shaking with anger.

My dearest Petra,

From my earliest days as your father, I was warned I would give you too much rein. And, God help me, I did. With your dear mother gone from our lives, and knowing little what to do with a girl, I treated you both as a second son and a reigning countess. I allowed you too much time in the stables, and did not have you much chaperoned around the stable lads. In short, my daughter, I trusted too much.

As of late, I have learned of my failures in raising you. From your uncle, I have heard them often, but it was not until I heard them from the gentleman you met yesterday, Mr. Luca Drysdale, and others that I finally felt compelled to take notice.

Mr. Drysdale is much in town, well-connected, and hears much of what goes on in society—though, admittedly, one could scarcely call him a gentleman, as his fortune is recent and self-made. But, as a wealthy man, he has come to the notice of the most influential men in society. My daughter, Drysdale has heard many stories of you—witnessing some of it himself—and has felt compelled to tell me some of the gossip that surrounds you, unpalatable as it was for him to share it, and, naturally, for your papa to hear it.

I will not relate all of it here, for I can scarcely think on some of what he said, but I will relate the least untoward of what I learned. That you use unladylike language in public. That you freely give your friendship to men who are of the back-door persuasion—and possibly to women of sapphic inclinations as well. Drysdale has also heard that you behave as an egregious flirt with a certain gentleman of some standing whom he did not name, that you gallop your chestnut horse on Rotten Row, and that you freely consort with street urchins.

But the two worst indiscretions I will put into writing here is that you were involved in some way in the murder of one of Her Grace's footmen! And as Mr. Drysdale related to me the erratic way you acted during the minutes he was in your presence— some of which I now feel I witnessed myself—he told me he believed you had come under the influence of the opium habit, with Annie likely helping you conceal it.

I wish very much not to, but I feel the need to take the reins from you before you make a fool of yourself and the Forsyth name. Thus, I have given the servants notice that Forsyth House will be closed up a fortnight from today and for the foreseeable future. Do not worry yourself, I have not dismissed any servants, though some have informed me they will seek out other positions to keep them in London.

You, my dear, will pack your things and return to Buckfields within five days. Until then, I expect you to comport yourself as not only a lady, but also as the daughter of the Earl of Holbrook.

Petra sat in her chair, shaking all over now, barely able to breathe. She went over her father's letter once, twice more, her anger slowly giving way to a determination like she had never felt.

Petra stood, refolded the letter from her father, and slipped it into the slit pocket of her dress.

"I am to act like a lady, am I?" she said to the place where her papa usually sat. "Well, so be it—but I shall think like you, your lordship, and make my decisions accordingly."

Much as she'd seen the earl do in times of decision-making,

Petra paced for ten minutes up and down her drawing room until she came to a stop with a firm nod of her head. She had a plan and would put it into action.

First, she spent the next half hour writing a letter and sealing it. The despondent underfootman, Allen, was dispatched to make the delivery.

Next, she called for Annie and told her to pack and to have Rupert ready the carriage to leave in three hours' time. Then she called all the remaining nine servants into her drawing room.

When they had assembled, everyone looking downcast, and the younger maids with reddened noses and eyes from crying, Petra told them that she was going to do her best to have the earl reverse his decision.

"He has given you two weeks to ready the house for closing up. I ask that you give me five of those days to change his mind."

"But how will you do that, my lady?" asked Mrs. Bing, wringing her apron in her hands.

"Yes, my lady. We will need all the time we can get to properly close up the house if it is not to be reopened anytime soon," added Mrs. Ruddle.

"Do you know who is to be in charge of the servants once we get to Buckfields, my lady?" asked Smithers.

"These are questions to which I cannot yet give you an answer," Petra replied. "All I ask of you is that you give me time before you do anything of great significance—and that includes those of you who may decide to look for a position elsewhere here in London. If I am unsuccessful in convincing his lordship to reverse his directive, then I shall help any and all of you who wish to stay in London to find a new position."

Her loyal servants looked both dubious and cautiously hopeful. Then, as they were filing out, Allen came racing into the room, sweating and a bit pop-eyed with exertion. He had clearly been running at a sprint for some time.

"Allen," Petra said. "I believe I sent you to Hillmorton House with a letter, and asked that you not return without the favorable reply I had requested."

"I did—my lady," Allen said through labored breaths. "I were—"

"I *was*, Allen," Petra corrected gently.

"Right—my lady," he panted. "I *was* halfway—there when I saw—Mr. Shawcross—riding this—way. I stopped him—and bid him—to read—your letter."

At that point, Smithers entered the drawing room again. He cast a stern look at Allen, who stood at attention, then said, "Pardon me, my lady. Mr. Shawcross is here and requests an immediate audience."

"Please tell Mr. Shawcross that he will wait until I have completed my task here," Petra replied.

The sound of boot heels announced Duncan before Smithers could say another word. Though even if Smithers had spoken, he wouldn't have been heard over the thunderous words delivered with more than a trace of angry Scotsman.

"You will talk with me *now*, Lady Petra."

Dismissing Smithers and Allen with a nod, Petra turned to Duncan, whose dark hair was mussed from the wind, and his striped waistcoat in dual tones of dark green and sea green made his furious eyes glow like a dragon's. The very second Smithers closed her drawing room door, he advanced on her, holding up a crumpled letter, his voice dropped to a deep growl.

"What the devil is this? You call me a traitorous friend, and then you say you are requiring my help?"

Petra crossed her arms over her chest. In vowing to act as the earl might, she had finally decided to confront Duncan, and she would.

"Do you deny it? Do you deny telling Drysdale of my most private moments with Emerson? For you were the only other person who knew them."

"Of course I deny it!" he roared. "I have never, ever been anything but true to you, Petra!"

"True to me?" she repeated, her incredulity nearly matching his anger and causing her to take a step toward him. "How can you even claim as such after the disagreement we had three years ago? After I wrote to you with the sincerest of apologies for the things I said in my grief and heartbreak, and in my fear. I bared my soul to you in hopes you would understand why I became so angry that you were leaving. In hopes that you would forgive me for the terrible words I said. And to hear nothing in return? Ever? Do you call that being true, Duncan?"

Dropping the hand that held her letter, Duncan's other hand ran through his hair in an agitated gesture as he paced three steps one way, turned, and came back again. He stopped directly in front of her, his free hand reaching into his coat pocket and extracting a small bundle of two letters tied with a thin ribbon.

"I have never given away any of your secrets, Petra," he said, setting the letters onto a nearby table. "And the last thing I would ever do—ever—is allow anyone the leeway to speak ill of you."

From another pocket, he pulled a second set of letters, setting them next to the first. He moved forward another inch, so close that she was forced to tilt her head back to glare up at him. His voice went the strangled quiet of someone struggling to keep hold of their emotions. From a pocket in his waistcoat, he pulled a third bundle. Then a single letter from the pocket over his heart. "And as for that disagreement, I was heartbroken as well. And monstrously fearful." His eyes were boring into hers, his voice gone ragged. The last letter dropped onto the table. "For I did not know how to reply to you in the same brave way that you wrote to me. I made attempts—" He gestured to the pile of letters—locked letters at that. She could see her name on all in Duncan's hand and the direction for Forsyth House, or for Buckfields, and there must have been twelve or thirteen in all. "But they never reached the caliber of what I felt in my heart. So I wrote them, but never posted them."

Petra's arms had dropped, though both hands now went to her belly as her breath left her.

Then, remembering that it was seen as a sign of weakness, as a sign of a nervous disposition in a woman, she clasped them together and let them hang lower so that she was standing in a most ladylike position as she pulled in air as silently as she could.

"What do they say?" she asked.

But Duncan just shook his head, then rushed a hand through his hair. Once more, he paced another three steps away and back again.

"There is something else I must impart first." He stopped, facing half away from Petra. He then spoke quietly. "I am not the only one who knows about your time with Ingersoll. You must know that, Petra. You yourself have told Caroline and your lady's maid." He immediately held up a hand. "You may cease before taking a bite out of me, for I know that Caroline and Annie are not likely to blame."

"Then who would be?" she snapped.

Duncan closed his eyes and, even in his profile, she could see he did not like to say the words.

"You must understand that I do not know for sure. However, in answer to your question, I believe . . ."

"Yes?" she said coolly.

"I believe that Emerson, in his joy of being with you"—Duncan turned fully to look at Petra, pain reflecting in his eyes—"in his excitement at being so close to marrying you, he may have forgotten to enforce my directive that you never stay beyond half past six in the morning."

It took Petra a long moment to think of why this would be important, but then understanding came.

"Your charwoman."

"Yes," Duncan said. "My charwoman did her job well. She was very punctual and quiet, but she was also nosy and very greedy."

"She must have truly been light on her feet, for I overslept two or three times and never saw or heard her."

"That was part of her appeal—for bachelors who wished to

sleep in, that is. She worked for other unmarried gentlemen at the time, including Lord Copeland, Mr. William Boyle, and Lord Wyncroft—or Tibby, as he was known before he married your cousin Lynley and she forced his closest acquaintances to call him by his given name of Breckville."

Petra sank down onto her chair. "Tibby," she said on a weary sigh. "Who had wished to marry me after Emerson passed and then proposed to my cousin when I rejected him." She then peered back up at Duncan. "But it has been three years. Why am I only hearing rumors of my ruin now? It is absurd. Do you think Tibby told Lynley, and it was she who offered up the scandal on a silver platter to Drysdale? It would be so very like her."

"Yes, I recall Lynley's mercenary ways," Duncan said dryly. "Yet on the other hand, I have learned since coming back to London that Tibby has taken more and more to the whisky. And when he does, it takes very little for him to speak out of turn. As of late I have heard him speak of details concerning scandals from the past, as if he had been holding them in whilst sober, and they are flowing off his tongue now with rather too much ease."

Despite it all, it was hard for Petra to be angry, or surprised, for she was now recalling that Tibby indeed became rather soused at Her Grace's ball—at one point pulling tulips from one of Her Grace's flower arrangements, sticking them in the front flap of his trousers, and whirling about by himself to one of the livelier dances. Lynley had been puce with anger.

"Papa always liked Tibby," Petra said, rising, feeling weary. "He did inquire as to why I refused Tibby's proposal, but I explained that while I found Tibby to be a very kind man, I did not find him sufficiently diverting, or intelligent enough, or passionate enough in his convictions. Or, if I may be so very shallow, indeed handsome enough to suit me. I should have been bored within one hour of our marriage."

She stopped, shoulder to shoulder with Duncan, and met his gaze. "And unless I can look to my husband every day and know that he is a kind man whom I can trust with my life, but who also challenges me and challenges himself, I shall never be happy." She smiled briefly, sadly, adding, "And if he cannot make me laugh until I snort like you and Emerson used to when you two teased me within an inch of my life, all the other things are worth little."

"You expect quite a lot from a man, my lady," Duncan said, though without disapproval.

"I admit that is true, and it is but one of the reasons I have decided to remain unmarried," Petra replied, gazing out the window to her garden. She swiveled her eyes back up to his. "Though would it help to know that I expect the same of myself? And that I would only give myself to a man to whom I could offer the very same qualities in return?"

"It does help," Duncan said, his eyes never leaving hers. "And to know that Emerson earned that from you . . . well, I always felt he was the best of men. I know it more now than ever."

Petra felt the prick of emotion behind her eyes while a fullness bloomed within her chest, but she willed them both away to ask about his letters again. Yet she did not get the chance.

Duncan's dark brows had come down to hood his eyes. "But we must return to the matter at hand. This Drysdale. Since returning from the Continent, I have heard certain men speak his name."

He had turned serious all at once, and it took a moment before Petra could collect herself and ask, "Would your brother, Lord Langford, be one of these men?" Petra turned to face him. "And Lord Whitfield? I could name others—Lord Potsford, Josiah Bellingham, Lord Milford."

Duncan regarded her for a moment. "My brother, yes. Of Whitfield, I cannot say. Of Milford, either. But, yes, Potsford and Bellingham were two others whom I heard mention him. When I left for the Continent three years earlier, Drysdale was known to no one—or, at least no one who was willing to mention him."

"But you have heard more."

"Some, yes. Langford was rather unhelpful as to what exactly this Drysdale did for a living," Duncan said, "but he did say that Drysdale had been with Admiral Nelson at the Battle of Copenhagen in 1801, where, though he was but a lowly surgeon's mate, he had been known for being both persuasive and rather cunning."

"Qualities he has not lost, and has honed toward the most evil of ways," said Petra.

"From the bits of your letter that did make sense, I can agree with you," Duncan said. Yet before Petra could retort, he continued.

"My brother implied Drysdale used those talents to earn money after leaving the navy and became a man of all work for an aged peer and his wife. A baron, I think, and one who preferred to live away from society, in Essex. There was something about the baron being scrupulously frugal and leaving Drysdale to look after his wife after he died. As there were no children and the title died with the peer, the house was left to Drysdale in payment for his loyalty and service."

"Fairwinds," Petra said in a quiet voice. "And I have discovered what Drysdale does there." Petra walked to the edge of the sofa to gaze out the window to her garden, somehow needing to be as close to the light and the beauty and the flowers as she could.

"Tell me," Duncan said. He had moved to her side again, but not too close. He was giving her space.

"He runs an asylum for women," Petra began, the color in her garden blurring before her eyes. "For women who are deemed insane or suffer from melancholia, nerves, hysteria. They are remanded by their husbands, fathers, or other male relatives to Fairwinds for a price." She looked up at Duncan. "He has also made it a place for women who are deemed mad because they are difficult, or unfeminine, or headstrong, or obstinate. Fairwinds is a place where men can pay to make the women in their lives disappear. Women like me, Duncan."

To his credit, Duncan did not bluster ridiculous excuses for these men, or suggest that some of the women may indeed be experiencing madness. He merely looked at her, let her talk. And shifted just enough that she could feel the strong hardness of his upper arm lightly touching her shoulder.

"Duncan, every strange thing that has happened started when I began searching for answers about Lady Milford. And she was there. Gwen was at Fairwinds, though she somehow escaped. Sir Hugh Thacker's late wife may have been sent there as well, and soon, possibly, Lady—"

There was a knock at the door, and Smithers entered.

"Forgive me for interrupting, my lady. Young Teddy has arrived at the servants' entrance. He said to tell you he has completed his mission and found this."

Smithers brought forth his right gloved hand and turned it over. In his palm, tied up in a cornflower-blue cotton handkerchief, was a roundish object about the size of a small lemon.

Smithers continued in his calm baritone. "Teddy asked me to explain that he was forced to wait until well past nightfall to retrieve it, as a man he had only seen once before had been surveilling the house. He said to tell you he'd seen the man with a Mr. Drysdale, but he knows not the man's name."

Petra thanked Smithers and asked that he and the servants take special care of Teddy.

Duncan looked amused. "You sent Teddy on a mission?"

"I shall explain once I see what is inside, but this is from Miss Arabella Littlewood," Petra said, then set to work untying the blue handkerchief and releasing the object within. It was revealed to be a small rock, overlaid with a piece of stationery.

Petra smoothed out the page, and she and Duncan both read the words that were scrawled in so much haste that splatters of ink decorated the page, the words appearing to end in mid-plea.

My lady, we beg of you to help us! We are being held prisoner! Lady P. has but three days before she is taken away if she does not agree to giving me in marriage to a horrible man. Do not trust Lord P. Help us

"What the devil—" were Duncan's words even as Petra clutched at his arm.

"Duncan, I had thought it was only Lady Potsford who would be sent to Fairwinds, but Arabella is saying she *and* Lady Potsford are both are in danger from Mr. Drysdale!"

TWENTY-SIX

DUNCAN HAD NOT REPLIED TO HER DECLARATION, BUT WAS reading Miss Littlewood's note again. Though it was not the time to become a foolish woman who gave into petty jealousies, Petra could not help herself. "If all that I have said to you thus far will not convince you to help me in my endeavors, possibly the saving of Miss Arabella Littlewood might persuade you?"

Duncan dragged a hand through his hair, but then turned to look at Petra. "Miss Littlewood is indeed a lovely young woman. She is bright, amusing, and worthy of saving in every way, if my opinion is to be taken into account."

"Ah. Excellent," Petra said, nodding like an automaton.

"But she does not have the qualities I have grown to feel are those best found in a woman I hold in the highest regard." He cleared his throat. "Now, what is it that you require of me?"

He would help her. Petra wanted to release a sigh of relief but simply nodded instead. Collecting herself, she then said, "I plan to travel there—to Fairwinds. And I hope you will accompany me."

"Go on," Duncan said with narrowed eyes, but she took great heart in the fact that he did not say no.

"Gwen has given us little information before she sank into her fever, but she spoke of there being a few women at Fairwinds who are sadly touched in the head, though others are not. Duncan, she spoke of Drysdale performing experiments on them."

"What kind of experiments?" Duncan asked, two lines forming between his eyes, but Petra could only shrug helplessly.

"There was not much time for explanations, Gwen was so feverish. Yet she said there is proof of Drysdale's misdeeds in a ledger that is locked in a desk. She wished to rescue these women, and now I wish to do the same. Gwen was adamant that the information be taken to your grandmother, the duchess, and I agree. For Her Grace has the Queen's ear, and she may be able to put a stop to this horridness. Especially as Lady Potsford is due to be sent there next . . . and so might I be."

"Surely you do not believe your father would—" He stopped when Petra pulled her father's letter from her pocket. He read it, his jaw clenching with anger.

"How do you suppose we get into Fairwinds?" Duncan asked finally.

"That I do not know," Petra said. "I thought we might travel to Essex and take a day or two to scout our surroundings, as it were." She gave him a quick grin. "And once we are inside . . . well, I am still excellent at picking locks."

"That is a very ambitious plan," said Duncan evenly. "And what do you wish of me first?"

Petra smiled for the first time that afternoon, but it was brief. She walked quickly to the shelves filled with books that surrounded her fireplace. Selecting one titled *Maps of Britain*, she handed it to him.

"I am told it will take us around two and one half hours with fresh horses going at a comfortable trot to reach Fairwinds. I know it is in Essex, and somewhere near the River Roding. I recall when we were children, I would give you just such vague directions, all conjured in my head, and you would look at the maps and tell me all the places in England we could go in that amount of time. Will you please do so again for me now?"

Duncan took the book, and the intensity in his face softened. "Ah, yes. You would pretend to be Lady Artemis Byerphin, the half goddess who gave both the Byerley Turk and the Godolphin Arabian to England, and I was Mr. Robert MacBruce, secret and true heir to the Scottish throne." He swiveled amused green eyes up to her. "I seem to recall I once took us into France with the parameters you laid out, Lady Byerphin."

Petra let out a laugh, delighted he would remember their silly names from so long ago, and it was followed by a soft snort. "Only to Calais, Mr. MacBruce." Then she bit her lip, realizing what she had just done.

"Only to Calais, she says," Duncan mimicked with exaggerated outrage as he flipped pages. "As if any other boy of ten years of age could have taken all the stops you laid out that day, the switching of a fast curricle to the post coach—*the bloody post coach*, by the very beard of Zeus—and have you end up in beautiful Calais instead of somewhere north of Birmingham. Ungrateful little . . ."

He'd found the map he wanted that showed London and points east to the Thames Estuary and the North Sea. "Fetch me the note Miss Littlewood left us and a pen, would you?"

Petra, catching sight of her reflection in the gilt-framed mirror near her writing desk, was grateful for a moment to compose herself, for she had been smiling again at how he'd teased her.

Dipping the quill in ink and using the legend at the bottom of the page to mark out the length of a mile onto the edge of the stationery, he said, "A carriage travels at between six and eight miles per hour at a trot, but we shall err on the side of caution and say six miles. Two and one half hours would mean it is about fifteen miles from London, but could be as far as twenty or more miles. You said the village where Fairwinds sits needs to be near the Roding." Pulling out a magnifying glass from his waistcoat pocket, he used it to better read the tiny print. Then one of his long fingers was tapping the map.

"There are two villages I'd wager would be the ideal place for Fairwinds. Abridge or Epping Banks, and I'd bet it's the latter."

"Why do you suppose that?"

He stood up and took the book to stand next to her. He had to lean down to hold the open map book where she could see it, and pointed out both places, his breath gentle on her temples. "Because Abridge, while still small, is not as small as Epping Banks. Just right for an old baron who disliked society, and the perfect place for a blaggard to run an asylum."

In the end, Duncan persuaded Petra to allow him to go on his own to Epping Banks to ascertain if they had discovered the exact location of Fairwinds.

"I shall go immediately, for that will allow me to be back this evening to oversee one of Grandmama's salons."

Petra was grateful, as this would give her more time at Gwen's side. And to pay a call to Caroline as well, for Petra was feeling she must warn her friend that Lord Whitfield may have ties to Drysdale. After seeing Duncan off, Petra spelled Frances for a while at Gwen's bedside, but not before collecting the letters Duncan had never sent her and locking them into the drawer of her writing desk. She wanted time to read them slowly and thoroughly.

"I am afraid she is no better, my lady," Frances said when Petra arrived and took in Gwen's pale, sleeping face. "And if she does not improve in another day or so, I fear we will lose her."

"We shall continue to hope," Petra said. "And I should be grateful if you would call me Petra, as I hope you feel as I do that we are now friends."

Frances smiled her agreement. "However, I believe I could take better care of Lady Milford if she were with me, in my own set of rooms above the apothecary." She went on to explain that her parents lived in a town house in Gracechurch Street, but in her own dwelling she had a cook and a maid, both of which were loyal and trustworthy. "There is also a back entrance where no one would see Gwen carried inside. Besides, I am needed in the apothecary. My father will notice if I am not there soon."

Petra agreed this was sensible, especially as the fate of Forsyth House was now in question. Arrangements were made to transport Gwen during the midday meal, as that meant the other tradesmen on Jermyn Street would be less likely to notice any goings on.

In the meantime, Petra located her lockpicks and spent time practicing her skills on various doors and pieces of furniture in Forsyth House, becoming so quick that she had the tricky lock to the wine cupboard open in mere seconds.

"Well done, my lady!" Annie said. Charles, Mrs. Ruddle, and Mrs. Bing concurred.

"One day, I shall have to thank Duncan and Lynley for locking me in so many rooms when we were playing as children, causing Edward, our former footman, to teach me the skill of picking locks," Petra said with a laugh, sliding the pick back into its spot in the small leather roll made specially to hold her picks and five skeleton keys. "Though in the case of Lynley, I was never completely sure she was playing."

At midday, Gwen did not awaken during the trip to Jermyn Street, where Charles carried her upstairs to a pristinely clean bedroom next to Frances's, with the cook and housemaid already invested in helping Gwen awaken and recover.

In an effort to keep up normal appearances, Petra met with Lottie near the Serpentine after lunch, where they spent a happy two hours letting Fitz and Sable play with some of Lottie's other canine charges. Then teatime was spent with Caroline in her friend's handsome drawing room, which reflected Caroline's personality with its bold upholstery colors and rich fabrics setting off elegantly carved furniture.

"You should not go about this on your own, dearest," Caroline said, after hearing Petra's plans.

"Your words, they mean everything, Caro. But I will have Duncan, and I somehow feel that the fewer people who attempt to access Fairwinds, the better. Lottie will be taking the scrap of pocket fabric to Chancery Lane tomorrow in hopes of determining the identity of Martin's killer. I have asked that she come to you if she requires further assistance."

"And I?" Caroline asked. "What am I to do?"

Petra reached out and grasped Caroline's hand. "If you are willing, I am hoping you will use your charms on Lord Whitfield to gather information. But you must take care in doing so."

"Whatever for? My Whitfield may look like quite the privateer with his black hair, blue eyes, and that delectable beard, but he is rather the pussycat in private."

"I am afraid he may be a pussycat who lies at the feet of Mr. Drysdale," Petra said gently. At Caroline's shocked face, she then explained how he was seen outside Drysdale's place of business. "I think you know many have heard the story of Whitfield and the opera singer," she continued. "I am concerned Whitfield may not be so gentlemanly when a woman attempts to defy him. I am hoping you will use this time to determine if he is worthy of being in your company."

Petra understood just how much Whitfield had come to mean to Caroline when her friend was far from her bright self as they met friends during the promenade hour, even leaving early complaining of a slight headache. Petra, suddenly feeling rather tired herself, collected Annie, and a hackney was hailed. They were about to board when a small figure appeared.

"'Allo, my lady," Teddy said with a grin.

"Your smile is just what I needed to see, Teddy," she told him. "And I thank you for all you have done so far to assist me. Now, what may I do for you?"

"I came about Forsyth House, my lady."

"Indeed? Whatever for?"

"Did you know that the house were being shut, my lady?"

Petra stilled. While the earl had stated in his letter that she had five days to return to Buckfields—something she was not intent on doing, not like this—he was not to have Forsyth House closed for another fortnight. Surely her father had not gone back on his word. "Why, Teddy? What did you see?"

"Watched it happenin' myself, I did," Teddy said. "Went there to see if you were in, just a bit ago. Didn't go no nearer when I saw that

Mr. Drysdale at the door, askin' for you. Another man was with him. Yer butler called him Lord Alling-somethin'."

"Allington," Petra said automatically.

"That's right. Weaselly-lookin' bloke. They went inside, and soon they were comin' out again. Allington said that he speaks for the earl, and the house was to be shut up by teatime. He also said you weren't comin' back. Are you not comin' back, my lady?"

Annie gasped. Petra pulled a coin from her reticule and handed it to Teddy along with a lemon drop, not wanting him to see how angry she was.

"Of course I am, Teddy. In fact, I shall be there directly. Now, be sure to find yourself something to eat, yes?"

Teddy assured her he would, popped the lemon drop in his mouth, and was soon out of sight.

TWENTY-SEVEN

"I do not like this, my lady," Annie said darkly as the hackney arrived at Forsyth House.

"Nor I," Petra agreed, "but I cannot allow Uncle Tobias to have a say in what goes on at Forsyth House. The earl promised a term of two weeks before the house is to be closed, and I intend to hold him to that promise—I intend to have him reverse it, in fact."

Annie offered to be the one to speak to the servants, but Petra declined. "I am mistress of this house, and I will honor my duty."

At the front steps, Petra banged the horse-head door knocker. In minutes, it was answered not by Smithers, but by Agnes, one of the scullery maids.

"Where is Smithers?" Petra asked, brushing past her.

"Gone, my lady. He were turned out by Lord Allington. Only ones here are me and two others, packin' up the silver for transport to Buckfields. Charles took Sable with 'im, as Lord Allington—well, Charles said he'd bring 'er by later."

Petra whisked off her shawl. "Please have whoever is still here meet me in my drawing room. Quickly, Agnes. There is no time to waste."

Agnes swallowed hard and said, "I'll bring up some tea, too, my lady, for he is already there waiting for you."

"Who is waiting for me?"

"Lord Allington, my lady." She bobbed a curtsy, grimacing almost as if she were in a mixed state of fear and pain, and was gone.

"My lady," Annie began. But Petra was furious and did not wait for Annie to say anything further. She strode away, and Annie went silent.

Entering her drawing room like a ship in full sail, Petra found Uncle Tobias lounging in her favorite chair, finishing a sandwich and drinking a glass of wine.

"Ah, my niece," he said, dabbing at his lips with his napkin and rising. "How are you, my dear?"

"I am thoroughly vexed, that is how I am, Uncle Tobias," she said. "What have you done? Why have you dismissed the loyal and longtime servants of this house? And without the earl's knowledge as well? How dare you attempt to speak for him?"

Allington merely smiled and gestured to the sofa next to him. "Why do you not sit and take some wine with me whilst I finish my meal, Petra."

"No, thank you," she said crisply.

But her uncle had picked up a second glass and brought it to her. The manners instilled in Petra made her take it. Then the idea of a bit of wine to calm her down made her take a sip. It was a claret that had not been allowed to breathe, for it tasted off. Still, by thunder, why not? She took another, bigger sip.

"Uncle Tobias, this—what you have done today—is beyond the pale," she said, putting the wineglass down on the pier table.

Something sinister passed over Allington's face. "Beyond the pale? And how dare I? You are the one making a mockery of your father and me, my girl. Making a mockery of our family and all we stand for—and have worked for over the generations."

"That is not true, Uncle," Petra retorted. "I love my papa and my family. I am proud of my family's past, and their legacy. It is my hope that my name will go down in the annals of our family history as a member of the Forsyth and Allington union whom my nephews and their families may say was a woman with spirit, intellect, great love, and abilities."

"You will be forgotten within months of your death if you do not marry and continue your lines, Petra," Uncle Tobias snapped. "You will go down as nothing but a spinster, about whom everyone wondered, 'Why? Why did she never marry? Did she not like men?

Did she not care for children? What was wrong with the Forsyth-Allington families that caused such a beautiful woman to live the rest of her days as a sad, pitiful husk of a woman?'"

Petra felt as if he had laid a hot poker over her soul. She had contemplated these very things herself, and had felt them in every corner of her body and spirit.

"I can only hope that will not be the case, Uncle. I can hope that my nephews will remember me fondly. Talk to their own children about me, and find some way to keep my spirit alive. Such as letting their little girls ride astride. Such as teaching their boys and girls alike to love the outdoors, to be proud of their intelligent minds, to love reading, and smiling and laughing, and to be kind to others. And to advocate for women and their ability to have rights, and teach their own subsequent children to do the same. Making it something that is passed down, in my honor."

Her uncle gave a cruel laugh. "Do you honestly believe that any man worth their salt will advocate for a woman's rights? Much less encourage their sons to do so?"

"My own papa does," she argued. "He may not shout it from the rooftops, or send letters to the *The Times*, or attend meetings, or any of those things. But he sees me as strong, as intelligent, as capable." She felt her throat tighten as emotion mixed with worry even as she continued. "The earl may not always be proud of me—for men and women both are complex creatures who cannot always do the right thing or be held up as the epitome of perfection—but Papa recognizes that I . . . that I *strive* to be a good and worthy person."

Her uncle's slack mouth crept upwards at the sides as he watched her face.

"Ah, but you are no longer certain of this, are you? For you know the earl is displeased, and greatly so. He is most concerned now that he has had time to think upon your decision to become a spinster. Never to marry. Never to give him another grandchild." He gave a soft, derisive tut that was laced with a lascivious gleam in his eyes. "Or do you wish to add the mother of a bastard to your list of sins?"

Petra's eyes narrowed. "Pardon me . . . sins? What sins have I committed?"

Her uncle took a step closer, picking up his wineglass as he did. "It would be my pleasure to list them. Dancing more than is proper at balls is but a start. For I heard you danced seven times at Her Grace's ball."

"Irrelevant. It may be frowned upon by some of the older generation, but it is not an issue amongst so many friends. The duchess herself bade me dance twice."

"Speaking your mind when no man asked for your opinion, then."

"That is exactly why I speak my mind, for a man needs a better opinion to which to listen."

Uncle Tobias smiled thinly, but kept going. "Using your fingers like that of a cat and scratching men who only wish to court you."

Petra did not let herself gasp that he knew this. "Lord Bellingham deserved it with his impertinence."

"Speaking of behavior, yours is most impetuous. Riding astride, and doing so in areas where anyone passing by in a carriage may see you, as I did not so many days ago."

"That lane is on Forsyth land," she snapped. "And no doubt you were looking for me with your Galilean telescope, for no one else would have seen me and known I was a woman."

"There!" He all but crowed. "You are constantly wishing to flout rules, and do so in a way that you justify by the use of loopholes."

"What does it matter if I do flout a rule on occasion, Uncle?" she asked, narrowing her eyes because he seemed to waver in front of her for a moment. "It is the only way a woman may be allowed any freedoms."

"Freedoms, bah!" Uncle Tobias spat. "Women and their freedoms. That is all I am hearing about these days. How women should be allowed to keep their own money after they marry. That they should be allowed to divorce a man they do not love. How they want this, or do not want that. These are tedious and ridiculous arguments that have no merit in the real world. For if women had those rights, then what rights would men have? How would we be considered the better, stronger sex?"

"More absurd a statement I have never heard!" Petra fairly shouted. She was dissatisfied with her reply, but her brain could somehow not think of something better. She must still be tired. Yes, that must be it, she thought as she picked up her wineglass and took another slug. There was not enough wine in the world to make her uncle's drivel worth listening to. Uncle Tobias, however, was already waving the argument away. He was back to her sins.

"And now I have heard you've befriended one of the so-called back-door gentlemen, not to mention that your closest confidante, Lady Caroline, is married to one. Yes, Lady Caroline, for all her good breeding, has become little more than a ladybird, cavorting with a different man at every turn, while assisting her captain in committing his disgusting acts."

"How do you know this?" She felt stunned, weak. *Why do I feel weak?*

"I only had to watch, as would anyone else," Uncle Tobias retorted.

Petra could only gape. She had to hold on to the pier table to keep from stumbling sideways. Her uncle's smile started small and widened. She thought he looked like a dead fish, with his pasty skin and ugly mouth. One that was shouting once more.

"And then declaring yourself a spinster would be at the top of your list of sins, I must say—but only after you spread your legs for your late fiancé first. Oh, ho, ho . . . you thought no one would know, did you not, niece? Indeed, the gossip took a bit to start going around, it is true, but I have it on excellent authority that your Lord Ingersoll himself was one of the first to crow about bedding—"

Smack!

Petra didn't remember taking a step forward, or bringing up her hand. Why, she did not even feel it as her palm slammed against her uncle's cheek. She saw redness blooming in his face, though, which looked farther and farther away, and blurred at the same time. She had the sensation of dropping. *Was that why it was called Kendal Black Drop?*

And she could recall no more.

TWENTY-EIGHT

OH, WHEN DID RHUBARB KICK ME IN THE HEAD?

Petra groaned as her temples throbbed. She lifted a hand to rub her face, but her arms felt too heavy, as if something were pulling them down.

"Annie," she croaked.

There was no answer, though she thought she heard footsteps from somewhere beyond her bed.

"Annie?" she called out again. She became aware that her eyes were not open. She cracked one. Only a sliver of light could be seen peeking through a gap in the drapery. Why was it to her right instead of to her left, as it should be? With another groan, this time accompanied by nausea, she tried to turn onto her side to grasp the bellpull.

Her head and shoulders turned, but her arm did not follow.

She tried again, and once more it was as if something had kept her arm from raising more than an inch or two. She tried to sit up, then sat back as wooziness took over, but it settled after a few moments.

Then the events at Forsyth House began to come back to her. Slowly, as if in a haze that became clearer with each blink. How her own uncle had drugged her wine with opium. For what purpose? And where was she?

Steeling herself, she made the effort to sit up again. Her head lifted, as did her shoulders. Then up to her elbows. Then nothing.

Fear shot through her, waking her better than a splash of cold water, and her eyes flew open wide. She started, felt her wrists jerk sideways, then snap back again to where they had lain a moment earlier. The very same action was happening simultaneously with her legs. They went sideways for a short way, then were pulled back into place.

A scream was building in her throat as she thrashed again. Then it died into silent horror when the thin counterpane that had been laid over her slipped sideways and she saw her left wrist. Encircling it was a thick leather strap secured by a buckle. The end of the strap drew away from her wrist and upward, where it was attached to a link of black iron chain. Her eyes followed the chain over the side of the bed, knowing without seeing it that the chain was secured to the floor.

Slowly, and with a wince at the pain in her skull, she turned her head. The other arm was the same. She tested her legs again, this time hearing the sound of metal chinks moving. She was held in place by restraints.

Emitting a shaky breath, she looked around her. Whitewashed walls without portraits or other adornment. One window with iron bars. A small washstand too far away to reach. A door that was undoubtedly locked.

There was no denying where she was, and fear was clenching her insides.

I am at Fairwinds.

Sounds could be heard out in the halls. Footsteps. From somewhere farther away came the sound of wailing. Then, closer by, came a screech, followed by a woman yelling, "No! No! Nooooooo! I do not want to! Do not make me!"

Petra heard the distinct sound of a slap, followed by shocked silence, then quiet crying. Then a woman's voice, sounding as if it were coming from someone rapidly approaching.

"We do not strike these women, Mabel." It was delivered in a tone that sounded distinctly like that of a head housekeeper. Brisk, brooking no argument, and authoritative.

"Himself does," came the sullen reply, sounding right outside of Petra's door, heard just above the quiet crying. "All the time from what I seen."

The first woman replied, "That's as may be, but *we* do not. I recognize you're new here, but if I see you behaving as such again, you will be dismissed. Now, take Lady Thacker downstairs. Mr. Drysdale merely wishes to observe her." The woman's voice softened marginally even as it increased a bit in volume. "Did you hear that, Lady Thacker? Mr. Drysdale only wishes to look at you."

"It ain't like she understands either way," came the reply, which Petra almost didn't hear over her own gasp at hearing Lady Thacker's name. *She was alive. Not dead from a miasma, but being held here, at Fairwinds!*

"Ow! I thought you said we don't strike round here."

"I said we do not strike *these women*, Mabel," the first woman said coldly. "You deserved a cuffing for your insolence. Take Lady Thacker downstairs to the treatment room, and then come see me afterward as I will reassign you to other, less difficult patients. Now, I must see if our newest has awakened."

It seemed Lady Thacker went away willingly this time, for all Petra heard was shuffling, then the sound of a key being inserted in a lock, and then her door was opened.

In stepped a tall woman with a thin frame and gray hair pulled back severely from her long, narrow face. Her dress was black serge with the lower, more fitted waistline of years past. A chatelaine hung about her waist and made a bright jingling sound incongruous with Petra's increasing level of fear as the woman closed the door and moved swiftly to Petra's bed, carrying a tray with a cup and a small bowl. She put the tray on the washstand and came to stand before Petra, revealing intelligent and soft gray eyes almost at odds with the harsh planes of her cheekbones, chin, and nose. She looked down upon Petra, her eyes seeming to assess every freckle on Petra's face, her eyebrows coming together, mouth slightly twisting, as if . . .

Almost as if she were disappointed in the Lady Petra Forsyth she had found. As if she had expected a version of Artemis, the warrior goddess, and had found nothing but a weak, entitled girl.

"You are awake, then, Lady Petra," the woman said, clasping her hands in front of her. "I am Mrs. Nance, the housekeeper here. You are at Fairwinds, which is an asylum for women. You have been relegated here for your own good by your uncle. Sit up, my lady, and I will give you some water and porridge."

These words sounded routine, and Petra attempted to sit up, but could only barely raise up on her elbows.

"But this is not correct," Petra whispered, her voice cracked and strained, coming from dry lips and mouth. "I do not require being here, Mrs. Nance. You must believe me."

Mrs. Nance looked almost pitying as she put a silver cup to her Petra's lips, as if she had heard those words from every woman in this place. "Drink, my lady. It is only water, I assure you." When Petra began drinking greedily, Mrs. Nance continued. "I have merely come to see if you are awake and to give you a bit of sustenance. Mr. Drysdale will be round to see you and evaluate you." She hesitated, as if she would say more. Then pressed her lips together and gave Petra a spoonful of porridge.

At first, Petra had not felt hungry—the thought of eating when she was restrained like this, plus the pounding in her head, made her feel as if she might vomit—until the porridge met her lips. It tasted good, with a dash of milk poured over the top, plus a small bit of jam. There were only four or five spoonfuls to be had, but Petra was grateful for them. Mrs. Nance dabbed at Petra's mouth with a napkin, picked up the tray, and then turned to leave.

"Wait," Petra said. Something within her was telling her to say something. Something specific, but her mind still felt woolly. What was it?

"You are here for your own good, Lady Petra," Mrs. Nance repeated. "Though I am sorry to have to say so."

"My uncle has no authority to remand me to this place—and my father would never consent to it," Petra said, feeling a new bout of hysteria coming over her even as she said the words, hoping they were true even as the memory of the earl's letter gave her little hope that they would be.

"True," Mrs. Nance said. "The Earl of Holbrook has not fully consented, but I understand he is taking the charges against you laid out by Lord Allington very seriously indeed." She studied Petra again for a moment, bringing her lips together into a thin line, then turned and began walking toward the door.

Petra had not heard any joy in the housekeeper's voice when she'd declared this. And was there not a sadness in the woman's eyes? Again, it was almost as if she expected more of Petra. As if there was something she expected to hear.

"Lady Milford!" gasped Petra when Mrs. Nance was one step from the door. "She managed to find me. She is alive, and she spoke of you."

Mrs. Nance stopped, but did not turn.

"I do not have an opium habit, Mrs. Nance," Petra said, even as her head throbbed with its aftereffects. "My uncle dosed my wine with laudanum."

"There are other reasons why you were sent here, my lady," Mrs. Nance said with a sigh, making Petra feel that the housekeeper was sticking to the lines of a play. Lines written by Drysdale himself, that Mrs. Nance must follow or risk losing her position.

Even through Petra's haze from wine and opium, she knew that it was not so simple for a woman to leave any position, no matter how odious. And from the little Gwen had managed to say before falling ill, Petra knew Mrs. Nance stayed on at Fairwinds to be the person who attempted to give these women some level of protection, even if she likely rarely succeeded.

And suddenly, Petra's mind began to clear, and things that Gwen had said the night Petra found her in her wisteria tunnel at Forsyth House made sense. Gwen had spoken of Drysdale's personal papers and how they could be used against him. However, there was likely no possibility that Gwen would know where Drysdale kept his papers. Not if Gwen were a patient here. Drysdale was undoubtedly too careful. She might have seen him writing things down. Might have guessed he would keep his documents in his office. But know that he kept them in a locked cabinet? No, that information must have come from someone else.

"You helped Gwen—Lady Milford—escape, did you not?" Petra said softly.

Mrs. Nance whirled round to face Petra, glancing quickly back at the door. Petra lowered her voice further.

"You knew Gwen did not deserve to be here—much like several women here, as I understand it—and you wished to help. You are the one who told her where exactly the documents that might serve as proof of Mr. Drysdale's misdeeds could be located. Those documents that might save Gwen, and others like her." Even as Petra said the words, something new came to her understanding. She tried to sit up further, her neck now aching with the angle, in an attempt to keep eye contact with Mrs. Nance, whose fingers had gone to her lips, her eyes wide. Petra knew she had hit at least one mark.

"Gwen must have spoken of me," she said to the housekeeper. "Of my ability to pick locks, possibly. That is why you helped her. So that she might find me. So that I could do what you and she could not."

Mrs. Nance lowered her hand, but did not move to Petra's side. Yet she spoke.

"Lady Milford indeed told me of your determination to assist those who have little ability to help themselves," Mrs. Nance said. "She said you were always kind to her on the days she felt at her lowest. That if you knew what was going on here, you would wish to help these women."

Petra struggled again to sit up, the effort making her want to scream from being restrained while gasping for breath from the exertion. "I do. I will. You must give me the chance. Please, Mrs. Nance."

But Mrs. Nance still hesitated. Her face was drawn and wan, and she wrung her hands. Then she seemed to come to a decision. She turned and walked swiftly to the door.

Petra's heart sank. She would not be able to release herself from these restraints on her own. And how long would it be before anyone noticed she was gone?

Annie's face filled her mind, and tears now burned behind Petra's eyes. What had happened to Annie last night? Petra now realized her lady's maid had gone silent as they strode down the hallway of Forsyth House toward her drawing room. And she only now realized that Annie had not joined her when she confronted Uncle Tobias.

Had Annie been set upon? Was she still well and whole? Was she thinking Petra had abandoned her? Oh, her dearest Annie!

Then, with her internal fortitude at its weakest, the darkest of thoughts managed to come skulking into Petra's mind. Could Annie have been complicit in Uncle Tobias's horrid scheme to drug her and bring her to Fairwinds? Or, could it be that Annie feared for Petra's sanity as well, and had somehow become convinced by Uncle Tobias and Drysdale—like her own dear papa had—that Petra needed to be in this horrid place?

Petra's lips trembled, even as another face with green eyes filled her mind and her heart. Duncan. Where was he? Would he come for her? Or had his mind, too, been tainted by Drysdale and Uncle Tobias?

And what of her papa? Though he had not yet fully agreed to keeping her in this place—had he given Uncle Tobias carte blanche to drug her and bring her to Fairwinds anyway? Her throat was closing with absolute despair, at the feeling of being all alone. She could barely breathe as her chest tightened.

Then the faces of her friends came to mind. Caroline, her dearest friend. Lottie and Frances, two people she had felt close to so quickly. Somehow, she knew they would be frantic when they saw that Forsyth House had been shut, the servants dismissed, and Petra gone. But would they know by now?

From the weak sunlight coming through the window, she knew Caroline would likely not even be awake. Frances and Lottie would, but Frances was still holding vigil at Gwen's bedside. And Lottie said she spent the early hours of her day exercising and working with her dogs. None of them would likely even yet know Petra had gone missing.

She knew that her friends would do all they could to try to rescue her from Fairwinds. And her deepest gut feeling said Annie would as well. For Petra realized she never truly believed that Annie, who had been loyally at her side for so many years, would do such a thing as to hand her over to an odious man like Uncle Tobias, much less an evil one like Drysdale. Not like this. Annie would have attempted to help Petra first. Attempted to set her to rights. Petra felt this with all her heart, and a small part of her constricted chest eased.

Yet there was something else Petra felt strongly, down to her toes, which felt icy in the cold room. Drysdale would know that she, Lady Petra, had allies. And that those faithful to her would wonder after realizing she had gone missing. And Drysdale would do what he could to keep them from rescuing her. For Petra knew she was more than just a patient to Drysdale. She had become a threat to him, to his newfound wealth and status, to his livelihood. And most of all, to his ability to subjugate helpless women, inflicting pain upon them with absolute impunity.

Yes, she, Petra, had been sent here to Fairwinds, but she had a feeling she would not live long to tell about it. Drysdale would make certain of it. Even as fear clutched at her, hot tears of anger welled in her eyes, blurring her vision to the point that she started when she noticed a form standing by her side.

Mrs. Nance. She had returned. Belatedly, Petra noted that Mrs. Nance had been listening at the door for sounds. Now the housekeeper's voice was barely above a whisper. Her thin face was drawn and anxious.

"I have been attempting to do what I can, Lady Petra, but there is so little I can accomplish without losing my position."

"I understand, Mrs. Nance," Petra said.

Something in Mrs. Nance's face seemed to relax for a moment, and then she was talking, as if she needed to unburden herself.

"I was the housekeeper here at Fairwinds when it was a fine house and belonged to the old baron, Lord Harling. When Mr. Drysdale first came here to work for his lordship, he seemed genuinely interested in maladies of the mind, in wanting to help those with afflictions. That was, until Lord Harling died, but three years ago now, and Mr. Drysdale was put in charge of Lady Harling's care. She was always a difficult one, with a nervous sensibility, and he began to practice on her, one would say."

"Like he does to the women here?" Petra asked. She recalled how Gwen could not speak of the things Drysdale had done, but Petra felt as if she must sound as if she already knew. Mrs. Nance nodded once, then canted her head as if to retract her statement in part.

"At first, it was merely different teas made from herbs. I, who am interested in herbal remedies as well, even helped him choose the ones I thought might be of assistance in her ladyship's care. But with each time she showed little improvement, and became more difficult, he began dosing her with laudanum." Mrs. Nance's jaw tightened. "And when it became clear Lady Harling was becoming increasingly unwell in body and spirit . . . well, at first I truly believed Mr. Drysdale felt there was no sense in not attempting new treatments, knowing her ladyship was not long for this world. But I soon began to feel as if he were . . ." She closed her eyes briefly, drawing in a steeling breath. "I felt as if he were enjoying himself every time he saw the baroness in pain. Every time he could produce an ill effect in her. Every time he could produce fear in her eyes. I confess I did not truly understand what I was seeing in him until after Lady Harling died, and he announced the very next morning his intention to turn this lovely house into an asylum."

Petra did not attempt to sit up again, but merely listened, giving the housekeeper her full attention.

"The rooms were quickly converted, and an iron gate erected around the property," Mrs. Nance said with some distaste, looking about the cold, small room, "and during that period he spent more and more time in London, coming back each time with a loftier accent and finer clothes, tossing about names from the highest echelons of society." She pursed her lips, her brows contracting with a memory. "And the first woman came. Then two more in the span of weeks." Mrs. Nance met Petra's eyes, seemingly wanting her to understand. "They were clearly mad, my lady. These poor souls hardly knew their own names, or where they were."

"Lady Milford indicated as much," Petra said.

Mrs. Nance nodded. "And Mr. Drysdale started up again with his experiments. I attempted to intervene when I saw the pain he inflicted, but I was given a choice. Either I could stay, remain head housekeeper, and do my best to make these patients comfortable after what he termed their 'treatments,' or I could be tossed out without a reference. I don't have any family left, my lady, so I have nowhere to go. And I wanted to do what I could." She looked down at her hands, clasped tightly in front of her. "Even if there is very little that I can do other than offer a kindness or two and ensure they stay clean and fed."

"And you offer them respect," Petra said. "Yes, indeed, Mrs. Nance. I heard you speaking outside my door a few moments ago."

Mrs. Nance opened her mouth to reply, but Petra kept speaking.

"Though it be but in a small way, I am acquainted with Lady Thacker. She purportedly died two months ago, but now I am sorry to understand that she is here. And I am even sorrier that she is not one of those women Lady Milford referenced as being remanded here without cause. However, hearing the way you demanded that her ladyship be treated well and with the respect she deserves no matter the state of her mind—the way you yourself spoke to her—has convinced me that the little Lady Milford was able to say about you before falling ill after her journey was the truth."

Two spots of pink appeared on Mrs. Nance's thin cheeks. "Thank you, my lady," she said quietly. But her eyes were troubled still. "Lady Milford—will she survive? I had overheard Mr. Drysdale saying that she had drowned at some point during her escape. I assumed it to be true."

"She is being well looked after, but I cannot tell you if she will survive. Though if her sacrifices, and yours, are to mean something, then I must ask you for your help. If you will simply untie one of my wrists . . ."

She lifted her wrist as far as it would go. Mrs. Nance's hands reached for it, then she brought them back as if she'd put them too close to a fire. Petra's stomach lurched. She wanted to thrash. Being tied to this bed was indeed making her insane. She was barely holding on.

"You will not help me then," she whispered, feeling her lower lip tremble with the words.

"I cannot," said Mrs. Nance. "For Mr. Drysdale told me he will kill me if I do. I am already suspected of helping Lady Milford escape, and he has enlisted some of the other servants to spy on me and report any instances where I could be seen as partial to a patient—especially those who might have the ability to escape if they had help." Her face was pale, but set with determination, and Petra knew. Mrs. Nance was going to leave her to a horrible fate.

Bile was coming up Petra's throat. She swallowed it back, and with it another urge to thrash like a wild thing. The wish to do so was so strong and her fingers were clenched so tightly into her palms that she could feel her nails piercing her skin. She was perspiring. Oh, Lord, she was too warm. The sweat was under the leather straps on her wrists and ankles, making them chafe as she twisted and pulled against her restraints. Mrs. Nance was looking at the watch attached to her chatelaine.

"Mr. Drysdale will be here soon," she said.

Petra could not look at the housekeeper. She stared up at the ceiling, clenching her teeth together for fear of lashing out at the housekeeper with cruel words—with anger that would only make her look and sound more like a madwoman. She would need Mrs. Nance's tendency toward giving small kindnesses after Drysdale began treatments on her, whatever those treatments would be. She wanted to ask Mrs. Nance what to expect but could not make herself do so. Maybe it would be better not to know. At least this first time.

No, she, Lady Petra Forsyth, was indeed no Artemis, no warrior goddess. She could do no more unless someone was willing to help her. She must resign herself to her fate.

I am strong. I will bear up as best I can against whatever Drysdale does to me. I must hold on as best I can, and hope someone will come.

She told herself this, even as she did not believe it. Even as she made herself think of Duncan. Of Annie, and her friends. Of her own father, who had always seemed to respect her strong will. Who only seemed to worry about her as of late, when he began to listen to the opinions of other men instead of trusting his own. Instead of trusting his own daughter.

Petra felt the muscles in her jaw ache with how tightly she was clenching her teeth. And then she bit her lip after she pulled in a shaky breath through her nose and heard the damp sounds that proved she was not strong at all. That she was crying.

She closed her eyes when she heard Mrs. Nance take a step back from her. And then she heard the sound of footsteps outside. The confident footsteps of a man. And her door opened.

TWENTY-NINE

"Well?" said Drysdale in that soft, smooth voice Petra had not been able to forget.

Her stomach contracted, and she did not think she was mad to believe she heard a sense of satisfied excitement in that one word. Like a cat who has finally trapped the bird that had been flitting away every time it attempted to pounce.

And now, as she smelled the scent of his shaving soap as he strolled languidly to her right side, she knew the cat had come to play with her. To frighten. To torture. And then, she felt sure, to kill—simply to prove to the little bird that he could. And to teach her a lesson at the same time.

"Lady Petra has just awakened, Mr. Drysdale," Mrs. Nance said in a tone so stony it sent every last shred of hope in Petra's heart tumbling as if it had been pushed down a set of stairs. "Though only just. She is in and out of consciousness."

Petra stiffened inwardly at these untrue words, then made a show of letting her head loll toward Mrs. Nance, her eyes fluttering open halfway. Mrs. Nance was staring hard at her, her mouth tightening a bit more, as if to warn Petra not to contradict her.

"Has she spoken?" Drysdale asked.

"Only mumbling thus far, Mr. Drysdale," answered the housekeeper. "She should be awake fully in the next few minutes. Shall I come fetch you when she is?"

Without warning, Petra felt thick, callused fingers on her chin, jerking her head to face center. She winced, closing her eyes again as if sleepy and only mildly agitated by an attempt to waken her.

And then her left cheek was on fire, her jaw screaming with pain. She hadn't anticipated the slap. Hadn't heard it, and hadn't even felt it until a heartbeat after it happened. Her head jerked sideways as her eyes flew open, watering as she gasped for air. Vaguely, she felt her wrists being lifted, felt them lighten for a moment, heard the sound of chains falling to the ground. Then her wrists were pulled together, linked by a shorter chain. It had happened so quickly, all in the few moments Petra had been stunned into doing absolutely nothing.

"I think you are awake now, Lady Petra, are you not?"

Luca Drysdale, with his cold blue eyes and rapidly graying dark hair, was standing with his hands behind his back, smiling down at her with great satisfaction. He was dressed in shirtsleeves and waistcoat the color of a fiery sunset shot through with golden threads that swirled and bent before her eyes, which were blurred with tears.

"Where am I?" she croaked. It wasn't hard to sound as such when her jaw was aching.

"Where are you?" Drysdale drawled. "Why, do you not know, Lady Petra? Does this happen to you often? Where you awaken and do not know where you are?"

In response to this, Petra merely attempted to move her arms and legs. Then, feeling that it was expected behavior, she frowned and began thrashing, feeling the straps cutting into her wrists and ankles again. She stopped after a few moments, breathing heavily. She did not have to feign the terror coursing through her. Drysdale's eyes were triumphant. It was what he wanted to see.

The counterpane that had given her a margin of warmth had finally slipped to the floor, leaving Petra feeling exposed, with only a thin cotton chemise that was not her own to cover her.

Drysdale's eyes traveled the length of her, looking almost aroused when they rested on the restraints and then the chemise that had risen up almost to her knees while its bodice barely covered her with each rapid rise and fall of her chest.

Petra tried again to bring her legs together but could not. She struggled again, wanting to scream, all while becoming angrier than she had ever been in her life. Indeed, at this moment, she felt as if she were losing her grip on reality. She was overwhelmed with emotions, and with the intense fear that came from being restrained and vulnerable. She swallowed them down as best she could.

Then Drysdale hooked the chain holding her wrists in front of her with one of his fingers and hauled her up into a sitting position. He was so strong, she so weak, that she came flying forward, off balance once more. Her hair had been taken out of the neat chignon Annie had fashioned the day before, and her reddish-blond curls came flying into her face. Petra was pathetically grateful when Mrs. Nance helped steady her, brushing Petra's hair gently from her cheeks.

Yet Drysdale shot the housekeeper a scathing look that had her stepping back. And when he jerked his head in the direction of the door with a "Go ready the treatment room," fear closed down Petra's throat. She tried to beg Mrs. Nance not to leave, but the housekeeper was out the door in three swift steps, never once even meeting Petra's eyes, or replacing the counterpane.

Drysdale's chuckle made her eyes snap to his as Mrs. Nance's footsteps could be heard fading away. "But where are my manners? I have not answered your question. You are at Fairwinds, Lady Petra. You have been remanded here by your uncle, who feels it is in your best interests."

"My uncle has no authority to do so," Petra retorted, though it sounded weak from her dry lips.

"Oh, but he does, Lady Petra," said Drysdale with no attempt to hide the smugness in his voice. "You see, Lord Allington was given the authority by your late mother before she died. Did you not know of the provision in her will? The will that left you monies so that you could shame your father and your family name by becoming a spinster of independent means?"

The smile grew wider, the voice grew silkier as Petra looked up at him. "No, I can see by your face that you were unaware of this truth. Your father, the earl, was not trusted to raise you properly, and thus, your mother appointed Allington as your guardian. And the inheritance left to you has several provisions, one of which is that it can be overturned if you are declared unfit to hold your own purse strings."

"You are a liar, sir," she snapped. "As is that odious man who is my uncle. There are no such provisions in my inheritance, and while my mama did ask Lord Allington to assist in my upbringing, he was never made my guardian. Therefore, I demand you release me this instant."

Drysdale gave a chuckle that gave Petra the collywobbles. "Oh, but while it may not have been the truth a few days ago, it is indeed the truth now."

Petra was rendered stupefied by this. And then, her haze clearing, she thought, *Lady Vera was right. Uncle Tobias had indeed found a way to take what was not his.*

"Damn and blast, Uncle Tobias, you rude, white-feathered, sneaking cur of the worst sort!" she exhorted, jerking so hard in an attempt to separate her wrists that pain shot through the muscles in her shoulders and upper arms in protest even as her back arched.

Yet this just made Drysdale tip his head back and laugh. "Oh yes, I knew you would be a fighter. That's what made me so intrigued when I met Allington and began hearing of your exploits. And I was proven correct when I met you at Forsyth House. You need someone like me to help you, Lady Petra."

Struggling against her leg restraints this time, Petra stopped instantly, watching again as his eyes roamed over her person. The disgust could not be washed from her tongue as she interpreted his words.

"You cannot be in earnest. You actually wish me to marry you?"

For a moment, Drysdale looked nonplussed then laughed once more, though this time it held a brittle quality at Petra's distaste.

"Now I am sure you need me more than ever, my lady, for your sense of self-confidence is overdeveloped and most unfeminine." His voice now included a singsong quality as he continued to taunt. "No, I would not marry a spinster like you, who I am certain is already drying up as we speak." Petra was horrified when his hand went to her ankle, thumb caressing her ankle bone for a moment, then moving slowly up her leg as he continued. "I, in fact, will soon be taking a lovely young woman as my bride, just as soon as her shrew of a guardian arrives here and learns that being an obstacle in my path is much more painful than giving her ward's hand to me in marriage. Though, until then, I expect you'll do for a time or two. After all, I understand you enjoy it."

Petra's skin was crawling from Drysdale's touch, but she knew he was baiting her. He wanted her to react to his words so that he could use her anger to his advantage. Thus, she focused on what else he had said.

"Lady Potsford is the guardian of whom you speak," she said. "You are planning to imprison her ladyship here in order to force Miss Arabella Littlewood to marry you."

Drysdale's pupils had grown large as his hand grasped her calf and moved up to her knee. She tried to jerk it away, but this seemed only to please him more.

"I knew you had been asking questions when you should not have been, Lady Petra," he said softly, caressing the sensitive area on the inner side of her knee. "Uncovering truths that your emotional female mind cannot possibly wrap itself around without becoming distressed. Proving you are reckless and impetuous enough to arrange to meet a footman out in public, causing him to lose his life in the process. And this after he'd already lost his position at Strand Hill because of me. But it had to be done, as I've found that having loyal servants around impedes my ability to extract a woman from her home in a peaceful manner." Drysdale's lips formed into a smirk. "Of course, a dose of Kendal Black Drop works wonders as well."

Petra stilled, her lips parting in a silent gasp as she did so. "You. It was you who had Lady Milford's servants dismissed. And you killed Martin. But the tailor said none of your coats had been damaged, that the pocket flap I found was not yours."

Drysdale began running a finger up the inside of Petra's lower leg. "I shall have to give my tailor a reward for leading you astray.

Oh, Lady Petra, you are not only suffering from a psychosis, but you are also naive. I knew better than to wear one of my good coats when I went to the Green Park to meet the talkative young footman before your . . . assignation with him. He needed to be silenced, you see. He was not only asking rather uncomfortable questions about his former mistress, Lady Milford, but he had also been underfoot too many times when my name was mentioned amongst certain men of rank. Oh, it was his job to be about and at the ready, naturally, but Lord Potsford did not care for the way the young footman looked at him when Potsford discussed me and my services with Lord Bellingham at Her Grace's ball. I understand the footman even had the impertinence to frown at hearing the Marquess of Langford speaking with another peer about me."

"With Lord Whitfield," Petra said, hatred bubbling in her at what Drysdale had said about Martin, while also sparing a thought for Caroline, who would be despondent when her lover's duplicitous nature was confirmed.

Yet Drysdale only chuckled wryly. "Ah, Whitfield. He is one of the few who has managed to elude me. He refrains from becoming frivolous with his money, or with his mistresses, thus giving me little leverage over him." His small eyes narrowed. "Unlike most of the men of the ton, who are so bored with their idle lives, who do not give themselves over to pursuits that keep them out of gambling dens and whorehouses that they offer me a veritable banquet of ways to keep me in the life to which I have become accustomed."

Petra gaped at him. "You mean to have me understand you are not merely wishing to take in women who truly require a stay here at Fairwinds. You also seek out situations where men become indebted to you. And you discharge those debts when their wife, daughter—or indeed niece—is remanded here to this asylum. So you may experiment on them."

Drysdale looked amused. "How else will I discover the mysteries of the mind and how it works if I do not have a varied group on which to test my theories?"

"Is that what you call what you do? *Testing theories?*" Petra asked, incredulous.

"You have no idea what I do here, Lady Petra," Drysdale said, his eyes going up and down her person once more, lingering at her chest, which she could not settle into a calmer rhythm. "Without my work, some men would not know if their wives' and daughters' inconsistencies are merely part of the female brain or some lack of proper functioning within the woman herself. I have given many a man a clearer understanding of the women in their lives."

He then made a gesture as if to encompass the house. "It is not as if I simply collect women here in order to treat them. I only have so many beds. I save the majority for those unwanted women of rank who need a place to go to live out their days. And the other beds? Well, they are for women like you, who are experiencing some level of madness that may not yet be incapacitating. Still, it is better for them, and all those around them, if said women are evaluated and, if possible, taught to control themselves and their impulses. Behave more femininely. Relinquish their headstrong nature. Submit to their men."

"Those men who you hope become indebted to you, again, you mean," Petra said coldly. "After succumbing to strumpets and cards once more."

"Precisely," Drysdale said. "I am glad to see the effects of your opium habit have not addled your brain too much, Lady Petra. Though in your uncle's case, it was mostly debt from losing consistently at cards, for even the whores want little to do with him. In fact, after he began losing to me, Allington went into further financial difficulty by buying the debts of a Mr. Brown from Chartham so that I might release Brown's daughter into his care in order to secure him a wife."

Somehow, this idea that Uncle Tobias resorted to buying himself a wife did not come as a shock to Petra. Drysdale was lifting one shoulder, as if this line of conversation was of little interest to him.

"Of course, he came to understand Miss Brown is only willing to lie with him until she is with child—and that she never wishes to lie with him at all, preferring the company of a Lady Amanda instead, thus making it highly doubtful a child will come to be anytime soon. Allington then found that if he could send you to me, he could reverse your inheritance, bringing it back to his own coffers, discharging all his debts, and ridding himself of a niece who was actively seeking to embarrass him and the Allington family with her announcement of spinsterhood. He would keep other Allington holdings in his hands as well."

When Petra blinked at this, confused, Drysdale deigned to explain.

"For you do know, do you not? That if Allington does not marry and bear a legitimate child, then by a portion of the entail that came about when the Earl of Holbrook married your mama and saved the fortunes of your grandfather, the former Lord Allington, you and your brother are to receive the Allington estates and monies?"

"No," Petra said in a small voice. "I did not know."

"Ah well," Drysdale said, sounding pleased to have shocked Petra with knowledge of her own family. "But it does not matter now. Allington will marry Miss Brown, and she will give him children, even if she will be dosing herself with the Black Drop and dreaming of Lady Amanda each time she lies with him. You have been legally remanded to my care, and even your father can do little about it—if he even wished to."

"Which he will!" Petra returned stubbornly, yelling the words as if doing so will carry her hopes all the way to Suffolk. "My papa will not stand for me to stay in this place and be mistreated!"

A cruelness came back into Drysdale's curving lips. "Do you really think so, Lady Petra? Because you should not. You should not expect that the earl will ultimately believe you are worth the amount of money he would need to cover Allington's debts to me. For your father has been incurring debts of his own and has little to spare." Then Drysdale made a brief motion with his hand, as if to shoo away a pesky fly. "Oh, but they are related to a string of underperforming racehorses, owners who have been late in paying their fees, and other such boring reasons, and not to other vices, but it is of no consequence. Holbrook knows that Allington is more than willing to use your monies to cover the earl's debts as well as his own."

"He will not require that assistance," Petra said, straightening her shoulders as best she could. "Once the owners pay and his next crop of thoroughbreds start to show their mettle and win, everything shall be well."

Drysdale's eyebrows rose up briefly even as the corners of his mouth turned down, displaying his lack of faith in her assertion.

"Yes, but the earl is most concerned with your behavior as of late. I made certain of it. And the knowledge that his racing stables could be saved by having your inheritance reversed is of great interest to him. Even as, naturally, he wishes to help you understand where you have erred in your choices, and hopes you will be willing to return to a better path during your stay here."

"So, I am only here on a temporary basis?" Petra asked quickly, hating herself for the hope that was rampant in her voice.

Drysdale seemed to find this comment amusing, tapping the leather cuff about her wrist with his finger.

"If you were any of the other women here, I might be inclined to tell you that is the truth, Lady Petra. But you have deliberately sought to undermine me and to disrupt everything for which I have worked. Thus, no, you will not be leaving here. And if you are believing Mr. Shawcross might come to your aid in time, then I may add that to your list of delusions. Allington knew Shawcross would come in search of you, as would your lady's maid and your friends. Thus, with the help of your dear cousin, Lady Wyncroft, who has quite the talent for writing in other hands, they all received letters from you, telling them that you have decided to go away for your health. To, oh, I believe it is your father's small holding in Cornwall. By the time they understand you did not, you will likely not be fit to return to society."

At the sound of a wail from outside the door, he laughed. "No, not if you respond to your treatments the way Lady Thacker and so many others have. You may end up just like Lady Thacker, and not even recall your own name."

With this, his hand moved swiftly upward and squeezed her thigh as he leered at her like Josiah Bellingham had at Her Grace's ball.

Was that really only four nights ago? Petra thought, her mind so full of fearful thoughts that it was happy to go back in time for a moment. The ball seemed like another lifetime ago. When things were sane. When her life was ordered. When the worst she must face was a daily reminder of her heartbreak in the form of a beautifully rendered miniature of Emerson that sat upon her writing desk, and a small worry that she would never again feel the touch of a man whom she cared about.

Duncan's face, his laugh, his voice, they were all suddenly in Petra's mind, and she felt the very real anguish that she might never see him again. Never truly resume the friendship that had been cultivated since they were children.

"I demand that you stop this instant," she said with as much authority as she could muster as Drysdale's pressure increased on her leg.

"Oh, but my lady, your days of being obeyed are over," Drysdale said. He ran his hand down her leg to her ankle. "But I will untie you, as it is time to go for your first treatment."

As soon as her right leg was free, Petra tried to kick out at him, but then her head was whipping sideways once more, stars bursting in her eyes. She felt a sharp sting and the trickle of blood running down her cheek. He'd used the back of his hand this time, allowing a ring that graced his third finger to inflict extra pain.

"Get up," he growled. Grabbing the short chain between her wrists, he hauled her from the bed. Petra stumbled out onto bare feet and icy-cold floors. Before she could get her bearings, she was being pulled toward the door, just as a bloodcurdling yell came from the other side.

THIRTY

"SHE'S GONE OFF 'ER 'EAD AGAIN!" SHOUTED SOMEONE AS there came sounds like a rampaging bull in the hallway. A crash. The sound of something breaking. More screams, sounding as if they were coming from the bedroom next door, and muffled as if from other rooms.

"Where's Mr. Drysdale?" called another terrified voice, which then cried out as if the person was struck by something.

"Mr. Drysdale! You must come quickly!"

It was Mrs. Nance. Then came another crash. Petra's eyes flew open as Drysdale gnashed his teeth, growled out a curse, and stalked to the door, yanking it open.

"What is—"

And a wraith in a white chemise flew at Drysdale with a guttural scream. Arms outstretched, dark hair flying wildly behind her, something in a pale, matte blue held fast in her right hand. Drysdale barely had time to react as she swung her arm up in an arc and lunged.

Drysdale made an angry sound and stumbled sideways. The wraith had caught him in the arm, and blood bloomed on his pristine white shirt.

The wraith had stopped, momentarily stunned after what she had done. Her hand opened, and what looked to be a long, jagged piece of a broken Wedgwood saucer—now stained with blood—could be seen. Hearing Petra's gasp, the woman looked up at Petra with huge hazel eyes and almost childlike curiosity through a curtain of straight brown hair, cocking her head to one side, as if some part of her mind was surprised to see another person. There was no overt recognition in her eyes, but Petra thought she saw a spark, as if somewhere, in the back of her mind, the woman recognized an acquaintance from her past.

"Run, Lady Thacker!" Petra yelled, seeing Drysdale righting himself, a look of absolute fury in his eyes.

Lady Thacker, whom Petra knew to be about her own age, turned and sprinted out of the room with the speed of a streetwise urchin like Teddy. She dodged the grasp of Mrs. Nance, a furious Mr. Drysdale not far behind, pulling Petra along with him into the wide hallway.

"Take her downstairs and secure her," he growled to Mrs. Nance, shoving Petra into the housekeeper's arms as Lady Thacker sped down the stairs, slapping aside the outstretched hands of another servant along the way and jabbing those of another with the broken shard of porcelain before disappearing. Another scream was heard, followed by a crash of crockery, and then someone yelling, "Betsy, you left the door open, you daft cow! You'd best go after her before himself finds out!"

"Get out of my way!" bellowed Mr. Drysdale a moment later. There was another crash, like that of two bodies colliding into a table. Then the sound of a slap, and of the injured party wailing. Betsy, no doubt.

"Go and help Mr. Drysdale!" Mrs. Nance ordered the two other servants. They had been dithering as to what to do, their eyes popping, glancing back and forth between the stairwell, the retreating Lady Thacker, and other doors, where sounds of wailing and even banging could be heard. Mrs. Nance took the arm of Petra, who was bloodied and still bound at the wrists, saying, "I'll take this one downstairs."

As the others scurried off, Petra and Mrs. Nance were still in the hallway, some ten steps from the stairs Lady Thacker had flown down, pursued by Mr. Drysdale.

There were closed doors all along the hallway, including several on the far side as the hall made a right turn. Some of the doors looked original to the house, while others were much newer. All had padlocks securing the women inside. Like Petra's room, the walls of the house were bare and whitewashed. No rugs adorned the floor, and no tables, chairs, cabinets, sconces, or any other fripperies graced the hallways. The only color came from the large Venetian window opposite the top of the stairs, where a glorious spring day brought in sunlight and showed riotous shades of green from the abundance of nearby trees that seemed to surround the house, hiding it from any outside eyes.

Petra could tell they were on the second floor of the house, as there were no other visible stairwells for what would have been any abovestairs residents, and Lady Thacker had made it to the outdoors quickly. That meant Fairwinds was only two stories, not including the attics, and was of a comfortable size for the former Lord and Lady Harling, but nowhere near the size of Buckfields. Or even Forsyth House, for that matter.

"Quickly," Mrs. Nance hissed. "We must be seen taking you downstairs and toward the treatment rooms. Then you will knock me down and escape. Lady Thacker is very fleet of foot, and it usually takes some time to capture her again."

"Will she be hurt?" Petra asked worriedly.

"You must not concern yourself with her fate at the moment, my lady," replied Mrs. Nance, but her tone was grim. "You can ride well, as I understand it?"

"Of course," whispered Petra as they took the stairs, Mrs. Nance holding on to the chain that secured Petra's wrists together. With the din all around them of yelling servants and unseen female patients wailing or banging on their doors, Mrs. Nance could barely be heard as she whispered in rapid short declarations.

"His horse is already being saddled. I saw to it. There are no men allowed on this property, except for Carver, the brute of a guard at the gate, and Wilkins, the stable lad. You must wait until I can send Wilkins in the wrong direction, and then you will ride to the gate. For the drive is too long for you to make it on foot without being caught. Carver will be assisting Mr. Drysdale in capturing

Lady Thacker. The gate will be securely padlocked, but there is a secondary key kept in Carver's gatehouse."

They'd reached the bottom step, where two servants were busy cleaning up crockery from the herringbone oak floor, another was leading a still-wailing Betsy off toward what was undoubtedly the servants' area, and Mr. Drysdale was nowhere to be seen. Mrs. Nance briskly told two other servants to go upstairs and help calm the patients, and they quickly obeyed. Then Mrs. Nance pulled Petra around a corner, and through another door.

The hallway went in two directions. To the left and some twenty or more steps in the distance, the bare wood floors gave way to a handsome carpet in rich shades of red, gold, cream, and blue. Light could be seen from more windows. And the corner of a sofa, offering the temptation of comfort, of reality, the familiarity of a grand home. In the other direction, and much closer, another door was opened to show the hallway narrowed to what appeared to be four more rooms.

Before Petra knew what was happening, Mrs. Nance had lifted one of the chains from her chatelaine. It held a key, and she swiftly unlocked the small padlock that held Petra's wrists together. The black iron links dropped from the leather cuff about her right wrist to dangle harmlessly from the cuff on her left. Petra then made quick work of unbuckling both.

She was free.

From behind the door, Mrs. Nance produced a simple cotton dress in an unattractive brown color, held it out to Petra, and pointed down the longer hall, toward the light and the color. Her voice was breathy with anxiety.

"Now, my lady, put this on. These are kept for women who . . . become unclean after their treatments. No one will think it odd if you are wearing it." Then she produced a pair of worn and scuffed half boots.

Grateful, Petra pulled the dress over her chemise. It was too large for her, but added extra warmth and modesty. The boots went on easily, and were just a bit too large as well, but Petra cared not. Mrs. Nance was still speaking, even as she handed Petra a small flannel, dampened with water, which Petra took and used to begin wiping the blood from her face.

"I will pretend you knocked me down and I twisted my ankle. You will go down this hall, where one of the windows is already unlatched. From there, you will need to hide behind the boxwood hedges and head in a southwesterly direction. The stables are not far. You must wait behind the hedges until I come running out and sending Wilkins in the opposite direction and then go for the horse. He is an easygoing animal, and you should not have any problem with him—though he is rather tall. I hope you can get on his back without issues. If not—"

But Petra stopped her, while continuing to dab at her face.

"I cannot leave yet, Mrs. Nance. Not without those documents."

"But my lady, you must," Mrs. Nance protested. It was clear from the sudden pallor of her face that the thought of Petra staying even a moment longer was not one she expected. "He will kill us both if we are found. And he might give one of us to Carver first."

"I fully understand how much you have risked, Mrs. Nance," Petra said. "But you must know that I cannot leave without proof of what terrible things are going on here. I must have them to ensure the safe release of those women here without cause. And to ensure more humane conditions for those women whose minds have rendered them in need of an asylum."

Mrs. Nance looked aghast. "You are determined to continue? My lady, you have a chance to escape this place. To find help and send those who might assist us. Some sympathetic men, perhaps."

Petra scoffed as she worked her sore wrists and ankles, which were chafed and burning, with cuts already oozing blood. She touched her cheek, which had stopped bleeding but was still smarting.

"And do you think I will be believed, Mrs. Nance?" she asked as she gestured to various parts of her person. "I well and truly look as if I belong here. Any man who sees me will no doubt seek to return me." She lifted one eyebrow. "For I would expect there is a reward for any escaped woman found, yes?"

Mrs. Nance pressed her lips together, but nodded. Then the years of training as a housekeeper, where being ruffled was a rare occurrence and quickly remedied, straightened her spine and sharpened her wits.

"You'll need to go to his study, then," she said.

Petra nodded. "Tell me what I should look for and take."

"All his documents are kept in locked cabinets," Mrs. Nance said. "The most recent files are in the cabinets located to the left of his desk. Older ones of past patients who have died here are in the cabinets to the right. There is also a ledger which contains damning information concerning men of rank who owe debts to Mr. Drysdale and such. If you wish to know my opinion, my lady, I would say you should take the ledger and several documents regarding those who are currently here, and a few of those who have died—though I truly believe that even one of the documents will be enough to raise an alarm with someone of integrity."

Petra glanced toward the room with the sofa. "His study is this way?"

"Through the door at the far side of the room is a hallway. To the left is his study, to the right, his bedchamber. My lady?"

Petra had already turned to leave. When she looked back, Mrs. Nance was holding something out to her. It was a small leather roll, tied at its center in a monk's knot.

"My lockpicks!"

"They were on your person when you were brought in by Lord Allington, my lady," said Mrs. Nance.

A shot of something—hope, maybe?—ran up Petra's spine. "Truly?" She had not had them in her pocket or in her reticule, so that must mean her uncle had gone through her personal effects in her bedchamber. *Odious, odious man!* "But why would he have brought them here?"

"I believe your uncle wished to use them as visible proof of your unfeminine ways." Mrs. Nance's eyes had rolled with irritation when she said this, and despite it all, Petra nearly laughed out loud.

Shouts could still be heard within the house, and Mrs. Nance held up one hand and went to look out the window.

"I can see Mr. Drysdale at the far edge of the garden. Lady Thacker has treed herself again," she said with a surprising touch of humor. Then she frowned. "Carver is approaching with a ladder. I have seen this scenario before, and it is an ugly one. I would say you have but ten minutes, my lady. Possibly a bit less." She removed a key from her chatelaine. "This will get you into his study."

"Thank you, Mrs. Nance," Petra said. "Now, if I do not make it back to this window in time, you must pretend as if I have attacked you. I could not forgive myself if you incurred his wrath in helping me. You must promise me you will do this."

Mrs. Nance, with her thin face, severe hair, and kind eyes, looked Petra up and down for one moment. "And I could never forgive myself if I did not help you, for you are their best hope for a better life. Until then, I will continue to do whatever I can."

Petra nodded. Then, on a whim, she curtsied to the housekeeper.

"What was that for, my lady?" Mrs. Nance said, two spots of pink blooming on her pale cheeks.

"Because you have the heart of a duchess, Mrs. Nance. And one always curtsies to a duchess."

And before Mrs. Nance could reply, Petra glanced out the windows, then dashed past them. Moments later, she was in Mr. Drysdale's study.

THIRTY-ONE

LOCKING THE DOOR, PETRA TURNED AND TOOK IN THE WHOLE of the room.

A large desk atop an Axminster rug, a smaller desk against the far wall, a door that likely led through to Drysdale's bedchamber, and cabinetry along the back wall. The one table between the windows held nothing but a clock showing it to be just after ten o'clock in the morning. Several paintings were on the walls, including a rendering of the house titled *Fairwinds, Home to His Lordship, the Eighth Baron Harling, 1807.*

Fairwinds was constructed of red brick with a hipped roof and three dormer windows beneath two chimneys. Decorative stonework was over the fluted portico front door. Five large windows faced the lawn on the second floor, and four on the ground floor. There were no outside stairs or any other decoration, natural or man-made, to give interest to the prospect. Except, she noted, for a few mature trees and shrubs on each side of the house, all of which had grown significantly taller in the eight years since the painting had been completed, further shrouding the house from any and all who wished to see it.

Yet that was the extent of the furnishings. The room was sparse otherwise and immaculately clean.

Drysdale likes control and order wherever he is, it would seem, she thought dryly, as she made haste to the cabinets.

Then she stopped when she noticed movement outside the windows. It was a group of five Fairwinds servants, all in dresses of plain dark brown with white aprons and caps. Their expressions were dour and their thick arms and necks spoke of the strength required to subdue a thrashing woman. Petra shivered involuntarily as she saw they were walking with—no, more like herding—a group of nine women out onto the lawn, all wearing thin, white chemise-like gowns topped with light shawls.

Once they were outside, the servants went to a set of benches near the house and sat, not interacting with their charges, nor seemingly caring when one lifted her dress all the way to her bare breasts and began twirling in a circle, singing a song Petra recognized as a nursery rhyme.

Petra watched, now understanding even more what Gwen had said. A couple of the women's faces were blank, as if walking around with little understanding of their bodies doing more than moving forward. One had soon sunk down to an ungainly position in the grass and started to slowly pick at the blades, one by one, her mouth open in a gape, like a drunkard after far too much ale. Or like Papa's old steward, who had experienced an apoplexy, leaving the left side of his face permanently slackened.

Petra wondered if this was what had happened to the woman as she saw yet another walking slowly, eyes wide and terrified even as her face was seemingly devoid of expression otherwise. Her shoulders were hunched and high as her ears, as if she feared a monster would leap out of the grass and devour her at any moment, but did not exactly know why she felt as such. It was a heartbreaking tableau to witness.

Yet the other six women were different. They paired off in twos, taking each other's arms, and began to stroll around the perimeter of the lawn, much like Petra and Caroline had done at the ball when taking a turn about the gardens. And while their expressions were sad and miserable, these women's heads were held high, and they were . . . What were they? Petra felt the word would be "cognizant," of themselves and their surroundings. They also seemed to be supporting one another, as if finding strength by banding together. And when one looked as if she had begun to cry, the other turned somewhat sideways so their keepers would not see.

Petra peered desperately at the women, wondering if she would recognize any of them as being the wives, daughters, and sisters of peers, yet she could not be sure. But the very sight of those six women holding their heads high in the face of not knowing if they would ever see their freedom again, or indeed would ever be allowed to be themselves again, gave Petra new determination.

At the wall of cabinets, she lowered herself to her knees, taking note of the locks that held them closed. They would be child's play to open, thank the gods.

She spun round to Drysdale's desk. Large and imposing, it featured a carved coat of arms in miniature at each corner. As the desk seemed long used and old, Petra surmised it had belonged to the dead baron. All its drawers, seven in all, had been fitted with locks as well, and ones that looked much newer than the desk at that.

Returning to the cabinets once more, she deftly inserted her picks and was relieved to feel the tumblers move easily. Inside, she did indeed find files, but they were relating to Fairwinds, the house, and the running of it. *Damn and blast, Drysdale must have rearranged some of his files.*

Petra unlocked other cabinets. More useless files. But then she discovered a large supply of laudanum, Kendal Black Drop, and other types of opium. But she had not yet found any files that seemed to be for the current residents.

She glanced at the clock. Almost five minutes had passed. She had but little time.

Swiftly, she moved to the desk, moving the chair aside. It was her last hope of finding any substantial proof.

The last drawer at the bottom left was a large one, and Petra found a thick sheaf of papers, rolled up and bound with a piece of black ribbon. They looked to have been hastily thrown inside, as if they were destined for the burn pile, but Drysdale had not yet found the time. Quickly, she loosened the knot and glanced at the documents. They were about past patients of Fairwinds, it seemed, for all had been marked with one word at the top: *Deceased.*

Fully untying the knot, Petra skimmed the documents' contents, her horror increasing with each one. Now she knew why Mrs. Nance had recommended she take even one page.

The first few lines of each document reminded her of the earl's notes on his racehorses, with descriptions of the women that listed everything from height and weight to hair color to any markings that made her unique. Then came a brief description of her background and pedigree, followed by notes on her temperament. Dates of her courses were also recorded, like proof of a mare in season. But then, *oh, heavens*, the documents veered away from that of any Petra had ever seen.

She began reading words and phrases such as "hysteria," "melancholia," "nerves," "visions," "belief in the supernatural," "sapphic tendencies," "delusions," "inability to control temper," "dual personalities," and others that made Petra's heart hurt for these women. Especially now that she knew that some, as in the case of Lady Thacker, might very well be true.

Then she saw notes pertaining to treatments that spoke of restraints being utilized, tinctures using varying levels of opium, the reactions to such, and also the surgical removal of certain organs—and it only became harder to read from there.

Somehow, for reasons she could not name, Petra had felt she would not know the women who were sent here to Fairwinds, save for Gwen and Lady Thacker. For she had not ever heard of any woman or girl of her acquaintance suddenly disappearing. But she was soon to learn this was untrue. She knew many of the names she read. Perhaps she did not know them well, but in reading about them, the women of Fairwinds had ceased to be vague souls she would never know and instead became all too real.

She teared up reading about Lady Tomkins, aged forty-two, who was put into a pillory in the dead of winter and left outside until she stopped screaming. Her ladyship finally did, and died of pneumonia two days later. Petra had heard of Lady Tomkins through her aunt Ophelia, but had never met her. Did her aunt know her friend had died? Petra thought likely not.

Another, a Miss Verona Ludbrink, aged nineteen, who constantly tried to scratch others during fits of temper, was whipped in an attempt to subdue her. After months of this, she died of gangrene from one of her wounds. Petra recalled briefly meeting Miss Verona four or so years ago when the young woman was presented at court. While Petra could not claim to truly know her, or much of her family, she *had* met her. As the Ludbrink family hailed from Cumberland, Petra had always assumed Miss Verona had simply never returned to London. Now she knew better. Verona had died from her "treatments" a mere eight months after her presentation.

With a heavy sigh, Petra turned the page over.

More women, more documents. Petra began to feel bile coming up her throat when she read of those subjected to "internal inspections pertaining to womb failure."

Drysdale went into great detail as to whether the women screamed, cried, or moaned as if they enjoyed the process. Mrs. Tabitha Kersey, whom Petra found to have been seven and twenty years old, was marked by Drysdale as "especially pretty and willing." Two months later, she had died after screaming through the night of pain in her womb. Drysdale's notes recorded her as having been "clearly delusional, as she held her hands over her stomach when I asked where the pain was located, and the womb is farther downward from the abdomen."

Petra had known of Mrs. Kersey as well. She was a distant cousin of Caroline's, in fact. Petra had recalled Mrs. Kersey being exceptionally beautiful, but looking most unhappy in society, not unlike Gwen. Mrs. Kersey had never been blessed with children, and per Drysdale's notes, after seven years of marriage and no children, Mrs. Kersey was sent to Fairwinds for "matters of the weakest womb."

Anger had now filled Petra to the point that she was shaking.

She saw Gwen's name on a document, but did not wish to read more of these poor women's plights. Quickly, she pulled some of the pages from the file, including Gwen's, and folded them into a letter-sized packet. Realizing she had no pockets or a reticule, she folded the packet once more lengthwise and slipped it between her breasts.

Quickly, she opened the other locked cabinets and found the files on the current patients. This time, she did not read them, knowing what horrors she would find. Instead, she pulled three at random, though she took the pains to find the documents for Lady Thacker as her third. Once more she folded them and slipped them into her bodice.

"Now to find that damned ledger."

She glanced at the clock as she picked the locks on Drysdale's desk. Through the window, she could see that the group of nine women was still out on the grounds. No one seemed to be craning their heads toward any sound coming from the back of the house. Was that a good sign or a bad one?

Petra was perspiring now in her haste to find all she needed, and it made the cuts on her face, wrist, and ankles sting. Finally, she opened the last drawer in the desk, that of the center.

"Huzzah!" she cried softly, finding a ledger lying neatly within, to the right of a small journal secured at its middle with a monk's knot, similar to that on her own set of lockpicks. While the journal was small enough that Petra could easily carry it in her hand, the ledger was not. Opening it, Petra found what she'd been led to expect. Pages of notes in Drysdale's neat hand with more names Petra recognized than not. Lists of their vices, of their debts, of how often they paid, of any scandals.

She had so little time left. Hurriedly, she flipped the pages until she found *Holbrook, Earl of (Thaddeus Forsyth)* and *Hillmorton, Duke of (Hugh Shawcross)*. She ripped out the pages without looking at them, and was about to stop when she saw *Ingersoll, Viscount Emerson*. She took that page as well, then flipped quickly through, looking for Duncan's name. His name was there, and she tore it out, though without reading its contents. There was only a bit of writing under his name, making him one of the few who had so little to report. Lastly, Petra went to the end of the ledger, and found *Wyncroft, Viscount Breckville (Tibby).*

"Lawks, Tibby," Petra whispered, and tore out two full pages.

Folding them was difficult, as the paper was thicker, but she managed it, tucking the packet inside her bodice. Then as she slid the ledger back into its place in Drysdale's desk—knowing full well he would notice the missing pages, but hoping with all her might that she would be far away when he did—she saw the little journal once more.

She knew she should not, for she heard more shouts throughout the house, but she pulled out the notebook and untied the knot, flipping at a rapid pace through its pages, her fingers coming up blackened from what she found inside.

"Caricatures," she whispered. All of the same woman, it seemed, and done in amateur fashion at best. She was about to close the little notebook, for it contained nothing but simple drawings . . . but no. Something was strange.

As she continued flipping the pages, the woman depicted seemed to change. On the first pages, she had been sweet-looking and maternal. In one, she was even beautiful. Then, as Petra went on, the woman was drawn raising a whip to a cowering boy with dark hair and a familiar countenance. *Drysdale. These were his drawings, his memories.*

Yet another caricature showed the woman lifting her skirts and baring her breasts as a lecherous man approached. In another, she looked satisfied, smug, ugly. Petra turned her attention to the woman's dress, looked to be drawn as coarse, of low rank, yet still with embellishments, like ribbons, lace, and pleats. Petra flipped back and forth a few pages, and saw something similar in each of the woman's dresses. Something she wouldn't have noticed looking at just one of the caricatures, but did when looking at many, and concentrating on the dress.

Crafted by his charcoal pencil into the pleats and creases of the woman's dress, as if it were formed out of the very way the fabric fell, was the word *MOTHER*.

A very small part of Petra felt for the young boy that Luca Drysdale had once been. Mistreated, frightened, and dismissed by the very woman who should have cared for him and protected him the most. Petra no longer wondered why he hated women as much as he did. Why he sought to control and torture members of the female sex. It was a constant, unending payment for the abuse he suffered as a child.

Only Luca Drysdale was no longer a helpless boy. He was a man, grown and with no little amount of intelligence. He had the choice to go in a different direction in his life once old enough to strike out on his own—one that might help other young children escape the kind of life he had endured, much like young Teddy did with the other street urchins in his care. And yet Drysdale had chosen not to. He had instead chosen hate and his own brand of retribution against his mother, to be suffered by countless women at his hands. While Petra could now pity the child that was Luca Drysdale and somewhat understand the man he had become, she could not accept that man, or forgive him.

From outside the windows she could hear voices. Hurriedly, she retied the journal and put it back in the drawer as she found it. She then locked the drawer again, wrapped up her lockpicks, and—

"Where is she? Damn it, you will find her, this instant!"

The bellow was so loud and angry that Petra felt as if Drysdale were right outside the study door. With a whimper, she raced to the door that she presumed went to Drysdale's bedchamber, wrenched it open, and shot through, closing the door behind her and finding herself in almost total darkness. The heavy drapes were closed, rendering her momentarily blind as she fumbled to turn the lock. Behind her, she heard the doorknob to Drysdale's study being shaken with the force of someone filled with fury and looking to punish.

Petra ran toward the small sliver of light peeking through the drapes, pulled one side back with a grunt, and stumbled back, a scream caught in her throat.

At the window was a hulk of a man, like an angry god with wind-tangled dark hair and blazing eyes. He pressed his palms against the glass of the window, baring his teeth, like he would swallow her whole.

THIRTY-TWO

"PETRA!" DUNCAN'S VOICE WAS A STRANGLED CRY.

"Duncan!" she gasped, and her palms went to the window, matching his, as if she could pull him to her through the panes with the sudden swelling of her heart alone. He'd come for her. And, judging by the cuts on his face and the leaves in his hair, not without cost to himself.

"Can you open the window?" Even through the glass, she could hear the Highlands in his voice, sounding nothing like the elegant, aristocratic Englishman he'd been taught to become. She loved it.

She loved him, and something told her she always had, and that love was what had fueled so much hurt in her heart when he'd left.

Grasping for the window latch, her palms sweaty and slipping, she tried to turn it.

"Damn," she whispered, panting. "And blast!"

Duncan was attempting to help from the other side, but the window was stuck fast.

From the direction of the study came a yell and the sound of a door swinging open so fast that the doorknob hit the wall. There was only one other door between Drysdale and herself.

"Lady Petra! You will not escape me!"

Petra looked over her shoulder, her heart racing. But no—there was another door, the main door to Drysdale's bedchamber. Could she escape and make it back to the drawing room, where she knew a window to be open?

Frantically, she pointed in the direction of the parlor, and before Duncan could but call her name again, she took a breath and then dashed to the bedchamber door, even as the connecting door to the study was rattling with Drysdale's furious attempts to unlock it. Petra slipped through the door and into the hall, just seconds before she heard the connecting door swing open. Lifting her skirts, and stifling a noise of pure fear bubbling from her throat, she ran, praying the window was still open.

It was, but feet away was Mrs. Nance, slumped against the wall, eyes closed, a trickle of blood running from her temple. She was too still, and a young servant with dark hair and widened brown eyes was tending to her with a worried expression. Uttering a cry, Petra ran to the housekeeper's side.

Mrs. Nance's eyes fluttered open. "You returned," she whispered. "Were you able to discover the documents?"

"I did. Oh, Mrs. Nance, what did he do to you?" Petra said with such anguish that Mrs. Nance gave a brief smile. She patted Petra's hand, which was attempting to ascertain the severity of the gash on Mrs. Nance's forehead.

"You must go, Lady Petra," whispered Mrs. Nance. "I will be well. Do not worry. Sally will tend to me."

"Yes, I will take care of her, my lady," said the girl, in an accent that was decidedly from the northern parts of England, flushing pink as she said so. Then the girl gasped as they both heard another yell of rage from the direction of Drysdale's wing. Then she let out a squeak, her huge eyes going to the window.

"Help has come, Mrs. Nance," Petra said, and turned toward the window. Duncan was there, filling the space. "I will find a way to come back for you," she added. "For all these women. You have my word."

With one last squeeze of the housekeeper's hand, Petra was at the window, grasping Duncan's hand as he pulled her through, and into his arms, if only for but a moment. Sally, showing a bright mind, was at the window, pulling it shut behind them.

Together, Petra and Duncan swung around, away from the window and to the side of the house, and ducked down behind a tall set of boxwood hedges. She pulled him down with her as they hid between the boxwood shrubs and the bricks of Fairwinds, noting the stables were in sight.

"How did you know . . . ?" Petra asked.

"Teddy," he said simply. "He knew something was amiss and braved Hillmorton House to find me late last night, not long after I'd returned from scouting this place. I then went to Forsyth House, and found Charles tending to Annie, who'd been given a bash on the head, likely by Allington's valet. You had been gone for several hours at that point. I assure you, Annie is well, and is waiting for you in your carriage. It is hidden by the river, on the outskirts of Epping Banks."

"Then you did not receive the letter Lynley wrote, disguised as my hand?"

"Oh, I did," Duncan replied dryly. "But though it has been a most painful three years without seeing it, I still know your hand as well as I know my own, and I knew you had not written what I read." His eyes crinkled at the edges. "But mostly, Lynley made the mistake of writing 'With greatest affection' as the valediction. Yours have always tended to be words such as, 'Remember, I am a better rider than you.'"

Petra smiled, taking his face in her hands, seeing now that he knew her better than she possibly knew herself. But there was no time for any sentiment, or the kiss she so desperately wanted. Drysdale's voice could be heard through the window, storming into the parlor.

"Where is she, Mrs. Nance?" he roared.

"She went that way, she did, sir!" squeaked Sally. "Toward the kitchens!"

"If you are lying to me, girl," snarled Drysdale, and Petra could hear a terrified yelp that wobbled, as if Drysdale were shaking the poor girl.

"He is hurting her!" Petra whispered.

"I will kill him with my bare hands," Duncan said through his teeth, straining forward, but Petra pulled him back. Another voice could be heard. One that was deep, male, and coarse.

"An intruder's on tha grounds, Mr. Drysdale," the man said.

"Mabel saw 'im after I'd come up here to pull that Lady Thacker woman outta that tree."

"It is the gatekeeper," whispered Duncan in Petra's ear as Drysdale swore. "Big brute of a man. I was about to bash him on his bald head as he was relieving himself in the bushes when he was called away by one of the servants. Something regarding an escaped patient who was off her head. I assumed it was you. Clearly not."

Duncan's arm was still in her grasp and Petra gave him a light pinch for that remark, which had been delivered with far too much amusement.

"What does this man look like, Carver?" Drysdale had snapped.

"'Bout my height, so Mabel says, but ain't half as stout as me. Dark hair. Clean-shaven. Green eyes."

From between the dense boxwoods, Petra had found a small space that enabled her to see a bit of the window, and caught sight of Carver. He was a truly coarse, ugly fellow with a bald head, a scraggly beard, and small eyes reminding Petra of onyx beads. She saw him curl his upper lip, giving Petra the impression that Carver did not appreciate Mabel noticing this fact about Duncan.

"It is Shawcross, you fool!" cried Drysdale. "Find him, and bring him to me!"

Petra watched Carver punctuate this directive with a nod and the lifting of something long and deadly looking.

"He has a shotgun," she breathed. "A fowling piece."

"Mmm, yes, I saw it earlier," Duncan returned grimly. "He also has a rather large knife. But then again, so do I." He looked down at Petra. "Were you able to secure the documents Gwen spoke of?"

To this, Petra pulled at her bodice, giving him a good look at more than just the three tightly folded sets of documents. "We must get them out and to the duchess. There is too much information here that would damage society if allowed to be printed in the newspapers. I have to hope Her Grace will know how best to rectify the situation without turning out the women who so clearly need a safe place to live out their days."

"And how are you planning to escape?" Duncan asked.

Petra put her head closer to his, her stomach doing a little flip when his eyes roamed her face, going down to her lips. She took his chin in her hand, and his mouth went slack for a moment. Then she turned his head away, so that he could see what she did.

"That is how," she said.

Some thirty steps away, the stable lad had come out with a bridled riding horse, looking unsure as to whether he should saddle the horse with the commotion currently happening. But the way the chestnut stood placidly, reins already over its neck, without needing to be tied, Petra knew it was their chance.

Duncan looked back into her eyes. "But the mounting block is in full view of the house. Petra, I know you can swing yourself up onto a horse's back, but you've always done so in breeches. And that horse is at least sixteen hands, if not more. How will you do so in a dress?"

Petra's smile faltered. "Why, you are going with me, of course, and you can give me a leg up."

Duncan was already shaking his head. "We have only a minute or less before Drysdale finds us here, and someone has to hold him off while you ride out with the documents. You must get to your carriage and away before Drysdale can find you again."

"No," Petra said. "I will not go without you."

"Petra, you must. I can take care of myself—and Drysdale," Duncan replied, taking her by the shoulders. "And someone needs to try to help Mrs. Nance and the other women here. Protect them from him." This, she could not disagree with, and Duncan made to stand. "Quickly, I will come with you and give you a leg up."

But Petra put her hand on his chest to keep him from being seen above the hedges. "No. I can get up on my own."

"How?" he asked, exasperated, but not before he covered her hand with his own. "And with the stable lad right there?"

Petra tutted. "For all the things you remember from our child-hood, Duncan Shawcross, you seem to forget that when I turned fifteen and gained bosoms, I used them to make you my own personal mounting block."

Grinning as Duncan looked momentarily unable to breathe at the memory, she took his face in her hands again and whispered, "Be careful, Duncan. I shall not be easy until I see you, whole and unhurt, again."

There was a commotion from inside, and Drysdale roaring, "Where is she? Where *is she, damn it!*"

"Go," said Duncan, his voice hoarse.

Petra turned, rising slowly to make sure no one else was around before brushing through a space in the hedges. Then she was hiking her skirts and dashing toward the stable lad, whose back was to her as he ran a hand over the chestnut's back. He turned upon hearing her approach.

She didn't give him a moment to speak. Her knee came up, hard and swift, between his legs. A moment later, the stable lad was bent double, unable to move, speak, or breathe.

"Thank you," Petra said as she hopped lightly onto the lad's back, grabbing the reins just as the chestnut tried to shift away, and then fairly leapt onto the horse, her skirt ripping at the side seam as she did. The next moment, she'd wheeled the chestnut around before the stable lad had even fallen to the ground in a combination of the pain in his manhood and the force of Petra leaping from his back to the horse's.

But then the servants' entrance was flung open, and two men rushed out, one holding a fowling piece. The first was Drysdale, and he sprinted toward Petra as the second, Carver, took aim at another target.

"Shoot, you idiot!" cried Drysdale. Petra saw the gun barrel tracking his quarry. Tracking Duncan.

"No!" she shouted, and turned the horse toward Carver.

It was a mistake. Drysdale was too close, and too angry. He leapt out, grabbing the right rein of the chestnut's bridle, yanking the horse's head around, its body following into a jerky circle. Petra, clinging on through a combination of skill and furious determination, registered smoke coming from the barrel of the shotgun as Duncan charged the shooter.

And then a chunk of brick exploded off the side of Fairwinds.

Petra ducked reflexively over the chestnut's neck, but the shot had gone high. From the corner of her eye, Petra saw Duncan and Carver tussling on the ground, and she could not tell which one had the upper hand.

The chestnut, spooked, dragged Drysdale some steps, yet he managed to hold on and contain it by forcing the direction of the horse's head. Drysdale's neck muscles were straining, and yet his fiery eyes were trained on Petra, uttering, "You will not get away from me, you little bitch!"

Petra aimed a kick at him and missed, nearly slipping off the chestnut's back as she did. Drysdale retaliated by attempting to grab her right leg and yank her off, but the horse shifted away, pulling her leg from his grasp almost as soon as he'd caught it.

Angrier now than she had ever been in her life, she dug her nails into the fingers Drysdale had wrapped around the horse's reins, but to little avail. Drysdale loosened his pull on the rein, but did not let go, further responding by grabbing part of her dress.

Again, Petra slipped as he pulled, yet Drysdale's abilities were hindered by the movements of the clearly upset chestnut. Weaving her fingers into the horse's mane to anchor herself, Petra clung on, tightening her left leg around the horse, her heel digging into its side as a consequence.

The chestnut suddenly did as all horses do and moved off from the pressure of its rider's leg. And with Drysdale's grip on the right rein lessening, suddenly the horse straightened its neck, stopped turning, and began stepping rapidly sideways instead, guided by Petra's leg. The horse moved laterally, like an equine wall, toward Drysdale, bumping the man and sending him stumbling backward with a grunt.

Drysdale was caught off-balance, but only for a moment. With one hand still holding the right rein, Drysdale used his other hand to pull something from a sheath on his belt. It was a dagger, its blade sharp and deadly. While the horse's movements had briefly pushed him away, toward the brick side of Fairwinds, now he came forward again, this time aiming the dagger at the horse's flank.

"No!" Petra cried out again, and kicked out her leg as Drysdale lunged. Her boot connected, sending the dagger flying from Drysdale's hands, even as the horse continued to sidestep, its head up, eyes wide, hooves clattering on the ground. Instinctively, Petra had pulled her left rein higher up on the horse's neck as well, encouraging it to continue shifting toward the house. Then she aimed another kick at Drysdale with an angry yell.

He attempted to shove her foot away, but the horse was moving too fast in his direction, giving her kick more power and causing Drysdale to stumble backward once more.

From in the distance, Petra thought she heard someone shouting, "Petra, go!"

But Petra did not put the horse into a gallop, toward freedom. She kept her leg on the horse's side, until its powerful shoulder connected with Drysdale's chest, the force of it slamming Drysdale against the house. Petra saw his cold blue eyes close tightly with the impact, then open wide with shock. His head was at her knee, his body pinned between horse and Fairwinds.

From her position on the chestnut's back, Petra looked down and saw nothing but the face of a man who had hurt so many innocent women. Who had enjoyed it. Who had cruelty in his heart, on his mind, and in his eyes.

And suddenly, Petra knew what it was to have a fit of insanity.

Holding the reins tight in her left hand, she reached out with her right, curled her fingers into the still-dark hair at Drysdale's forehead, and slammed his head back with all her might, against the bricks of Fairwinds. She heard a sickening sound, but didn't stop, grinding out a word or two with each time his head met the bricks.

"You. Shall never. Hurt. A woman. Again!"

Her fingers opened. Drysdale had gone slack beneath her hand, eyes rolled up into his head, body going limp. When Petra moved the chestnut away, she watched in satisfaction as Drysdale slumped slowly and inelegantly to the ground, the back of his head blooming scarlet with blood.

"Duncan?" Petra called, swinging off the chestnut's back, and landing on shaking legs before going down on all fours, weak in every inch of her body.

"Duncan!" she said again, her eyes beginning to brim with frustrated tears when he didn't call back. The chestnut had trotted off briskly. A few feet away was Drysdale's dagger, and she crawled toward it, keeping an eye on his unconscious form the whole time. She could see his chest rise and fall; Petra would not make the mistake of allowing this man to make one more attempt on her life—or anyone's life—ever again.

And then someone was at her side. A man, from the tall boots, shined to perfection, on his legs. He had not come from the direction of where Duncan and Carver had been fighting. Instinctively, Petra went to lunge for the dagger, but a hand had come down to grip her arm.

THIRTY-THREE

"Be easy, my dear. Shawcross is unhurt," said a voice. It was gentle, but strained, and she knew it well. Petra looked up. Into blue eyes exactly like hers.

"Papa?" she whispered.

And the earl was pulling her up. Were his eyes, too, filled with tears? Was it because of the daughter he'd found, looking the very portrait of a madwoman with her dirty hair and face, on all fours on the ground, and having just assaulted a man? Was her father here to take her inside and shut her away, back into Drysdale's charge?

When he untied the cravat from his neck and held it as if he would use it to bind her wrists, her heart sank. Yet she was still too tired to run.

And then her father went down on one knee, deftly pulled Drysdale's wrists together, and bound them, finishing by tying the ends of the pure white silk in three successive knots, pulling each one tighter than before with a certain amount of relish.

The earl rose and turned once more, cupping Petra's cheek with his hand, taking her in, anguish written all over his face. And then he was gathering her into his arms, holding her close.

"Please forgive me, my dearest Petra. I have been weak," he said into her hair.

Petra tilted her head back and looked up into her father's face, with his graying brows and hair, and the lines about his eyes, all looking more pronounced than she'd ever seen them.

"I have been most weak indeed," the earl continued. "I was allowing myself to be swayed by the opinions of other men—especially of your dratted, conniving uncle—over my trust in you. Over my faith in your strength and intelligence. Over my own knowledge of seeing the kind and capable woman you are in every way." He shook his head sadly, looking up at the walls of Fairwinds, and then down at Drysdale, who seemed to be stirring. "And I did not understand the full extent of this horrid place, or this monster of a man." He looked at Petra again, and this time she knew the tears were his. "I am so very sorry, darling Petra, and I beg your forgiveness. And whether or not you do forgive me, I shall endeavor to earn your trust again."

Petra clasped his hands, her throat tight with emotion. "Oh, Papa," she whispered.

Sounds were coming from behind her father's back. She peeked around and saw his favorite bay riding horse grazing near the chestnut, who had calmed and now seemed wholly unbothered by the events of moments earlier. Yet she also heard barking and saw a carriage coming smartly up the drive. Out of the window hung the anxious faces of Annie, Caroline, and Lottie, who was holding back both Sable and Fitz as the dogs wiggled with excitement. Yet it was her father's carriage, not her own from Forsyth House, or Caroline's.

"Lady Caroline, Miss Reed, and I discovered your carriage with Annie and Rupert on our way here," he explained.

Her papa had not only come for her, but had brought her friends. He explained that he had returned to London to tell her uncle Tobias that he would not consent to send his daughter to Fairwinds. Instead, he found Forsyth House closed, the servants gone, and a worried Caroline on the doorstep, holding the fake letter from Petra's duplicitous cousin Lynley.

"Charles is tracking down every last servant as we speak to return to Forsyth House if they so wish. And Miss Bardwell is still tending to Lady Milford," said the earl, "who I am instructed to tell you is awake and showing much improvement."

A smile was coming to Petra's lips, which increased when she turned to find Duncan striding toward her, holding Carver's shotgun under one arm, a large knife in the other, and indeed looking very well save for a few minor scrapes and part of his shirt ripped away to expose one very muscular arm.

Behind him, out cold and trussed up with some of Drysdale's own restraints, was Carver himself. Standing guard over him was Mrs. Nance, who was leaning on young Sally and another woman, both of whom who were holding cast-iron pans. From the red bump visible on Carver's bald head, it seemed one of them had helped Duncan in his subduing of the brutish guard.

More servants were gathering behind them, a few looking wary, but the bulk of them relieved. All seemed to view Mrs. Nance as their leader, which made Petra's heart glad. She was hoping the housekeeper would be willing to stay and look after the women— and if she did, she would need all the help she could find.

"And what of Uncle Tobias?" Petra asked her father.

The earl's expression darkened. "As for Tobias, my dear, he has always been my problem, not yours, and he is one I should have righted long ago. You should know I also received a letter from Lady Vera yesterday morning, relating a most unusual sighting of Tobias in London."

"At the solicitor's by the name of Fawcett," Petra said quickly, to which the earl nodded.

"Lady Vera said she recounted as much to you on Rotten Row. And that you appeared concerned, but were inclined to give your uncle the benefit of the doubt. Lady Vera feels Toby does not deserve such praise." The earl's mouth thinned into a line. "And I am whole-heartedly in agreement. Thus, I have begun to make inquiries. Especially after the last time I saw him, when he first brought Drysdale to Buckfields and was more smug than he should have been, considering the potential ruination of his niece and my beloved daughter. I now believe I know what he may have attempted to do, and I will not have it. But on this, I wish you to let me confront your uncle."

Petra already knew what her uncle had done regarding her inheritance, and she told him as much. Petra rarely saw her father angry, but when he was, it seemed sparks flew from his eyes.

"Then I will have it undone immediately," he said, gripping Petra's hand. "And I shall ensure Tobias never darkens your doorstep nor any corner of Forsyth land ever again. You have my word."

Petra gripped her father's hand tightly in return. He was well on his way to earning her trust once more.

THIRTY-FOUR

"Is this true, Lady Petra?" Her Grace's eyes were narrowed as she studied page after page with her quizzing glass. But her nose was wrinkled up. "And why do you smell like you have been bathing in muck, sweat, and horse?" She snapped her fingers at Trenworth. "Bring some of the Floris eau de toilette in the night-scented jasmine for Lady Petra. It is one of her favorites, and will make me feel less like I may faint from her *odeur*."

"I do apologize, Your Grace," Petra said, bringing her arms closer to her sides. Duncan snickered, earning him a glare through Her Grace's quizzing glass.

"And you are twice as bad, my boy. Go and have a bath, now. I wish to hear the details of this from Lady Petra."

Duncan attempted to protest, but his grandmother called out for another footman, saying, "Have Mr. Shawcross's valet run him a bath immediately. He is on his way."

When Her Grace held up one document to better read it, Petra made a triumphant face at Duncan and then pinched her nose to show just how bad he smelled.

"*You wait*," he mouthed. But when Her Grace snapped, "Shawcross, I can still smell you," he gave her a wickedly correct bow and left with a grin as his grandmother called him incorrigible.

A splash of jasmine eau de toilette and some tea had Petra feeling a bit better even though the entirety of her body was beginning to ache with the day's exertions. Yet she sat, straight and still, like a lady should, as she explained everything that had happened, from the day Uncle Tobias had come to Buckfields until the moment she left Fairwinds in her father's carriage—thankfully, dressed in a fresh gown brought by Annie—with her father and Duncan following behind on horseback, Duncan riding Drysdale's chestnut. Some of Duncan's own men, who he would only say were his men of security, had arrived not long after the earl's carriage. They took away Drysdale and Carver, both awake, furious, and in shackles, to somewhere only Duncan knew. Word had been received that the two villainous men were under lock and key, and Duncan's orders on how to proceed were being awaited.

Petra was also able to tell the duchess of welcome news delivered by Annie.

"It seems my footman, Charles, has a cousin employed as a housemaid at Potsford House. Charles, having heard of my concern for Lady Potsford and Miss Littlewood, made contact with his cousin. We understand that Lady Potsford and her ward remain locked in their respective rooms but have not yet been moved or harmed. Duncan has sent one of his men to keep watch on the house until a plan can be devised to ensure the safety of both women." Petra did not add that Teddy had been enlisted by Duncan as a second lookout and was already proving himself useful in reporting Lord Potsford's comings and goings.

"Well done," Her Grace said, nodding with approval. "And what of the women at Fairwinds? Who is looking after them?"

Petra explained that Mrs. Nance had been left in charge. "The servants whom Mrs. Nance trusts to treat the women with kindness were kept on. The others, well, we found a great deal of money upon my second, more leisurely, look into Drysdale's office. Those being dismissed were paid handsomely to go, to never return, and to look for employment elsewhere that did not include being cruel to helpless individuals."

"Excellent," said the duchess.

"Of the six women who, we were assured, were not a danger to themselves or others, Duncan and two of his men removed the locks from their rooms. They were told they may stay there—and encouraged to do so—until something could be worked out to their advantage. The lock was removed from the gates so they knew they could leave at any time, if they so wished. A local man with an excellent reputation has been installed at the gatehouse, merely for protection for the ladies, but not to keep them in. The other poor souls did not seem to know the difference, I am afraid, including Lady Thacker. They will need constant supervision. And a qualified physician to treat them. One who will show compassion and respect."

"I agree," Her Grace mused, then straightened her shoulders and announced, "I think I shall buy Fairwinds myself. I shall turn it into a house for women who need a special place to go. But no one there will be a prisoner. They may come and go as they please. And those who are ill like Lady Thacker, well, we will work with physicians and the families to find the best possible solution."

Petra beamed. "Your Grace, your idea is simply splendid."

The duchess held up some of the documents she'd been reading with such distaste.

"I know what I would like to do with this information, Lady Petra. But what would you have me do with it?"

Petra had been thinking on this the whole way back in the carriage, discussing options with Caroline, Lottie, and Annie, all feeling with certainty that Frances would agree with what they decided. Now she explained their wishes to the duchess.

"Lady Caroline, Miss Reed, and Miss Bardwell would like to help me, for we were all affected by this in some way."

The duchess's eyes were full of mirth by the time Petra finished voicing her ideas. "You may have decided to remain a spinster, my girl, but you are indeed one to be reckoned with," she said. "You have my permission, not that you really truly need it. But do not get caught."

"We do not plan to, Your Grace."

Then she called out for Trenworth and whispered something. The butler said, "Yes, Your Grace," and Petra was instructed to write down what she required. After that, Petra and Annie were seen safely home, where the servants of Forsyth House, everyone having returned, welcomed them and the earl with a feast—but only after Petra took a long and luxurious bath.

THIRTY-FIVE

Thursday, 27 April 1815
London

LORD BELLINGHAM CAME OUT HIS FRONT DOOR, BRUSHING A stray bit of lint from his coat and looking with satisfaction upon the nearly healed marks barely showing upon his left wrist. He straightened his cuff once more. The backhand he'd given his unwilling chambermaid after she'd sunk her teeth into his flesh a fortnight earlier had soothed his rejected ego. Well, that and turning the little trug out onto the street. The salve from Bardwell's had done the rest. He would have to make certain Lady Petra knew how well it had worked. If he ever had to lay eyes on the spinster again, that was.

He smirked as he went down the stairs toward his waiting carriage. Rumor had it that Lord Allington had convinced the Earl of Holbrook of his daughter's numerous instabilities, and Lady Petra was now ensconced at Drysdale's Fairwinds. And in the coming weeks, Fanny would follow, whether she wished to or not. Soon, Bellingham thought, he would be free.

His footman opened the carriage door, smartly moving aside as he said, "May you have excellent weather for Lord Milford's stalking party tomorrow, my lord."

"And may I kill more deer than I can count," Bellingham drawled. He lifted a leg to the step, and then let out a bloodcurdling yell at the sudden pain in his buttocks. He began spinning, yelling, as the jaws of two dogs clamped tightly onto his backside, one on each cheek. The footman, so startled, cowered at the sight of the snarling, growling beasts digging their teeth into his lordship's trousers and the flesh beneath.

Then, just as suddenly, the dogs released their hold and sprinted away, almost as if someone had given them a command. He saw two brown blurs, one larger than the other.

"My lord!" the footman cried out.

Bellingham had gone down onto the pavement, blood streaming from the rear of his well-tailored trousers. "*Bloody hell! My arse!*"

Around the corner, the door of a terrace house under renovation opened at the sound of a call, like that of a bird. Two dogs rushed inside, followed mere seconds later by a tousle-headed boy with bright blue eyes.

"Well?" Petra asked when Teddy came skidding to a halt in front of them, his grin stretching wide.

"That were the best thing I ever seen, Lady Petra, Miss Lottie! Fitz an' Sable were brilliant!" He went down on one knee to stroke the heads of both dogs, who were looking right proud of themselves. "Drew blood an' everything! His lordship were writhing on the ground, gushin' blood from his backside by the time I left. He won't be goin' on no hunt tomorrow, I can tell you that. And won't be sittin' right for a while, neither!"

"Well done, my darlings," Lottie said to Fitz and Sable, feeding them both bits of roast chicken. Fitz had to spit out a piece of Bellingham's trouser to best eat his.

For his part, Teddy was handed a large parcel containing more chicken, apples, and Mrs. Bing's best ginger biscuits, which had become Teddy's favorite. Petra knew he would share it with the other children he looked after.

"And well done you," Petra told him.

"No, my lady. Miss Lottie," Teddy said, taking in the both of them with a look of awe. "Well done *you*."

Friday, 28 April 1815
The forests of Strand Hill
Wickhambrook, Suffolk

"Your Royal Highness, I must say how splendid it was for you to suggest this stalking party," said Lord Milford, attempting but failing to keep his obsequious tone to a minimum as he followed Prince George to a spot amongst the trees where they would establish themselves and wait for their prey. "For the weather is excellent, and my man said the deer are not far."

"Yes, yes, Milford. It was a grand idea of mine, if I may say so," said the prince with a sigh that marked him as already a bit bored. "All of the best men of society are here, of course, ready to watch you fail. But if you do not, I shall appoint you to assist in the building of the street that shall be named in my honor from Charing Cross to Portland Place. It leads to Papa's estate in Marylebone Park, don't you know."

Milford was all but salivating. This would finally elevate him from the poor relation of the former Baron Milford who inherited a title and married a frigid, insane woman to a respected widower who was in the rarefied circle of Prinny himself.

"Thank you, sir. I appreciate it most ardently."

"Of course you do," said the prince, tossing back his thick head of dark hair. "And the food this morning—most excellent. Well done, Milford."

"I am most pleased you think so, sir," Milford replied silkily.

Prinny raised a languid, beringed hand, and pointed. "Oh, look. There is Potsford and Holbrook. What do you suppose they are reading?" He narrowed his eyes. "And what do you suppose is upon the trees? Is that an—"

There was a light *whoosh* and then a cry from Milford as an arrow pierced the tree by which he was standing. He ducked belatedly, but the arrow, still quivering, was a good two feet above him, as if it had never been aimed anywhere but the tree. Chaos ensued with the prince's men as they looked about for the archer, but Prinny merely walked to the tree and pulled out the arrow. Wound tightly around its shaft, and sealed with a dab of bloodred wax, was a pamphlet. The prince removed it and unfurled the short page, and his eyebrows rose.

MEN OF THE TON SENDING
WIVES AND DAUGHTERS
TO BE IMPRISONED AND DIE
AT THE HANDS OF CRUEL SHAM PHYSICIAN

Milford, who could see over the prince's shoulder, gasped at the headline. By the time he had finished reading the details contained in the single page with no printer's marks and no address, he was perspiring. Brief accounts of the horrible deaths of women belonging to well-respected families leapt out at him—all the women being deemed mad by their husbands, fathers, nephews, and uncles—like clawed fingers looking to sink into him from the beyond.

And then there was mention of those women who were not mad at all. Those who were headstrong, impetuous, who suffered from the vapours, or black days of sadness. Those who had not been blessed with children, and those who did not enjoy lying with their husbands. And those who had been sent to a hell-like place merely so the men in their lives no longer had to be saddled with someone whom they found difficult. Where they were restrained. Subjected to tortures. Where they lived in constant fear. Where some were to never leave.

Their names were all listed, including those who were soon to be relegated to Fairwinds, according to Drysdale's own records.

Lady Tomkins, Miss Verona Ludbrink, Mrs. Tabitha Kersey, Lady Potsford, Lady Bellingham, Lady Thacker, Miss Alice Brown, *Lady Milford*, and many more.

The list went on for a total of twenty-two names. Some were dead, some were still alive. Some did indeed have illnesses that meant they needed special care, though not torture. And the rest were merely women who had been discarded by their men and who had become prisoners of Fairwinds and Mr. Luca Drysdale.

The names of the peers in question did not have to be printed. Those of their wives, daughters, and nieces sufficed. Or, in the case of the surprisingly absent Lord Allington, who had been preening about his upcoming nuptials to anyone who would listen, the name Miss Alice Brown would ring many bells. Yes, the connections were made all too clear.

Then Milford stumbled back a step. At the very bottom, one man's name did appear, leaping out via a short sentence: *Lord Milford is confirmed to have been the connection between Drysdale and most of the men of the ton.*

Milford looked up to see every one of his guests rushing in his direction, holding the pamphlet like it was concocted from belladonna. Some, like Lord Potsford and Lord Tomkins, looked like they wished to run. Others, like Ludbrink and Sir Hugh Thacker, looked as if they would swoon like the frail women they had relegated to Fairwinds. Young Juddy Bellingham shook his head in disgust, while Tibby, Lord Wyncroft, blinked bemusedly and took a swig from his flask. And then others, such as the Earl of Holbrook, the Duke of Hillmorton, his grandson, Mr. Shawcross . . . Christ, they looked furious. Even His Grace's other grandson, the philandering Marquess of Langford, looked disgusted at what he read.

Prince George turned to Milford, giving him one long look up, and then down, and then turned his back. Some of the men gasped.

Lord Milford had been given the cut direct.

Through the trees, a herd of red deer could be seen walking gracefully in the distance. Then came an unexpected sound. Another *whoosh* of an arrow flying through the air. It landed mere feet from the deer, sending them bounding away into the mist.

"Find that archer!" Milford shouted to his men. Two of them, both with pained expressions and hands at their stomachs, stumbled off in the direction from which the arrow came. Milford scowled at their ill composure, but he would soon know the cause.

As his guests began moving off, a grunt of pain was heard from one man. Then another, followed by rude noises of flatulence, and cries of "Oh! My gut!" from seemingly everywhere.

Potsford was doubled over, as was the earl. His Grace and, oh, the prince, too. Shawcross's face was screwed up as he held one hand to his stomach. Sir Hugh looked about ready to retch. And then Milford felt the cramping.

"You've bloody poisoned us, Milford!" shouted the prince, as he grimaced in pain before a loud, rude noise issued from his royal buttocks.

And then, like the deer, the most highborn men of the ton were running, to find privacy for what would be a most painful and low next twenty-four hours.

From farther away than any of the men would expect, if they ever knew, Petra lowered her telescope and grinned at Caroline.

Friday, 28 April 1815
One half hour later, in a dog cart
Two miles from Wickhambrook, Suffolk, heading north

"How long must I lie under this tarpaulin? It is dirty under here. And it rather smells."

"As I told you, dearest, until we can reach our carriages and our lady's maids," Petra said to Caroline from beside Rupert, who was dressed as a farmer, with a hat pulled down low. Petra, too, was wearing a simple cotton dress, apron, and a large bonnet that concealed her features. "But may I tell you again how absolutely brilliant you were? Of course, I have always known this, but it has been far too long since I have seen your skills so well displayed."

"Go on," said Caroline from beneath the tarpaulin. "Continue your praise of me. It shall help me pass the time."

Petra exchanged a suppressed grin with Rupert. "Why, to shoot as straight as you did, with those pamphlets Her Grace's personal printer made for us? Oh, Caro, I wanted to cheer with every one.

However, I did not think you needed to scare off the deer, too. It was a bit showy, was it not?"

"I did not wish any of the men to shoot in anger and hit a defenseless deer," Caroline returned.

"Quite so," Petra said. "I cannot wait to see Duncan, Papa, and Juddy later and hear the tale of how well Frances's licorice-root drops worked! And that Papa was the one who administered them into the coffee last night, knowing they should take effect in the morning! Well, if I had not forgiven him for ever doubting me, that would have done the trick. Of course, he and his fellow conspirators will have to pretend to feel the same effects as the other men, but that just makes the anticipation of hearing their stories even better."

"Dearest," drawled Caroline. "While I am most happy that you and the earl are back to your usual solid footing, I should like to return to the subject of this archeress, who is currently dressed as a man and hiding beneath a tarpaulin that smells vaguely of wet dog. It will be much more diverting."

"And is your satisfaction at a job well done all the better knowing that your Whitfield's claims that he was not in league with Drysdale are confirmed? I am glad to know the same can be said of Lord Langford, who appears to have only known Drysdale through evenings at his club. And that Whitfield had only taken the advice from Langford to speak with Drysdale in order to discuss the proficiencies of the solicitor, Mr. Fawcett. Though I confess I am relieved to know Whitfield chose to use Lady Vera's solicitor instead after Fawcett's dealings with my dratted uncle."

"Mm, yes, it is very satisfying," Caroline purred. "And my Whitfield plans to make sure I know how much he worships me when I see him tomorrow. How I wish I could have told him about our endeavors, though!"

"We have agreed to keep them secret, dearest. Just as we did with the maid we assisted last year." Petra then smiled. "Though I, too, wish we could shout about it. Especially that Her Grace has already secured Fairwinds and the surrounding lands. And knowing of the relief of those women who were imprisoned there! And that Gwen continues to improve under Frances's ministrations by the hour! Did I tell you Gwen wishes to return to Fairwinds and help the other women like her? Oh, it all makes my heart soar with happiness."

"Mine as well, dearest," Caroline said. "In all, this was a bit of an adventure for all of us. I must say, I learned from it as well."

"I could not agree more," Petra replied, thinking of all the ways she had been too trusting—and yes, sometimes even rather fool-hardy. She would need to be better in many ways if she were to ever attempt to right another wrong again.

The knowing tone was back from the voice under the tarpaulin. "And what else might make your heart soar, dearest? Hmm?"

"Oh, look," Petra said loudly, glad for her bonnet so that Rupert could not see her pink cheeks. "We are nearing the carriages. No one is about, Caroline. You may rise from your hiding place now."

And as Caroline threw off the tarpaulin and sat up, a wide smile upon her face and her bow held high, Petra laughed. Then they both ran to her carriage as Lottie and Frances alighted, both turning to help a weak but smiling Gwen step down as well.

"I suspect your husband will leave the country as soon as His Grace and my papa follow the prince's suit and give him the cut direct," Petra said, taking Gwen's hands and giving them a squeeze. "Congratulations, my dear friend."

For the first time in a very long time, Petra saw a true smile on Gwen's face, and Annie came forward with a bottle of champagne for all to toast.

Saturday, 29 April 1815
Early afternoon
Buckfields
Newmarket, Suffolk

Petra's hair was flying behind her, loose and untethered, gleaming in the afternoon sun. She leaned forward, hovering over the neck of the handsome gray, her legs gripping its sides, her buckskin breeches and tall boots feeling like they were one with her skin.

At her side raced a magnificent dark bay, its head at her own horse's shoulder. Deep laughter made her look back. Duncan's dark hair was whipping off his forehead with the speed of their gallop, his smile wide and elated.

One heady moment later, Petra flew past the pear tree that marked the entrance to the forested lands of Buckfields. It was the agreed-upon finish line, and she had won. As they slowed to a trot, Duncan bowed at the neck and admitted his defeat. "You are still the better rider, my lady."

Petra laughed and held out her hand for a lemon drop. Duncan gave her one and popped a second in his mouth, his green eyes crinkled up in mirth.

"Where are we going?" he asked, as Petra entered the woods, guiding her horse between trees.

"You shall see," Petra said. "And do not make that face. I knew you were wishing for your breakfast, and I made sure we would have some." She reached back and patted the saddlebags tied to the back of her saddle.

"Excellent," Duncan said. "Are we going to the stream?"

"No, we are not."

"Then to the far fields? I expect my steed could race again. He would likely win without the slight incline he had to suffer." Petra looked back to see Duncan patting the bay's neck and looking at her with challenge.

Petra snorted, even as she rolled the lemon drop to the other side of her cheek. "That was no more an incline than you are a judge of good sweets. I cannot believe that your very favorite sweet is still the lemon drop. Have your tastes not matured in twenty years?"

"Apparently not," he said, in a low voice, making a delicious shiver run down her spine and her fingers flex tighter on the reins, just for a moment.

She turned her horse at the lichen-covered rock, her lips curving up as she saw the tree ahead that grew nearly at a right angle. Soon he would know that she had made the choice to bring him to the little secret glade in the forest that she'd finally found one day and had never shown anyone else. It had always been her place of quiet refuge, with its carpet of tiny white daisies that gave the space a magical feel and the blackberry bush at the far edge offering up the fattest, darkest, sweetest berries she had ever seen or tasted.

It was there, early that morning, that Petra had finally read the letters Duncan had written, but never sent. Though they were as badly expressed as he had claimed, Petra had come to understand the man that Duncan had been during their three years apart.

When Petra was in such mourning, Duncan had been as well. Not only for the loss of his friend Emerson, but also for Petra's pain and loss. And he was mourning a side of himself, too. One that had long felt he simply cared for Petra in the uncomplicated way of a friend. Until the day not long before Emerson's death, when he had realized he had loved Petra since the moment he first laid eyes on her, when they were both so young.

Duncan's letters told Petra that he'd thought he would have to live forever without being able to express his true feelings. To live only as Petra's friend. And when Emerson—the man who had Petra's heart—died so suddenly and shockingly? It had opened up feelings of guilt in him that made it difficult to be around her, especially as a new sense of hope bubbled beneath the surface despite it all. And this was something Petra understood all too well.

Petra now knew that Duncan felt he must leave England, to give both himself and Petra space. It was lucky his grandfather had already offered him the position as an agent, and it helped further to know Petra was so angry with him. Knowing he was unwelcome in Petra's life kept Duncan on the Continent instead of confessing his love to her, knowing she might not wish to be in his arms.

After her ordeal at Fairwinds, Petra had thought much on the way Duncan had looked at her during the most tense moments hiding in the shrubbery outside the window. His look had told her he would welcome an advance on her part, but would give her the time to be sure of herself. To decide for herself. Yes, Duncan may still enjoy teasing her and taunting her as much as ever, but he had never acted like she was his possession. And somehow, Petra knew he never would.

Now, as she guided her horse deeper into the woods, with Duncan following close behind, her feelings and wishes had gained clarity. And if the timing was right—and she felt decidedly certain it would be—she would kiss him. And if she chose to lose her virtue—again—this time in the private little field carpeted with daisies, that was her choice as well. No one need know, and her true friends would not care.

After all, she thought, *even headstrong spinsters who flout the rules are allowed some secrets, are they not?*

EPILOGUE

Two months later
Very early morning
London

PETRA SMILED AS DUNCAN'S SLEEPY HAND TRIED TO PULL HER back against him, but she slipped out of his bed, pulled his white shirt over her naked body, lit a candle, and made her way downstairs to the library.

The renovations to Duncan's new town house had finished barely three weeks earlier, and Petra had spent all but a handful of nights here since. The two were discreet to the highest degree, with Petra arriving in a series of hackneys driven by trustworthy drivers, and leaving for Forsyth House well before those of the ton awoke in the mornings. And always—*always*—before Duncan's charwoman came to clean.

Though if anyone did discover their romance, Petra felt sure the scandal would be short-lived. Indeed, Caroline had said it best.

"Dearest, there is nothing that would interest the ton less than a spinster having a liaison with a man who respects her." She'd raised one languid eyebrow. "Dare I say respects *and loves* her? Regardless, I cannot think of any topic that would bore society more."

As Duncan had never used a valet unless at Hillmorton House— and Annie was happy to have evenings free to spend in the company of Charles—there was no one for Petra to worry about if she desired to walk naked through Duncan's lodgings. Or if he wished to walk naked, which he did with regularity, usually in search of Petra for another romp. Often Petra's early morning detours to

Duncan's library occurred after she'd slept the sleep of the gloriously sated and then arisen early for a bit of time alone with a book and some tea she had made herself.

It was true; Lady Petra Forsyth could now make her own tea. Already proficient as a fine lady should be at measuring the proper amount of tea into the pot and knowing the best length of time to brew the leaves, she'd also learned to light a fire under the Register stove in the library fireplace so that the water in the teakettle sitting on the cast-metal plate could boil. In all, she'd found there was something infinitely satisfying and calming about the whole process of making tea, and she always enjoyed it.

Once the ritual was complete, Petra would then settle in for a spot of reading. On the sofa, under the tartan throw that smelled like Duncan, while she sipped tea and nibbled biscuits.

Eventually, Duncan would find her and the warmth of the fire would further warm their two bodies as he showed her again how much he enjoyed every inch of her. And she was vocal in her appreciation of his talents, to be sure. She looked forward to his appearances each and every time.

But this morning, she would be glad of a bit of time to herself, as she would have a long day ahead of her later.

She had the honor of the Duchess of Hillmorton asking her to oversee the opening of the refurbished dining hall at the charity for young orphaned women in St. George's Fields, Lambeth, known as the Asylum for Female Orphans. Though, oh, how Petra wished never to hear the word "asylum" again, even if in this instance it was meant in the word's truest and most philanthropic sense.

For, indeed, the refuge helped to shelter and educate nearly two hundred young orphaned girls until the age of fifteen, where they would be apprenticed into trade or domestic service. Until then, they were overseen by the patrons and patronesses and taught all manner of skills. And as Queen Charlotte herself was a patroness of the refuge, with one of her younger sons, Prince Adolphus, as its president, the Asylum did great work for a number of girls who would otherwise have little chance at a good life.

Petra had also been charged by Her Grace with two other tasks. One was to keep her eyes open for one or two girls of apprentice age whom Her Grace might assist in finding positions at one of the duke and duchess's properties in the country. The other was the true reason Petra had been asked to stand in for Her Grace.

Something untoward was going on at the Asylum for Female Orphans, as evidenced by the matron who was found dead on the floor of the chapel last week. To keep the scandal from reflecting badly on Her Majesty and the prince, Her Grace recommended Lady Petra Forsyth, spinster, to investigate. The Queen, having heard of how Petra helped save the women of Fairwinds from death at the hands of Mr. Drysdale, was only too quick to give the scheme her approval.

With a contented sigh, Petra tucked her feet under the tartan rug, put half a ginger biscuit in her mouth, and picked up the book she had started two months earlier, the very day after that horrid time at Fairwinds. However, she had found she could not concentrate on its story then, for she'd needed time to think on all that had happened.

Therefore, she'd stuck a folded piece of paper, the contents of which she hadn't felt the need to read, in as a bookmark and had set the book aside. Then it had been rendered completely forgotten when, soon after, she traveled with her friends to Suffolk to help disrupt a certain stalking party attended by the Prince of Wales. She'd only picked the book up again yesterday, decided she was ready to enjoy it now, and packed it in the small valise she brought with her to Duncan's.

The spine cracked open with a satisfying crackle, and out dropped her makeshift bookmark, landing on her stomach. Taking another bite of her biscuit, Petra picked up the page and unfolded it with mild curiosity. Then she stopped mid-chew as she saw the handwriting of Mr. Drysdale.

It was one of the pages from his ledger that Petra had torn out when she'd believed she would only be able to abscond with a few documents detailing Drysdale's tortures of the women at Fairwinds. At the time, she could only hope to make the most of them. Instead, she'd vanquished the odious man and had brought back the lot to the duchess.

Briefly, Petra's lips formed into a smile. Fairwinds had changed significantly in the past two months, and all for the better. Mrs. Nance was helping the women there with the assistance of a kind physician. Gwen, too, had found a new purpose in life, as both a benefactor of Fairwinds and in assisting the physician in determining the best courses of action, while learning at the same time to understand her own dark days better. Gwen was now free to do all of this, as the disgraced Lord Milford had fled for the Colonies, not recalling a provision in Gwen's ample dowry secured her monies from Milford's hands should he abandon her.

As for Drysdale himself, his neck had met the noose in a swift manner. Certain men of rank had been instrumental in bringing it about. Petra was glad none of the women tortured by Drysdale would ever have to see his face again, or hear his voice. They would no doubt see him in their nightmares, she knew, but Petra fiercely hoped those would rapidly diminish in time. After all, she had not had a nightmare about Drysdale in at least ten days.

But seeing his handwriting again nevertheless sent a shiver down her spine. And then she recalled why she'd kept the page. It had been the one piece of the ledger that pertained to Duncan. There had not been much written, and Petra had felt no need to read it at the time. After all, what horrible things could be contained in a few sentences?

Pulling the tartan rug aside, she got up and went to put it in the fire. Yet her eyes were pulled downward. It was as if Drysdale were having one last laugh.

Shawcross, Duncan (Honorable)

Illegitimate son of Marquess of Langford (Lord Robert Shawcross) and unknown Scottish whore.

Particular favorite of Duke and Duchess of Hillmorton. Entrusted with overseeing His Grace's properties on the Continent. Entrusted with security of Her Grace.

Vices: Gambles, drinks, and takes snuff all on minor levels. Little of interest.

While Petra knew Duncan would take considerable umbrage in his mother being called a whore—she had been merely a simple country lass, wooed by the powerful and handsome sixth Marquess of Langford—there was nothing Petra did not know here. Holding the page closer to the fire, she let her eyes travel down to the last notations, looking to be almost written in haste.

Lent lodgings in 1812 to Lord Ingersoll and Lady Petra Forsyth (now declared spinster) for purposes of sinful fornication prior to marriage. Ingersoll died three weeks before wedding from fall down Shawcross's stairs. Broken neck.

Am told no accident. Contrived by Shawcross himself.

ACKNOWLEDGMENTS

THIS BOOK HELPED FULFILL MORE THAN ONE LONG-HELD dream for me, and I hope the joy I felt in writing it shines through its pages. The gratitude in my heart is overflowing, and I'd like to point out those who are at the forefront of the stream.

To my two stellar agents, Christina Hogrebe and Jess Errera of Jane Rotrosen Agency, who are so encouraging, and enthusiastically helped me hone my initial idea for *Act Like a Lady, Think Like a Lord*—and helped in coming up with the best title, too! Thank you both for continuing to be two of my biggest cheerleaders.

To my incredible editor, Hannah O'Grady, for loving Lady Petra and her friends with so much delight, for all the rereads of various parts of the book, for all her patience and upbeat emails, and for spreading her excitement about my book to others. You're such a joy to work with; thank you for all you do for me and my books.

To my copyeditors and my sensitivity reader. Thanks for helping me to make Lady Petra's first adventure that much better.

And especially to my parents, who are the most wonderful, supportive, and loving people, and who are always so excited for me with each book I write. I'm beyond lucky and so grateful for both of you.

I also send out many thanks to all those Regency writers who blogged about their research online for other writers like me to find, enjoy, and utilize in some way in our own novels. I send a curtsy to each and all of you.

As a lover of historical adaptations, I have grown up watching and reading about other periods in history through the occasionally anachronistic viewpoints of a storyteller wanting to entertain as much as bring a certain time period to life. If and when I noticed historical errors, I was and still am almost always happy to over-look them and simply allow myself to be swept into the story.

I certainly didn't set out in my book to incorrectly depict a point of history—whether it be major events, etiquette, food, types of dress, or any society rule of the day—but I allowed myself the lee-way to simply enjoy writing my story. That means I know there may be points that might not line up completely with the Regency period of history. Nevertheless, I hope you will see fit to add me to the long list of storytellers who write to be as faithful as possible to the time period, while still letting the simple act of entertaining be their top priority.

Thus, as always, any errors—including any anachronisms—are mine and mine alone, though I hope you'll enjoy Lady Petra's adventures regardless.

Turn the page for a sneak peek at
Celeste Connally's new novel

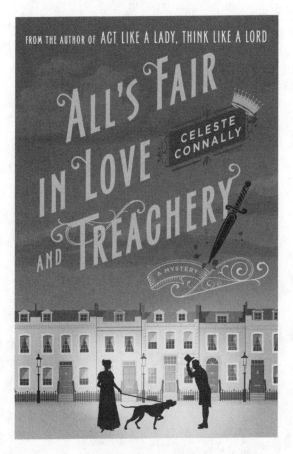

Available Fall 2024

Copyright © 2024 Celeste Connally

ONE

Wednesday, 21 June 1815
3 Bruton Place
Mayfair, London, England
The four o'clock hour of the morning

THE DAMNING WORDS FOLDED IN ON THEMSELVES AS THE PAPER crumpled in Lady Petra's fist. Flames danced merrily in the fireplace until one log split under the crushing heat, sparks flying like the spitting of an angry cat.

From beyond the window shrouded in heavy curtains came the rumble of thunder. Numbly, Petra pulled the tartan blanket tighter about her body, her mind crowded with too many thoughts. Her gaze fell to the handle of the fireplace poker, the brass glowing in the firelight as if beckoning her.

You could be an avenging angel, it seemed to say.

The implement was long and well crafted, ending in a point almost as sharp as a dagger. She crushed the paper tighter in one hand and reached out with the other to close cold fingers around the warm brass handle, casting her eyes to the ceiling and the bedroom above.

Would he deny the veracity of the words she had just read?

A crack of lightning made Petra start, her hand reflexively loosening, then tightening on the poker. Outside the small, warm library in which she stood, a bolt of brightness speared the transom window above the heavy oak front door and lit up the foyer of the town house.

In that moment, she could see the foot of the staircase clearly, and her memories flared just as brightly to that horrible early morning three years earlier when she came down a very similar set of stairs. When she made the terrible discovery of her betrothed— her darling Emerson—his neck at an unnatural angle, all life gone from his body.

Petra had been assured it was an accident. That the young, handsome viscount must have missed a step as he rushed down-stairs. Or slipped in his stockinged feet, perhaps, as he went to an-swer a knocking at the door that Petra had not heard. She had been cocooned in their bed, slumbering as only one who was blissfully exhausted from lovemaking can.

The explanations for Emerson's fall had been believable—all too easily so, in fact. For the theories had come from a man she trusted with her life. The man who had helped her slip away into the darkness of London before anyone could bear witness to Lady Petra Forsyth, the unmarried daughter of the Earl of Holbrook, emerging from a bachelor's lodgings, half-dressed and with her reddish-blond curls hanging loose down her back.

Petra lifted her eyes to the ceiling and the bedchamber above, imagining that man as she'd left him a mere half hour earlier. Green eyes, so startling, hidden behind lids closed with deep sleep. His thick, wavy hair, mussed from her hands, would look black as night against the white linen pillow. Duncan Shawcross was the man who had helped Petra sneak away that fateful morning three years ago. The man who Petra had more recently realized she had always loved; whom she had known and trusted since they were both children. Even recently when she feared their friendship lost, Petra's faith in him had never truly wavered.

Now it seemed to be crashing down around her.

She whispered an agonized oath, stumbling backward until her shoulder blades rested against the bookshelf. The fireplace poker was somehow still in her hand, its pointed edge having dragged through the thick blue carpet with swirls of rust, cream, and goldenrod.

Petra turned over her right hand, unfurling her fingers. The paper, being of fine quality, retained some of its integrity despite being compressed. Slowly, it began to open like the petals of a night-blooming jasmine flower. Not fully, but enough so that she could read the words once more.

It was but one page in a ledger full of information gathered for the purposes of blackmail. The handwriting was of a man named Drysdale, a sham physician who was as cruel as he was clever.

At the top of the page was written *Duncan Shawcross (Honorable)*. Beneath were a few sentences regarding his background and minor vices. Then followed a mention of Duncan lending his lodgings to Emerson, Viscount Ingersoll, and Lady Petra Forsyth for their scandalous premarital liaisons. And how, three weeks before the nuptials, Emerson had died of a broken neck after falling down the stairs of Duncan's town house. Then came two short, final sentences.

Am told no accident. Contrived by Shawcross himself.

A hot tear Petra had not realized had formed dropped down to the page, landing atop one word. She watched as the letters blurred, the ink retreating and swirling, bleeding out Duncan's name.

Thunder came again, so loud and close that Petra felt it deep within her, saw how it made her fingers tremble. Or were they already trembling?

Clenching the page once more, Petra lifted the fireplace poker. Her knuckles whitened as she gripped the handle, the spear blackened from stoking fire after fire. Despite the intense heat it faced, the sharp point had never bent. And neither would she.

The tartan blanket began to fall away, but she stopped it at the last moment. Lifting her chamberstick, its candle lighting her way, Petra made her way up the stairs, fireplace poker at the ready.

Silently, gently, she pushed the door open, eyes going across the bedchamber to the mahogany four-poster bed.

Her lips parted. The fireplace had long gone dark and cold, but a finger lamp burned atop the round carved-marble table at the far corner of the room, next to the bed. She had not lit it before going downstairs, but now it gave her all the light she needed.

Hangings of moss-colored velvet that had created Petra and Duncan's nightly cocoon, and from which Petra had slipped for some reading in the library, were now open and tied back at each of the four corners. She saw rumpled linens, but the bed was empty. As was the bedchamber itself, with its dark oak-paneled walls on which hung evidence of Duncan's penchant for landscape paintings, including Runciman's *A View Near Perth*.

She took two quick steps to the right and peered into Duncan's dressing room. The wooden valet stand holding his breeches, shirt, and coat had been freed from every bit of clothing. His haversack no longer sat on the wooden stool in the corner.

Duncan was gone. Only the scent of him lingered, a mixture of saddle leather, green grass, fresh air, and lemon drops.

No doubt he would have escaped her by using the hidden staircase at the corner of his dressing room that wended down to the servants' entrance at the back of the house. It was the same way she would exit in an hour when the prearranged hackney arrived, the driver having been paid handsomely to keep his eyes averted and his mouth closed.

Still, even with her face concealed by a poke bonnet and her attire by a full cloak, the drivers of London's hackneys were canny men. The driver would know he was collecting Lady Petra Forsyth from the town house of Mr. Duncan Shawcross, the son of the late Marquess of Langford and the grandson of the Duke and Duchess of Hillmorton.

If word of where she spent her nights began to infiltrate society, it would not matter that Lady Petra had declared herself as never wishing to marry, or that she had a fortune of her own. Most of society would simply ignore the fact that Duncan and Petra had known each other—even loved each other—for the bulk of their lives. Society's view would be harshest on her. They would say that Lady Petra Forsyth was still an unmarried woman risking an illicit liaison with a handsome, rakish gentleman. She was staking her reputation, and that of her family's name as well.

But was she now risking her life, too? Was she having a scandalous affair with a man who was not only a liar, but also a killer?

Though she had indeed known Duncan her whole life, for the past three years, as she mourned Emerson's death and slowly healed her heart, Duncan had been traveling around the Continent at the behest of his grandfather, the duke. In truth, however, he had all but fled Petra's presence and England the very day after Emerson's funeral.

Realizing she'd had her back to the staircase when she made her discovery only minutes earlier, she had to wonder: had Duncan witnessed her discovery of the accusations against him? It was easily possible. Duncan had more than once slipped down the stairs before without her knowing, always in search of her touch, her kisses, her body.

If so, did he at first watch with languid amusement as she opened her book and the long-forgotten page from Drysdale's ledger fell out?

She could imagine his eyes widening with apprehension when she read the page, watching her go still and pale, whispering in anguished tones, "No, no. *No!* This cannot be!"

And had it been then that he had fled like a coward?

She felt a vexing swoop of emotions. Duncan Shawcross had never been a coward, ever. Yet only someone guilty would act as he had.

With a sigh, Petra set her chamberstick atop Duncan's chest of drawers. Then a movement made her start; in the pool of candlelight, a shadow began to grow from the far side of the chest.

Instinctively, she shrugged off the tartan blanket and raised the fireplace poker with both hands, aiming it like Diana about to spear the stag that was Acteon.

"Make yourself known, whoever you are," she said, her heart thudding in her chest.

Someone was rising from the chair set against the wall. Petra squinted as the form—a small man or a boy—moved better into the light.

It was indeed a boy. A street urchin, by the frayed trousers, bare feet, and dirt-stained shirt. Yet his face remained in darkness, as if he had no face.

She blinked twice. Were his hands shielding his eyes? They were, presumably from her state of wearing nothing but one of Duncan's own shirts.

The fingers of one of the boy's hands splayed to reveal a sliver of an eye.

"'Allo, and good morning, my lady."

The end of her fireplace poker tipped and fell to the marquetry floor.

"Teddy? Is that you?"

ABOUT THE AUTHOR

Annie Hewitt Photography

Celeste Connally is an Agatha Award nominee and a former freelance writer and editor. A lifelong devotee of historical novels and adaptations fueled by her passion for history—plus weekly doses of PBS Masterpiece— Celeste loves reading and writing about women from the past who didn't always do as they were told.